The Body in Nightingale Park

Nick Louth is a best-selling thriller writer, award-winning financial journalist and an investment commentator. He self-published his first novel, *Bite*, which was a No. 1 Kindle best-seller. It has sold a third of a million copies, and been translated into six languages.

Freelance since 1998, he has been a regular contributor to the *Financial Times*, *Investors Chronicle* and *Money Observer*. Nick is married and lives in Lincolnshire.

Also by Nick Louth

DCI Craig Gillard Crime Thrillers

NICK LOUTH

THE BODY IN NIGHTINGALE PARK

First published in the United Kingdom in 2023 by

Canelo
Unit 9, 5th Floor
Cargo Works, 1–2 Hatfields
London SE1 9PG
United Kingdom

A CIP catalogue record for this book is available from the British Library.

Print ISBN 978 1 80436 439 0
Ebook ISBN 978 1 80436 440 6

This book is a work of fiction. Names, characters, businesses, organizations, places and events are either the product of the author's imagination or are used fictitiously. Any resemblance to actual persons, living or dead, events or locales is entirely coincidental.

Cover design by Jem Butcher

Cover images © AdobeStock and iStock

Look for more great books at www.canelo.co

Printed and bound in Great Britain by Clays Ltd, Elcograf S.p.A.

1

MIX
Paper from
responsible sources
FSC® C018072

For Louise, as always

Chapter One

Craig Gillard lifted the last of the packing cases out of the van and carried them up the garden path into the hall of his new home. Resting the box on top of another, he sighed and wiped his brow. It was six o'clock, and already dark, the February air chill and damp. Sam would be over in her car with the last of the essential items for the birth of their baby, due in a week. She had been adamant that she did not want to bring their child up in their old semi, with Gillard's awful aunt Trish living opposite. So they had put the house on the market just before Christmas, and encouraged by the level of interest and some positive early viewings, had themselves put in an offer on a delightful and already vacant place in a leafy street in Guildford. It all made sense: much closer to work for both of them, and putting a good twenty-five miles between their child and the baleful influence of Trish.

He went into the kitchen, grabbed a can of lager and returned to the doorstep. As he swigged from the can, he looked out at the silhouetted roofs and chimneys of Parkmead Crescent. A pleasant tree-lined street of 1930s mock-Tudor homes, sloping gently down towards Nightingale Park. That at least was what the estate agents' brag sheet had said, and it was true as far as it went. However,

Gillard, being in the business, was aware that there had in the last couple of years been two serious sexual assaults in the park. A casual mention of this fact during their second visit to see the home had secured a small but not insignificant discount to the price of the house. It was just as well, because they had not yet sold the old place, and had secured a bridging loan of a frightening size. Once their child was born, Sam would pretty much have to go back to work immediately her maternity leave finished. They needed the money.

Gillard listened, and heard only the faint noise of the traffic in the distance, and the reversing beeps of some lorry on the main road.

Just three days before they moved in, there had been a third attack in the park. He'd said nothing to Sam of the details he'd heard at work. This time, a seventeen-year-old girl was dragged into the bushes and raped. It was a similar MO to the previous attacks. There was no place in this world that was one hundred per cent safe, but part of him felt that this was a case of frying pans and fires. For the average resident of this area, particularly women, hearing of another attack would provoke anxiety and fear. There was nothing that they could easily do to protect themselves. But for Gillard, it was different. He was in the business of catching criminals. And with Sam, and their precious child on the way, he had an even more personal reason to make the streets safe again.

In the fading light, he saw a sizeable and presumably unseasonal moth flutter through the glow of the street-lamp at the bottom of the front garden. It made him smile. They were going to be happy here. He was going to make sure of it.

Sam arrived half an hour later with her mother. She would be staying with them until a week after the birth. Gillard had always got on with Mary Phillips, a woman of warmth, common sense and good humour. She had brought with her the now elderly black labrador Boris, the very same dog that had engineered by its misbehaviour Gillard's chance meeting with Sam more than five years ago. Gillard had been rock climbing in the Lake District and spotted a young woman lying prone with what appeared to be a twisted ankle, having chased her errant dog well above the main path to Scafell Pike. With the weather worsening, he felt obliged to abandon his ascent and rescue her. The rest, as they say, was history.

The two women and the dog made their way laboriously into the house, clambering around boxes and misplaced furniture. Boris, now twelve, immediately headed off upstairs to explore, even though his arthritic hips didn't quite allow him to bound up the steps as fluidly as before. Sam, her pregnancy bulge now enormous, was carrying two heavy bags, which Gillard rushed to relieve her of.

'Come on, let's get the kettle on,' Mary said.

'Ah. I haven't managed to locate it yet,' Gillard said. 'It was in box K3, but I haven't seen it.'

'Maybe the removals people put it in the wrong room,' Sam said, sitting down on one of the boxes and holding her back.

'There's a coffeemaker here,' Mary said, from the kitchen.

'No coffee,' Gillard replied.

'I've got milk,' Sam said, making her way into the kitchen. 'And a few emergency teabags.'

'We can do it in the microwave,' Mary said. 'If you've found that.'

'Ah, box K2. I do remember seeing it,' Gillard said, turning to a large cardboard box which had been shoved under the breakfast bar. Boris, now downstairs again, shuttled between the three of them, pushing his nose between their knees, and wagging his tail. Every time a box was opened, his nose would be the first into it.

'Have you found it, Boris?' Mary asked, as the labrador sniffed energetically in the top of the box. Gillard lifted out the spice rack, and found the microwave underneath. It was just a few minutes before they were sitting round the breakfast bar, with a mug of tea each.

'You've got a lot more space here,' Mary said, eyeing the spacious kitchen diner, with its large window onto the garden.

'It will be when we get rid of this monstrosity,' Sam said, nodding at the aged American double-width fridge. 'The new one's coming next week.'

'Sam, do you remember me telling you about moving into my first flat, with John and Ian when I was nineteen?' Craig asked.

'I do,' she eyed her mother. 'When you didn't have any furniture.'

'Not a stick. We sat on our crash helmets on the floorboards watching football on a second-hand black-and-white portable TV. We were so broke we ate baked beans on toast every night for a fortnight.'

'Luxury,' said Sam, in a fake Yorkshire accent. 'When I was a lass, aye, we had it tough...' She giggled.

'Enough of the Monty Python,' said Mary. 'Let's just hope you can complete the sale of the other place quickly,' she added.

'You may remember that when we had it on the market previously,' Sam said, 'Trish did everything she could to sabotage the sales.'

'Yes, I remember you telling me,' Mary said. 'Didn't she keep telling buyers that the place had subsidence?'

'That's right. Nice little typed flyers, popped under the wipers of visiting cars,' Sam said. 'Of course there was no evidence, but we lost every buyer, even the ones who believed us. Who on earth wants to move opposite a neighbour as nasty as that?'

'You should have moved while she was in hospital,' Mary said.

'Yes, I suppose we should,' Gillard said. 'Still, this time we never told her about the sale, and didn't have an estate agent sign. With any luck she didn't know, until the removals van arrived.'

'You've got a cash buyer haven't you?' Mary asked.

'Touch wood,' Sam said, resting a hand on her husband's head. 'Oh, by the way, Craig, we've got a cleaner booked, once Mum goes. The agency is sending someone round tomorrow to get acquainted.'

'She was all set to try to do the housework herself,' Mary explained to Gillard.

'Well, we're strapped for cash, aren't we?' Sam said. 'A bridging loan you could span the Amazon with...'

The letterbox clattered, and Boris rushed out to see what was happening. He returned with a local free newspaper in his mouth. After a brief tug-of-war with Sam, he released his hold, and she opened the paper. There was only one article in it, the rest being advertising. But the headline was stark enough: 'Rape Terror After Third Park Attack'.

Sam showed it to Gillard, with a downturned mouth.

'Did you know about this?' Mary asked.

'We knew about the previous two,' Sam said, reading the piece. 'They've started calling the assailant the Nightingale Knifeman. Because of the way he threatens his victims.'

'It's a bit worrying, isn't it?' Mary asked.

'Guildford is not a high crime area,' Gillard said. 'We will catch this guy. There are extra patrols in the evening, and there have been undercover officers in place at weekends for a couple of months.'

'Here's hoping,' Mary said, resting her hand affectionately on her daughter's swollen belly. 'Don't worry. Your daddy will sort it.'

Gillard smiled, hiding an inward anxiety. He was aware that the initial police response to the first incident had been slow. Even with best practice, sporadic attacks of this sort were often very hard to solve. But in this case there was an added problem. No DNA evidence had been found, and the assailant had worn a mask, gloves, and in the only actual rape, a condom. Such meticulous forensic awareness by the perpetrator was only going to make it harder to catch him.

In theory, this was someone else's problem. It wasn't his case. But now, by the sheer proximity to his family, Gillard felt he owned it.

–

It was seven o'clock when Gillard took a call on his mobile. It was DI Claire Mulholland, calling from her work phone. She was his closest friend in the Surrey force, and they had worked on many cases together. She had managed to combine being a busy mother of three adult but still dependant kids with a successful career as a detective. He knew it must be urgent for her to disturb him when he had a rare weekend off. In fact it felt more than that; even as he picked up the phone the ringtone seemed unusually intense and demanding.

'Hi Claire.'

'Have you heard?' From the background noise, it was clear she was on her hands-free in the car.

'No, heard what?'

'Ken Stapleford is dead, murdered.'

'What!'

'Yes. With a knife buried in his chest, at home.'

'I can't believe it.' It was only two years ago, almost exactly this week, that Gillard and about a hundred others had attended Stapleford's retirement party at the Olde Black Swanne in Guildford. Stapleford was one of the bigger characters who had passed through Surrey Police. Old school, definitely, but a huge personality and just the kind of guy you needed by your side when a drugs raid went wrong. He was a uniformed sergeant, and had tried but failed to get further promotion. He had left it a little too late. Common sense policing had given way to a more academic and policy-based approach, which he detested.

'He was watching football with a friend, at home this afternoon.' Claire said. 'The friend, incidentally, is a serving PC from the Sussex force. At half-time, the friend goes out to get some more beers from the local corner shop, and comes back to find Ken sitting on the settee, dying, blood everywhere. His last words were to accuse a neighbour with whom he'd had a long-running dispute about parking. He died before paramedics arrived.'

'I'm totally shocked,' Gillard said. 'Who's doing the scene of the crime?'

'Yaz Quoroshi. They didn't know each other. He's told me it's a shocking scene. Anyway the big news I've left to last is that I'm leading the case. I'm just on my way down there right now.'

'Hang on. Didn't he retire to the south coast somewhere, in Sussex?' Gillard asked.

'Yes, Hove. But the chief constable of Sussex wanted an outside force to look at the case, seeing as one of their own may be implicated.'

'Of course, with CSI he had no choice.' Surrey and Sussex shared a Crime Scene Investigation department.

'Yes, but it has all got to be seen to be above board,' Claire said. 'Rigby volunteered me, because I never really knew Stapleford.'

'Makes sense,' Gillard said. The Surrey chief constable had a finely tuned political antenna, and choosing a female to investigate was smart. After the Sarah Everard case, in which a serving Metropolitan Police officer abducted a young woman from the streets of London and brutally murdered her, cases where an officer may have committed a serious offence were undertaken with the utmost care. The independence of having an outside force involved would also play well. Stapleford's thirty-year career was mainly spent at Redhill, in the far south-east corner of the county. Although she lived in Staines, Claire was mainly based in Guildford, and the west.

'I have to admit I'm nervous about it, Craig. I'm on my own for now, until Rainy and Michelle can join me in the morning.'

'I'm not surprised you're a bit jittery. It's going to be very high profile. Make sure you are on good terms with the PR people in Sussex, they'll have your back with the press.'

'The good news is they've already got a suspect, so hopefully it will be open and shut. The thinking is that it is a neighbour dispute.'

'Good grief.'

'Look, Craig. I know you're off on leave for two weeks, because of the baby. But I was still wondering if I could occasionally bounce ideas off you?'

'Of course.' Gillard felt a warm fuzzy feeling that Claire would open up to him, and trust his judgement this much. There was no greater compliment. She had always been a safe pair of hands, good at the big picture, as well as having a keen eye for detail. Claire's solid physique belied her former career as a dance teacher and Taekwondo instructor. The day after finishing training as a WPC, the five-foot-five blonde had been put on a drugs raid, with instructions to stand at the back and keep out of the way. But when the gang's six-foot-three-inch enforcer tried to stab a fellow officer, Claire had famously taken him down with a single kick to the stomach.

Claire thanked him and cut the call.

'What was all that about?' Sam said. 'You've not been called in, have you?'

'No, don't worry.' Gillard knew that Sam's biggest fear was that Surrey Police couldn't help making demands of him, even when she needed him most. She was terrified of giving birth, of the agonising pain she had heard so much about, and what she most wanted was to have him by her side holding her hand. Surrey Police had owned him for decades, year in year out, and now it was her turn. He knew that he could not let her down on this. He had personally asked Rigby to reassure him that his two weeks' leave would be sacrosanct. She had agreed.

For all that, his curiosity about the killing of Ken Stapleford was intense. This was a man who pretty much everybody in the force liked. Gillard recalled from anecdotes retold at the leaving do that Ken was briefly a professional footballer for Brentford and then later, after an ankle injury ended his career, had been in the England Olympic squad as a hammer thrower. His jovial nature, wicked sense of humour and huge voice made him well known throughout the force. Since retirement, he had taken up coaching a junior football team in Hove, standing in the driving rain bellowing them on, driving the minibus, raising funds, attending to grazed knees and twisted ankles, and generally dispensing an avuncular care. This begged the question: who on earth would want to plunge a knife into such a man? To end this light of community service?

Chapter Two

Claire Mulholland arrived at Fir Close at eight o'clock. The cul-de-sac was the shape of the figure nine, with Stapleford's modest semi-detached home on the left, roughly where the loop rejoined the down stroke. The entire front of the house was covered by a white tent. Five police vehicles were parked at angles all over the road and pavement, blue lights playing off the neighbouring homes. Parking her unmarked white Renault in one of the few remaining spaces, she walked twenty yards to the tape which cordoned off Stapleford's house. Yaz Quoroshi was there in his Tyvek suit, looking like a giant white jelly baby. The same CSI unit served both Surrey and Sussex forces. She greeted him, but his response to her was subdued.

'It's a grim scene in there, Claire,' he said. 'I'd look at the photographs before going in, if I were you.'

Claire followed him into the CSI tent, brilliantly lit by LEDs. On a folding table was an iPad, and Claire swiped away through the gory pictures. The settee on which Stapleford was laid out was drenched in blood. His face was cut and bruised, his eyes open, his bloodstained mouth gaping. His salt and pepper beard was matted with gore.

'It was a savage attack,' Quoroshi said. 'Dr Delahaye has already been, and will be doing the post-mortem tomorrow morning.'

'Is the body still in there?' she asked.

'No. It was removed half an hour ago to the mortuary at Redhill. We've lifted most of the samples we need, DNA, fingerprints and so on.'

Claire returned to the photographs, swiping through. The murder weapon, a wicked-looking knife a good foot long, lay on a coffee table, coated in blood, next to a plastic evidence marker. In the background of one picture she saw the TV, still on, a fine spray of crimson on the screen. She had seen plenty of scenes of crime in the past, including murders, but this seemed particularly shocking, and not just because Ken Stapleford was a man she had heard of.

Turning away, she opened a cardboard box and helped herself to a Tyvek suit, booties and gloves, pulling up the hood so it covered her hair. She fitted a face mask over her nose and mouth. When she was ready, she took a deep breath, and walked in through the open front door into Ken Stapleford's home. In the dazzling light, it was clear that there were bloodstains even in the hallway, on the Anaglypta wallpaper, the beige carpet, on a light switch. Treading lightly, as if she might wake the dead, she took four paces in on the plastic stepping plates, which brought her to the 1980s-style lounge. Glass shelving units with an outdated stack stereo system, plus team pictures that covered the years of his footballing life. Grinning youths in tight shorts with tousled hair and arms folded across the chest, then more solid individuals from his Brentford years, mullet-haired and firm of jaw. Behind the units were wall-mounted football pennants from his favourite Brighton and Hove Albion, and a couple of classic schmaltzy landscape pictures, of rolling waves across an empty shore, the last light of the setting sun piercing the foam-flecked water.

The settee, originally some textured wheat colour, was already on a plastic sheet, ready to be taken away and bagged for evidence, and cushions from the two matching chairs had also been removed. The flat screen TV now unplugged was lying on one edge, propped against the wall. As she was taking in the scene, two male CSI technicians crackled past her, gave her a brief greeting and went to either end of the sofa. They then wrapped it in the plastic sheet, and wriggled the entire thing into a gigantic polythene bag, gaffer taping down the billows. She stood aside as they manhandled the three-seater onto its end and, like experienced removals men, eased it round the corner into the hallway. One of them winked at her as he passed, and said, 'What you reckon to the decor? Ickier than IKEA, wouldn't you say?'

She managed a brief smile. Black humour was a way of coping. She was sure that a few of this team would end up down the pub this evening, sinking a pint or two and exchanging bad jokes to cover their shock at this death. She retreated from the living room to let the technicians continue their work, peered briefly into the kitchen, where a slice of half-eaten pizza still lay on a plate on the breakfast bar, a plastic bag of unopened beer cans next to it. No bloodstains were apparent, except for a large red stain on a towel rail next to the oven. The connected dining room seemed untouched. She saw Quoroshi, and asked him whether anyone had looked upstairs.

'The photographer has been round. Seems undisturbed.'

'I'd still like to take a quick look myself,' she replied. The stairs were adjacent to the front door, and apart from a gory handprint on the newel post at its base, seemed uncontaminated. Gingerly she climbed up the thick pile carpet. The landing looked pristine, except for a clotheshorse bearing recently laundered referee kit, and some baggy male underwear. She moved past, into the master bedroom, and saw a queen size bed, with a dishevelled duvet, and a scattering of clothing. There were more framed photographs of football glory days on the wall. She didn't touch anything, but she was beginning to learn a little of what was important to the late Ken Stapleford. The beautiful game was clearly front and centre. It seemed like a bachelor pad, which was fair enough for a divorced man. No pictures of kids, if he had any. Maybe they would be grown up by now. She hadn't had time to read more than the first two paragraphs of the briefing she'd been sent about him.

A man adored by all. Apparently killed in a dispute about parking.

She made her way out and into the second bedroom, which sported an exercise bike, some fairly meaty-looking hand weights stacked on a metal shelving unit along with a couple of pictures of Stapleford throwing the hammer. Making her way into the bathroom, she saw plastic crime scene markers indicating the toothbrushes that had been taken, presumably for DNA. The final room, a box room, was used for that intended purpose. Packing cases, suitcases and a receipt from a removals company. It showed that Ken Stapleford had only lived there for eighteen months. She looked out at the back garden. Small and tidy with neat borders, a shed and a vegetable plot marked out with string. There were no neighbours beyond, just the south coast railway line. Heading downstairs, she exited through the kitchen door and made her way across the garden up to the shed. It was in good repair, with a hefty padlock. She marked it for examination. The rear panel fence was recently creosoted, and solid. Standing on tiptoe, she could see over to a thick bank of brambles, and a vertical drop to a cutting in which the railway line ran. Climbing onto the fence cross rail she saw that the embankment brickwork was sheer for thirty feet down to the track. Very hard to get in this way.

Once she emerged from the house, she checked her phone. She been texted by her de facto boss Detective Chief Superintendent Russell Mills, who reminded her a little tersely that the principal witness PC Liam Lewis was waiting for her at Brighton Police Station, along with the neighbour who had been implicated. She messaged him back to say she would be there in half an hour.

That was fast work. She looked across the street, and saw that there was indeed a uniformed officer stationed on the doorstep of a neighbouring property. That must be the one. Could this really have all been about parking? There had been cases in the news where such neighbour disputes had turned into murder. She'd be in a better position to judge when she'd seen the statements of the other neighbours, and spoken to all concerned.

A uniformed sergeant called James Anderson, young enough to be her son, approached her and told her that they had tracked down the next of kin, Stapleford's brother Colin, who lived in Weston-super-Mare. 'We asked the force in Bristol to dispatch a family liaison officer,' Anderson said.

'No wife, ex-wife, girlfriend?'

'Two ex-wives, we're still chasing down the details. No current girlfriend, apparently. There is a daughter, from his first marriage.'

'Can I leave it to you to contact them all?' Claire asked. 'To look for any skeletons in the cupboard?'

'Yes, ma'am. This is a terrible business, isn't it? Such a peaceful neighbourhood, and such a lovely bloke by all accounts.'

'Murder always is a terrible business, sergeant. Whoever the victim is.'

When she arrived at Brighton Police Station, she introduced herself to the desk sergeant and asked to borrow a uniformed PC. A fresh-faced male recruit was found, who leapt to attention when she addressed him. 'Good evening officer. Does your bodycam work?' she asked indicating his tunic camera.

'Yes, ma'am, it's brand new,' he replied.

'Okay, make sure it's on, and come with me.'

The desk sergeant led them to the rape suite on the ground floor and let her in. 'She's arrived, Liam,' he said. Clearly she had been a subject of some conversation. Liam Lewis was standing and eating a lasagne from a plastic plate, in conversation with a female PC that he seemed to know. He turned around to look at Claire as she entered, openly appraising her. Lewis was in his late thirties, tall and athletic-looking, and was wearing a T-shirt, tracksuit bottoms and a pair of Crocs. Bloodstains were still visible under his fingernails, and dried on the matted hair of his arms.

'I'm DI Claire Mulholland of Surrey Police, and I'm the SIO.'

He shrugged his plate up. 'Do you mind if I finish this? I'm starving.'

The female PC said: 'I had to get him some clothes from home, as all his were taken for evidence.'

'And you are…?'

'PC Karen Rayner. We live together.'

'I see.'

'No need for you to stay, Marcus,' Lewis said to the young recruit.

'I'm in charge here,' Claire said. 'This is an urgent interview, and is being recorded on his bodycam.'

'That's a bit over the top,' Lewis said.

'PC Lewis, I think we'd just better get off on the right foot. It's of the utmost importance that I treat you just as any other suspect, which is why I was brought in from another force.'

'What? I'm not a suspect.'

'He's not, it was him that called 999,' Rayner said.

'PC Rayner, I think you had better leave us now. You can take with you the remains of the food.'

'Yes, ma'am,' she said, exchanging a glance with her boyfriend, and then glaring at the young recruit with the bodycam. After she had left with the plate, Claire said, 'I'm here to do this by the book, which in the long run will be better for you as well as for me, and much better for the chances of justice being seen to be done.'

'Yeah, but look, are you saying I'm a suspect?' He pointed his plastic fork at her.

'As I understand it, your fingerprints are on the murder weapon. You were, it seems, the only person there when Mr Stapleford died. I think you can see why you have to be treated like a suspect. For that reason, you are going to be held overnight, and I and another officer from Surrey will interview you formally first thing in the morning.'

Lewis groaned, and rolled his eyes. 'Look, as I said, when I got back from the offie, he was lying there dying, with a knife stuck in him. He gestured for me to pull it out.'

'Gestured?'

'He couldn't move; he was too weak. He just pointed at the knife, and kept coughing up blood.'

'I take it you've attended a first aid course. You will recall that medical advice is not to pull out any object stuck in the body.'

'Yeah, I know. But if you'd seen him suffering, begging, you would have done it too.'

'And when did you call the ambulance? Was it after that?'

'Yes. When I could see how much blood was coming out. To be honest, I panicked.'

She said nothing for a moment, then: 'So what happened next?'

'I was trying to staunch the blood flow with towels from the kitchen. It was already coming out of his mouth, like a spray. I knew he was done for.' Lewis emitted a sob, and his shoulders began to tremble. 'And he said, "It's him opposite, about the parking."'

'And you're absolutely sure he used those words?'

'Yes.'

Claire completed her notes, and glanced across at the recruit, who was looking nervous. She hoped that they could get a quick confession out of the neighbour, because if not things looked pretty bleak for PC Lewis. She left with the young recruit in tow, told him he could turn off the bodycam, and went out to look for the custody sergeant, a grizzled veteran called Jones. When she told him that Lewis was to be detained overnight, he gave her a look as if she was about to torture a puppy. 'He's probably in shock, ma'am. He needs to go home.'

'And if it turned out that Liam Lewis did kill Ken Stapleford, how would you defend your decision to give him bail?'

'Right you are, ma'am,' he said with a sigh. 'I'll bang him up downstairs.'

'While you're down there, can I see the neighbour?'

–

Jones led her down a flight of stairs to the cells, and then into a dismal adjoining corridor, before unlocking a metal door halfway along. Stapleford's neighbour, Robert Harkins, had been left on his own in one of the dingiest interview rooms she'd ever seen. No lasagne, either. When she walked in, he jumped to his feet and demanded to be released. He was in handcuffs.

'I've been here six hours,' he shouted. 'It's gone ten o'clock, and I haven't been able to phone my wife, or my solicitor, and I haven't been charged.' Harkins, a retired college lecturer, was an upright white-haired, bearded sixty-year-old with ruddy features. According to his brief statement, given to a uniformed PC at the time of his arrest, he had been gardening, and knew nothing about the attack on Ken Stapleford.

'Lift up your hands,' Claire said.

He did so, showing the handcuffs. She could see dark marks under his fingernails. Soil? There were also a few surface abrasions on his wrists and arms. No signs of blood. Still, a guilty murderer would wash his hands thoroughly. Lewis apparently hadn't done so either.

'I assure you I didn't do this,' Harkins said.

'Is there anyone who could back up your story?'

'An alibi? I was on my own!'

'A neighbour perhaps?'

'We have high hedges; the neighbours can't see us. Look, my wife was out seeing our daughter. She is probably sick with worry.'

'I'll make sure that your wife is made aware of what's happened.'

'Well, actually, I don't *know* what's happened. All I know is that somebody attacked Ken Stapleford. I don't even know how he is.'

'Do you care?'

'I resent that accusation, detective inspector.'

'Well, I have to tell you that Mr Stapleford has sadly died of his injuries.'

'Christ almighty!' Harkins lifted up his hands to his face, and flopped down into the chair.

'Have you been offered something to eat?' She was pretty sure that the desk sergeant hadn't given him the lasagne option.

'No. I just want to go home.'

'I'm afraid that's not possible tonight, given the gravity of the crime we are investigating.'

'Oh, this is outrageous. Have you got all the rest of the neighbours in here? No, you haven't, so why me? I demand to speak to my solicitor, and I shall be writing to my MP.'

'Fair enough. I'll see you are allowed to make a phone call or two. In the meantime, would you like something to eat? I'm told there is a reasonable lasagne available.'

'Is it vegetarian?'

'I imagine not. Let me see what I can get you.'

'I'm also lactose intolerant,' he added.

'Right,' she said. 'I can't promise anything.'

'One final question. Why is Surrey Police investigating this when Stapleford used to work for that very force?'

'Because the man found with him when he died is a serving officer from Sussex Police.' She knew that that element would bound to be in the papers by tomorrow anyway.

'Oh, *now* this is all beginning to make sense!' He was clearly outraged. 'And I suppose he's at home with his feet up, while I'm banged up here. You lot always close ranks.'

'Actually, no, we've detained him too.'

That knowledge seemed to deflate Harkins' anger. 'Well, at least it's not just me. I suppose I'm here because of the argument about parking spaces?'

Ah, that's better, Claire thought. Now we're getting somewhere. 'What argument was that?'

'Oh, it's been smouldering away for some time. He only moved in eighteen months ago, and within two days began to park his motor caravan in front of our house.'

'It's not restricted parking, is it?'

'That's not the point. It blocks the evening light into the lounge. He'd already got his own gas-guzzling four-wheel-drive cluttering up the close, and quite often the football club minibus too. He's basically taken up all the spare parking. Parking is a community commons, and when one person decides to take more than their share it causes friction.'

'So what did you do?'

'I went round and politely asked him to move the camper van next to or on to his own property.'

'What was his response?'

'Pretty much the same as yours. That nobody owns the street outside their own house, and it was just tough luck basically.'

'So what did you do then?'

'I asked him again on numerous occasions. But when he went on holiday in his camper van, we moved my daughter's old car, with a small trailer, into the space in front of our house. Things rather deteriorated after that. He blocked our drive with the camper van on a couple of occasions, and he took to parking that horrible planet-destroying Land Cruiser thing on the pavement. I called the council about it, and they refused to take action, would you believe, because it wasn't "causing an obstruction". I thought pavement parking was always illegal. It certainly used to be when I lived in London, but not anywhere else apparently. Besides, it *was* an obstruction. If anyone here had a young child in a pushchair they would never get past it.'

'Did you ever threaten him?'

'You mean with physical violence? No, of course not. Have you seen the size of him? I tried to appeal to his reasonable side, but soon discovered there wasn't one.'

'Did you kill him?'

'Of *course* not! I abhor violence in all its manifestations. I believe in negotiation, but of course this requires a certain level of reasonableness on behalf of your interlocutor. Sadly, the authoritarian and bullying nature of the British police force was fully manifest in him.'

'All right, I'll return with a colleague for a formal interview tomorrow morning. You can have a solicitor with you, and hopefully we will have some forensic input by then.' Claire left him, and arranged with the desk sergeant for Harkins to have a couple of phone calls. 'And you can remove the handcuffs,' she told the sergeant. 'Unless you prefer to handcuff Lewis as well.'

'Harkins was handcuffed because he was resisting arrest.'

'Well, he's not resisting it now.'

As she was leaving, the sergeant asked: 'Has he admitted it yet?'

'No, and I don't think he will. CSI are going through his house, so hopefully if there is any corroborating forensic information we should have it by tomorrow.'

—

Sussex CID had booked Claire a room in a seaside B&B just down the road from the crime scene. She didn't get in until nearly midnight, dumped her overnight bag on the bed, and took a quick glimpse of the panoramic sea view. She breathed a huge sigh and thought about her challenging day. Brighton Police Station had been like an ants' nest, stirred up by the very idea that one of their mates could be accused of such a vicious crime. When she'd gone to the refectory, she'd endured hostile glances and derogatory comments from the Sussex officers, and not just the men. One female officer in the queue to pay behind her had muttered 'interfering bitch'.

Trying to clear her head, she watched a few minutes of the news on TV while she cleaned her teeth. She wished now that she'd partaken of the lasagne that seemed to be in good supply at Brighton Police Station. In the end, she only had time to gobble down an apple and a couple of satsumas she had brought with her plus a bar of chocolate from a vending machine, consumed while she rang Barry and texted her kids.

She'd missed the start of the news, and only caught part of the latest instalment of the tabloid saga that was gripping the nation. The ongoing court case between trendy handbag mogul Gary Wray, the man behind De Marr Couture, and his estranged girlfriend and former model Tia Whitlock. Ms Whitlock appeared from her expression to have lost the latest round in the case. With the sound down, she didn't get what today's developments had been, but there was plenty of coverage of a glum-looking Ms Whitlock emerging from a taxi, showing her long tanned legs, and of her ascent of the steps outside the High Court, accompanied by a shaven-headed minder who steered her through the press melee. Claire recalled Ms Whitlock was claiming that it was her designs that led to the success of the company, and that she had been short-changed in the contract. Wray was a good-looking man, a slightly more rugged version of David Beckham, with a dazzling smile and light beard, in his mid-thirties and now on the lower rungs of the *Sunday Times Rich List*. DC Michelle Tsu had been in secondary school with him in Guildford, and had been following the case avidly. No doubt Claire would get the full details tomorrow, when Michelle arrived to help on the case. With the newly promoted DS Carrie 'Rainy' Macintosh, plus Jill Haynes as evidence officer, it would be an all-girl team, which again seemed to be one of the great ideas of Alison Rigby. The Surrey chief constable knew that in the post-Sarah Everard world, anything that stepped away from the stereotypical macho police culture would be a useful bulwark against the media. Trouble is, it didn't help dealing with the police themselves.

The first line of the weather report predicted high winds and driving rain along the south coast tomorrow. The typical British seaside experience. With a groan, she clicked off the TV, slipped her pyjamas on and slid into the large bed. She had a final check of texts and emails. There was one from Craig Gillard, wishing her the best of luck for tomorrow.

Nice. She clicked off the lights and was asleep within a minute.

–

While Claire Mulholland was getting ready for bed, Craig Gillard was standing in Nightingale Park, Guildford, talking to two members of the community police team. PC Harris Floyd, beanpole thin and bespectacled, was with PCSO Nita Basu, who Gillard recalled meeting just a few months ago in the case of the missing pub charity box. The park was unsurprisingly deserted, given the recent events.

'So you've just moved in?' PCSO Basu asked him.

'Yes, just round the corner at Parkmead Crescent.' He pointed.

'That'll put the wind up our rapist,' she said. 'Our top cop living in the area.'

'Well hopefully he won't get to hear about it,' Gillard responded. 'My wife is just about to give birth and I'm on leave, so I won't be around a lot, but you can always ring me in an emergency.'

Floyd nodded appreciatively. 'That's really good to know, sir. It's actually been really quiet. It gets dark around five, all the female parkrun joggers have gone, just get a few commuters taking a shortcut, and then later on the usual bunches of lads sitting around on the benches. We've generally moved them on.' Floyd had a slight West Indian lilt, mixed with London tones.

'I wouldn't be in too much of a hurry to do that,' Gillard said. 'They have eyes and ears too, and could provide vital information.'

'We have spoken to them, sir, and they are aware there is more patrolling going on,' Basu said. 'But the last thing they want to do is hang around anywhere there might be police. Most of them now meet up behind the community centre on Wavertree Road.'

'So there is a lot less litter now,' Floyd said, with a smile.

'But probably more in Wavertree Road,' Gillard responded. 'What's the latest on getting an undercover team?'

'No one tells us anything,' Floyd said.

'I'll make some enquiries,' Gillard said, adding, with a hint of exasperation: 'Surely they have the budget for this.'

When he got home, he went to what would become his home office, at the moment still a stack of boxes. He sat on a packing case, and opened his laptop on his knees. He logged on to the Surrey crime database, and then carefully closed the door. He certainly didn't want Sam to see the details of the sexual assaults in Nightingale Park.

The first victim, a nineteen-year-old legal receptionist, had been waiting for her boyfriend on a park bench just after ten o'clock at night, when she was attacked from behind, dragged into the bushes, and a knife held to her throat. She was warned not to scream, so did not. She was blindfolded with duct tape during the attack, but described an athletic male with a slight London accent. The man who was on top of her, in her own words 'interfered with her', took her underwear, but penetration did not take place. She thought he had been disturbed by a noise.

The second victim, a thirty-seven-year-old call centre manager, had a similar experience, dragged from behind from the very same bench to the undergrowth, and threatened with a knife. Again, she had not heard the approach until the final moments, and was taken by surprise. Like the first victim, she was blindfolded with tape, but her contact with the assailant's face indicated that he was wearing either a mask or a balaclava, and gloves. The assault took less than a minute, and included penetration with a gloved hand. The description of the voice and accent concurred with that of the first victim.

The final victim, a seventeen-year-old schoolgirl who was repeatedly raped just a week ago, was attacked in a different part of the park, around midnight, and suffered a much longer ordeal. Her description of the assailant, his voice, the presence of a mask, matched that of the others. The attacker had worn a condom, and no DNA was recovered from the victim. Her underwear had been taken.

A violent, athletic, stealthy and forensically aware rapist. And Gillard had just moved Sam in round the corner.

Chapter Three

Sunday

Sussex Police had taken over a community centre five minutes' walk away from the crime scene, to use as an incident room. Claire Mulholland had called the first meeting for eight a.m. on the Sunday morning, which was as soon as Rainy Macintosh, Michelle Tsu and Jill Haynes could get there. She had hoped that the fact it was only five minutes' walk would give her enough time to sample the cooked breakfast the B&B claimed to be famous for, but she discovered a note been put under her door saying that 'off-season catering' was limited to 'help yourself' tea and toast. She felt robbed of her sausage, bacon, black pudding and fried egg, though the package left for her downstairs at least included Marmite, which masked the tasteless white mass-produced loaf.

She arrived at the community centre at 7.40 a.m., having already read up all she could, and having made a couple of quick phone calls tracking the forensic evidence. A good-looking young male uniform was already there, stowing away the table tennis tables. Claire admired his firm behind as he bent over a stack of chairs. The pool table had already been edged to one side, and a couple of whiteboards set up. He hadn't heard her approach and jumped when she called out to him. Tea and coffee had already been arranged, he said, and proper curtains have been installed so that the local youths could not peer in and see what was on the whiteboards. 'Is there anything else you'd like ma'am?' he said with a nervous and rather fetching smile.

'There is,' she said. 'Would it be possible to get some breakfast delivered shortly after eight o'clock? I have three hungry female officers arriving soon.'

'It's a Sunday,' he said.

'I know what day it is. I just need you to show a little initiative.'

'Yes, ma'am.' He looked a bit surprised, but did not demur.

'Make sure there's at least two rounds of bacon sandwiches, some orange juice, croissants and fruit. Oh, and a couple of *pains au chocolat.*'

'We'd normally order in, ma'am, but I'll have to go to the supermarket for some of that lot.'

'It's not beyond you, is it?'

'No, ma'am.'

It was ten to eight when the others arrived, having shared a car. Rainy and Gill had both worked the evening shift the day before, and dozed in the car on the way down while Michelle drove. They were all smartly dressed, trouser suits and white blouses, aware that they would be on show. 'Och, I do like to be beside the seaside,' Rainy said, rubbing her arms against the cold. 'Aye, it's almost as chilly here as in Glasgee.'

'It's going to get worse,' Michelle said. 'Rain later, and lots of wind.'

'Aye, but we can produce our own hot air,' Rainy said.

'Right, let's get on, breakfast should be here shortly,' Claire said. 'I hope no one's become vegan overnight. There should be some bacon sandwiches.'

There was a chorus of approval. As Claire had guessed none of them had enough time for anything to eat before leaving. 'I come from the land of the deep-fried Mars bar,' Rainy said. 'A wee bacon sandwich is the healthy option.' Rainy had been a junior doctor in Glasgow, but fed up with the long hours and the abuse and chaos of A&E, made the fateful choice of coming south and joining the police. Out of the frying pan into the fire was a common opinion.

Claire stood at the first whiteboard, in the centre of which was a picture of Ken Stapleford, held on by smiley-face magnets. 'Right, ladies. This is our victim, aged sixty-three, retired two years ago. Liked by all, is the general impression. Found, with a knife embedded up to the hilt in his chest, by this man.' She pointed at the picture beneath. 'PC Liam Lewis, currently serving officer with Sussex Police. Pristine record.'

'Aye, yon fella dinnae look like a chibber to me.'

Claire looked quizzically at her.

'A stabber, a knifeman,' Rainy explained.

'Right. Here's the timeline. Lewis rang 999 at 4.03 p.m. to say he had found Stapleford with a carving knife in his chest, still alive. The paramedics arrived at 4.17 and declared Stapleford dead at the scene at 4.40. Lewis' story is that he came round to watch football with Stapleford, a match that began at three p.m. At half-time, 3.45, he said he went to fetch some beers from a convenience store around the corner. He claimed to have returned before the second half started at four, to discover the crime scene.

Sussex Police has already secured CCTV footage, which clearly shows Lewis in the shop at the time he claims.'

'Were they supporting opposing sides?' Rainy asked.

'Good question. Brighton was playing away at Newcastle, and was two–nil down at half-time. I haven't checked Lewis' affiliation, but it could be a motive.'

'You are joking, aren't you?' Michelle asked. 'Two friends falling out over a game?'

Rainy laughed. 'Och, you've obviously never been to A&E in any big city on a Saturday night. If I had a pound for every stitch I put into the face of some wee supporter who had been glassed by a mate in a row over an offside or penalty decision, I'd be a millionaire. No, a multi-millionaire. I'm no' kidding. I read somewhere, some famous manager who said: "Some people believe football is a matter of life and death. I am very disappointed with that attitude. I can assure you it is much, much more important than that."'

They all laughed. 'It's a line of inquiry, anyway,' Claire said. 'What we do know, is that the only fingerprints on the murder weapon, on the settee, in the kitchen, the glass tables, hallway, front door and any other surface, apart from that of the victim, belong to Liam Lewis.'

'Done and dusted, then,' said Rainy, miming the action with her hands.

'Ha ha,' said Michelle. 'When's the post-mortem?'

'Later this morning, and by chance it is the good Dr David Delahaye. We should have the DNA results by then too.'

'So who is the other guy?' Michelle asked, pointing to the third mugshot on the whiteboard.

'That's Robert Harkins. According to Liam Lewis, the victim's last words were to implicate his neighbour, with whom he had a long-running disagreement about parking spaces.'

'Amazing,' said Haynes. 'Talk about the banality of evil. So the decision to plunge a knife into another human is either inspired by an offside decision, or where to park the car.'

'Most killings are like that,' Michelle said. 'Ingredients: trivial disagreement, plenty of alcohol and a handy weapon.'

'And a man,' Rainy said. 'Don't forget, it's almost always a man.'

They looked up at a noise, and saw the young, uniformed PC in the doorway, laden with a brown paper bag, dark with grease.

'Breakfast is served,' he said.

'How much do I owe you?' Claire asked, going to a desk and reaching for her purse.

'It's £16.75.'

'Here you are,' she said giving him a twenty. 'Keep the change, for having such a nice smile.'

The young officer looked shocked.

'What's your name, son?'

'PC Snowdon, ma'am. Keith Snowdon.'

'You probably think running off to get breakfast for us is a waste of your time, and being patronised, or should I say matronised into the bargain adds insult to injury. And you're right. It's just that, it happened to me so many times in the early years, I just had to see what it felt like to be on the other end. You can see my point, yes?'

'Errm, absolutely, ma'am,' he smiled winningly.

'Aye, but you really do have a canny wee smile, Keith,' Rainy said, as she tucked into a sausage sandwich. Once he was out of earshot, she added: 'And a bahoochie tight enough to clench a pencil.'

They burst into laughter. 'It'll be all round Sussex Police in five minutes that the coven of cackling witches has arrived,' Rainy said.

'Right,' said Claire. 'CSI has already taken a quick look at Harkins' home, we have his phone and laptop computer. Nothing seemed out of the ordinary at first glance. Michelle, I want you to co-ordinate the house-to-house, and oversee the Sussex officers. Find out if anything was heard around the time of the attack, check to see if there is any CCTV or doorbell cameras that might have covered the entrance to Stapleford's home, or indeed that of Harkins. I also want you to look at the CCTV from the convenience store where Lewis was seen.'

'Righto.'

'Gill, I need you to get a firm grip on the evidence. Sussex Police has agreed to give us a storage room here at the community centre. Make sure everything, absolutely everything, is locked away and only you have access. They have promised us a deep freeze for anything perishable. I don't think that anyone who worked with Lewis would try to interfere, but we have to be proactive and err on the side of caution. This is going to be a high-profile case and it's all about optics.'

'Aye, that's what they say at my local gin palace,' Rainy said.

'I've already spoken to my opposite number,' Gill said. 'All the photographs are catalogued already, and everything with bloodstains on it in the house was removed, including an entire settee, a section of carpet, a coffee table, several tea towels and of course the murder weapon. The first thing I will do is to cross-reference from the photographs to make sure we're not missing anything.'

'That's good work. Rainy, you and I are going to interview Liam Lewis, and then Robert Harkins. They've both already been cautioned, and we're going to do this by the book. And Michelle, your other job is to dig into the background of both Stapleford and Lewis, find out everything about them. We'll hold our next meeting at five, when hopefully we will have more to go on.'

Michelle Tsu sat next to the pool table with her laptop open, reading through Ken Stapleford's employment record from police files. Born in 1961, he had a middling academic record at school, left at sixteen then studied electrical engineering at a further education college. He did four years with a local electrical firm near Gatwick Airport before joining the police at the age of twenty-three. He was already married, to Elaine née Smith, but the marriage ended in divorce in 2006. They had one daughter. Stapleford then married Elizabeth Pearson in 2010, but stayed on site in Mount Browne in a police house. The records noted that the second Mrs Stapleford left within a couple of years, and Ken was moved to a smaller home on site. He was commended for bravery in 2002, when he entered a burning house and incurred second-degree burns trying to rescue a toddler. Although he brought the boy out, the child did not survive his injuries. Notably, he was involved in the long-running girl F case, in which a catalogue of abuse against a vulnerable teenager was ignored for a number of years until the girl's suicide in 2009. Stapleford was one of a number of officers criticised in an inquiry about the girl's death, though in truth there was an enormous amount of blame to go round. In his case, he was criticised for ignoring her initial complaint. The most damning evidence against him was his assertion about the complainant, noted by a female officer who appeared before the inquiry, that: 'She [girl F] is just a lying little scrubber trying it on.'

Michelle ran the cue ball gently up the baize, and waited for it to bounce back into her hand. Then she sent it down a pocket, listening to the satisfying clunk as it rattled through the interior of the table.

That Ken Stapleford was old school was not in doubt. A handful of complaints had been made against him over the years, principally of excessive force during arrest. Separately he was reprimanded in 2004, for ordering a strip search of an arrested female, supposedly in pursuit of concealed drugs. The search should have been conducted by a female officer, but as none was immediately available, Stapleford and another officer did it themselves. They stopped short of a cavity search, and each denied the complainant's allegations that she was requested to do a slow striptease. There was no evidence of this either way, and as the complainant was subsequently jailed for drug offences, the matter went no further than a reprimand.

Michelle sighed. Just not good enough. She knew that it would go a great deal further these days. She closed the document and clicked on the file of statements from officers who had worked with him. There were dozens, almost all of which eulogised him. Skimming them, she got the impression that Stapleford had spent an enormous amount of time down in the police sports and social club. He was definitely one of the lads, a big man with a big voice, and a great sense of humour.

She picked up the phone and rang Sergeant Anderson, who'd been checking on next of kin. She introduced herself and asked how he'd been getting on.

'I've spoken to the brother, Colin, and to the ex-wife, the second one that is. Name of Elizabeth Pearson, aged fifty-nine. She lives in Warwickshire, Henley-in-Arden, and remarried to an estate agent. She'd already heard the news.'

'How did she take it?'

'She said she was shocked. She displayed what to me seemed genuine sadness. "I won't speak ill of the dead," she said. She wasn't aware that her former husband had moved house to Hove. She asked when the funeral would be, but I got the impression she wouldn't attend.'

'That sounds reasonable for a failed marriage,' Michelle said.

'We've also been in phone contact with the daughter from his first marriage, Helen Smith. Her mother is apparently deceased. There's not been much contact with Stapleford in recent years.'

'Interesting that no one seems to have kept the Stapleford name.'

'It's the modern way, isn't it? Women keeping their own name.'

'Perhaps that, or reverting to a maiden name. If you hate your ex, you would hardly want to have the constant reminder of his name, like an albatross around your neck.'

'I see what you mean.'

She thanked Anderson and hung up. She thought about it, and realised what she had heard so far about the victim wasn't a world away from the average male police officer of his age. She knew dozens of officers with failed marriages. Stress, the dislocation of shift patterns, plenty of opportunities for cheating. All these things contributed. Then she thought about the manner of his death. A big man overpowered in his own home, repeatedly stabbed and beaten up. It was a long time after either of his divorces. While there had been dozens of murder cases inspired by a split-up, it was usually the rejected male doing the killing, and it would usually be soon after the split. Neither of those things seemed to apply in this case.

Which left other types of enemy. Every police officer has a hatful of enemies, normally but not exclusively the criminals they put away. They just rarely got a chance for revenge.

But this time might be different.

–

Claire and Rainy drove over to Brighton Police Station, and caught the nine o'clock local news on the car radio. The airwaves were full of the story of the killing of a much-loved policeman in his own home. Two arrests had been made, the report said, but gave no details. The two detectives had already been buttonholed by a reporter on their way out of the community centre, and then had to run a gauntlet through a crowd of journalists on arrival at the station. Claire as aware not only of the obvious public interest in the case, but the scrutiny of senior officers both in the Surrey and Sussex forces.

They made their way through the station and down-stairs to the interview rooms. The one-way glass showed PC Liam Lewis sitting with his arms folded next to a female solicitor. His body language conveyed a sulphurous mood. Claire wasn't surprised. A night in the cells, the very same lock-ups that he had over the years consigned many suspects to himself, was a humiliation. Undoubtedly, other inmates would soon have realised that they had a VIP neighbour. She had once heard the bloodcurdling verbal threats and intimidation meted out to a suspected paedophile locked up at Staines. She had no doubt Lewis would be treated in similar fashion.

When Claire and Rainy entered the room, Lewis scowled at them.

'PC Lewis, stand up when a senior officer enters the room,' Claire said.

He climbed reluctantly to his feet. Rainy then prepped the tape, identifying everyone who was there, and ensuring the video camera was set. Claire then allowed him to sit down, and ran through some basic details of his eleven-year career in the force. It was largely unblemished, but for two incidents several years ago.

'You were reprimanded for excessive force when arresting Mr Christopher Johnson back in 2014. It was alleged that you put him in a painful arm lock for an extended period.'

'I was exonerated by the police complaints board. Johnson was a psychiatric patient who had stopped taking his anti-schizophrenia medicine.'

'It was alleged by him that you were excessively violent.'

'He was a complete nut job, and had already injured a WPC who tried to restrain him. If you want to prove I'm a violent individual you will have to do better than that.'

'Three years later, Mr Dermot McCann complained…'

'That was total bullshit. He was so drunk he couldn't even stand up.'

'…that you repeatedly banged his head against a cell door…'

'He banged it himself when he fell over. Again, I was exonerated.'

'Not exactly. The Independent Office for Police Conduct simply found no compelling evidence. The fact that you and he were engaged in a brawl was not contested.'

'He wouldn't go in the cell.'

The solicitor interrupted. 'Detective inspector, there is no point rehashing these outdated charges, of which my client was cleared.'

'Every copper gets complaints, it comes with the territory,' Lewis added. 'This is all bullshit, and just shows the force has been taken over by the woke brigade.'

Claire held her ground, and fixed him with a stare. 'It would be remiss of me not to investigate complaints against you. I've got your statement here, and I've reviewed the footage of your brief interview with me yesterday. I'd like you to start at the beginning, and tell me exactly what happened yesterday afternoon.'

Lewis described how he had arranged to go over to Stapleford's home to watch the Brighton match, and had arrived at ten to three, bringing with him a few cans of beer.

'Is this something you regularly do? Visiting his house?' Rainy asked.

'Not normally. Ken had a season ticket, so he went to all the home games that he could, and would usually go to the away matches too. But this was away in Newcastle, and he had a training session for the youth team that he ran on Sunday morning, so the logistics would have been a bit tricky. Other times this has happened we have gone to the Rose and Crown to see the game, but with the big

Man United fixture, we knew that the landlord would have that on.'

'How many beers did you take with you?'

'Four.'

'What brand?'

'Staropramen. Look, I wasn't drunk.'

'We recovered eighteen cans from the crime scene, including those four. There were also two Carlsberg Special Brew, six cans of Guinness, and six unopened tins of San Miguel. Which of those did you drink?'

'Ken offered me one of the Carlsbergs, when I first arrived. And I also had the four Staropramen and a Guinness.'

'Is that typical of your consumption over a forty-five-minute period?' Claire asked.

'Yes, when there's a match on, otherwise no.'

'By my calculations,' Rainy said, 'Yon swallies exceed the weekly safe limit for a man. And you guzzled it in less than an hour.'

He shrugged.

'And yet you claim you weren't drunk,' Claire said.

'No. I can handle my drink. Ken drank most of the cans.'

'Would you describe him as being drunk, at the point when you went off to the convenience store?' Claire asked.

'No. Ken could drink a dozen pints during the course of a match, and you wouldn't know to talk to him.'

'Did you have a disagreement, during the course of the game?' Rainy asked.

'No.' He paused. 'I mean, I ribbed him when Newcastle scored, and when the Brighton goal was disallowed. It was all good natured.'

'What team do you support?' Rainy asked him.

'Southampton.'

'So why were you watching this match?'

'The Saints aren't playing until tomorrow evening. Of course, I wanted Newcastle to win because that would put Brighton below Southampton, and give us some breathing space above the relegation zone.'

'So in short, you were rooting for opposite sides.'

'Not exactly. Well, yes, I mean I liked to torment Ken a bit, especially when Brighton wasn't doing very well. But I personally couldn't care less how well Newcastle do overall.'

The solicitor leaned forward. 'Is this really relevant?' she asked.

'I'm trying to establish if they had an argument,' Claire explained.

'Of course we didn't.'

'PC Lewis, you had both been drinking heavily,' she said. 'You supported opposite sides. I don't think it's unreasonable to assume the likeliest conclusion is that you had an argument which escalated.'

'This is total crap! I went to the off-licence, was away maybe ten minutes, and when I got back he'd been stabbed.'

'So you are suggesting that someone waited until you left, sneaked into Ken Stapleford's home, plunged a knife into his chest, and then exited without leaving gory foot-prints or being seen by you or any of the neighbours?'

'I told you who it was. The neighbour, Harkins.'

'Let's assume you are right,' Rainy said, 'That Robert Harkins nursed such a mighty wee grudge about the parking issue, that he was willing to kill. In those circumstances, would he nae have assaulted Stapleford immediately after an argument?'

'Not necessarily.'

'Would he nae have chosen his time a bit better? Rather than rushing in during the gap between two halves of the match?'

'Perhaps he was trying to frame me.'

'Did he even know you?'

'I don't know. But if he saw me leaving to go to the offie, he might think that I was a suitable person to take the rap.'

'Even so, don't you think the wee rascal would have brought his own knife?' Rainy asked.

'Not if he wanted to frame me.'

She looked across at her boss. 'Aye, this tale is from a galaxy far, far away.'

'I agree. PC Lewis, are you sure about what you heard?'

'Look, all I know is that Stapleford told me Harkins did it. They were his dying words.'

Claire looked down at the statement Lewis had given. 'What exact words did Stapleford use?'

'I told you, he said "It's him opposite, it's about the parking."'

It was near enough. Naturally, as a policeman Lewis would know that consistency in his story was going to be essential.

'You are the only person who could have witnessed that.'

'I know, I know! You've got to check Harkins' house. There's bound to be bloodstains, DNA. All you have to do is look for them, *please*.'

'I don't need to be told how to do my job, constable,' Claire said.

'You killed him, didn't you, Liam?' Rainy said. 'And you made up this wee fairy story about his last words to deflect the blame.'

Lewis sobbed, and his shoulders began to shake. 'No, No! You've got to believe me.'

'It's not us you'll have to convince,' Rainy said. 'It's twelve good men and women.'

'You're not going to charge me, are you?'

'Not yet, no. We'll see what the forensics say.'

They terminated the interview, and the two detectives went to the anteroom, which had one-way glass. The desk sergeant and three other uniforms were gathered there, including Lewis' girlfriend, PC Karen Rayner.

'When are you going to release him?' Rayner asked.

'There's no way he did this,' said one of the male uniforms. 'I've worked with him for five years, and he's a solid bloke.'

Claire smiled tightly, and turned to look at Lewis through the one-way glass. He was slumped over the interview table. 'Perhaps you'd all like to step outside, so we can continue our work,' she said to the four officers. They grudgingly shuffled out, and Rainy closed the door after them.

'The wee laddie radiates innocence,' Rainy said.

'We don't have any alternative lines of inquiry, do we? Not unless forensics turns up something from Harkins' house.' She took out her phone and logged on to her emails. Sure enough, there were a couple from the lab. She opened them.

'It's the DNA results from Stapleford's house. There's not a scrap of Harkins' DNA in there, but there is plenty of Lewis'.

'What about Harkins' house?'

'CSI was a few hours later filing those samples. We should know by late this afternoon.'

Rainy shook her head. 'Och, if you release Harkins but not Lewis, this place will be like the hornets' cocktail bar during unhappy hour,' Rainy said. 'They'll go fucking carnaptious.'

'I know,' Claire said. 'We've got a few hours left yet.'

Her phone buzzed, and she picked up. It was Michelle Tsu, who had been re-interviewing the other residents of Fir Close and checking the statements taken by uniforms.

'No one seems to have seen or heard anything,' Michelle said. 'However, there is a doorbell camera at number one. I'm getting the data now.'

'That's good. Anything else?'

'They're mostly elderly here, and they loved Stapleford. He fixed one old lady's electrics when they went off at ten o'clock at night, and gave another a lift to A&E and waited with her for nine hours. Didn't charge her a penny for the petrol.'

'Sounds like a saint,' Claire said.

'Not quite. It was well known in the close that glamorous young ladies were dropped off by taxi outside his house couple of times a month. I traced the taxi company, and can confirm that they were escorts. I spoke to the head of the escort agency, who confirmed this. There was nothing in the last three weeks.'

'That's maybe an area to look at in more detail when we've got time.' Claire hung up and grabbed her coat. 'Right now I'm off to the mortuary to see what's left of our heroic former colleague. I'm not looking forward to it.'

'I've got some Valoid in my desk,' Rainy said. 'Take some now, if you think you might boak. Wouldn't do to chuck up on Dr Delahaye's shiny brogues.'

–

Claire travelled over to Redhill Hospital, where Dr David Delahaye was carrying out the post-mortem on Ken Stapleford. She was shown into the examination room by a technician, and spotted the shiny domed forehead of the Home Office consultant forensic pathologist as he leaned over a sink, washing his hands. He looked over his shoulder and called a greeting to her, as he lathered up to his elbows, between his fingers, and around his wrists. He reminded her of a praying mantis.

'Ah Claire, good to see you.'

'I was hoping to get here earlier.'

'Family all right? See much of Gillard recently?' Small talk seemed incongruous in this necropolis, with dozens of bodies chilling in the stainless steel cabinets that lined the walls.

'Not for a while. Sam is due to give birth in the next few days.'

'Do send him my regards,' he said, finishing his laborious rinsing, and reaching for some paper towels. 'I've just finished,' Delahaye said, indicating with his chin the examination table behind him, where a second technician was unwrapping a fresh body bag. 'Feel free to come and take a look.'

Feeling a little queasy, Claire advanced up to the table. She had seen the photographs, but her first glance at the face made her bile rise. Even setting aside the hairline scalp cut the pathologist had made to remove the brain, it was clear how severely beaten up the retired police sergeant had been. There were scrapes and bruises all around his eyes and mouth, and his nose was broken and displaced. His chest, marred by the Y-shaped incision to remove the vital organs, showed a half-dozen parallel vertical cuts, each a couple of inches long.

'He was given a right going over, wasn't he?'

'Yes. Seven deep stab wounds to the thorax, puncturing numerous vital organs, and in three cases exiting the back. There was damage to the spine. In addition, as you will have noticed, there are numerous sites of blunt force trauma to the face, with some extravasation, as you can see.'

'He was punched?'

'Possibly, or struck with a weapon. Either way considerable force was used, and there are abrasions and lacerations beyond what one would normally expect with the naked fist. The lack of swelling indicates they were either inflicted post-mortem or immediately ante-mortem.'

Claire glanced at the hands. 'It looks like he may have been caught by surprise.'

'Yes, a good observation. There are no signs of any defensive cuts on the hands, nor anything significant caught under the fingernails, which in this case were short and well trimmed.'

'According to our only witness, the victim was found in the middle of his own settee, apparently still alive, with the knife embedded so deeply that it connected with the wooden frame of the sofa. He said he removed the knife with some difficulty, and moved the victim so he was lying full length on the settee.'

'Yes, I read the statement. Is this police constable a suspect?'

'Unavoidably,' Claire said. 'There is only a small time window for this killing. Between when the witness was seen at the convenience store, without any signs of blood-stains on him, and the arrival of paramedics, we are talking about less than fifteen minutes. We have a doorbell camera catching the suspect returning. Fingerprint and DNA tests show only the presence of the victim and the witness at the scene of the crime.'

'I'll have my full report for you tomorrow, however there is one element of significance. I have retrieved several textile fibres from lacerations on the face. I shall be sending these away for analysis. You might want to get CSI to take samples of the fabrics within the house for elimination purposes.'

'Yes, I'll get that done.'

'In terms of toxicology, we're talking mainly about alcohol. He would have been at least three times the drink-driving limit at the point of death. There was clearly a pattern of such consumption, with the liver showing early signs of cirrhosis. I'll send away some samples for wider toxin testing, if you think is it worthwhile.'

Claire smiled. 'We've got a good budget for this. I don't want us to skimp on any tests, however peripheral they might seem, because this is going to be a high-profile case. It's a case of leaving no stone unturned.'

'Indeed. Lead item on the ITV news this morning,' Delahaye said.

Claire nodded. 'One tabloid was headlined "PC accused of knifing retired cop in half-time soccer row."'

'That's jumping the gun a bit.'

'But I suppose they would argue it's a great story.'

Delahaye shrugged. 'The British tabloid press wouldn't know a caveat if it fell on them.'

After the mortuary visit, Claire Mulholland drove back down on the A23 from Redhill towards Hove. The rain was lashing down, and she had the wipers on full. She checked in with Rainy on the hands-free, who told her that the forensic results from Robert Harkins' home had just this minute come in from the lab.

'There's nae trace of blood, or Stapleford's DNA. Seems like the wee laddie's in the clear.'

'Thank you.' Claire said nothing more for a moment, concentrating on overtaking a heavy lorry, which was throwing out spray in all directions. It seemed she had no alternative but to release Harkins, which pretty much ensured she would have to charge Liam Lewis. It gave her butterflies just thinking about it. Was she missing something? It would be good to have a chat with the Crown Prosecution Service before she made a decision. Perhaps she should ring Gillard, to bounce some ideas off him. Seeing another call coming in, she thanked Rainy and hung up.

'Russell Mills here. Just seeing how you are getting along.' Her butterflies intensified as she spoke to her new boss. The detective chief superintendent listened carefully as Claire listed the lines of inquiry, and detailed the lack of evidence for any involvement by Robert Harkins.

'It comes down to this, sir. Liam Lewis is the only individual forensically connected to this crime. His fingerprints are on the murder weapon, and by his own admission he was there at the moment that Stapleford died. I think we have to set aside Lewis' contention about Stapleford's last words. It's completely self-serving.'

'Yes, I can see that.' He sighed. 'What about the post-mortem report?'

'Delahaye's full report will take a day or two, but everything he told me is consistent with the idea that Stapleford and Lewis were drinking heavily and watching football on the TV. They began to argue, Lewis stormed out to buy some more cans, and on his return – possibly during the replay of highlights at half-time – the argument resumed. Lewis went out to the kitchen, grabbed the biggest knife from the block on the countertop, walked back in, and stabbed Stapleford repeatedly. He then finished off by punching him several times in the face. Only when he realised what he'd done, did he call 999 and invent this nonsensical story about Stapleford's accusatory last words.'

Mills sighed. 'It's just that it's so hard to believe. I could name you half a dozen officers who are known to have issues with self-control. But Lewis isn't one of them.'

'We have to follow the evidence, without fear or favour. And we have to remember the role of alcohol in personality change, which as we know can turn a lamb into a leopard.'

'Of course we do,' Mills conceded. 'It's your decision, and I shan't interfere with it.' He thanked her and hung up.

A moment later, the call she had been dreading came through. Her own chief constable. Alison Rigby went through a little perfunctory small talk, asking about the accommodation Claire had been given, and the level of co-operation from Sussex Police. She then asked: 'When are you going to charge Lewis?'

'I was going to speak to the CPS first, ma'am.'

'That's fine, but they don't know anything that you don't, Claire. If we have the evidence, you need to have the courage of your convictions. The big picture, as you

49

know, is whether we as a police service have the balls to charge one of our own with murder. The press coverage, if you've had chance to see any of it, has largely been lurid rather than accusatory. If we don't get our skates on, that may change. You will see it first in the *Guardian*. Everyone is thinking about police culture...'

'Yes, I'm aware of that ma'am.'

'Good level-headed female officers, who can perform under intense pressure, are few and far between. I think you are one of them, and you could go far. I've got your back, Claire. One hundred per cent. I know you will do the right thing.'

Rigby hung up, leaving Claire's worries to evaporate. *Did she just promise me a promotion?* She clicked on the radio, Planet Rock, and turned up the volume. AC/DC's 'Highway to Hell'. Not normally her kind of music. But it wasn't a normal day. With a smile on her face, she pressed the accelerator.

Chapter Four

Sunday

Craig Gillard was sitting in his home office, sorting out his various files and papers, checking out stuff that probably should have been tossed years ago, but in their hurry to move just got stuffed in the boxes with everything else. Sam was downstairs, having just interviewed the cleaner.

'What was she like?' Gillard asked, coming downstairs.

'Okay, but late. She wouldn't walk through the park. Had to go the long way.'

'Understandable,' Gillard said, returning upstairs with the agency paperwork.

'You've got to catch him,' Sam called up to him. 'Or this will be a no-go area for women.'

'Doing my best,' he muttered to himself.

Nothing was said for a moment.

Then there was a crash, as of breaking crockery. He called out to her, then heard her call his name. He jumped up and thundered downstairs. Sam was standing next to the kitchen worktop, mouth open, her hand on her back. She was breathing hard, her swollen belly straining against the maternity dress.

'Are you okay?' He asked, looking at the fragments of crockery around her feet.

'It's painful. I was stupid, I bent down and I shouldn't have done. It's just a mug.'

'I can take you to the hospital,' he said. The car was preloaded with everything that Sam might need for a stay in hospital, or if she was forced to give birth en route.

'No, don't worry. The pain is easing already.'

'Okay, let's forget all about this stuff now,' he said, indicating the box of kitchen items. 'I can do this later.'

Sam's mother Mary was up in London for the day, and would be back by five. Gillard looked out of the kitchen window. 'The rain's eased up now, why don't you come with me for a walk around the park? It'll make a change from the exercise bike.'

'If, kind sir, you'll promise to be my protector.'

He gave her a lopsided grin. 'Of course.'

They embraced and she said: 'It's weird, but even now, I feel slightly anxious about it.'

Gillard went to the hallway and helped her into a raincoat. The buttons wouldn't all do up over the front of her tummy, but the belt would reach. He slipped on a leather jacket and a baseball cap. The wind was too strong for an umbrella. He dug in the drawer by the front door, and found a cloth cap, of the type worn by the country set. It was his, but he fitted it over Sam's head. It was a tad large but still looked good on her.

They made their way down to the park, where the bare trees dripped over them, and puddles on the paths were rippled by the gusty wind. There were few others about, just a couple of male dog walkers and an athletic-looking runner in all the gear. Gillard made a beeline for a particular bench near the play area, and looked around as Sam caught up.

'You're at work. I recognise that expression,' she said, reaching for his hand.

'This is the bench where the first two assault victims were sitting. The bushes behind have been cut back, but there's still dense undergrowth.' He indicated a dense stand of laurel. 'There's been a debate between the crime prevention team and the council about whether to remove it entirely.'

'I suppose you can't have a park without bushes, can you?' she said.

'That was the council view, and I do sympathise.'

Gillard's phone rang. 'It's Claire,' he said, as he answered. He listened to the details she gave him about the case.

'It sounds like you have to release Harkins,' Gillard said.

'And I have to charge PC Liam Lewis. But interviewing him, my gut tells me he didn't do it,' Claire said.

'Then wait, if you can. Explore other ideas.'

'I'm running out of time for that. Rigby rang me, and is encouraging me to press the button. Even DCS Mills, who I'm seconded to, is hinting that I should do it.'

'All right. Maybe it's helpful to wargame the other possibilities. If Lewis didn't do it, from what you say, the assailant must have had less than fifteen minutes…'

'More like nine, from the doorbell camera sightings…'

'So nine minutes, to walk into Stapleford's house, without a suitable weapon, take one from the kitchen, stab him to death and leave. All without leaving any DNA, or being observed by the neighbours.'

'That's pretty much it. Of course none of the neighbours saw Lewis come or go either. The doorbell camera is on the first house in the close, and caught a few vehicle movements, but none at the right time. The only pedestrian caught on it was Lewis, on his way to and from the offie. You'd have to pass it to get in.'

'Any number plates?'

'No, only distant side views.'

'Is there access from the back of the house?'

'Only for Spiderman. The property backs onto a railway cutting, with vertical brickwork and a nasty bank of brambles to get through.'

'All right, if Lewis' story is true, then the assailant is either a neighbour or was in one of the vehicles which passed the doorbell camera. Is there any other CCTV nearby?'

'No. It's a very low crime area. The nearest ANPR is miles away.'

'And no one saw any unusual vehicles parked there?' Gillard asked.

'Nope. There would have been precious few spaces for a stranger's car anyway. It's a typical problem for a cul-de-sac, that there are a lot of big properties, but very little road frontage.'

'What about parking on the main road?'

'It's restricted to either side of the turning because of visibility, and there is a primary school to the right, with zigzag lines. There used to be a public safety camera near the school, but it was taken away last year, because of concerns about pupil privacy. The nearest parking to the left of the close, from recollection, is about a hundred yards away after the railway bridge, and would not be in sight of Stapleford's home.'

'Okay then,' Gillard said. 'You can't get any further without a list of registrations for vehicles using the close.'

'But how do I get it?'

He laughed. 'This is what I would do.'

Claire listened to his idea and then said, 'My God, that's brilliant. I would never have thought of it.'

—

DS Rainy Macintosh and the Brighton police custody sergeant had just released Robert Harkins from his cell. If Rainy had expected him to be thankful for his release, she was disappointed. As he left in the company of his wife, Harkins threatened legal action for wrongful arrest, and an official complaint.

'Bloody *Guardian* readers,' the sergeant muttered after he was out of earshot.

'Aye, but it was a horrid wee cell you found for him.'

'Thank you,' he said, with a wicked smile.

'It wasnae intended as a compliment.'

She turned away and left the building, planning to head back to Hove for the five p.m. incident room meeting. She was just heading out to her pool car when her mobile rang. She didn't recognise the number, and answered it cautiously.

'Detective Sergeant Macintosh? This is Detective Constable McIver of Police Scotland.'

'What can I do for you?' She couldn't think what they would need her for.

'I just needed to confirm your date of birth, and your national insurance number.' The cautious and deliberate way these verification questions were asked made her nervous. She rattled off the answers, convinced they were going to tell her that something had happened to her elderly mother.

'I understand that you are a former partner of Mr Ross Macintosh, of High Bank, Alderley Lane, Kirkintilloch.'

Then she knew. It could only be one thing.

'I'm afraid I have to inform you that Mr Macintosh has sadly passed away.'

A hundred thoughts and emotions crowded into her head simultaneously, until she thought it would explode. She grasped at the railings at the entrance to the station to steady herself.

'Was it a stroke or a heart attack?' Her medical brain was in overdrive. Ross was the classic hypertensive, a brilliant but furious man, who didn't suffer fools nor indeed anyone gladly. He was medicated for it, as well as taking statins. Even as her brain raced, part of her realised how pointless this was. The man was dead. Ewan's father, absent, capricious and domineering, would no longer cast a shadow over both of their lives. She had loved him and hated him, quite often at the same time, and now he was gone. Twenty years of her life demolished.

'I'm afraid I don't have that information. It was, however, the result of an incident.'

'What incident?'

'He was involved in an RTA on Saturday night, and was declared dead at the scene. I have asked Surrey Police to assign a family liaison officer, particularly as I understand you have a teenage son.'

At that moment, Rainy felt her legs begin to give way. She cut the call, with the briefest of thank yous, leaned against the railings, and howled. A young female officer, clearly not realising who she was, rushed up and asked if she was all right. She was so racked with sobs and gulps, she couldn't reply. When hatred had become so much of the scaffolding of her existence, she wondered what would hold her up now. Eventually she managed to show the young woman her lanyard, but she persisted.

'Come back inside, ma'am, and I can get you a coffee.'

'You're too kind,' she rasped through thickened throat.

It was only after she had sat down in an unused rape suite that she was able to gain her composure, and let her analytical brain back in. There was only one reason why a detective, rather than a uniform, would call her about Ross' death. Because there was something suspicious about it.

–

The inquiry team hadn't asked for Stapleford's colleagues to forward their own theories about who might have liked to kill him, but the Surrey Police Facebook group was full of conversations from current and former officers speculating about his death. Michelle, who joined the group in order to find out more about Stapleford's past, made a note of numerous names of criminals that he had put away, but kept finding the same name mentioned again and again.

Tommy Hollis.

She'd heard the name before, but looked him up on the system. Thomas Francis Hollis, thirty-nine, a drug dealer and gangster, who had been receiving cocaine supplies smuggled through Gatwick Airport cargo facilities for a number of years. A man with a history of violence and intimidation going back two decades, Hollis had been arrested in 2012 at a pub in Redhill by a team led by Stapleford. It had been something of a pitched battle, with glasses thrown, and knives wielded. While a handcuffed Hollis was being led by Stapleford to a police van, he had made bloodcurdling threats, recorded word for word on the phone of a passer-by, and used in evidence. She found the video file, and played it. Hollis was a nasty piece of work, and muscular. It took Stapleford and three other officers a couple of minutes to manoeuvre him into the van.

'If it takes a hundred years, I'll get you. I'll find where you live, and I'll fucking kill you, rape your wife, and dissolve your kids in acid. I've got friends all over, who'd be more than happy to make you suffer, to make you plead for your life.' Then he turned to the witness, whose phone he could see. 'Just look at what happened to Dennis Wheeler.' Then he winked into the camera.

Wheeler had been a minor rival to Hollis, and had been found dead in a shipping container on an industrial estate just outside Felixstowe in 2014. The container had been set up as a torture chamber, with electric drills, power saws and oxyacetylene cutters. By the state of his partially dismembered body he must have suffered enormously.

Michelle quickly switched screens to the Ministry of Justice database and searched for Hollis' prison record. He was still inside, and would be until 2035 at the earliest. Still, that didn't mean he couldn't have arranged Stapleford's killing. Many of the worst murders were ordered from inside, known as the revenge Deliveroo, a dish always served cold. It was another possibility. Somebody should interview him.

—

Claire was on the phone to Sainsbury's, and had already spoken to Tesco. Michelle had got through to Asda, and had already spoken to Waitrose. Gillard's idea had been so brilliant and so simple, that she wondered why nobody had ever thought of it before. The doorbell camera only caught passing vehicle movements in the periphery of its fish-eye lens, but if they wanted to trace which vehicles had been parked in the close in the days leading up to his death, there were other sources of information.

'Hello, yes.' Claire had been kept on hold for half an hour until a senior Sainsbury's manager was available. 'We have information that a delivery of yours took place in Fir Close on Saturday at 2.12 p.m. Was there nothing later on Saturday? Oh, yes, of course, the police roadblock. So you weren't able to get in to make the evening deliveries. Understood. Can you forward me the data by email for all deliveries in the week leading up to that?' She took down the details, thanked him and then hung up.

'So Michelle, how is it going?'

'We saw the Waitrose van on the doorbell camera. The previous one was on Wednesday.'

'We still want it, Michelle.'

The door to the incident room burst open, and a tearful Rainy Macintosh walked in.

'What's the matter, Rainy?'

'My ex has been knocked down and killed in a hit-and-run.'

'Ross?'

'Aye, the wee bastard. I cannae believe it. A detective from Police Scotland just rang me, and I've spent the last half an hour trying to get more details. I've got to break the news to Ewan, and I don't know how.'

'Sit down,' Claire said, dragging a chair over. 'Let me make you a coffee.' It was a sickening realisation that she would have to grant Rainy compassionate leave. Just at the time she needed more hands on deck, she would have fewer. Nevertheless, it was the right thing to do. The woman had suffered a horrible shock.

'How did it happen?' Michelle asked.

'In the road outside his own house, apparently. Whoever did it just drove clean away.'

'Any cameras, anything like that?' she asked.

'In our old hoose, that would be nae bother, but a year ago he moved out to a wee village in the middle of nowhere.' Rainy blew her nose, sighed and scooted the chair over to her desk. She began to log in.

'Forget all this,' Claire said. 'Your mind won't be on it.'

'It's okay, just give me an hour to get my heed straight.'

'No, Rainy,' Claire persisted. 'Take a couple of days. I'll see if I can draft in Carl Hoskins to replace you. We've got some evidence that is right up his street.'

'Yes,' Michelle chuckled. 'Hours of dashcam footage from supermarket delivery vehicles. He'll enjoy that.'

Rainy finally agreed, and went off to make arrangements.

'That's awful news,' Michelle said, peeking through the curtains at Rainy standing in the entrance hall of the community centre on her mobile.

'Well, she's finally rid of him,' Claire said. 'They're halfway through a court case contesting the split of assets. I better ring Gillard and let him know.' She paused. 'I suppose she gets all the money, unless she's been cut out of the will.'

'Wouldn't be surprised if that is the case from what I've heard,' Michelle said. 'You know he assaulted her, don't you?'

'Numerous times, from what I heard. Most recently after the family wedding last September. Craig urged her to press charges, but she never would.'

'It's the usual story,' Michelle said. 'Any kind of confrontation with an ex is too frightening to contemplate. When I was on the domestic violence team we had so many cases that evidentially were easy, but when we got within a couple of weeks of the court date, the women would bottle out.'

'I don't know what the answer is,' Claire replied, returning to her screen to reread some of the neighbours' statements.

'Speaking of which, have you heard the latest about Gary Wray?'

'No. I've been just a tad busy to catch up on the latest celebrity gossip.'

Michelle continued: 'Tia Whitlock reckons Wray insisted on checking her phone every day. He used to delete her friends. Eventually he gave her a dumb phone with only one number in, his own. I don't know how she put up with it.'

'Mm.' Claire replied neutrally. An email had just come in from Waitrose, and she was keen to see what it contained.

'He also bought her a Prada dress, two sizes too small, and insisted she slim her way into it. I think that's disgusting.'

'Has anything come back from Tesco?' Claire asked.

'No, not yet. Anyway, you know he raped her don't you? Repeatedly, over the course of years.'

'Allegedly. She is trying to get more money, after all.'

'So you don't believe her?'

Claire rolled her eyes. 'I have no opinion. Neither of us were there in court to hear all the evidence, let's not rush to judgement.'

There was a pause of a few seconds, then: 'You know he asked me out once, don't you, in the sixth form?'

'Yes, you told me.' Claire decided this was getting beyond a joke. 'Don't you have enough work to do, Michelle? We've got an incident room meeting in half an hour, and you'd better have finished all the tasks I've allotted you.'

'Sorry, Claire.'

Perhaps it was a mistake to encourage such an informal work team. Claire was happy for everyone on her team to be on first name terms, but this kind of distraction was the price you paid. Gillard was a little stricter, and never had to put up with this nonsense.

After ten minutes with no further conversation, Michelle asked: 'So are we going to charge Liam Lewis?'

'I'm still thinking about it. DCS Mills has already given me permission to have an extra twelve hours, until five a.m. tomorrow, but as it is such a serious offence, he says he's open to allowing a further twelve hours on top making forty-eight. By this time tomorrow, we should know for sure.'

'Why are we waiting?' Michelle asked.

'The CPS said we should go ahead, but I'm trying to see if we can stand up an alternative line of inquiry. Okay, Harkins is off the hook, but if somebody else killed Stapleford, we need an idea of who that might be.' Claire was scrolling through the dashcam footage from the Waitrose delivery vehicle. She had now found the moment that it turned in to Fir Close. She had hoped that with three onboard cameras, two front and one rear, each supermarket delivery van would capture every parked car in the street. Some of the parked vehicles were so tightly bunched, their number plates were not visible. Nevertheless, it should be possible to take screenshots of each car, show them to the occupants of all twenty-two homes in Fir Close, and get each of them identified. Any left over, which no one recognised, might conceivably be a vehicle connected to an unknown assailant or at least someone conducting surveillance for the attacker. This was Gillard's idea, and it was brilliant. But she would have to get it completed in twenty-four hours.

–

Claire called the incident room meeting to order. Apart from her and Michelle, evidence officer Jill Haynes was there, along with Rainy Macintosh, which was to be her last duty before heading off to break the news to her son that his father was dead. DCS Mills from Sussex Police was there along with half a dozen uniformed constables who had taken statements from the neighbours. They included two officers posted respectively on the doorsteps of Stapleford's home, and until recently, that of Robert Harkins. Both had been ordered to keep their body cams on for the duration, and to make a note of any vehicle that came and left.

'All right, everybody,' Claire said. 'As you will know, we have released Robert Harkins on police bail. He surrendered his passport, but I can tell you that his involvement in this killing is no longer an active line of inquiry.'

There was a groan of disbelief from some of the uniforms.

'Look, I know many of you know PC Liam Lewis, and I can understand your shock that he may have been involved. But I must emphasise we are being led by the evidence, and everything we have so far points to him.'

'Why haven't you charged him, then?' One burly PC asked from the back. 'If you have all this evidence.' There were murmurs of agreement.

'Maybe there is no evidence,' muttered someone else.

'Let me run through it for you, then,' Claire said, turning to the whiteboard. 'The only DNA and finger-prints we have found in the victim's home are Liam Lewis'. They are on the murder weapon, on the victim's body, on towels used to mop up the blood, on wallpaper, light switches, telephone and TV. There are only nine minutes between the time that Lewis was captured leaving the close on the doorbell camera at number one and returning from the convenience store. If someone else killed the victim, he was a) very quick, b) very clean, forensically, c) passed unnoticed to and from the address on that Saturday afternoon and d) got into the house without forcible entry. Make no mistake, I will follow where the evidence leads without fear or favour. Your job is to do the same.'

When she finished, Rainy and Michelle applauded softly, but nobody else did.

'The reason I haven't yet charged PC Lewis with murder is to see if we *can* substantiate an alternative line of inquiry. So if Stapleford's killer was someone else, there would have to have been surveillance. With a lack of access to any of the homes in Fir Close from the rear, this almost certainly means surveillance from a vehicle. In addition to the doorbell camera, I have obtained CCTV footage of Fir Close over the preceding three days from supermarket delivery vans, which all have dashcams, and when reversing, rear cameras are operative.'

She saw some softening of the expressions of the assembled officers. This tough crowd had presumed her stupid, and now they were being forced to reconsider.

'Evidence officer Jill Haynes is in the process of screen-shotting each vehicle captured from the footage, and transferring it to your iPads. What I would like each uniformed officer to do, is to return to the door-to-door interviews, and get these vehicles identified.'

'What about fibres, ma'am?' asked the burly officer. 'I've heard that fibres were found in the wounds.'

'Yes, those fibres are being analysed at the moment. However, your job is not to second-guess my management of this case, it's to do what I tell you to do. Is that understood?'

'Yes ma'am,' the officer said.

–

It was seven o'clock when Michelle looked up and through a gap in the curtains saw Detective Chief Superintendent Russell Mills emerging from his car outside the Hove incident room.

'Bandits at ten o'clock,' Michelle hissed to Claire. Jill Haynes, who had just potted a frame on the pool table, dropped her cue on the baize and scampered back to her desk.

The door opened. 'Evening ladies,' he said softly, as they scrambled to their feet. 'How are you doing tracing the vehicles at the crime scene?' The soft rumbling of the cue ball, loitering on its way back to a resting place within the table's entrails, seemed to distract him.

'It's complete, sir,' Claire said. 'Thanks to the camera footage from the supermarket delivery vehicles, we have a complete number plate list of all vehicles in the close at any time in the seven days leading up to the murder.'

'Good.'

'After checks with the DVLA and follow-up phone calls to registered owners, none seem suspicious. Of the three vehicles unknown to the residents of Fir Close, a white Transit rental van turned out to have been used by a roofing contractor working at number one, a silver Peugeot 106 belonged to a health visitor to an elderly resident, and a small blue Renault van belonged to a boyfriend of the Harkins' student-age daughter.

'Any of them present at the time of the killing?'

'Yes, sir. The Peugeot, but it was still there when CSI arrived, so hardly evidence of a getaway. It was only removed on Sunday afternoon. It's not suspicious.'

'Tell me about the health visitor,' Mills said.

'I interviewed her,' Jill said. 'A fifty-eight-year-old female. Not a candidate for the kind of damage done to our victim.'

'And do we have DNA checks for the remaining residents?'

Claire replied. 'None of them match the traces inside the victim's house. Only his immediate neighbour, and she's eighty-six. She says she delivered him a cake four days previously for fixing her electrics.'

Mills nodded, and walked over to the pool table. He extracted the cue ball from its bay, and rolled it up the baize, where it bounced off the far edge and returned to his open palm.

'So we've run out of alternative theories, have we?' he asked.

'It seems so,' Claire said. *Yes, Lewis is toast.*

'DI Mulholland, I'd just like to say I thought you handled the incident room meeting very well. Not surprisingly there's some resentment in the ranks about the arrest of PC Lewis. But you are absolutely right, that we have to follow the evidence. I've called in some of the more vocal individuals who challenged you, and put them straight on a couple of matters.'

'I appreciate that, sir.'

'Now I understand we have another detective from Surrey joining us to replace DS Macintosh.'

'Yes. Carl Hoskins. A very steady individual.'

'Good. If as seems likely you do charge Lewis, I'll back you up. It's not going to be a popular decision, so you'll need all the allies you can get.'

'Thank you, sir.'

'You've not been dropped in anything this political before, have you?'

'No.'

'This is what it's like at senior levels the whole time. Political firefighting. No time to catch criminals.'

'Well, I am trying to catch criminals.'

'Of course you are. We're all impressed with the work you're doing so far, and that goes for all of you.' He thanked them and left, clicking the door quietly shut behind him.

'Of course, if you do screw up,' Michelle added softly, 'you'll be left to drown.'

Claire looked across at Michelle. She was right, of course.

Chapter Five

It was nine on Sunday evening, and the kettle had still not been found. Gillard scratched his head. The box it was supposed to be in was now completely unpacked, as were all the kitchen cartons. They had found pretty much everything else they were looking for, so they'd switched to drinking microwave coffee. Looking around the place, everything looked more organised now. Sam's mother had been brilliant, helping her daughter unpack some of the bedroom items, hanging pictures, and putting aside items that were to go in the loft. He leaned against the breakfast bar and looked around him. This was going to be a great place to live, he thought. A bigger and better laid out home, good schools nearby, and even a large park at the end of the road. He felt like a beer, but realised that he might be required to drive Sam to hospital at any time. Best not.

He walked into the lounge, where Sam was resting lengthwise on the sofa. 'How are you feeling?' he asked.

'Bloated. I just want it over with now, Craig. I've got backache, and I'm walking like an old lady.'

'Sam, I'm just going to go for a walk. I'll have my phone with me. I owe Rainy a call.'

'About work?'

'No. Remember I told you her ex-husband had died?' He'd only told her that afternoon.

'Oh, yes, of course. Sorry, my head's all over the place.'

'Your mum is just upstairs. Is that okay? I'll only be fifteen minutes.'

'Of course. Take a break, you deserve it. I'll be fine. But you'd better take a coat. It's vile out there.' She indicated the rain pattering against the window.

Gillard smiled, kissed her on the cheek, and went out into the hall. He donned a gabardine mac and a baseball cap, and grabbing house keys, wallet and phone opened the front door and stepped outside into the cold and wet. It was a brisk three-minute walk down to the park, and the reflection of the streetlamps quivered in the windblown puddles. He slipped into the park, having seen no one so far, and made his way down to the main entrance.

–

No one was around. The bare branches of trees stood out against a bronze sky, lit from below by the lights of the town. He took the main route along an asphalt path to the bandstand, where a young couple were smoking in the shelter. There was no sign of the PCSOs. Gillard stood under a conifer, which offered some shelter from the rain, and pulled out his phone. He rang Rainy on her work mobile, then her personal phone, leaving messages of condolence each time. He had always felt protective of her, a talented and hard-working colleague, always full of jokes but underneath the ebullient exterior prone to depression because of the agonies of the break-up of her marriage. He made a mental note to get a condolences card tomorrow, and shrugging up his collar, set off down the path.

Further down, into the thicker woodland, he heard a dog snuffling, before crashing out through bushes, and heading back up the hill towards its owner, a man with a torch in one hand and what looked like a couple of filled dog bags in the other.

As they passed each other, they exchanged greetings. The dog, an English bulldog, sniffed at Gillard, and then wheezed off in the other direction. 'Come back, Henry,' the man called, then turned to Gillard. 'He probably thinks he can smell the rapist.'

'It would be a useful skill,' Gillard replied.

Just then a piercing scream tore the air. It seemed to come from the far end of the park, and was followed by another shout, less loud.

'Ring 999,' Gillard said to the man. 'I'm going to investigate.'

He didn't wait for the dog walker to answer, but sprinted off down the path towards the sound of the noise. As he was doing so, a stocky figure in a motorcycle helmet on an electric scooter emerged from the darkness of the trees, coming towards him at silent speed.

'Stop,' Gillard yelled, trying to flag the scooterist down. He stepped in front of the scooter, waving his arms. The rider dropped the vehicle, ran as if to go past Gillard, and turning slightly away did some kind of martial arts kick aimed at his head. Gillard partially blocked the heel of the motorcycle boot with one arm, but staggered backwards with the force. The next blow, a kick to the ribs, knocked all the wind from his body. As he tumbled backwards, an arc of metallic sky flew past his vision until his head hit the ground, leaving him with an upside-down view of the approaching bulldog, and the cold shock of the puddle he had fallen into. By the time he had scrambled to his feet, retching, his assailant and the scooter had vanished.

'Are you all right?' asked the dog walker, who had rushed over. 'The police are on their way.' Henry stood nearby, panting asthmatically, with a Churchillian look of defiance on his face.

'Where did he go?' Gillard mumbled dizzily.

'Up there,' the man said, pointing to Gillard's own street.

'Into Parkmead Crescent?'

'No, past the entrance, there's a footpath behind the bushes there. Are you okay?'

Gillard noticed his arm, hand and knuckles were badly grazed from parrying the kick, but the pain from his midriff made him feel sick, and a headache was coming. The man felt in his pocket, and brought out a wad of tissues, handing them to Gillard for the blood that was seeping from his hand. 'Such violence. You only asked him to stop. What is it with the youth of today? Look, do you need an ambulance?'

'No, I'll be fine.' He felt for his phone, but couldn't find it in his pocket. The man shone his torch, which showed the iPhone lying in the same puddle Gillard had fallen in. The screen was cracked and showed no signs of life.

'I think there is somebody down there,' the man said, shining his torch into the trees. Gillard could see it too, a dark recumbent form, the white and orange flashes of a pair of trainers reflecting the torchlight.

'Maybe we just disturbed the rapist,' the man said, heading off towards the shadows. Taking his cue, Henry raced ahead.

'Can you stay back and hold your dog, please?' Gillard said. 'I'm a police officer, and this may be a crime scene.' He felt in his pockets for his warrant card, but it wasn't there. Like the phone, it had probably fallen out of his pocket when he was knocked down.

'Gosh, yes of course.' The man seized the bulldog by the collar and held him back, and let Gillard take his torch. The figure was face down, spread-eagled, near a bench, wearing black running gear. Gillard knelt and felt for a pulse on the neck underneath a mass of pale hair restrained by an Alice band. Expecting a woman, the breadth and hairiness of the neck showed this was a man. He was still warm, but there was no sign of life. Gillard gradually eased him into the recovery position. But one look at his face made clear. He was dead. His right eye was missing, and the socket was oozing blood. It looked like he'd been beaten up, and stabbed in the face for good measure.

'Dead?' the dog walker asked, leaning over to look, and then recoiling. 'Oh, good God.'

Gillard looked up at him. 'I need you to stay away.'

'So are you working undercover to catch the rapist?' the man asked.

'No. I was off duty.'

The sound of sirens in the distance made them look up. Gillard was impressed. That was less than five minutes.

—

In two more minutes, there were three squad cars, an ambulance and a CSI van parked across the path. Gillard woozily recounted to a uniformed female officer called Nolan what had happened. He identified himself, but refused her attempts to get him to go with a paramedic to be checked over.

'You've almost certainly got concussion, sir,' she said. Her face was flashing on and off in the strobe of blue lights, which seem to be adding to his monumental headache.

'I'll be fine.' He looked at the paramedic, similarly illuminated, who was shaking his head. No you won't.

'We'll take you in to A&E. Get you looked over, get that arm attended to,' the paramedic said.

'Look, my wife is expecting me back, and is due to give birth any time. I can't afford to wait two hours sitting in a hospital.'

'To be honest, sir, you'll not be much help to anyone in this state.'

The bile rose in Gillard's throat, and he leaned over, gagging on a sour acrid taste as if he was going to throw up. He swallowed it down, embarrassed to be in this state.

'Who's the victim?' Gillard asked, through thickened throat.

'Don't you worry about that,' she said. 'It's all under control.'

Gillard felt another wave of nausea, both from his bruised diaphragm, and the patronising attitude of the PC. He tentatively explored his mouth with his tongue. All he could taste was the metallic tang of blood. Had he bitten his tongue when he fell? It seemed swollen. Luckily, he still seemed to have all his teeth.

'My phone isn't working,' he said, brandishing the ruined device. 'I need to call my wife.'

'You can use my personal phone, sir,' said a male PC. 'I'll fetch it from the car.'

'This is the golden hour,' Gillard whispered hoarsely to Nolan. 'Get some detectives here. You need to trace that electric scooter. See if there's any CCTV, video doorbell footage. Get someone along that path, behind the bushes near the Parkmead exit.'

'I'm sure there's somebody from CID on their way,' Nolan said. 'You just take it easy, sir.' She stepped away to answer a message on her radio. Gillard could hear the crackly sound but couldn't make it out. He turned to look over his left shoulder, where the CSI van was just visible beyond the ambulance. The paramedic was offering him a wheelchair, and he waved it away.

'I want you to go to A&E right now,' the paramedic said. 'You banged your head, and you could easily have a bleed on the brain which might kill you. I've seen it many times. You'll be doing your wife and unborn child no favours by refusing,' he said.

The fresh-faced PC passed across his phone. Gillard thanked him, tapped out the number, and Sam answered almost immediately.

'Where have you been?' Sam asked, before he had time to speak.

'I'm in the park, I'm all right, but they want to take me to hospital.' Even as he said it he realised it didn't make sense.

'You sound drunk, and slurring. What's happened?'

'There's been a murder.'

'Oh no! Is this the rapist again?'

'Possibly, but the victim is a man. I heard a scream, went to intervene, and got a good kicking for my troubles.'

'Craig! You poor thing.'

'Never mind about me, I'm thinking about you and the baby.'

'Well, don't. We are absolutely fine. Mum's here, she can drive if anything happens. You look after yourself, do you hear me?'

'I hear you,' he said thickly.

'I love you,' she whispered. 'But you can't do everything all by yourself, you have to understand that.'

'I love you too, Sam.' He cut the call, handed back the phone with thanks, and turned to the paramedic. 'Okay, you better take me in.'

—

Gillard sat in the accident and emergency department of the Royal Surrey County Hospital, awaiting his turn for attention, and trying to get his phone to work. Some ibuprofen from the paramedic had cut the headache to a dull throbbing. Being a Sunday the place was only medium busy, and he couldn't see anyone who was obviously drunk. A slightly built young doctor, wearing a hijab, had been working away along the rows of mainly elderly people waiting to be seen. Rainy Macintosh, formerly a hospital doctor herself, had described the delights of working at the front line, using a triage system to spot those who really were in need of urgent treatment. The doctor was trailed by a sizeable woman with a bandaged leg, who had spent some time on the phone to her daughter describing in unnecessary detail the diabetic sores that were the bane of her life, intermittently button-holing any member of staff who might be able to see her more quickly.

The doctor finally came to Gillard, and asked him what had happened. She was taken aback to hear that he was a police officer, and took him into a curtained cubicle, where she shone a light into his eyes.

'Any vomiting?' she said, as she got him to move his eyes.

'Not as such,' he responded.

'Your pupil reflexes and eye movements seem normal,' she said. 'But I think we'll need a scan, to be on the

75

safe side. I'll prescribe you some paracetamol for your headache. No driving or alcohol for twenty-four hours.'

'How long to wait for the scan?'

'It's not too bad. Half an hour. If it's all clear, you should get someone to take you home. Take a few days off work.'

'I'd love to,' he said. As she moved to the next patient, Gillard replayed in his head those few seconds of the attack. His assailant, stocky and muscular, really knew what he was doing. He had been assaulted quite a few times over the years, especially during drug raids. All he could be certain of was that this man was a highly experienced fighter. Assuming it was his assailant who had stabbed the victim, he had remained composed and focused.

He emerged from the cubicle and went to sit in the waiting area, where he saw PC Nita Basu smiling at him.

'How are you doing, sir?' she asked.

'I'm absolutely fine. I'm going home as soon as I've had my scan. My wife's expecting a baby any time.'

'Before you do that, I was wondering if you'd be able to answer a few quick questions. Is there somewhere we could go?'

Gillard looked around him. There were trolleys with patients in the corridor, and a steady stream of staff and patients going back and forth. 'Let's go outside.'

He made his way laboriously out through three sets of doors to the entrance, where a man in a dressing gown and a surgical boot was smoking under the porch, right by a sign which said that he couldn't. Gillard shuffled along closer to the car park ticket machine. The rain had died away, but there were still plentiful puddles and the breeze was damp. After the cloying heat of A&E it felt refreshing.

Nita brought out her notebook, and took a complete account of the incident.

'So how long after you heard the scream would you say it was before you saw the man on the scooter?'

'Just over a minute, I suppose. I made a note of the time of the scream, 9.13 p.m.'

'And you say you couldn't get a look at his face?'

'He was wearing a full-face motorcycle helmet, which was white with black and blue stripes on it. A bit like my head feels.'

She smiled. 'Was there any kind of logo on the helmet?'

'Not that I could see. The visor was tinted too, so I couldn't see his face.'

'I was just going to ask you that.'

'Have there been any other sightings of the assailant?'

'Not that I've heard of.'

Gillard managed a slight chuckle, which hurt more than he expected. 'The last I saw of him he was heading towards the street that I live in, although the witness said he went past it. If it had just been a few days later, I would have installed the video doorbell, assuming I could find which storage box it was in.'

'We'll be doing a house-to-house on all the streets leading to the park from tomorrow morning. We haven't had any witness sightings apart from the dog walker, who just basically backed up your story.'

'Who is running the case?'

'DI Perry.'

'I see.' John Perry was a decent enough detective, but lacked imagination and drive. No doubt he was given the case because Claire Mulholland was tied up with the Hove murder.

'Everyone is asking after you,' she said.

'That's nice, but I'll be fine. Have you got an ID for the stabbing victim?'

'Yes,' she said, lowering her voice and eyeing the smoker. 'It's the celebrity divorcee.'

'What! You mean Gary Wray?'

'The very same. It's not been made public yet.'

–

The first hint that his mobile wasn't broken was when it rang. The number was marked private, but turned out to be Chief Constable Alison Rigby, calling from home. Given that it was nearly one a.m. it had to be something urgent. He had a horrible feeling he knew what it was.

'Yes, ma'am.'

'I hear you've been assaulted, Craig.'

'Yes, in Nightingale Park, Guildford. I'm just here at A&E waiting for my scan.'

Rigby then asked a few questions about Sam and the baby and the expected date. He knew what was coming.

'You sound crisp and clear to me, Craig, which is good news. Because, pending an all clear on the scan, I'm going to make an exceptional request—'

'You want me to take on the Wray murder case, don't you, ma'am?'

She laughed, 'Craig, as always, you're one step ahead. Yes, it seems a shame to waste your unique knowledge of the case, and I know you will do a very rapid and effective job.'

'Sam is going to have a baby, any time. I promised her, and ma'am, you promised me—'

'I know I did, and I'm extremely sorry to have to break my promise. You have to look at my operational difficulties. This is going to be a huge case, and I need my safest, most capable pair of hands.'

'But what about Sam?'

'I understand she is not due for a week, and you know how first births are normally a few days late. If I'm wrong, I'll let you go. I'd never forgive myself if you weren't by her side when your child is born. But we have a few crucial days and you can make a real difference.'

'But, ma'am—'

'Thank you, Craig, I knew you'd see it my way. The incident room meeting is set for nine a.m. tomorrow.' She cut the call.

He stared open-mouthed at the cracked screen of his phone, then looked up to see Sam and her mother approaching him.

'The mountain has come to Mohammed,' Sam said, tapping her now huge bump. 'I couldn't sleep, anyway. So how are you?' She flopped down into a chair opposite.

Gillard explained what had just happened. Sam listened carefully and then shook her head with incredulity. 'That woman is literally going to work you to death, isn't she?'

'Hopefully it will only be a couple of days,' he said.

'I just don't believe it,' she said. 'You. Are. On. Leave.'

'I know. Look, if you go into labour or your waters break, then I'm bailing out.'

She stared at him. 'I suspect you actually prefer to be at work than sitting at home with me, waiting for our daughter to be born.'

'Look, most of the time while working I actually will be sitting at home with you.'

Mary Phillips was smiling enigmatically at him, but he felt he was being judged.

A nurse hove into view. 'Mr Gillard? Please follow me for your scan.'

As he walked away, he felt a hot pang of guilt. Sam was right. He had got bored at home, once the unpacking was finished. She knew he was a workaholic, and so did Alison Rigby. The outcome was inevitable.

Late Sunday

Rainy Macintosh stared out of the window as the Euston to Glasgow train whooshed and rattled through the night. Her carriage was half full; tired-looking people idly scrolling their phones, or asleep with their mouths open. Her insides were completely knotted. Before she'd left, she'd broken the news to Ewan about his father's death. At first he seemed to take it well. But she knew her son, all bravado and no communication. A bit like his father. Every hurt and every pain buried, walled off in the garret of his psyche. He hadn't wanted to come up to Glasgow with her, and she was relieved. She had some investigating to do. Something that her son should have no part in. Stuck in her head, immovably, was a horrible suspicion that she knew what had happened, that it was her own hurt and anger that had indirectly led to his death. For all that, she prayed that she was wrong, that the bizarre circumstances of his killing would turn out to be just an accident.

She steepled her hands over her nose, closed her eyes, and hyperventilated to try to stabilise herself. She had been told Ross was found dead on a country lane outside his own house, having been run over. Not simply knocked down, but driven over, by a so-far unidentified vehicle. The alarm had been raised by a passing motorist, who had seen the body and dialled 999.

Tomorrow morning, Monday, she had a meeting with DCI Harry McLeod at the mortuary. She just hoped he could set her fears to rest. Because if what she feared had transpired, she didn't think she could ever reveal it. The consequences would be just horrific. It would not simply be the end of her career, but much worse than that. She would lose Ewan. And that she could never bear.

No, there had to be some other explanation.

Chapter Six

Claire woke up in her seaside bedroom when it was still dark, to the scream of gulls overhead. She checked her phone, and saw it was not yet seven. She hadn't slept that well, and dreamed of being forced to address thousands of angry male police officers at some rally. She got up, showered quickly and put the TV news on while she dressed. There had been a vicious attack, apparently racially motivated, on an elderly shopkeeper in Birmingham. She really didn't need to hear any of that, she had enough on her plate. When the latest headlines on Gary Wray and Tia Whitlock flashed across the screen at the bottom, she groaned and switched channels, finding a programme about dolphins, which was at least more cheerful.

She made herself a cup of tea in her room, and ate the two small biscuits wrapped in cellophane which sat on the tea tray. Hopefully there would be something more of a breakfast downstairs than there had been yesterday. She quickly texted her kids, reminding Collum about his dental appointment later that day, and Tom about the letter she had seen on Friday about his motorcycle insurance. Being a busy mum didn't stop just because you are working on a murder case. She'd had a long phone call yesterday evening with husband Barry, a plasterer, and had got off her chest all of the frustrations of having to make a decision about when to charge Liam Lewis. Barry was always the first to say that he couldn't possibly judge what she had to do but he listened carefully, and concluded that she should keep her options open for as long as possible.

With the approval of DCS Mills, she could hold Liam Lewis in custody until 4.30 this afternoon. But then she would either have to charge him or release him on police bail. All the evidence was that he was guilty. She had to charge him, there was no alternative. But her gut instinct, and that of her entire team, was that he didn't commit the crime. But who did? How on earth had they got into Stapleford's home without effort, committed such a savage attack, and escaped without anyone seeing a thing?

She looked out of the rain-speckled window, where the first rays of sunshine were peeping through leaden clouds. She wasn't looking forward to today. Not at all. An innocent cop was going to be charged with a crime she was convinced he didn't commit. And without fresh evidence she could do nothing to stop this legal jugger-naut. But there was no fresh evidence. She just couldn't work out what she had missed.

–

Gillard was at work at seven, easy enough now it was only a five-minute drive. He had kissed Sam goodbye, but she had turned over grumpily and waved him away. She wasn't sleeping well anyway, and in the middle of the night had woken up to say: 'You know Craig, I'm beginning to feel I'm losing you to another woman. A woman who *really* controls you. By comparison, as your wife, I feel I have no power.'

He didn't argue, and indeed could find little to contest about her point of view. He just needed sleep, and to be on top form the next day. That was why he'd gone home with Sam straight after the scan, ignoring the doctor's advice to wait for the results. He'd googled subdural haematoma, what the doctor said they'd be looking for on the scan, but as the headache had receded and he no longer felt nauseous, he thought he'd take the chance. If there was a problem, the hospital would surely ring.

As he slid his car into the Mount Browne car park, he noticed that Alison Rigby's vehicle was already there. He saw the chill condensation on the bonnet, and realised she must've been there for some time. No surprise, really. In media terms, the Gary Wray murder was going to be huge.

He went into CID reception, greeted the night officer, and made his way upstairs to his glass box on the first floor. John Perry, who was the duty DI, was sitting at his desk, along with DS Vikram Singh.

'Ah, are we glad to see you!' Perry said, wiping a hand across his forehead. Gillard knew that Perry would be out of his depth. Originally a schoolteacher, he had a good intellect, but lacked the edge of steel required to be lead on a major case.

'Isn't your wife having a baby right now?' Singh asked. 'I thought you were on leave?'

'I was, but our chief constable had other ideas. Where's the rest of the team?'

'Well, Claire Mulholland as you know is down in Hove with Michelle, and Rainy Macintosh is in Glasgow after the death of her husband...'

'Do we have a research intelligence officer?'

'Rob Townsend will be in at nine,' Singh said. 'He didn't get off until midnight.' Singh then listed three other

DCs who were on the case, but Gillard recalled that two of them had only recently finished their probationary period.

'We need more bodies,' Gillard said.

'We've got three off with Covid,' Perry said, defensively, then looked at his watch. 'And I'm off home myself.' He picked up his jacket.

'Where's Hoskins?'

'Allocated to the Stapleford case to replace Rainy,' Singh said.

'Right,' Gillard said, and picked up the phone. In the next half-hour he had arranged for two of the three Covid sufferers to work from home, had arranged for uniformed officers to conduct a fingertip search at the crime scene, and had spoken to press chief Christina McCafferty, to find out what she had planned in the way of press conferences. He'd left a message for the chief constable pleading for more bodies, and had rung the hospital to see who was the duty forensic pathologist. He also juggled some shifts to ensure DC Gabby Underwood was available to be family liaison officer with the Wray family.

In a final few minutes before the nine o'clock incident room meeting, he sat in the loo and googled Gary Wray. Originally Gary Radu, of Ukrainian and Romanian parentage, his family had come to the UK when he was a toddler, and made their home in Chertsey in Surrey. He left school at sixteen, avoided joining his father's fabric business, and instead began hustling in the rag trade, buying and selling ex-celebrity clothing, before appearing on *Dragon's Den* and making his name on social media. He'd worked his way up the hard way, always a route oozing with motives for revenge and jealousy.

Finally, as the incident room meeting began, the case was looking in some kind of order. Gillard had whiteboards populated with details of Gary Wray's last movements, next of kin, and a list of investigative leads to chase down. There were three officers on Zoom, and four there in person, including a uniformed inspector, a bureaucratic desk jockey named Geoffrey Holt. Definitely a second division team.

'All right everybody, let's get going,' Gillard said. 'The circumstances of Gary Wray's death are as follows. His black Mercedes was caught on his home security system leaving Walton-on-Thames at 8.27 p.m. At 8.46 p.m. he was captured on CCTV jogging towards Nightingale Park from Churchill Terrace, where his car was later found parked. It was 9.13 p.m. when a scream was heard, by me amongst others, less than a minute after that when the electric scooter appeared, and my own little argument with the rider. Now although we have no evidence to say that the rider is the perpetrator, that is I think we can agree the most reasonable line of inquiry, which is why we need to find out who he is soon as possible.'

Geoffrey Holt put up his hand. 'I've got half a dozen officers doing door-to-door, in Parkmead Crescent, on Churchill Terrace and the properties in other streets which border on the park. I'm not optimistic on getting any witnesses to the electric scooter, seeing as they are nearly silent, and they wouldn't turn your head.'

'How many houses back on to the park on that side?'

Holt looked down at his notebook. 'Erm. Maybe a dozen, or two.'

'How many of them have rear gates into the park?'

'I don't have that information yet.' He looked up. 'Did the scooter have a headlight, sir?'

'There was a small LED cyclist-type lamp on the handlebars, from memory.'

'In my experience most of these effectively illegal road users do not have correct illumination,' Holt continued.

'Well, once we catch him, we can do him for that as well,' Gillard said. 'In the meantime I want to find some image of this scooter, either coming in or out of the park. There's a couple of A roads nearby, and at least one road safety camera, as well as a parade of suburban shops. I think there must be a good chance. If we get an image, we've got something to put out there for the public.'

One of the newly qualified DCs, a tall woman called Liz Tufnell, put up her hand. 'Are we assuming Mr Wray was simply in the wrong place at the wrong time, or are we thinking this might be related to the court case in which he was involved?'

'That's a good question, and one I was coming to. If it was targeted, then you'd have to know exactly what his jogging routine was. He may have been seen here before.'

'Why drive all the way to Guildford to run?' Tufnell asked.

'Another good question,' Gillard said. 'Maybe he had some other reason to be there. It would be good to find out.'

'Given that he was very fit, he would have taken quite some killing, wouldn't he?' Singh asked.

'Quite possibly. We're not expecting the post-mortem to take place until later today, but I can tell you that in addition to other injuries he looked to me to have been stabbed in the eye.' There was a collective *eeeugh*. 'I'm no pathologist, but I guess that wound alone would be fatal.' He turned to Holt. 'Right, Geoff, I'm hoping we get enough uniforms to do a proper door-to-door for all the roads adjoining the park, particularly around the pedestrian exits. I want every house with a rear gate on to the park visited, and the gardens checked for a discarded weapon or even the scooter. We will be looking for domestic CCTV, doorbell cameras, anyone who heard anything, and any witnesses to either the movements of the victim, or our presumed assailant.'

'I'll see if we can get any more bodies,' Holt said.

'Christina McCafferty has arranged a press conference for five p.m. and we need to focus ourselves on having something to say.' He turned to the three officers on Zoom. To one, a female DC called Kim Leighton who had coughed her way through the conference so far, he allocated the task of finding out every scrap of information online about Gary Wray, and particularly to establish if his address and location were well known. The second, a pale-looking male, he asked to ring round every business with premises bordering the park to seek out CCTV. 'If you look at Operation Safety Net, which you will recall was put in place to catch the park rapist, you will see somebody has already done the hard work for you. There is a list of premises, and I want their latest footage by lunchtime at the latest.' The final Zoom participant, a glum-faced officer with a bad case of bed-hair, he asked to take detailed statements over the phone from any witness referred to him by the uniforms.

'Right everybody, I've no need to tell you this but it is essential that nobody talks to the press. All we are putting out is that Mr Wray was found dead in the park, and that we want to speak to the rider of an electric scooter who may have witnessed it. Refer any enquiries you may get to Christina McCafferty and her colleagues.'

The meeting broke up, and Geoffrey Holt came over to Gillard. 'We've already had a couple of reports from the door-to-door, mainly of people hearing the scream.'

'I know there were two 999 calls.'

'We've also had one eyewitness sighting of the electric scooter, someone with an upstairs window overlooking the park,' Holt said. 'It was just a glimpse, apparently.'

'If we can get a route for the rider, that will help.' Gillard turned away to take a call from the coroner's office. He then followed up by ringing the Royal Surrey County Hospital, to find out when the post-mortem would take place. Eleven. He would be there for it. As he hung up he saw DS Vikram Singh was waiting to see him.

'Have you got time to look through the evidence bags with me?' Singh asked. 'I've just signed them out from the store.'

Gillard nodded, and followed Singh into the evidence examination room on the ground floor, where a female technician was already waiting. There were half a dozen paper evidence bags, and the two detectives donned plastic gloves before opening them. The largest contained Wray's training shoes, Nike Vaporfly Elite. 'This is superstar footwear,' Singh said. 'Where I grew up, these would be enough motive for a robbery.'

Gillard hefted the bag. 'Light as a feather,' he said. Using magnifying glasses, they peered at the laces for signs of blood, and carefully inverted them to inspect the soles.

'I've taken prints already, and samples from mud caught in the treads,' the technician said.

They moved on to a smaller package, which contained Wray's fitness tracker, and mobile phone. 'We've already downloaded the data, and it's just awaiting analysis,' Singh said.

'That's a priority,' Gillard said. 'If he'd received threats or anything like that it could be significant. Did he have a wallet with him?'

'None was found. No wristwatch, either,' Singh said. 'A single door key was found in a sleeve pocket on his tunic.'

'No car keys?'

'No. The clothing itself is still in place on the body, and will be cut off in the mortuary. They know we want it back for examination.'

Gillard nodded. 'I want to find out who else's DNA was on him.' He checked his watch. The e-fit artist was due upstairs in a moment. 'Vikram, get over to Gary Wray's home, and collect all his computers and phones. I'll want a match to any DNA found there, and what is recovered at the crime scene. And I want to know where he left his car keys once he got to Guildford.'

'Got it.'

Gillard thanked the two, and headed for the stairs. As he did so he rang Gabby Underwood, who should be on her way to the home of Tia Whitlock, the estranged partner of the victim. What she had to say would be very interesting. If anyone had a motive to kill him, she did.

–

Gillard drove over to Pinkneys Green, near Maidenhead, to the seven-bedroom Georgian home belonging to Tia Whitlock. He eased the car through a crowd of reporters at the gate, and drove up the gravel drive. He saw that Gabby Underwood's vehicle was already there. He was met on arrival at the grand front entrance by Ms Whitlock's business manager, Jürgen Kempf. A former member of the German Olympic diving team, Kempf was impeccably dressed in an expensive suit, and apologised for the press presence. Gillard was guided past a beautiful, tiled hallway, into a walnut panelled office on the ground floor which gave views over rolling parkland.

Tia Whitlock was dressed in an ivory-coloured sheath dress which showed off her tan. In person she was even better looking than she appeared on TV, although her countenance was grim.

Gabby Underwood made the introductions.

'I'm very sorry for your loss,' Gillard said, far from certain how much of a loss Wray's ex-partner would consider it.

'Everyone is blaming me for this,' she said, tearfully, gesturing to a sheaf of newspapers on the desk between them.

'We're not assuming that,' Gillard replied. 'But—'

'No? A bunch of uniformed officers swooped on me first thing this morning, and snatched all my mobile phones and computers.'

'Ms Whitlock, we have to—'

'Just because I lost the High Court case last week, and haven't yet appealed, everyone is assuming I bumped him off. I'd never do that!' She slammed her hand down on the newspapers.

Self-pity first, grief later, if at all. Gillard wasn't surprised. Gabby Underwood had already relayed Ms Whitlock's alibi, which was certainly a solid one. At the time of her ex-partner's killing, she was in Colchester addressing a group of female businesspeople about how to break the glass ceiling. Of course, anyone with the money that Tia Whitlock had wouldn't have to get their hands dirty. A fast, virtually silent assassin, dressed in motorcycle gear, could presumably be obtained for the right fee.

'I think you have to understand that these are obvious checks we have to make,' Gillard said. 'But we are keeping an open mind.'

'So how did he die, then?'

'I'm not at liberty to share those details. The post-mortem will be conducted this morning, and then we will have a better idea of what really happened.'

'But you were there!' Tia said, brandishing a copy of the *Daily Mail*. 'It says here that an off-duty detective actually witnessed the attack, and was assaulted when trying to tackle the assailant.'

'I have no comment to make on press reports.'

'What about this then?' She picked up a copy of the *Daily Mirror*. "Police sources declined to confirm reports from neighbours that the detective in question was Detective Chief Inspector Craig Gillard, who had recently moved into the area."'

Gabby Underwood shifted uncomfortably in the seat beside him.

'I'll let you know the details as soon as I can,' Gillard said. 'In the meantime, there are some questions I'd like to ask you.'

'Fire away, then.' She glanced at her watch, the gems on the bracelet catching the light.

'To what extent do you stand to benefit from Mr Wray's death?'

'You mean financially? I've no idea what his will says. I have a half share in a number of businesses, which as you know is a subject of court action, and I was trying to wrest control of the intellectual property that underpinned them. There isn't any clear outcome, as far as I'm concerned,' she said.

'You don't seem very upset,' Gillard said.

'Well, you didn't look at my Twitter feed, then. Look, I'm certainly shocked. I don't love him anymore, but he was a big part of my life, and I'm sure it will hit me at some stage. Right now, I'm fighting for my reputation and my livelihood. I don't have the time to be upset. I have to function.'

Kempf leaned in, and said: 'Ms Whitlock has another meeting in a few minutes, so if you don't have any more questions…'

'What meeting is that?' Gillard asked her.

'It's with the managers of the various businesses, we have to adopt an emergency continuity plan. Gary was at the centre of everything, and he won't easily be replaced.'

That seemed reasonable. He thanked her and made his way out with Gabby. They had a brief meeting in his car. 'I spoke to Gary Wray's father this morning,' she said. 'He didn't waste much time before blaming Ms Whitlock.'

'You can see his point. If the killing was deliberate, it meant somebody knew where to find him, when and where he went jogging.'

'There's something else, you may already know about.' Gabby swiped through her phone. 'Look at this, it's from the *Sun* last week. "Tia Whitlock ex on assault charges. *Love Island* contestant Aaron Randall, former partner of handbags-at-dawn businesswoman Tia Whitlock, was on Wednesday charged with assaulting three men and a woman in a nightclub. Former cage fighter Randall, 33, was charged with head-butting Jerome Smith, 19, and punching Leroy Noades, 22, Harvey Davies, 28, and Mr Davies' girlfriend who cannot be named for legal reasons.

Randall, of Waverley Road, Liverpool, met Ms Whitlock on the reality TV show after she broke up with designer gear entrepreneur Gary Wray. They had a two-year on–off relationship, before Ms Whitlock began dating *Britain's Got Talent* contestant Mark Hagan, brother of TikTok influencer—'"

'All right, that's enough,' Gillard said. 'I'd got Randall on the interview list, along with a number of others. But this celebrity stuff makes my head spin.'

'Maybe Wray had other business enemies?' Gabby said.

'It's always possible. But not many are angry enough to do this.' He swiped through his iPad to show her a photograph of Wray's battered face.

'Ugh.' Gabby looked away.

'To me, Gabby, this looks personal, not business. This wasn't a clinical killing, it was vindictive.'

Chapter Seven

There was no such thing as a celebrity post-mortem. On the cold uncompromising slab the human body shrugs off all affectations and aspirations. In the all-pervasive light of the mortuary lamp, Gillard could see Gary Wray may have had professionally shaped eyebrows, a perma-tan and a regular manicure, but his face was a gory mess. His nose was clearly broken, teeth missing, lip cut in three places. Otherwise, the waxy flesh of which he was constructed was not a great deal different to that of any more ordinary mortal, from the greying roots of his dyed fair hair, to the various plasters on his heels and toes – evidence of the afflictions of a regular runner.

Dr Vicky Montague, the duty Home Office forensic pathologist, had not yet begun the evisceration, but was already intoning into the suspended microphone some of the more obvious findings when Gillard walked in. She ordered the voice-controlled device into sleep mode, and turned to him.

'Hello Craig. The report won't be ready until this evening at the earliest,' she said.

'I understand that, and I've only got a few minutes myself. I just wondered if you could give me a few clues.'

'The cause of death looks to have been the violent penetration of an object into the left hemisphere of the brain. There is considerable damage to the face, including a broken nose, a fractured eye socket on the other side, and some substantial abrasions and contusions. From a lack of swelling, I would suggest they were inflicted immediately pre- or post-mortem. CSI has already sent face swabs for testing, to see if we can get the DNA of the attacker.'

'Is there any evidence of fightback?'

'No. Very little material found under the fingernails, though I will get it tested. No defensive cuts on the arms. My guess is that he was caught by surprise. From the damage caused, I would suggest an unusually powerful assailant. Three ribs were broken, possibly by a kick.'

'Gary Wray was very athletic, an Ironman contender, and had once been a fitness instructor.' He glanced at the plastered feet. 'Maybe he'd been overdoing the running.'

'That's as may be. But look at the state of him. He had clearly met his match.' She reached up and with her rubber glove moved the face of the corpse to the left. 'There is, however, a slightly unusual wound just here.' She pointed to a pair of pea-sized silvery marks on his neck, about an inch apart.

'Are they burns?'

'Yes, I think so. I've taken a biopsy. I have my suspicions, having seen something a little like this before, but await confirmation.'

'Can you give me a clue?'

'The only time I've ever seen an injury like this was on a man who died of a heart attack after being Tasered by a police officer.'

'So that's an electrical burn?'

'I think so. The keratin on the surface has melted a little. If my suspicions are correct, we will find basal cell joule burns from the steam created by moisture vaporisation.'

'And a Taser can do that?'

'Well, it's not intended to. If this burn turns out to be relevant to the attack, then it may have been a modified device to give a substantially larger wallop.'

Gillard steepled his hands across his nose. The idea that someone was running around with a stun gun, possibly from police resources, was a nightmare. It opened up a wholly new and worrying category of suspect. Someone within the force? Another Liam Lewis? Surely not.

Back at Mount Browne, Gillard was looking over the shoulder of Vikram Singh at his terminal, watching some interview footage with Gary Wray, taken a month ago by Sports Fitness News. A reporter in running gear was jogging side-by-side with the millionaire, asking various questions about the court case. The introduction to the report began with: 'I'm here on the regular running route of Britain's greatest handbag entrepreneur, a man who is now involved in a multi-million-pound court case against his estranged partner. And I've come here to ask him: "Just what is it about regular running that drives a man on to become a successful businessman?"'

Gillard hadn't heard of the channel, and thought the whole piece rather crass, PR puff masquerading as news. Wray had clearly co-operated fully, even slowing down to give the breathless reporter a chance to ask his questions. Gillard recognised Nightingale Park as the location, though most viewers would presumably not have, until the final reporter's sign-off. 'This is Kevin Bailey, Sports Fitness News, reporting live from Nightingale Park, Guildford. Now back to the studio.'

Digging this up was a pretty good piece of research by one of the Covid-afflicted officers. It showed that any sufficiently interested member of the public could have discovered Wray's running route. Wray had even told the reporter that he did the same route every day, at the same time. For an assassin, even a casual one, this was a gift.

'So what do you think, sir?' Singh asked his boss.

'Well, excellent evidence though it is, we have just enlarged the pool of potential suspects. We can no longer assume that it was only close family, friends or intimate enemies who were involved with this. It could even be some Internet troll.' Gillard left unsaid his bigger worry. That because of the Taser burn, the culprit was someone connected to the police.

'His social media accounts certainly show a big spike in hate mail as the court case progressed,' Singh said.

'Let's check on the CCTV situation,' Gillard said, logging into his emails. They were gradually accumulating links to the various bits and pieces of footage from businesses and road safety cameras around the edge of the park, chased down by another of the officers working from home. Since he had last looked, there were two more, including one that he had been looking forward to. A convenience store whose camera covered part of the main road leading to the far end of the park. However, the email said that there seemed to be no sightings of an electric scooter in the hours leading up to the attack.

Gillard rubbed his chin. In the hour since the publication of an e-fit of the scooter rider, there had already been more than a hundred calls and messages from the public. He suspected that many of these would turn out to be general complaints about inconsiderate scooter riders, rather than any specific intelligence about the person they were looking for. One of the trainees was going through them now.

'So what did you get from Gary Wray's house?' Gillard asked Singh.

'Ah boss, what an amazing place. Right by the river at Walton, four levels of lawn going right down to the Thames and swans nesting on the bank. The house is a split-level Art Deco job, with massive windows. There's a huge kitchen which runs the entire length along the waterside, with the thickest granite top counters I've ever seen—'

'It's all right Vikram, I don't want to buy the place.'

'Sorry. The De Marr Couture business is run from a converted Victorian greenhouse in the grounds with a couple of hipster staff. They kicked up quite a fuss when I unplugged the servers, talking about legal action.'

'It's par for the course, unfortunately.'

'We had a team doing his home office, on the second floor. Wray's father, who is a director, stood around and glared at us. The company has a small office in Covent Garden, and secure warehousing in Hatfield. It will take months to go through everything, if that's what you want.'

'No problem. Wray is going to be dead for a while yet.'

'Wray's solicitors say they don't have a will for him on file, and his father believes there isn't one.'

Gillard nodded. 'The economic crime unit has taken a quick look at his bank records, and there is nothing that looks unusual. They'll get on to the company accounts later.'

Singh gave him a lopsided smile, then said, 'I also briefly met Wray's current partner Nooraya, well, who is just...'

Gillard watched the Sikh, his eyes widening, mouth moving silently, clearly struggling to articulate the effect on him of proximity to beauty. Nooraya, who went by just one name, was a rising Bollywood star, frequently voted amongst the world's top ten most gorgeous women. The connection with Wray had begun a year ago when she was recruited as a brand ambassador for De Marr 'armwear'. This was turning out to be one of the few crimes Gillard had investigated where tabloid celebrity news was essential background reading.

'How do you assess her motives in this, Vikram?'

He looked puzzled. 'Oh, I'm sure she had nothing to do with it. She said she'd just flown in from Mumbai, and seemed really upset.'

'Vikram, snap out of it! You're bloody mesmerised. Can I just emphasise this is one of the most high-profile cases you will ever work on? It's time to use your head, not your heart, nor whatever is stirring in the trouser department. By the end of the day I want to know whether Nooraya is in debt, what happened to her previous husband, and whether she has a financial interest in De Marr Couture Ltd. Do you think you can manage that?'

'Yes, sir.'

'And I don't just mean sitting reading the latest copy of *Hello!* magazine.'

'Right you are, sir.' Singh retreated to his desk.

It was almost lunchtime, and Gillard was feeling a recurrence of the headache he'd had after the attack, and remembered he was supposed to ring his GP to get the results of his scan. He tapped out the number, found out he was twelfth in the queue, and despite his call being 'very important to us', as the surgery robot insisted, he didn't actually have time to wait.

He returned to his desk to seek out some ibuprofen. As he swilled down a couple of tablets with some water, he saw DC Kim Leighton walk into the CID office after her lunch break.

'Kim, just the woman. Can you chase up my urgent request to get hold of Aaron Randall?'

Her eyes widened. 'What, from *Love Island*?'

Gillard laughed. 'Don't worry, you won't need an extradition request. He lives in Liverpool. Can you chase up Merseyside Police?'

'Absolutely. I'm on to it. Is this about Gary Wray?'

'Yes. Mr Randall is our prime suspect,' he said, as he picked up a call. 'Really? Okay, I'll be right over.'

'What's happened, sir?'

'Merseyside Police must be employing mind readers. They've already got Randall in an interview room. All right, off you go.'

Fifteen minutes later, Gillard sat down to a big screen terminal in the CID room with DC Liz Tufnell. 'Merseyside Police have already had Aaron Randall in for interview, and they've already sent me the tape.' He had only made the request four hours ago.

'Ooh, let's see,' said DC Kim Leighton, looking up from her desk. From the speed she crossed the room, it would be hard to guess that she had severe Covid just a week ago, and had been coughing like a TB victim all through one of the incident room meetings. Three other officers and a couple of female technicians also crowded round behind him to gaze at the celebrity.

It took a moment for Gillard to realise why Merseyside had been so efficient. Randall had initially been held in custody after last week's nightclub assault, and when released police bail conditions would have kept him on a tight chain. The video gave a bird's-eye view of a grim interview room with two officers. The interviewee was flanked by a male solicitor, and the tabletop held one of the more antiquated official tape recorders Gillard had seen in recent years. Randall's charisma came through, even in such circumstances. He was dressed in white T-shirt, tight grey jogging bottoms and high-top red trainers. The celebrity heart-throb sported a carefully razored blond skin fade and sizeable beard, and his six-pack was almost visible through the tight T-shirt. Even his piercing blue eyes were clearly visible.

'It's a world away from *Love Island*,' said Kim Leighton.

'I think it's meant to be,' said Gillard, laughing.

After the formalities had been concluded, Randall was asked some of the questions that Gillard had emailed: Where was he on the night when Gary Wray was murdered? Could anyone vouch for him? When did he last see Tia Whitlock? Had he ever met Gary Wray? All these questions were answered calmly and confidently. Randall claimed to have been in London at a casino, which should be a good alibi, given all the CCTV cameras casinos had. He claimed never to have met Gary Wray. His body language was relaxed, and he even laughed when he was asked about his relationship with Ms Whitlock.

'Tia is for me water long under the bridge,' he said, shaking his head.

'Yeah, and that's one fast flowing river,' Kim muttered.

Gillard turned to look at her, quizzically.

'I just mean he's had a lot of girlfriends… supposedly,' she explained.

Gillard sighed. 'I think it's very important that you all block the feeling that because of television or social media you actually know this person, because you really don't.

We all have to apply the law, dispassionately, based on evidence.'

'Yes, sir,' they said, almost in unison.

'He was a cage fighter, though,' Kim said. 'So, just putting two and two together. He could easily be the person who beat you up, sir,' she said.

'Thank you for that, Kim.' Gillard said. 'Perhaps you could see if there are any of his fights on YouTube. I've got an appointment at the hospital and I need to prepare.'

Right on cue, his headache had returned.

Gillard looked on his phone at an email from the forensic pathologist. It included a number of photographs of Gary Wray's battered face. Dr Montague described having discovered interesting contusions on Wray's jaw, which was broken in two places. After he had speed-read the jargon-laden email, and looked at the attached photographs, he had an idea. He hurried off to the gents' toilet. Stripping off his shirt, he pushed his chest as close as he could over the washbasin towards the mirror. The whole of his left side was bruised blue and purple. He turned one way then the other, so he was sideways onto the light, but couldn't find what he was looking for. He pulled out his phone and took several photographs of his chest, just as the door opened and Vikram Singh walked in.

'Sorry, sir,' Singh said, and started to back out.

'It's all right,' Gillard said, slipping his shirt back on. 'I'm just looking for a particular mark in my bruises.'

'What kind of mark?'

'From being kicked yesterday.'

'Looks pretty nasty,' Singh said, having seen the rainbow colours.

'I think I'm going to let the forensic pathologist have a look at me this afternoon.'

'Feeling a bit peaky, are we, sir?' Singh said dryly, inspecting his beard in the mirror.

Gillard laughed. 'I'm expecting to be alive throughout. No, I'm hoping to compare bruises with the late Mr Gary Wray.'

–

Gillard had arranged to meet Dr Montague at the Royal Surrey County Hospital, having been given directions to her consultation room, and wondered whether he should stop off to try to get his scan results. Certainly he seemed to be spending enough time here. Finally arriving at the forensic pathologist's office, she invited him in and showed him on a high-resolution screen the images she had taken.

Gary Wray's face, shown at three times normal size, was an almost archaeological record of violence. 'We discussed this already in general terms, but I have made an interesting discovery. There are certain injuries not quite visible to the naked eye, but using a specialist photogram-metric camera in ultraviolet light, I was able to determine the arc of an impact.' She clicked onto a close-up which showed a crescent impression in purple. The calibration device in the photograph showed a length of 104 mm.

'This impact was almost certainly caused by the heel of a heavy boot, and although it didn't tear the skin, an array of tiny blood vessels underneath have been ruptured. Now, if you would be good enough to take off your shirt.'

Gillard stood and stripped to the waist, while the pathologist sat on a chair, pressed a dermatologist's close-up lens against his ribcage, and put her eye to it. 'Yes, I think we've got something here. I'll send you to the technician who uses the ultraviolet camera. She's just down the corridor, and is a dab hand with all the various filters. It could turn out to be powerful evidence.'

Gillard agreed. If the shape and size of the kick he received could be shown to exactly match that on the corpse, then it was compelling evidence that his assailant was indeed Gary Wray's murderer. Hardly a surprise, but clear forensic evidence nonetheless. If Merseyside Police had, as requested, seized Aaron Randall's footwear, they really might be getting somewhere.

–

Rainy had steeled herself for the identification of her ex-husband's body, and it was just as bad as she had feared. After years as a junior doctor she had a strong stomach, but this was hard to take. It was clear, even from the lopsided shape of the sheet over his body, that his ribcage had been crushed. His face, however, look surprisingly peaceful, even the faint hint of a smile on his pale waxy features. A couple of seconds was enough to confirm his identity.

DCI Harry McLeod met her outside the mortuary.

'My profound condolences on your loss, Mrs Macintosh,' he said in his rich Highland burr. After a restorative coffee in the hospital cafe, he drove her to her ex-husband's address. She had seen pictures of High Bank before, googling the place Ross had bought with the money he wouldn't share with her. The five-bedroom detached house was on the main road leading out of the small town of Kirkintilloch, with a steeply rising drive and substantial holly hedges shielding it from public view. It was the last house before agricultural land began, and a hundred yards outside the 30 mph speed limit area. With no immediate neighbours it was quite isolated.

McLeod stopped his unmarked car just a few yards short of the drive. He pointed to the road ahead of them. 'Your husband's body was found here in the early hours of Sunday morning, on the carriageway. He was wearing just a T-shirt and corduroy trousers, slippers but no socks, which given the temperature at the time leads me to believe that he hadn't intended being outdoors for long. Likewise, the door to the house was found ajar.'

'So are you thinking he heard an accident, and came out to see if he could help?'

'Aye, that indeed was my initial thinking. However, if there was an impact loud enough for him to hear, there's very little sign of it on the road. My men did a fingertip search, and though there is a little bit of broken glass in the gutter, it seems old. There are no recent skid marks, either.'

'Maybe he just heard a car horn,' Rainy said.

'It's possible,' McLeod said, simultaneously indicating that he thought it was unlikely. 'We think it must've been after eleven in the evening, to explain the delay in finding the body. We've put out an appeal for witnesses, but none has come forward bar the woman who found him.'

'What time was he found?'

'Ten past midnight, according to our witness. Her own dashcam recorded it, so we have no doubt she is telling the truth.'

'Have you identified the vehicle that ran him over?'

McLeod cocked his head. 'We think it was a four-wheel drive. The tyre width, and apparent vehicle weight, seem indicative of that. The body wasn't dragged on the road, so the speed seems likely to have been low.'

'Then why did they hit him? Why on earth didn't they stop?' Rainy said.

'These are questions I have been pondering. We all know that there are some terrible drivers out there, but even so, it just doesn't add up.'

—

It felt odd that a stranger was showing Rainy round the home of her former partner, as if McLeod was an estate agent and she a potential buyer. The furniture was familiar, most of it having been bought by her over the years. There was her grandmother's corner cabinet, full of Ross' single malts. The exercise bike, barely used by either of them, the wedding dinner service. Quite an investment in a failed marriage. When they broke up even the stuff he'd agreed to let her take she'd had to leave because the new flat in Reading had so little space. She recognised his prized old-fashioned but high-fidelity German record player, the huge collection of opera CDs and vinyl, and the framed maps of the Munros he'd bagged. Ross had always enjoyed his mountain walking. Then there were the professional certificates, and the many framed collections of children's thank-you cards for his decades of work as a paediatrician.

'We have no hint that anyone else came into the house. There were no fingerprints on the door, nor any DNA apart from his and that of his cleaner.'

Rainy nodded.

'Does anything here look out of place or strange to your eye?'

'Well, as I say, I've never been to this house. It's tidy like he always wanted it, and more than I could ever keep on top of...'

She watched McLeod, who was admiring the collection of greeting cards, the kids' paintings. Look at this lot, and you could only think he was a good man. A paediatrician. So much care for the children of strangers, yet a strange neglect of his own, a kind of parental vacancy as if after all there was no love left for Ewan. While Ross' ferocious temper and withering sarcasm was known to colleagues, and put down to the stress of his job, the occasional violence she so feared was – as far as she was aware – known only to her and the few friends she had confided in. These Krakatoas of anger were often preceded by a glowering silence. Maybe it was only once a year when a mug was thrown at her, or the infamous October 2008 demolition of the glass shelving units from a hurled chair, but it was corrosive all the same. The actual violence had been rare, but the expectation of it almost constant. It was a punch in the face five years ago that broke her glasses, and cut her eyelid, that finally forced her to leave him. She wanted an end to the fear that had confined her life for decades. That inward cringe, the inevitable limitation to how she expressed herself, that ever-present fear of provoking him. That was exactly how intimidation works, and how it was intended to. The anxiety, gnawing away at her self-confidence and her happiness. And even after all that, at the family wedding last September, he had reminded her what she had escaped. While they were talking upstairs in her hotel room about dividing their possessions, he had suddenly seized her by the throat, forcing her to the ground until she couldn't breathe.

She shook her head to clear the vision, as McLeod spoke. 'As I say, crime scene investigators have finished, so this...' He waved towards the evidence of Ross' professionalism. 'This is all yours, and his family's. As I say, I'm sorry for your loss. He seemed like a wonderful man.'

Rainy nodded, and squeezed out a smile.

She peered into his home office, with its neat inbox and out tray, and the plastic anatomy models of children's spines, his speciality. She took in the laptop, the mobile phone, and the high-definition screen on which he would sometimes examine X-rays.

'Did you examine his mobile phone records?' she asked.

'I think CSI did a quick examination at the time, but more to find next of kin than anything else. It's still thought to be an accident, albeit aggravated by a failure to report.'

'I hope you're treating that as a serious crime.'

'Aye, we are. There's an unlimited fine and up to six months' jail on conviction.'

Part of her was relieved to hear that his death wasn't suspicious, but she couldn't imagine quite how Ross had been lured down to the road on a cold evening in February, to be there for some maniac driver. No, there was more to this, and she had a growing suspicion what it was.

Chapter Eight

DC Kim Leighton had found plenty of YouTube cage fighting videos of Aaron Randall. She and Gillard watched them together, and to him at least it was uncomfortable viewing: barely constrained violence; barefooted kicks, vicious punches with gloves much smaller and less padded than those used in boxing. Consequently there was blood, lots of it, flowing very quickly in most cases from cuts to eyes and noses. He found it hard to watch. Randall used a wide variety of wrestling techniques as well as kicks and punches, and defeated several opponents by gaining submissions. Gillard finished off by watching the bout that ended Randall's career six years ago against a Brazilian nicknamed 'Fera', beast. The speed and savagery of Fera certainly made him live up to his name, and after one minute of the second round, the referee stopped the fight. Randall was pouring blood from his mouth, and clearly didn't know where he was.

'I don't know why anyone would watch this stuff,' Gillard said.

'It's quite exciting, sir,' Kim countered.

'You would have been in your element in the Colosseum,' he said.

'In Watford?' she asked.

'No—'

'I've never seen any punch-ups there. I only went to see panto.'

'I mean in Rome. Christians and lions, gladiators, that kind of thing.'

'Oh, right,' she said. 'That was before my time.'

After he'd finished watching, and Kim had returned to her desk, Gillard leaned back in his chair and considered whether Randall was the person who had assaulted him, and killed Gary Wray. He was fighting in the lightweight class, less than 155 pounds, roughly eleven stone, and was listed as five foot nine, all of which tallied reasonably with his assailant. At the time, his impression of the man who attacked him was perhaps a tad shorter. But with motorcycle gear it was hard to be sure.

As it neared six, a lot of the day shift left. It was a quiet moment in a hectic day.

After a trip to the canteen for a coffee, Gillard pulled up the picture of his own torso, enlarged on his PC, when he felt an imposing presence behind him. He turned to see the chief constable, and gave an involuntary jump. For a tall woman Alison Rigby had a stealthy approach, quite often putting the fear of God into junior officers that she surprised. Something to do with her footwear. Flat shoes with a soft sole.

'Have I caught you looking at porn, Craig?' she said.

'Actually, that's me,' he said, nervously. 'It's the ultra-violet image of the kick I sustained on Sunday.'

'Ah yes,' she said looking closer. 'The impact of the heel is quite distinctive. That must have hurt.'

'It did, but it was the speed that was amazing. One moment I was standing up, and the next I banged my head as I fell.'

'Have you had the all clear from the scan?'

'To be honest, ma'am, I haven't had chance to really chase it down.' He wondered whether to mention to her his on-off headaches. He decided against it; she would only think he was trying to get time off to be with Sam.

'How is Sam?' Rigby asked, seeming to read his mind.

'She is very tired, and a little short tempered. She just wants the birth to be over now.'

'Well, let's just hope she can hang on for a few more days until we've caught the killer of Gary Wray, eh?'

We? Gillard thought. Until *we've* caught him?

'So are we thinking a professional killer?' she asked. 'With those martial arts skills?'

'It's certainly a line of inquiry.'

'What about Aaron Randall? He seems to fit the bill.'

'Well, his DNA was already in the system, and none of it was found at the scene,' Gillard sighed. 'Really, ma'am, we could really do with more witnesses. Nobody seems to have seen the scooter approach the park or leave it.'

She looked around. 'I thought Yaz Quoroshi might be here. I need to speak to him.'

'If I see him, I'll let him know.'

'Okay, thank you.' As she turned away she pointed at the screen. 'It's good to see you are keeping in such good shape, Craig. It seems half the male officers in the county have a paunch. Not so useful when you need to chase a suspect. But with you, I have no worries.'

As she left the CID building, Craig felt a smile creep onto his face. He looked at his own image afresh. Certainly he couldn't boast the six-pack that he'd had in his youth, but he still did enough swimming and cycling to be in reasonable condition, and yes, he was quite broad across the shoulders. He still didn't think it could be mistaken for porn.

He rang Quoroshi, whose number kicked in to voice-mail. He left a message to warn him that the chief constable was after him. Gillard was keen to discover the results of the DNA tests on Gary Wray's body. Modern techniques were so sensitive that there was a good chance that any physical contact would leave a trace of the attacker on his body. There was nothing showing in the CSI email inbox, so he rang the lab, to be told that a retest was being made. The admin assistant didn't have any more details.

Quality control was a vital issue in forensic examination, given that so many trials hinged on the details of tests. Still, it was frustrating.

He was just considering this when his mobile rang. 'Vicky Montague here. I'm just writing up the post-mortem report, but I thought you'd be interested in a couple of things. First is that I discovered a second pair of burn marks on Wray's body. The first, as you recall, was at the base of the neck. The second was on the right lower back.'

'Are they definitely electrical?'

'Yes. They show identical characteristics of significant electrical discharge, to the point where water within the basal layer of the skin was vaporised, causing steam damage to surrounding tissue.'

'Painful.'

'Excruciating, and probably immobilising too, in the same way that a Taser is. However, it's not impossible that the burns were caused in some other way, and may have been suffered several days before his death. High voltage burns heal slowly. Consequently, linking these burns forensically to the fatal attack would be problematic to say the least.'

'So the actual cause of death definitely remains the stab wound?'

'Yes, the weapon used was narrow, almost certainly too narrow to be a knife, and from the depth of the injury was at least 257 millimetres long. That would be commensurate with a sharpened screwdriver or something similar.'

'Going back to the electrical burns,' Gillard said. 'I'm trying to imagine what happened. It could be that while Wray was running the assailant attacked from behind, with this home-made device, to stun him, and perhaps used it a second time to stop him struggling long enough so he could stab him in the eye.'

'That's entirely plausible, but there is nothing in the damage to the body to tell me that that is how it happened. We couldn't exclude the possibility that, for example, Wray had injured himself previously in some electrical scenario. Imagine, for example, leaning back against a workbench, where some live wire is exposed, being stunned, and then falling so that a second connection to the charge was made on the neck.'

'Sounds very unlikely to me,' Gillard said.

'I didn't say it wasn't unlikely, I merely said we cannot exclude the possibility.'

'I'll ask his family if they know anything. When we get his medical records, we will know whether he sought assistance for a burn of that nature.'

'If he did,' Montague said.

'One other thing, I noticed the DNA swab samples from Wray's body aren't ready, and are apparently being retested. Do you know why?'

She chuckled, a surprising sound from a woman of such seriousness. 'It sounds like an issue of contamination.

The relevant samples are now being sent to a different laboratory.'

Gillard groaned. Evidential screw-ups were always a nightmare. 'Do you know exactly what happened?'

'Yes. The results seemed hopeful, because they got two DNA matches on one of the swabs taken from Wray's face. Obviously, one of them is the victim's. The second match came up on the database as Kenneth Stapleford.'

'Stapleford? At Gary Wray's crime scene? He was already dead and almost fifty miles away!'

'Yes. I shouldn't give it too much thought. It's unlikely to be a lab problem. Let's hope not, anyway. In my view it's much more likely to be cross-contamination within the CSI evidence-gathering process.'

Gillard thanked the pathologist and hung up. It made sense. Surrey and Sussex police forces shared the same crime scene forensic resources. Still, almost every tool involved in CSI investigations was disposable. Nothing was re-used on a second crime scene. That was basic. But it would only take some contaminated speck of dust, a smear from a plastic bag, something like that. The sheer sensitivity of tests these days cut two ways: making it much harder for criminals to leave no trace at a crime scene, but also requiring ever more diligent crime scene care. Yaz Quoroshi, as head of the unit, would be in the firing line if this turned out to be an obstacle to either prosecution.

No wonder the chief constable was trying to get hold of Quoroshi. She must already know about the forensic mix-up.

He thought about it again. Facial swabs are routine for victims of violence because they often capture blood from an attacker's grazed knuckles. But it seemed to suggest that the former policeman, a day after his own death, had punched or attacked Wray in Guildford, forty-five miles away. Was there any logical way that could happen?

No. Stapleford was not Lazaraus. But what possible way could his DNA have got on Wray's face? A forensic mix-up would be a disaster, but it actually seemed the preferable explanation. The wild card was that someone in the force had sabotaged the evidence, perhaps someone who also had access to a police Taser. But who?

Chapter Nine

Monday evening

It was gone nine that evening before Claire had chance to return Gillard's call. When he answered his mobile, she was surprised to hear in the background the hubbub of work. She had expected him to be at home with Sam.

'You've not been dragged you into the Wray murder case, have you?' she asked.

'I'm afraid so. It seems that Rigby is incapable of keeping her promises.'

Claire was surprised to hear this, because Gillard had hitherto been appreciative of the chief constable's talents. 'Sam must be furious.'

Gillard laughed softly. 'With me, mainly. She doesn't quite understand that it's impossible to say no to the woman.'

It was Claire's turn to chuckle. 'I think it might be worse because Rigby is a woman. In case you hadn't noticed, Sam will be going through a lot of emotions now. I know that I was a seething mass of jealousies with Barry when I was expecting. It's a Darwinian protection mechanism, I suppose.'

'Thank you for the tip-off.' He cleared his throat. 'Now, on to other stuff. I see that you charged Liam Lewis and remanded him in custody.'

'I did. We'll see if the magistrate agrees tomorrow.'

'That was a tough call, but I think you did it right. If the magistrate decides he can get bail, then you're off the hook. You went in hard, which you had to. Maybe the judiciary still bend over backwards to favour the police, but at least you can hold up your head and say you didn't.'

'Thank you. It wasn't easy, there was a heck of a lot of pushback.'

'I've no doubt about that. Okay, that's the nice stuff over, Claire. We've got something developing here which threatens both our investigations. I know it's late, but I need you on Zoom at nine thirty.'

'Tomorrow?'

'No, tonight. In fifteen minutes.'

'Okay. Is this about forensic contamination?'

'It is. I've got Yaz coming in for an evidence review of the Wray case. I'll be there with Vikram Singh, and it would help if you could be there. If we can't get to the bottom of this, both our cases could be utterly compromised.'

–

Once Claire was up on Zoom, CSI chief Yaz Quoroshi laid down twenty paper evidence bags on Gillard's desk, while DS Singh looked on. 'These are all of them,' Quoroshi said. 'Swabs from Gary Wray's clothing on knees and elbows, then his fingernails, and so on. It's this one,' he said, picking up and unsealing one envelope. He extracted a clear plastic vial, which in turn contained a small cotton bud swab. 'I knelt down by the body and as the label details, swabbed his facial injuries. Right cheek, mouth, left eye and nose where the lacerations and bruises were.'

'Did that swab include the stab wound to the right eye?' Gillard asked.

'No. That was a separate swab, because I could see that it was a stab wound. In each case I followed the usual procedure and used a sterile swab. It's what I always do. I mean there's no way I would ever do anything else.'

Gillard looked across the array of carefully labelled evidence. 'We don't have any evidential connection between Gary Wray and Ken Stapleford, do we Claire?'

'No. Ken never arrested him, and as far as we know never met him. They lived nowhere near each other.'

'Well, the sample's been double and treble-checked,' Yaz said. 'It isn't a lab issue, and I don't see, hand on heart, that CSI could have screwed up either. All the Stapleford samples were dispatched to the lab by Sunday morning, hours before the attack on Wray, and the used PPE bagged up and labelled. Okay, yes, it was messy. My Tyvek, gloves and booties had the victim's blood on all of them. But I went home, showered, and changed. So when I was called in to the Nightingale Park crime scene I was wearing a fresh Tyvek from a different batch, and booties, mask and gloves from stores in a different CSI van.'

'Could Gary Wray have killed Stapleford?' Singh asked. 'There would have been time for him to get home after doing so.'

'Remember, it wasn't Stapleford's DNA on Wray's fist. It was on his face,' Gillard said.

'Head butt?' Singh said.

'I didn't swab the forehead, as there were no cuts or bruises there,' Yaz said.

'There's no motive as far as we can see,' Claire responded. 'And no one showed up on the doorbell camera but our current suspect, Liam Lewis.'

Gillard steepled his fingers. 'I don't think we can make the heroic assumption that a celebrity handbag mogul killed a retired cop, unless we have some other evidence.'

'I agree,' she said.

'There are parallels in the MO,' Gillard said. 'Speed, surprise, rapid and effective violence against capable victims, who apparently had no opportunity to defend themselves.'

They all murmured their agreement.

'In fact, given that Stapleford was dead *before* the attack on Wray took place, there is only one realistic alternative to the idea of forensic contamination,' Gillard continued. 'That the same assailant killed them both, or at least the same weapon was used. First on Stapleford, then Wray.'

'But what weapon?' Singh asked.

'Yeah,' Yaz agreed. 'There was no screwdriver injury on Stapleford, like there was on Wray.'

'Gloves,' Gillard responded. 'In typical assaults with an unidentified assailant, we swab the faces of victims to try to get evidence of blood from knuckle grazes, right?'

'Agreed,' Yaz said.

Gillard held up the problematic vial. 'From my recollection, the attacker in the park was wearing gloves. I couldn't tell you what kind. But it occurs to me that if this same assailant had previously punched Ken Stapleford, with the same gloves, then he could quite easily still have Stapleford's blood on them and deposited it in turn on Wray's face, without leaving any of their own.'

No one said anything for a moment, until Claire said: 'That has staggering implications.'

'It certainly does,' Gillard said, turning a pen over and over between his fingers.

Quoroshi was shaking his head. 'I'm not sure. Gloves tend to cushion blows, but Wray was surely hit with something harder, I mean if you've seen the lacerations—'

'Maybe it was Stapleford's screwdriver Wray was stabbed with?' Singh said. The suggestion was greeted with a collective head shake.

'It didn't show on the stab wound swab,' Yaz pointed out. 'But on another one.'

Claire chipped in. 'Craig is right. If it was a knife we were talking about instead of gloves, and the two victims were at the same crime scene, you wouldn't be at all surprised to find blood from the first victim in or around the wounds of the second victim.'

'True,' Yaz admitted. 'But who would want to kill them both, within a day of each other? And this thing about gloves—'

'Hold on,' Claire said. 'There *were* fibres recovered from the face of Ken Stapleford. They were wool, and only had his DNA on them, and as you recall, Yaz, we both thought they weren't significant.'

'I read the report too,' Gillard said. 'Didn't they show traces of resin in the fibres?'

'Yes, I think so.'

'In which case I can reveal my theory. A friend of mine in Greater Manchester Police is couriering down some evidence to me. I had hoped it would be here today, however it will certainly be here first thing tomorrow. When I show you I think you'll understand. I got hit pretty hard myself, and I think I now know why Gary Wray took such a battering.'

Chapter Ten

After McLeod left, Rainy found herself sitting alone in Ross' kitchen. She recognised her own coffeemaker, and various kitchen utensils that had been divided between them when they split. A plastic spatula with a burned edge. She was surprised he hadn't thrown it away. The fridge contained a large amount of food, neatly arranged, including milk, cheese and a farmhouse loaf. There were the usual home-made salads in plastic containers, and an unopened fruit smoothie.

Perfect for lunch.

She took out a bean, radish and pasta salad which had various fresh leaves in it. She added granary bread and some mature Dutch gouda, again one of Ross' favourites. She munched her way through slowly, all the time her head spinning through the possibilities. Something had enticed Ross to leave the house and go into the road. Maybe somebody had rung the doorbell, or maybe he had just heard some kind of disturbance. He took his respons- ibilities as a doctor seriously, and was always quick to offer assistance. She recalled one occasion when they had both been in a shopping centre with Ewan on a Saturday, when a child playing on the escalator had fallen and gashed his head on the ridged metal of a moving stair. The mother had been impressed to find not just one doctor but two offering their help within thirty seconds.

A car went past, a distant swoosh in the kitchen. There was no other sound, bar the rain.

The nearest neighbours were a hundred yards away up the road but, according to DCI McLeod, hadn't heard anything. Once she had finished lunch, she wrapped herself up against the elements, and went to investigate the next-door property. Was it possible that Ross had fallen out with them? There was no roadside pavement between the two homes, and the little traffic that use the road did seem to travel at quite a speed. She made her way carefully on the carriageway up to the next driveway and saw that the car in the drive was a big Mitsubishi four-wheel drive. She walked past, up to the front, and rang the doorbell. A woman of about forty-five came to the door, and after Rainy introduced herself as Ross' former partner, she was invited in for a cup of coffee. The house had a light and airy feel, and they stood in the kitchen.

'I was so shocked when I heard,' said the woman, whose name was Margo Thomson. 'We didn't really know him at all, he seemed to keep himself to himself. All we saw was his car heading off at strange times, day and night. The police told us he worked at the hospital so I suppose that would explain it.'

'So you never actually spoke to him?'

'A couple of times I think, once about wheelie bins, and the second time about badgers, when one was knocked down on the road.' Margo then asked carefully about the family, and Rainy told her about Ewan, fifteen, who lived with her in Reading.

'He didn't mention family, but then I suppose you don't when you're discussing roadkill.' She put her hand up to her mouth, realising the faux pas. 'Oh, I'm so sorry. That was thoughtless.'

She sounded convincing enough to Rainy but there were questions she still needed to ask, hopefully without giving away that she was a police officer. 'I suppose the police gave your own car the once-over?' she said.

Margo turned to look at the Mitsubishi as if she had not seen it before. 'I don't think so. Why would they do that?'

'It's just a routine thing I imagine. To compare tyre marks with those on his body.'

She looked horrified. 'You mean he was actually run over?'

'Yes, they told me that the vehicle actually went over him, and crushed his ribcage. At low speed.'

'Well they certainly didn't tell us *that*,' she said, folding her arms. 'That's horrific.'

'It makes me think it was deliberate,' Rainy said.

'Well, I can assure you that we didn't do it.' She sounded slightly affronted.

'Och, I'm sure you didn't. It's just that the police don't seem to be taking it seriously enough. They seem to think it's an accident.'

'Well, it's a terrible business,' Margo said. After another few minutes, Rainy made her excuses and left. Once the door was closed behind her, she went halfway down the drive, and quickly doubled back towards the car, crouching down and using her phone to photograph the two front tyres. Hopefully she hadn't been seen, but if she had, well, tough.

Roadkill! So that's what Ross had become.

She felt a stab of anger, but didn't know what to do with it.

Back in the house, she prowled around, exploring the various rooms, discovering possessions that were once hers, or theirs, in new places, new settings. She found herself lamenting the lost time, the wasted years, the marital wrong turning that had consumed so much of her life. It was still raining, and the hills were shrouded with tendrils of curling cloud. She had intended to go on to visit Ross' surviving sister Aileen in Dundee, and they would no doubt come to an accommodation about the house, and whatever else was in the will. But it was a fair way to travel, and if she was going she should have set out hours ago. Besides, she was tired. Maybe she would go back to Glasgow and stay in the same anonymous budget hotel where she had spent last night. But actually, she could stay here.

It would be an odd experience.

Rainy didn't quite have the courage to sleep in their old marital bed, for all the fact it was a comfortable and expensive king size. She instead chose a small and so far unredecorated bedroom, which from the wallpaper had clearly belonged to a child. It looked out over the back, towards the golf club, with a simple single bed, clearly new and not made up. She found sheets and a duvet to fit it in the airing cupboard, along with a pillow and pillowcase. As she made the bed, it began to rain hard. The drumming of the downpour on the roof made the room seem cosy, and somehow she felt like she was revisiting childhood. She was quite tempted just to curl up there and then, and go straight to sleep. But so much was playing on her mind, so many unanswered questions.

She had a list of calls to return. Her boss, Gillard, had left her a lovely supportive message but she didn't yet feel strong enough to talk to him. HR at Mount Browne, ditto. She'd had long chats with a couple of close friends on the train, but despite their warm words, she still felt guilty. There was one person who could offer more, to whom she had poured out her heart and who could perhaps offer some answers. Rachel. She had missed one session of the Reading Domestic Violence Support Network because of the Stapleford case, but was due another group discussion meeting on Monday, which she should be able to get back for. It was late in the evening, after a pasta bake and a couple of glasses of wine, before she plucked up courage and rang her at home.

'Rachel is that you?' Rainy asked.

'Yes, Rainy. I've been expecting your call.'

'You heard?'

'I only know what you texted Anna, but I put two and two together,' she said. 'How are you feeling?'

'Raw, I suppose is the best description. I hated the bastard, but...'

'You are bound to be experiencing complex emotions, Rainy,' Rachel said.

'I feel I left him to die alone.'

'All feelings have validity, but you know this one is misleading. You did right to leave him. The courageous women are the divorcees, not the widows.'

'I think you're right. I'm sorry I missed the last session, but I hope I can make next Monday's. I'll be back down in a few days.'

'Good. Continuity is important. We're all feeling for you, thinking about you. And you have a lot to share.'

'I have. Right now, I'm at his house. I feel like Goldilocks, eating his food, sleeping in one of his beds.'

'But that particular bear isn't coming back to get you, is he?'

'No. He's gone, except maybe in my dreams.'

For a moment she was lost for words. Only thick, strange noises escaped her throat.

'Do cry, Rainy. Don't hold back. Tragedies aren't straightforward. There is guilt, pain, and the crumbling of a shared past.'

'Part of me has died too,' she sobbed.

'Of course, and there's good in that too. Be positive. Remember our session on unwanted emotions? Say goodbye to the worry that was part of you, say goodbye to the pain that was yours. Wave rage off the premises, it's not needed anymore.'

'On that subject, Rachel, I was just wondering...'

'About what?'

Rainy's courage failed her. 'Sorry, nothing.'

'Reassurance is what we are here for. If that's what you were wondering, let me tell you. It was simply a therapy. It was about you letting go. Rainy, go to sleep now. Celebrate the new you.'

But she couldn't sleep. She kept thinking back to the root of it. And the gathering sense of guilt.

Chapter Eleven

Tuesday

PCSO Nita Basu rang the doorbell of the Victorian terraced house and waited. It was not quite eight a.m. and the curtains were drawn. She gazed around, taking in the neat front garden, set for minimal maintenance with slate chippings where the lawn would normally be, and just a few shrubs around the edge. This was one of the dozens of homes on Churchill Terrace that backed on to the park, and one of just seven where police had failed to make contact with the occupants, despite three separate door-to-door inquiries. Gillard had rightly said that if no one had seen the scooter come or go through the main or pedestrian entrances of the park, then it was certainly possible that the assailant had escaped into one of the back gardens. Her boss Inspector Holt had under Gillard's instructions already arranged for DNA swabs and fingerprints to be taken from the rear garden latches of each of these homes.

On a previous visit to this house, she had spoken to the young couple next door, who had said that they thought the house had been rented a year ago, but there had been nobody living there for a few months. They didn't know who the landlord was. The couple had been kind enough to let her into their back garden to peer over the fence.

The rear garden was paved, supported a large barbecue, partially shrouded by its plastic cover, a glass-topped picnic table, some garden furniture and builders' supplies.

She checked the wheelie bins. Empty, and clean. Maybe nobody was living there. She peered through the letterbox. There was a sheaf of flyers on the mat, and a tidy carpeted hallway leading through to a kitchen beyond. Giving up, she marked her clipboard with a question mark, and then headed down to the next of the no shows.

It was a hundred yards further down, a very similar house although the garden was much more conventional, with a small square of neat grass and rose bushes.

She rang the doorbell, and immediately heard footsteps inside, a door opening. The woman who opened the door was in her mid-forties, blonde, smartly dressed. She had a slice of toast half wedged into her mouth, and gesticulated for Nita to hang on a second. After she had swallowed most of it, she held the rest in her hand.

'Sorry about that,' she said, licking a crumb from her lip.

'Sorry to disturb you so early. We leafleted you earlier about getting access to the garden, about the attack in the park.' She checked on her list 'Are you Ms Meadows?'

'Yes, I'm Rachel,' she said, eating the remainder of the toast. 'I'm a bit pushed for time, I've got to fetch the child minder, could you come back later?'

'I'm sorry. It will just take a moment.'

'Okay.' The woman shrugged, and beckoned her in. Nita could hear the sound of a child playing upstairs. The woman led her through a cluttered hallway, past various framed certificates on the wall.

'What business are you in?' Nita asked, staring at them.

'I'm a cognitive behavioural therapist, specialising in trauma and abuse,' she said. She led Nita through the kitchen, and unlocked the back door which led into a small, narrow and toy-strewn garden, bounded by high holly hedges. The woman slipped on green wellingtons, and led the PCSO across the short paved patio and down onto the grass.

'You'll have to watch out for Action Men underfoot, as well as the odd toy tractor.'

Nita noticed some damp wheel marks on the patio, but then saw a small child's scooter nearby, which may well have left them. There were no obvious footprints in the grass, and the rear exit was a well-maintained wooden gate with a padlock and bolts top and bottom, set within the hedge. 'Do you ever use this to go out into the park?'

'No. I don't like to advertise that it is usable access to the house. We had a couple of burglaries ten or so years ago, so once my husband left, and of course after the attacks in the park, I added a meatier padlock and grew the hedge even higher.'

'Holly is a very effective deterrent, isn't it?' Nita said.

'Hopefully.'

Nita crouched down, and donning blue nylon gloves searched through the grassy area leading to the gate. There were no obvious footprints. She got out her DNA kit and swabbed the padlock and latch. 'Just in case somebody did get in,' she said by way of explanation. She was aware that the woman was anxiously checking her watch.

'It won't take long,' she reassured.

'We've had all these rapes and sexual attacks, and it seems nothing was done. But, hey, when a famous man gets murdered, the police pull out all the stops.'

Nita felt she had to stand to respond to this. 'With all due respect, madam, we have tried very hard to nail the rapist. A lot of today's police force are female; we have no higher priority than making women in the community feel safe.'

'Well, I'm afraid we just don't. I used to go running in the park, I don't dare to do it now except in a group.'

'I do sympathise,' the PCSO said, putting her swabs away. 'We're doing all we can.'

The woman folded her arms. 'You know, I went to London for the Sarah Everard demo...'

The conversation was interrupted by the arrival of a small blond boy of perhaps six years. 'Are you a police lady?'

'I'm a police community support officer,' she said.

'Look.' He showed her a much-loved toy police car hardly any bigger than his hand.

'Ooh, that's lovely,' Nita said, and knelt down to examine the die-cast model.

'Jack, this lady is much too busy to play with your car,' said his mother.

'Okay. Would you like to play with slime instead?' he asked winsomely.

Nita grinned, and looked up at his mother. She shook her head, with a bit of a grimace. 'It's disgusting stuff at the best of times, and his has got bits of Lego caught up in it. Best avoided. Jack, go inside now and stop pestering her.'

The child left, and Rachel showed Nita out.

As she exited the front door, the PCSO ticked off the home from her list. Just one to go. She decided to go back and have one last go at finding out who owned it.

The couriered package Gillard had expected arrived a little before nine, just in time for the incident room meeting. He tore open the cardboard packaging, and pulled out a polythene bag with a pair of woollen gloves within.

'Is that what you've been waiting for?' Vikram Singh asked, as a number of other officers gathered round.

'Yes. An old colleague of mine from Manchester CID has come up with the goods. Some of the gangs up there used to make their own knuckledusters, and it was as I remembered: they started with a pair of rubber washing-up gloves—'

'You mean kitchen marigolds?' Kim Leighton asked.

'Yes.' Gillard pulled out one glove, and folded back the wrist to show the rubber lining. 'Just like this one, from the 1980s. You can see how it's cut down to match the woollen glove.' He started to pull the glove off the lining, revealing a hard layer of brown residue above the knuckles, in which were embedded a dozen nuts and washers.

'Ouch! That would hurt,' Leighton said.

'Yes, it's rock hard.' Gillard tapped the brown layer. 'This is resin, probably made from one of those hobby fibreglass kits. Glass fibre is dissolved in resin, to build up knuckles across the back of the glove.'

He slid his hand into the glove, flexed it, then folded down the woollen outer. It looked just like a normal glove. Leighton caressed her boss's knuckle. 'It feels really hard, sir.'

Gillard scanned her face for hidden meaning in that curiously intimate gesture.

'A punch from these would do a heck of a lot of damage. It could easily explain why there was so much damage to Gary Wray's face. It could also explain how DNA from Ken Stapleton's face got transferred to him.'

'I think Yaz was assuming much softer gloves,' Singh said.

'Yes. If I'm right, the possession of these not only ties together the two crimes, but it gives us a potential gang-land flavour, wouldn't you say? These are not the tools of some casual mugger. Someone wanted to inflict as much pain as possible.'

DC Carl Hoskins parked the pool car, and gazed up at the forbidding Victorian walls topped by modern razor wire and dozens of CCTV cameras. HMP Wakefield, a.k.a Monster Mansion, was arguably the toughest jail in Britain, home to some of the most violent and dangerous criminals in the land. Tommy Hollis was in the maximum security F wing. The gangster's public threats to Stapleford and his family had to be checked out. Although Hollis himself had decades to run in his own sentence, he had boasted of his contacts on the outside, and it was not uncommon for gangland figures to be able to settle scores from the comfort of their own cell.

It was a while since Hoskins had undertaken a prison interview, and despite his credentials, he underwent an intrusive search by a large and unsmiling female prison officer. Even after he had dumped his wallet, briefcase and all metal items in the tray by the security gate, and passed through, a light flashed above him. The subsequent scan with the wand found a paperclip in his jacket breast pocket, and a two-pence piece lodged in the turn-ups of his trousers. She glared at him, and he shrugged. After she had finished delving into his pockets, and had searched his briefcase, he cracked a smile and asked: 'Was it good for you too?'

She rolled her eyes, and pinched his cheek playfully, all without smiling. 'The old ones are the best,' she said. She led him along a series of corridors and through at least half a dozen locked gates, which echoed into the background noise of jeering inmates. He'd always had a frisson of fear every time he went into a jail, and this was more intimidating than most.

Hollis was sitting on a plastic chair which was screwed to the ground, at a similarly rigid metal and plastic table. The interview room was as grim as any cell, as high as it was wide, with a ghostly yellow light from a flickering incandescent tube.

'Who's this wanker?' he asked, as Hoskins walked in.

'Mind your mouth, Hollis,' said a large prison officer who was standing by the door.

'I'm Detective Constable Carl Hoskins.'

'One of Stapleford's bum boys, eh?'

'Hollis,' warned the prison officer. 'Any more of that talk and you'll be back in the cells.'

'Suits me,' said Hollis, glaring at Hoskins. 'I didn't ask to be here.'

Hollis, though not tall, looked even wider and more muscular than on the video. Of course in prison there is little to do except work out. He certainly had been busy. In this sallow light, he resembled the Incredible Hulk, right down to the skin tone and even the odd pudding bowl haircut.

'Mr Hollis,' Hoskins said as he took the seat opposite, and took out a digital recorder. 'I won't take much of your valuable time.'

'Good. I'm a busy man.' He flexed an arm, and a bicep the size of Hoskins' thigh popped out of his discoloured T-shirt, which had darts of extra material sewn in at the sleeve to accommodate it.

'You may be aware of the unfortunate death of retired Sergeant Kenneth Stapleford.'

Hollis began to laugh, his huge torso shaking with genuine mirth. 'Yes, very sad news. I was fucking gutted to hear it. Ruined my day.' He resumed laughing.

It was a few moments before Hoskins could make himself heard. 'At the time of your arrest in 2012, you made certain threats to Sergeant Stapleford—'

'They weren't threats, they were promises.'

'I have here a recording of the threats you made at the time of the arrest.' He got his iPad out of the briefcase, and played the short section of video. Hollis seemed to enjoy watching it.

'These threats played a key part in your conviction. I just want to know whether you have carried out these threats, seeing as you claim to have friends on the outside who would do this.'

Hollis grinned. 'I honestly wish I could answer "yes". He got divorced again, so no point killing his missus, as it would only make him happy. I found out where he lived, but then he retired and moved, didn't he? Eighteen months ago. The trail went cold, as they say. But obviously, I wasn't the only bloke whose nose he clambered up. Someone has got there first, and kudos to him. I'd like to shake his hand.' He offered his own huge paw. 'The world is a better place without Stapleford.'

'So you had nothing to do with this?'

Hollis shook his head. 'Naw. I'd like to claim the credit for it. But no, it wasn't me or mine.'

Hoskins tried a few more questions, but Hollis wouldn't play ball.

'Just one final question, Mr Hollis. You've been arrested a number of times over the years, by numerous officers, and while I'm sure none of them are your friends, I need to know what Sergeant Stapleford did to make you issue that threat?'

Hollis said nothing, the muscles on his jaw bulging, as he focused on some far distant point, way outside the interview room. Somewhere in the wider world.

'Well?' Hoskins asked.

There was clearly some memory troubling Hollis. 'I told 'em at the time.'

'Told who?'

'Senior officer, when they interviewed me after arrest. Don't remember his name.'

'Told him what?'

Hollis stared at him. 'Disappeared from the records, has it? Well what a surprise.'

'What exactly did Stapleford do?'

'When he raided my house looking for me. He violated my daughter Kaylee.'

'Violated?'

Hollis leaned across the table. 'Burst into her room, closed the door behind 'im. Dragged her out of her bed, held her against the wall by her neck, and put his fucking filthy cop hands into her pyjamas, and...' He held up his fist and slid two fingers inside. 'She was only fifteen.'

'Why would he do that?'

'He said "I bet you hid some drugs in there, didn't yer?" Then he said: "You complain, darling, and I'll make sure your daddy goes down for even longer.'"

'So what happened when you mentioned it to the senior officer at interview?'

'He said it was bollocks, words to that effect.'

'Did you make an official complaint to the IPCC?'

He laughed. 'Fat lot of good that would do. You lot stick together. Nah, mate. I wanted real justice, not the stuff you lot would dish out.' He held up a giant fist in front of Hoskins' face. 'Whoever done Stapleford, kudos to 'im. I hope it was fucking agony.'

–

Important details can often be missed in plain sight. Gillard stood with Inspector Geoffrey Holt and PCSO Nita Basu outside the Churchill Terrace home that she had been trying to investigate earlier. It was a short street of imposing Victorian terraced homes, half of them backing on to Nightingale Park, and bisected by a public footpath into the park. Gillard's own home in Parkmead Crescent was only a two-minute walk away. There, prominently parked in a residents' parking bay, was the pristine black Mercedes GT63 belonging to the murder victim Gary Wray.

'So when the car was found, Geoffrey, none of your officers seemed to think it strange that a man who lived in Walton-on-Thames would have a residents' parking permit for a street here in Guildford, and be parked in a reserved bay?' Gillard tapped the bottom right-hand corner of the enormous sloped windscreen where the permit could be seen.

Holt scratched his head. 'I don't think they were thinking outside the box.'

'Well, the box they were thinking inside of wouldn't be big enough to hold a brain cell. I'm not asking them to be detectives, but information like this should be recorded so that my investigative team can see it.'

'I couldn't agree more,' Holt conceded.

'Has anyone looked inside the vehicle?'

'Not to my knowledge,' Holt said. 'However, thanks to Wray's PA we now have the spare keys,' he said, bringing out a bunch and handing them to Gillard. He pressed the fob, and the orange lights flashed. He put on blue nylon gloves and eased open the driver-side door, to be met by a waft of faux citrus. The interior was very tidy, and had the indicative sheen on the dashboard of a recent valeting. After delving in the glove compartment and the seat pockets all that he recovered was a pair of designer sunglasses, a half-consumed packet of Strepsils, a cloth Covid face mask and small bottle of hand sanitiser. Opening the boot, there was nothing but a plastic jerry can, half full of fuel.

'All right, time to look in the house then. Nita, how did you track down that Wray owned it?'

'Well, there was no response any time I rang, and the neighbours didn't know, so I checked with the Land Registry. It's owned by a foreign-domiciled company. But when I looked through the letterbox I recognised the green and yellow envelope on the mat from a local letting agent. They are the same people I rent from. So I rang them. Turns out they had been dealing with Gary Wray. They no longer have it on their books, but they gave me the key cabinet combination, which turned out to be unchanged,' Nita said, offering him a silver Yale. 'Wray's PA knew nothing about it.'

'Very enterprising,' Gillard said. 'Perhaps I should put *you* in charge of the investigation.'

'Look, I'm sorry—' Holt began.

'I wonder if this key is the same that I have here, recovered from Wray's body.' Gillard held up a clear plastic evidence bag. He compared the two and decided they were identical. He used Nita's key and opened the door. The hallway was carpeted, and tidy apart from the scattered post.

'How far did you go inside?'

'Only as far as the kitchen,' Holt said. 'I'll head back now, if you don't need me. I've got the rest of the door-to-door teams to organise. Nita's got the door for you.'

'Okay.' Gillard closed the door behind him, and took a careful sniff. You can tell so much from the scent of a home: everyday questions like whether it's been heated recently, whether there's mould, or what was the last meal cooked; but matters of life and death too, like the reek of decay, the metallic taint of blood or the sickly stench of flesh. The first inhalation was vital. If you don't get it in the first couple of seconds, you'll miss it. The brain rapidly adjusts to the olfactory background. Gillard knew that Holt was baffled by his insistence on digging so carefully into Gary Wray's movements, when it was the perpetrator they were after. But Gillard's nose was leading him elsewhere, perhaps to a different crime.

And he could smell something.

He advanced along the hallway, which had been redecorated within the last couple of years. No yellowing of the gloss paint where the light fell. The carpets were older than the paint, proved by the odd spot on the tufts by the skirting board, and slightly faded in a few places. The kitchen was a galley style with better than average fittings for a rental. There on the countertop were a set of Mercedes car keys, identical to the ones they had just used. Wray's keys.

Nita Basu's research at the agency showed that the last tenant had left just over five months ago. Gillard opened the fridge, which was pristine. If anyone had been here since the tenants departed, they had certainly cleaned up well after themselves. The lounge was magazine perfect, down to the oatmeal carpet, the steel and glass shelving units, the three-piece suite in ivory fabric.

He could definitely smell something.

He gingerly lifted up the seat cushions, repository of a million missing items. Beneath he found hairs, a comb, two shirt-type buttons and a torn foil fragment. The serrated edge indicated it was from a condom wrapper. The other side of the seat cushions was stained. It had clearly been cleaned, but the shadow of the stain remained. The fact it was a reddish grey rather than brick red indicated wine, not blood.

Now he'd lost the scent. Standing up, turning around, was there anything to indicate this was anything other than a vacant rental house? No. He passed through the dining room, IKEA throughout, and into the utility. The bins were empty, as had been the wheelie bins outside.

It was while coming back via the hall to the base of the stairs that he got another scent. Stale drains, or worse. Upstairs? He padded carefully upstairs, his plastic booties scrunching as he did so. The landing had five doors, of which a bathroom and a bedroom to the rear were open. There was definitely a stale smell here, but the more familiar one of human sweat. He started in the bathroom, and spotted contact lenses, a toothbrush, paste, and a blue Bic disposable razor. There were no other toiletries. The back bedroom sported an unmade bed, rumpled sheets, an old-fashioned alarm clock and some clothing. Gillard fished out a small polythene evidence bag from his pocket, and inserted into it a few longish dark hairs from the pillow. Gary Wray was light-haired. So was this a love nest, away from prying eyes?

He peered out of the window into the small high-hedged rear garden. Here there was no usable exit into the park; the rotting gate was barred by brambles, clearly unused for months if not years. The small patio was crowded with a glass-topped picnic table, and several unopened bags of cement or similar, as had been previously recorded by Nita Basu peering over from next door. An encrusted spade stood nearby. Building work of some kind was clearly planned. He turned away and passed back onto the landing and to the third bedroom, which looked out over the side of the house. It had a single bed with a bare mattress on which were a pair of socks and a pair of men's underpants, and on the floor next to them a pair of loafers. A small filing cabinet stood adjacent to a table, below which a couple of charger cables were plugged into the wall. A copy of the De Marr handbag catalogue and sheaf of paperwork related to the house rental lay on the desk. Only then did Gillard turn to see the back of the door. On a hook hung a hanger, on which was a jacket, shirt and trousers. Office clothing. The jacket seemed weighty, in both side and interior pockets. There he found a Breitling wristwatch and Gary Wray's wallet, seemingly intact.

So this was where Wray came to change before jogging. It made sense. It was another missing piece from the jigsaw. He left Walton-on-Thames dressed in work clothes, and changed into his jogging gear here. But why come here to run? That was still a mystery.

Gillard turned to the rental paperwork with the same yellow and green logo that Nita had seen on the doormat. The envelopes had been opened. The first letter was clearly a sales push, dated September the previous year, addressed to Gary Wray, saying they would offer a fee-free month if he wanted to resume letting through them. The second concerned some matter of an unreturned deposit. The tenant had been making representations to them. Gillard tossed the letters back onto the desk, but then snatched the last one up again, when he realised who it concerned.

He'd read it as Mr Kemp. In fact it was Mr Kempf, with an F.

Could that be Jürgen Kempf, Tia Whitlock's business manager? A man working for Gary Wray's estranged partner? There was a motive. He was just getting ready to ring the letting agency when a call came in from the CID room. The chief constable wanted everyone in for a briefing about unifying the two cases.

'Okay, I'll come in,' he said.

He descended the stairs and went out to see Nita Basu, who was on the doorstep, blowing on her hands to keep warm. 'I'm heading off now,' Gillard said. 'I can see you're freezing. Do you need some gloves? I can nip home and get some.'

'That's okay. I'm off shift in half an hour.'

'Who's replacing you?'

'I don't know.'

'All right. Get Holt to ring me. I need someone on the door for now. I don't want anybody coming in here until I finish looking around, hopefully later this afternoon.'

'Righto, sir.' As he left her he heard her on the radio, passing on his request.

It was eleven a.m., while he was on his way back to Mount Browne, when Gillard took a call from Claire Mulholland.

'Sorry I couldn't get back to you earlier,' she said. 'I'm standing on the steps of the magistrates' court, in the middle of the biggest crowd of press I've seen for many a year. Liam Lewis has been remanded in custody, on our recommendation.'

'Well done,' Gillard said.

'There was uproar in the public gallery. Family and others. The defence wanted bail, with the surrender of a passport. But we argued that the seriousness of the offence should prevail regardless of the occupation or status of the accused. Justice should be blind.'

'Well said.'

'That's exactly what the magistrate said. Anyway my name is mud amongst the Brighton constabulary. The whole team has been getting the silent stare routine in the canteen, and some of those on adjacent tables have got up and walked away. It's quite nasty, Craig. I'm glad to say, however, that senior officers have generally been much more supportive.'

'As they should be. It's their job to see the bigger picture. How are the British police ever going to throw off the perception that they see themselves above the very same laws that they themselves enforce, if not through cases like this?'

'That's exactly what I think,' she said. 'Anyway, it's out of my hands now. Just as well, considering the allegation Hollis made about Stapleford.'

'What was that?'

She told him what Hoskins had told her about the alleged assault on Hollis' daughter.

'That's appalling, if it's true.'

'Well, it probably is. I checked who the senior officer was that ran the investigation, and it was Kincaid.'

'Christ Almighty.' Paddy Kincaid, a detective superintendent and for a while Gillard's boss, had himself been unmasked as a child abuser and murderer five years ago. He was in Winson Green prison, Birmingham, with years still to serve. 'Have you told all this to DCS Mills?'

'Yes, he was horrified, but warned me not to share it.'

'I bet it will get buried,' Gillard said. 'Bureaucratic instinct kicks in, every single time.'

'Yes. Now Lewis has gone down, the forensic evidence is in secure storage and the CPS is happy they've got a bulletproof case. Alison Rigby has just called me. The whole investigative team is heading back to Mount Browne to help you.'

'I'd heard. We can certainly use the extra bodies. Something very odd seems to have been happening in a house opposite Nightingale Park, and I've a feeling this case might soon get a whole lot bigger.'

–

'All right everybody, we'll make this brief as everyone has a lot of work ahead of them.' Alison Rigby, dressed in white blouse and black trouser suit, stood in front of a whiteboard on which the details of the Gary Wray case were written in various colours of marker pen. A dozen detectives sat or stood in a semicircle around her. Gillard, Singh, Mulholland, Tsu and Hoskins, plus the various recent recruits, along with a couple of uniformed sergeants. There was no sign of Inspector Geoff Holt.

'We are wrapping up the Ken Stapleton murder case, and as you will have seen, brought back the team that has done such an excellent job. Only Jill Haynes will remain in Brighton, as evidence officer and liaison with the Sussex force. I'm fully aware of the misgivings that some of you have about Liam Lewis' guilt, and having seen evidence that the Hove murder and the killing in Nightingale Park may be linked, we now have to unify our resources to find a suspect.'

She turned to the whiteboard and with a marker pen wrote a big red question mark against the name of Gary Wray.

'I have had the Home Secretary on the line earlier, and she is very keen, to put it mildly, that we crack this high-profile case. But I have to say that for all the theories, the insights, the hunches and not least the resources we have poured into finding his killer for the last two days, we have got very little to show for it. That has to change. Do you understand? I don't care if you have to work twenty-four hours a day, this case has to be solved, and solved fast.'

There was a murmur of assent across the room. Claire Mulholland gave Gillard a sympathetic smile. Not much of a break for an expectant father.

The chief constable continued. 'I had originally planned to have a press conference this evening but that will now be deferred for at least twenty-four hours. Until then nothing will be said to the press, do I make myself clear? No hints, no tips, no nudges. There is a news blackout until I say otherwise.'

She turned to Gillard. 'I understand we have found a new home next to the park owned by our murder victim, is that correct?'

'Yes.'

'I have to say that's the kind of basic intelligence that should only take two hours after the crime to establish, not two days.'

'I couldn't agree more, ma'am.' He resisted the temptation to publicly blame Geoff Holt. 'Nevertheless, we may well have some significant new leads as a result. It seems that Jürgen Kempf, business manager of Mr Wray's estranged partner Tia Whitlock, had been renting the house. He may well have a motive for the killing.'

Her gaze remained steadily on Gillard. 'Let's get him interviewed, as soon as possible.'

'That's my intention, ma'am.'

—

It was dark by the time Gillard drove past the house on Churchill Terrace. There was nobody on the door, but he could clearly see a light on upstairs. There was no room to park nearby, so he left his unmarked Vauxhall outside his own home in Parkmead Crescent, two minutes' walk away. He had planned to pop in to see Sam at home, but that could wait now until he had investigated the light. He didn't recall seeing any timer switches when he was there, so did this mean someone was in there now? He was pretty sure he hadn't left any lights on.

He took his forensics grab bag from the boot, and after locking the car made his way rapidly through the alleyway between the two roads. Geoff Holt hadn't returned his earlier call, which was annoying enough, but if an officer was now inside without having rung him, that was worse. He rang Holt's direct line, which was busy, and left a message. He then called the control room, to find out who was posted on the door. The answer was: no one. He was told a request had gone in from Holt for a police padlock, but the locksmith was busy on another job. Slack. He'd have words with Holt. He thanked the operator, and cut the call. He then put in a quick call to the letting agents, and asked if any of their staff were there. The answer was no, the agreement had finished months ago.

The moment he emerged from the alley into Churchill Terrace, he could see no upstairs light at Wray's house. He was positive it had been on just five minutes ago. A single string of crime tape hung forlornly across the gate. Wray's Mercedes was still there, right outside. He ducked under the tape, and went up to the key cabinet by the front door. He soon had a single Yale key in his hand, and after putting on booties and nylon gloves, let himself back in.

Once again the stale odour assailed him. He made his way into the kitchen, and noticed a vacuum cleaner, plugged in, its long tube leaning against the worktop. It had not been there before. He felt the motor. Still warm. The sink had traces of suds, the neatly folded J cloths still damp. Heading back upstairs, he saw all the doors were closed. He started in the rear bedroom as before, and saw that the bed had been stripped. There was no sign of the linen. In the bathroom the toothbrush, razor, and contact lens equipment was gone, the whole place wiped down.

Maybe somebody was living there, and just came back to clear up. A friend of Gary Wray's? A casual tenant?

The side bedroom looked no different from before, so Gillard headed to the master bedroom, which he hadn't previously visited. He eased open the door, and turned on the light. It was an attractive room, with a king size bed, the mattress bare but for a protector. The fitted wardrobes held a variety of upmarket jogging gear, and a second pair of the Nike Vaporflys. Gillard turned to the bedside cabinet. The top drawer contained a packet of household candles, one of which was missing, a box of condoms, a half-used tube of personal lube gel and an eye mask. The middle drawer revealed a roll of silver duct tape, a coiled length of plasticised washing line, a pair of handcuffs and their keys, plus a cigarette lighter. The bottom contained half a dozen pairs of women's underwear. None of them obviously laundered, and a few intimately soiled. Using a sterile forensic swab, he lifted a couple. They weren't all the same size. He didn't have to get any closer to detect the reek of sex.

Trophies, or something worse? Thousands of happy couples up and down the country indulged in bondage, dominance and submission. You couldn't draw a conclusion from the equipment here, not at least until you found the first bloodstain, knife, hammer or worse. Here was forensic evidence galore, but probably useless on its own.

Consent, after all, carries no scent. It has no unique chemical, no DNA marker, no thumbprint. If only it did, hundreds of thousands of rape accusations that failed to make it to trial would be prosecuted.

Was this evidence of Wray's hidden life, one with an unusual sexual element? Or of some other occupant who had recently been there? It would be odd to leave this stuff lying around if there was a cleaner coming in regularly.

And the big question. Could the answer to Wray's murder be found here?

Undecided, Gillard retraced his steps, returning down the stairs to the hall. He got another whiff of decay. Where could it be coming from? He looked about him. Kitchen and utility rooms and been checked, as had the dining room and lounge. The only door he hadn't tried was what he assumed to be a cupboard under the stairs.

The door was sloping at the top to fit the profile of the stairs, and only five feet high at its tallest. Perhaps it was a route to a basement. It fitted snugly into the frame, clearly painted many times. It had a keyhole at waist height, partially clogged with paint. Fresh paint. Gillard could feel a draught from it. He knelt, and put his face against it. On that air was an unmistakable putrid smell. Rotting flesh.

At that moment the doorbell rang. Gillard opened it to find the bespectacled face of PC Harris Floyd. 'Hello sir, Inspector Holt sent me.'

'Right, better late than never. Let me borrow you for a minute?'

'Yes sir, of course.'

Gillard beckoned him inside and closed the door. 'Can you smell something?' he asked.

'I don't think so.'

He guided Floyd over to the door under the stairs and got him to sniff at the keyhole. 'Eurgh, something died in there!'

'Yes, it's simply a question of what. Normally, I'd call CSI now, but if it turns out to be just a dead rat in the cellar, I'll be wasting their valuable time. So I need to go down myself.'

'The door looks painted in,' he said.

'Quite recently, I'd say. The gloss still smells a bit. What I need now is a screwdriver, to lever it open.'

'I've got a toolbox in the car,' he said. 'It's just round the corner.'

'Excellent. That's quicker than me nipping home for my tools.'

The officer was back in just a couple of minutes. Gillard got to work with a big meaty screwdriver, breaking the seal on the paint. Gradually the woodwork relented and could be pulled open, and as Gillard did so the horrible putrid stench made him gag.

He knew it came from something much worse than a dead rat.

The open door revealed a surprisingly roomy cupboard to the left, where the stairs were highest, and to the right a steep set of stone steps descending. A light switch was set into the lintel above the staircase, and when Gillard flicked it on a naked bulb suspended from the low ceiling gave enough light to see part of the room beneath. The cellar appeared to be quite basic, with an original floor of diamond-shaped black and brick-red tiles. Descending carefully, and crouching so he didn't bang his head on the rough brickwork above, Gillard peered into the wider room.

Just a glimpse confirmed his worst fears.

Chapter Twelve

The basement was the full width of the house, and at the far side away from the stairs was a newly constructed concrete platform, against the far wall. On the plinth was a plastic-wrapped package the size and shape of a human body. The smell was almost overpowering. The only other thing in the basement was an empty plastic sack of builders' aggregate, for making concrete, and the marks on the floor where it had been mixed.

He took out his phone, and began to take some pictures, pinching his nose with his other hand. The plastic was thick builders' sheets, securely wrapped with brown parcel tape. He was ninety-nine per cent sure this was a human body, but wanted to be absolutely certain before calling in crime scene investigators. Crouching down, he searched around the package for loose ends or untaped corners, before admitting defeat. But under the tape, in his light, he saw a couple of long, fair human hairs. Thinking of the cement bags outside, and the aggregate here, it seemed fairly clear that at some stage the killer had been planning to build this body into the basement. But something had changed his mind, because the painted-in cupboard door spoke of finality. Walling off an act, never to be thought of again.

He looked at his phone and hit the number for CSI. After that, he rang Vikram Singh to get him to get hold of Jürgen Kempf. Right now.

–

Jürgen Kempf lived in a two-bedroom ground-floor flat in Camberley, and was just letting himself in at 7.12 p.m. after a long day at work when Detective Sergeant Vikram Singh and Detective Constable Liz Tufnell emerged from an unmarked police vehicle. They introduced themselves, and asked if they could come in.

'Yes, but what is this about?' he said, as he ushered them in, closed the front door and led them into a spacious modern kitchen.

'It's about your tenancy at 57, Churchill Terrace,' Singh said.

'Am I finally going to get my deposit back?' He walked to the counter, his broad muscular back moving under his jacket, and then asked: 'Coffee?'

'No, thank you,' Tufnell said.

'It's nothing to do with your deposit, that would be a civil matter,' Singh said. 'We need to know the exact date when you left the house for the last time.'

'You've found something there, haven't you? Something criminal.' He laughed, running his hands through his sleek hair. 'Bad boy Gary Wray, eh? Up to no good.'

'It might well be you that was up to no good,' Singh responded.

'I moved out of there six months ago, August bank holiday. I can check the date. So what have you found?' He couldn't help the smile that slipped back on his face.

'Where were you last Sunday evening around nine?' Singh asked.

'Here, working on some spreadsheets ready for a meeting on Monday.'

'Any witnesses?'

His face creased, and he said: 'The system would have logged me as using it.'

'Do you own an electric scooter?' Tufnell asked.

'What? No, I don't. What's that about?'

'Do you still have keys to the flat? Did you cut a set before you returned the originals to the letting agents?' Singh asked.

'No, and no. Besides, there's a key safe. Anyone with the number can get in.' He looked more worried now. 'What the hell have you found there?'

The two detectives looked at each other and then at him. 'We are not at liberty to disclose that.'

Liz Tufnell reached into her jacket and produced a swab sample tube. 'We need to take a sample to eliminate you from our enquiries.'

He inclined his head as if considering whether to comply. 'Okay.' He opened his mouth, while Tufnell reached forward with the swab stick and wiped the inside of his cheek.

As they left, a few minutes later, his unanswered question hung in the air. *What the hell have you found there?*

–

Gillard arrived at Churchill Terrace just after midnight, to find CSI well at work. After donning a Tyvek suit, mask, gloves and booties he made his way through the tent which now domed the front garden. He found CSI chief Yaz Quoroshi in the brilliantly lit basement, crouching over the plastic-wrapped body, aided by Kirsty Mockett, who was taking photographs. Even wearing a mask, the stench hit him like a hammer.

'You've arrived at just the right time,' Quoroshi said. 'We are just about to unveil our victim.'

Quoroshi carefully removed the tape holding the plastic in place, and revealed the corpse. The smell, bad enough before, was now almost overpowering. The victim was clearly female, with long silvery blonde hair, some of which had become entangled with the adhesive tape. Her flesh was leathery, her closed eyes having shrunk back into their sockets, her lips cracked and receded around her teeth, which gave her a predatory appearance.

'Very dehydrated. She must have been here for weeks,' Quoroshi said. 'Probably lay awhile before being wrapped.'

'Any indication of age?' Gillard asked.

'She's got wisdom teeth,' he replied. 'So probably in her twenties at least.'

Gillard watched as painstakingly, Kirsty swabbed each piece of tape removed, then placed it in individual evidence bags. 'We are very hopeful on fingerprints,' she said to Gillard.

'Yes,' Quoroshi added. 'Parcel or gaffer tape is an excellent repository of forensic evidence. Extremely sticky, and hard to use when gloved up.'

When he got down to opening the full length of the plastic, the odour was so overwhelming that even with all his years of experience Gillard felt himself heaving. He beat a retreat to leave the professionals to their task, and after stripping off his protective suit and depositing it in the sack, made his way home to Sam, just two minutes away in their new home.

Rapes and murder in the park. Now a body in the basement, just round the corner. Not quite the desirable area he had assumed.

Chapter Thirteen

Wednesday

Gillard awoke suddenly in the dark. Next to him, Sam was gasping and holding her tummy. 'Are you all right?' he said. He could feel the incredible heat of her through her nightdress, like a radiator set on max.

'I don't know, there's something happening,' she said. 'My back hurts.' She looked sweaty, her damp hair stuck to her forehead. She climbed out of the bed and grasped the headboard, arching her back to ease the pain.

He looked at the bedside clock. Quarter to five. He was supposed to be at work for eight. 'The car's ready to go. It has the goodie bag inside, we can be at the hospital in fifteen minutes. All you need to do is say the word.' He got out of bed his side, clicked the bedside lamp, and squinted through the harsh light. He made his way around the bed and embraced Sam from behind, his hands reaching over her swollen tummy, kissing her neck and hair.

'What about work?' she said.

'Work will have to wait,' he said. 'I love you, and this is the most important thing in our life.'

'I've had some contractions,' Sam said. 'It's supposed to be normal to have some, but it's scary. The feeling is so powerful, as if something is taking over your body over which you have no control.'

A bit like Alison Rigby, he thought to himself.

'Just say the word,' he said.

'It's eased a bit now. Oh, Craig,' she said, turning to embrace him face-to-face. 'I love you so much, but everybody seems to want a piece of you. But I really need you right now.'

'I know, and I feel the same way.' He kissed her gently, on the forehead and the nose. 'I'll work from home until two p.m. at least. There's a press conference at six. It's the first for the case, so I will definitely need to be at it. Apart from that, I can be pretty flexible.'

Half an hour later, he was sitting in his home office while Sam balanced on her inflatable birthing ball down-stairs. It was still dark outside, and he felt like he hadn't slept at all. As he logged on to the Surrey Police system, he started munching away on some of the enormous amount of fruit that Sam's mother had been accumulating in the house. A banana seemed to be one of those things you can eat at any time of the day, likewise kiwifruit, which he ate with a teaspoon like a boiled egg.

Looking through the crime log on his iPad, he saw a series of photographs of the corpse in the basement. The body had been examined in situ by Dr David Delahaye, then removed to the mortuary, where it was scheduled for a post-mortem that afternoon. CSI chief Yaz Quoroshi had attached detailed notes to the images. Inside the plastic sheeting, the body was naked. There were no rings, earrings, nose studs or anything in the way of distinguishing features. There was one abrasion on the back of the left shoulder which largely obscured a small tattoo. Quoroshi thought this was probably undertaken post-mortem. There was otherwise no obvious damage to the body, and no clear cause of death. If this woman had been murdered, then the killer had gone to some lengths to try to conceal her identity.

Front and centre in Gillard's mind was that whoever this killer was could well have been the rapist in the park. Either Gary Wray, or just possibly Jürgen Kempf.

Gillard swallowed the last of his fruit, and swiped to the next case note, this time from Research Intelligence Officer Rob Townsend. Data downloaded from Tia Whitlock's phone and computer had been examined, and nothing incriminating found. It would take a little while longer to recover any deleted texts and emails, but Gillard didn't expect these to yield any result either. If Ms Whitlock had arranged the killing, she presumably wasn't so stupid as to do it in a way that could be traced electronically. Other entries showed that Aaron Randall's footwear had provided no match to the marks on Wray's body, nor indeed Gillard's own. Randall didn't own a motorcycle, and appeared not to possess motorcycle leathers or boots. The only plus was that the footwear Merseyside Police had found was a male size nine, roughly the same as that imputed from the marks on Wray's body.

Scanning through the other items, he could find no other new forensic developments on the killing of Gary Wray. No new witness sightings. CCTV footage had been chased down from half a dozen premises at the bottom end of the park by the main road, but there was no sign of anyone on an e-scooter in the four hours which straddled the time of the attack, nor of anyone wearing that particular combination of motorcycle helmet and leathers. The half-dozen motorcyclists who did appear on the footage were being contacted to eliminate them from enquiries, even though none of them seem to be dressed quite the same as the assailant. He rubbed his hands over his face and stifled a yawn. It was hardly surprising there was nothing new. It wasn't yet six a.m. He had last looked at midnight.

He reread the witness statement from the one person who had spotted the assailant on his electric scooter. Mrs Gladys Evans, whose home looked out over the park. She had been looking out of an upstairs window, when she saw a black-clad figure whizz silently by. Her description perfectly tallied with what he had seen.

The e-fit was already prepared, ready for that evening's press conference. A white motorcycle helmet and dark leathers. He'd estimated the assailant's height as five foot nine with a stocky build.

Who was this man? Powerful, fit, extremely violent. Professional, gangland possibly. That all made sense, whether Tia Whitlock had contracted him or somebody else had. It was hard to see that there could be any connection between this person killing Gary Wray, and being involved in the death of Ken Stapleford. Professional killers plan carefully, they don't race from one killing to another within twenty-four hours. That's the way that mistakes are made.

The sound of Sam's mother moving into the bathroom dragged him out of his reverie. The whole household was up now. He was feeling tired, and had a challenging day ahead of him.

He heard a bang downstairs. He called out to Sam, heard nothing, and then ran out of the room and thundered down the stairs, followed closely by Sam's mother, still in her nightdress. He found Sam sprawled on the floor in the living room, rubbing her elbow. The birthing ball was nearby.

'Are you okay?' He said, kneeling down at her side.

'I fainted, when I was sitting on the ball. I smashed my elbow on the TV stand.'

'How did you fall?' her mother asked. 'Was it on your side?'

'Yes, sideways and backwards. It could have been a lot worse.'

'You should see the doctor,' her mother said.

'I've got an appointment tomorrow anyway, I'll tell her then.'

'Have you had any more contractions?' Gillard asked.

'Not in the last two hours, no.'

'I can still take you to hospital,' he added.

'It's fine.'

For the next hour, they both kept an eye on Sam, who half watched TV while stretched out on the settee.

'I see they've had that policeman in court, charged with killing his friend,' she said.

'Yes. At least that's finished up, and I've got some reinforcements back in the office.'

–

It was gone eight, and Gillard was making himself a bacon and grilled tomato sandwich. Something about the early start had upset his body clock, and even though he'd had plenty of fruit, he now felt in need of something more substantial. Boris, no doubt feeling exactly the same, waddled in to investigate the waft of meat, wagging his tail, looking hopefully from cooker to chef. Gillard smiled at the dog, then returned to scrolling through his phone.

An email had just arrived, detailing the various e-scooters sold in Britain over the last few weeks, including partial lists of buyers' addresses. Long before he got to the conclusion, there was a sharp crackle and spit. He looked up from the phone, and pulled out the grill pan. The bacon was nice and crispy. The dog whined and pawed the ground excitedly, a sense of anticipation rarely justified by events. Gillard picked up the rasher of hot bacon between finger and thumb, and tossed it quickly onto a slice of granary bread. The halved tomato, two molten hemispheres sagging on the grill, were too hot to touch so he moved the pan close to the plate, and flipped each with a knife onto the bread. He then mashed them in, added a dash of Worcestershire sauce, and pressed the other slice of bread onto the top. After cutting it into two, he lifted the plate towards his mouth. Boris sat on his haunches and watched with undisguised envy as Gillard took a tentative bite of the sandwich. The tip of the labrador's tale swished backwards and forwards across the kitchen tiles, a movement that Sam had termed 'the economy wag'.

The sandwich was delicious, if a bit too hot. As he chewed, Gillard returned to his email. There was no evidence that the scooter had been purchased recently, and no chance they could chase down and interview the hundreds of people on this list. No, it was a hopeless line of inquiry. What they needed was to find the actual scooter. Or the helmet, leathers or gloves. Particularly the gloves.

Of course, for all their suppositions about gangster gloves, it was still only a hunch. One that was needed to explain why the DNA of one murder victim ended up on the face of another. And now there was the body in the basement too. The Gary Wray case was one of the most high profile he had ever been involved with, but that discovery in the cellar had already complicated it. If the same assailant was involved with Wray and Stapleford it could get bigger still.

He had almost finished his sandwich when the landline rang.

Sam's mother picked it up. 'No, I'm sorry, he's not here. You should ring him at work,' she said. Gillard looked at her, as she mouthed across to him the word 'press'.

'No, I can't give you his mobile number. Nor his direct line at work. I do have the number of the press office if that would help.' She then stared at the receiver. 'So rude. He hung up.'

'You're doing a great job, Mary,' he said. Ever since Sunday, reporters had been calling his newly registered and unlisted landline. How they got it so quickly, he had no idea. Sam's mother had been tasked with answering the phone, which she did with formality and courtesy. She and Sam had taken half a dozen calls yesterday and today looked to be even worse.

'Maybe we should unplug it,' Gillard said.

'Then you would miss some of your distant relatives,' Sam said. 'You've been getting quite a lot of get-well calls and cards from the elderly ones, since news of the assault hit the papers. Even one from Trish. And she sent this to me.' She waved at him a tiny knitted teddy bear with a wonky face, which his aunt had named Grizzly in the accompanying card.

'We should get Grizzly checked for hidden microphones,' he said.

'That's a bit ungrateful, Craig,' Mary said.

'Ah, but you've never met her,' he said. 'You may recall the serious crimes she stood trial for.'

'Wasn't she acquitted?' Mary asked.

'Hung jury,' said Sam.

Since moving, Gillard had deliberately not passed on contact details to his malicious and interfering aunt, but undoubtedly she had called somebody else in the family and got the address.

The phone rang again, and Gillard lifted the receiver and immediately hung up. 'I don't want you being disturbed, Sam. We should disconnect it.'

'Whatever,' she said, with a groan, turning sideways on the settee.

'Are you okay?' Mary asked.

'Just another contraction,' Sam whispered.

Gillard looked at her, and then at Mary. Just then the landline rang again. It wasn't even nine o'clock. Mary answered it, and went through the same rigmarole before hanging up. 'A gentleman from *The Times*,' she told Gillard. 'A lot more polite than the last one.'

Gillard's mobile rang. It was Alison Rigby. 'How are things?' she asked gently. Despite the dulcet tones, he knew not to be seduced into thinking this was a social call.

'Sam is doing fine, but otherwise it's a little crazy at the moment. As Sam's getting closer to her time, I'm trying to work from home, but we keep getting press calls.'

'You might find it quieter here,' Rigby said.

'Ma'am, I'll be there this afternoon, well in time for the press conference.'

'I don't want anything revealed yet about the body in the basement,' she said. 'Make sure your team is aware of that.'

'I will.'

'We don't want anyone jumping to conclusions. I hear that the body had been there for some time?'

'Weeks, certainly. The post-mortem is this afternoon, so perhaps we'll learn more then. CSI is going to see if there's a DNA match between the body and the underwear found in the drawer upstairs.'

'I've read the details, and I'm baffled. If the killer went to all the trouble of abrading away a tattoo to impede identification, why would he leave such incriminating evidence in a drawer for anyone to find?'

'It points to Gary Wray, doesn't it, ma'am? Wray appeared to still be using the house and, to state the obvious, wasn't expecting to be murdered. That's why I really don't think Kempf could have been behind this. He wouldn't have left all this evidence to find. Anyway, CSI has taken DNA swabs all over the house, and is currently undertaking a Bluestar analysis for blood. I'm sure we'll get more information by the time of the press conference.'

'And this theory you have about a single suspect for both the Wray and Stapleford murders?'

'I'm saying nothing about it yet, we need much more.'

'We most certainly do,' she said. 'I was really hoping that by now we have some clear leads on who killed Wray. I don't want you going off on some speculative investigatory jaunt.'

'No, ma'am.'

'Are you aware that Tia Whitlock was interviewed in this morning's *Daily Telegraph*?'

'No, I wasn't.'

'The paper showed photographs of her meeting Randall in a pub near Ashford in Kent—'

'He's on the radar, ma'am. Merseyside Police interviewed him on Monday, at my request.'

'I know that, Craig. The *Telegraph* said that photo was taken a week before Wray was killed. They put to her the suggestion that she hired him to kill Gary Wray, which of course she denied.'

'He claims to have an alibi—'

'Nevertheless, Craig.'

'I'll get on to it.'

'You should already be on to it.'

'The press office normally calls at nine thirty with any press coverage I need—'

'That's much too late. It shouldn't take me to be briefing you, I've got better things to do. Now buck up and make sure you have something to say about this at the news conference because you're sure to be asked.'

She hung up. Gillard cursed silently, then rang the office, and spoke to Vikram Singh. The detective sergeant confirmed that the *Daily Telegraph* had called late last night, asking for comment on the piece they were about to run. 'They'd already got a "no comment" from the press office, so I left a note on your desk. I'm sorry I've been so busy I didn't have chance to let you know.'

'Anything new on electric scooter sightings?'

'No.'

'Anything from the door-to-door interviews?'

'No, nothing significant.'

'Any luck tracing the motorcyclists?'

'Half of them have been eliminated, we're still working on the rest.'

'Has the e-fit been published?'

'Oh, I forgot that. Are we still on for a ten a.m. Zoom?' Singh asked. 'DI Mulholland confirms she is coming in for it.'

'Maybe. I'm actually going to put the incident room meeting back to eleven, to give a chance for the Churchill Terrace DNA results to come through.'

'When are you coming in, sir? We could do with you here.'

'So I keep hearing,' Gillard said. 'I'm coming in at two. In the meantime, let's get Tia Whitlock in for a formal interview.'

'Ah, did you not read the *Telegraph* piece?'

'No, not yet,' he said through gritted teeth.

'She's in Milan for some big fashion conference. That's where they interviewed her.'

Gillard muted the phone while he swore. 'Look, Vikram, we're supposed to be ahead of the press. Contact her business manager and get her brought back ASAP. Failing that we need her personal mobile.'

'The *Telegraph* reporter would have it—'

'No, *you* find it.' He hung up. The moment he did so, the landline rang. Cursing under his breath, Gillard walked up to it and pulled the socket out of the wall, before Mary Phillips had chance to answer it.

'And I thought I was in a bad mood,' Sam muttered from the settee.

–

There were three detectives at Mount Browne and six, including Gillard, joined remotely for the eleven a.m. incident room Zoom call. Yaz Quoroshi was expected to join them in person later, with the latest from the CSI investigation of the basement of Churchill Terrace.

It began depressingly. DS Singh recounted that there had been little progress getting fresh witnesses or evidence near the Gary Wray crime scene. None of the gates from the rear of houses adjoining the park had produced any DNA matches on the national database. No one had seen anything, very few had heard anything. It was as if the scooter-borne assailant had simply vanished into the bushes after attacking Gillard. However, when it came to the contribution by Merseyside Police, there was a break-through in checking Randall's alibi. Randall had been seen at a central London casino on the evening of the attack, first appearing on CCTV at the Barracuda Club entrance to the Grosvenor Casino on Baker Street at 11.15 p.m. That would have left enough time to have committed the attack in Guildford two hours earlier. Better still, they had traced Randall's Audi through ANPR, which showed it coming on to the M25 from the A30 at 10.04 p.m. If Randall had been the attacker, that might well have been the route he would have taken from Guildford.

'It's good,' said Gillard, when concluding the meeting. 'But it's not enough. We need direct and compelling evid-ence that Aaron Randall was at the crime scene. His DNA isn't there, and neither are his fingerprints. Maybe he's extremely careful or lucky, or maybe he just isn't our man.'

Kim Leighton put up her hand. 'If it's not him, it's another martial arts expert, isn't it? How many people are out there, who are capable of doing this?' She held up a photo enlargement of Wray's damaged face.

'That's a very good question,' Gillard said.

It really was. DC Leighton was a promising recruit.

'In fact, Kim, I'd like you to contact some of the martial arts associations, local gyms, trainers, and see if we can get any clues.'

'How local? I mean this person could've trained anywhere,' she said.

Another good point. 'Start with those in a fifty-mile radius. Send them the e-fit.' Even as he said it, he realised it was a long shot. An e-fit of someone in full motorcycle gear could be anyone.

The CSI chief then appeared on the conference call. 'I'm sorry I'm late,' Quoroshi said. 'The labs have been rather overwhelmed by the volume of tests. However, we finally have some clear results. Number 57, Churchill Terrace is as we would have expected, full of positive samples of Gary Wray's DNA, and some of Jürgen Kempf's too. However, in the basement we only found Wray's. There were fingerprints on the plastic, the tape securing it, and minute traces of his DNA on the body.'

'What about the victim?' Gillard asked.

'She's not on the database. However, samples from one pair of underwear in the master bedroom drawer do match her. I think we'll have to pass it to you to look on the missing persons list.'

'Right,' Gillard said. 'Was there any other DNA in the house? I'd seen evidence of an intruder yesterday.'

Quoroshi looked at his notes. 'Yes, we do have traces. From the hairs in the back bedroom that you collected, and on the vacuum cleaner and taps in the kitchen. They don't match anyone on the system.'

'I really need to know who that person is, Yaz,' Gillard said.

'I understand that.' He looked down again at his notes and then said: 'Ah yes, perhaps I should have mentioned this at the start. We also tested DNA on the rest of the trophy underwear, and one pair matches someone on the database. One of the Nightingale Park rape victims, and Wray as well.'

'Well, that's pretty conclusive then,' Gillard said. 'I think we've found our park rapist.'

There was some cheering from the Mount Browne end.

'Sounds like someone got him before we did,' Kim said. 'And I can't say I'm sorry about that.'

There was a general murmur of agreement. Gillard said: 'Look, if whoever killed him was a vigilante, and there is no particular evidence of that, it doesn't make the police look good, does it? Someone took the law into their own hands because for two years women have been attacked in that park. Our job was to catch this rapist, and we failed. This isn't a time for congratulations. Not yet, anyway.'

The press conference was set up in the grand oak-panelled room in the main Mount Browne building. Seating for 300 journalists, a place for TV camera tripods, and a cordoned-off area of the car park for the satellite trucks. Gillard had left most of the arrangements to press chief Christina McCafferty. His biggest problem was the lack of progress in finding the assailant. An e-fit of a stocky bloke wearing motorcycle leathers and a helmet was hardly going to make any difference. The lack of any CCTV coverage of him or the electric scooter was baffling. Purely based on his own recollections, they had been able to narrow down the make of scooter to five different models, principally based on the position of the lights. This was hardly much help, as tens of thousands had been sold in the last year, and unlike registered road vehicles the names and addresses of purchasers were less rigorously retained. Indeed, these were essentially illegal vehicles on both the road and particularly on the pavement, and the law had yet to catch up. Likewise there was no database of tyre treads, if indeed these lightweight vehicles left any traces. Technology, as so often, ran far ahead of legislation and policing practice.

There were just five minutes to go. The room was buzzing with conversation, packed with journalists, and there were even a couple of reporters doing their pieces to camera. His mobile rang, and the screen showed it was Sam's mother. He didn't have time for the call, but prayed that it wasn't anything related to the birth. Three minutes later, just as he was sitting down, there was a text from Sam. 'Waters broken. She's coming.'

Looked up just as Alison Rigby took a seat next to him. 'All set then, Craig?'

'Bear with me,' he said, getting up. Christina McCafferty, just sitting on the other side, looked alarmed. 'Two minutes,' he said and made his way out of the room at the back. He rang Mary, who answered immediately.

'I'm just taking her to the Royal Surrey. It could be any time,' she said.

'That's brilliant, Mary, I'm so glad you're there for her. I've got a press conference and will hopefully be there in an hour. Actually, I'll slip out earlier whatever Rigby says. Maybe half an hour.'

'I'd still make it quicker than that, if I were you,' she said. 'Got to go now.' She hung up. He didn't have time to dwell on her slightly terse tone. He'd promised to be there, and he wasn't. There was still time to put it right.

He made his way back to the desk, between the chief constable and Christina. The moment he was there, Alison Rigby opened a brief statement describing the shocking and apparently unprovoked attack on a public figure. 'We have our top team on this,' she said, glancing towards Gillard. 'But it's very important that the public help us to catch this most dangerous assailant.'

She passed over to Gillard, who showed the e-fit of the suspect, and a picture of an electric scooter similar to the one used. 'So far we have almost no sightings of either the suspect arriving or leaving on the Sunday night, nor of the electric vehicle used. I would ask all residents in the vicinity, particularly those with gardens adjoining the park, to search for anything that may have been discarded by the assailant. That could be a murder weapon, or even the scooter itself—'

'Have you interviewed Tia Whitlock?' interrupted one journalist on the front row.

Christina whispered in Gillard's ear. 'That's Howard Walker, *Daily Mail*.'

'Yes, we have, and she is co-operating.'

'You let her leave the country?' shouted someone from the back.

'We're not currently viewing her as a suspect.' There was a ripple of laughter, and a few of the tabloid hacks rolled their eyes at each other.

'What about her meeting with Aaron Randall?' called somebody else, from the back.

'We are currently keeping an open mind,' Gillard said.

Howard Walker spoke up. 'No arrests, an e-fit that could be anybody, and the main person with a motive has escaped abroad. Wouldn't it be fair, DCI Gillard, to see this investigation as a bit *Keystone Cops*?'

'I wouldn't characterise it that way,' Gillard said.

A female journalist, all glossy blonde hair without a strand out of place, interrupted. 'I understand you were in the park at the time the attack took place, and attempted to tackle the assailant. Is that correct?'

'Yes. I didn't actually see the attack take place, but the person I attempted to stop managed to evade me.'

'I heard he got a right kicking,' Walker muttered to a reporter on his left.

Rigby interrupted, staring down the entire audience. 'Can I just emphasise that we are being led by the evidence, and not by celebrity gossip and rumour? Our officers are working night and day to bring the attacker to justice. It would certainly help us if the press didn't put out its own pet theories in order to juice up the story. Yes, I'm looking at you, Mr Walker,' she said, pointing her pen at the *Daily Mail* reporter.

'Well, pardon me for existing,' Walker muttered.

The press pack looked a little stunned to be addressed in this fashion 'Right, we have work to do,' she said. 'We don't have time to take questions.' She stood up, and unclipped her lapel mic.

'Aren't you going to tell us about the body found in Churchill Terrace?' called someone from the back. 'That was Gary Wray's house, wasn't it?'

Gillard peered at the reporter, one from a local paper.

'That is a separate investigation,' Rigby said. 'We don't have any comment to make at the present time, but we will update you on any developments.'

The local reporter was surrounded by journalists from the nationals, which gave Gillard a chance to make his exit. As he did so, Rigby followed him, and said: 'You mustn't let them take control. What I'd like you to do now—'

'Sorry, ma'am. I'm off to the hospital. Sam's waters have burst.'

'All right, off you go. Can you be back in a couple of hours?' She looked at her watch.

'I doubt it, ma'am, I need to be there with her. You promised me.'

She softened. 'Of course. I don't want to steal the first day of fatherhood from you. But I want you on Zoom first thing in the morning. DI Mulholland will hold the fort, but I want you to be directing the operation, even if it's from Sam's bedside.'

They headed off in different directions, she upstairs to her office, and he downstairs and out of the building. There he ran into a melee of reporters, who peppered him with questions about the body as he headed towards his car. As he sped out, he passed half a dozen satellite trucks. Heading up to the Royal Surrey, he immediately ran into a traffic jam which took several minutes to resolve. As he reached the head of the queue, he saw in the middle of the junction a car on its roof, another nearer to him on its side. An ambulance, two fire engines and a police patrol car partially blocked his view. The road was strewn with broken glass and twisted panels. He got a second glimpse of the inverted vehicle. A metallic green Toyota Sienna. An uncommon colour. Identical to the one owned by Sam's mother. He slewed his Vauxhall to a halt, and flicked on the blues and hazard lights. It was only when he got out, and was able to see the number plate, that he was sure.

It was her car. *Oh God, Sam!*

Chapter Fourteen

Gillard sprinted across to a uniformed policeman, who was on his radio. He flashed his warrant card, but the officer held his hand up until he finished getting the message. 'I believe my wife may have been in the green car. Sam Gillard. Is she okay?'

'I'm sorry, sir, I've only just arrived. Bear with me.'

He could hear on the radio mention of 'life-changing injuries', and his heart sank. Leaving the officer to do his job, he made his way to the ambulance where a paramedic was just putting away some equipment. Again he brandished his warrant card.

'Are you able to tell me anything about the occupants?' he asked.

'We're just clearing up now, sir,' he said, as he closed the rear doors. 'I'm told there's one dead at the scene, one with life-changing injuries, the other two walking wounded.'

'Which from which vehicle?' Gillard said, glancing at the crushed roof, shattered windscreen and cutaway passenger-side door of the Toyota.

'I don't know. I'm just clearing up. You need to speak to someone at the hospital.'

Gillard made his way over to the Toyota, but was barred from getting any closer by two very young uniforms. He again flashed his warrant card. 'Sorry, sir,' said one of them.

Despairing of getting any clear information, he crouched down until he could see into the car. He recognised Sam's birthing bag, embroidered with red and blue butterflies, lying on the road. The contents, everything she might have expected to use during the hospital stay, were littered amongst fragments of window glass and shattered plastic. He spotted the wonky-faced teddy bear.

'My wife was in the car; she is expecting our first child.'

The two policemen glanced at each other.

'Sorry for your loss, sir,' one blurted out.

'Is she dead?' Gillard said. They didn't say anything. 'For God's sake, does nobody know anything?'

Chapter Fifteen

Gillard made half a dozen calls, some to the hospital and some to his colleagues, as he stood in the middle of the road, traffic queuing around him. Numerous passers-by and car passengers filmed him and the other emergency workers as the traffic queued to get past. Getting nowhere, he returned his car, found a side road with a decent cut-through, and headed off to the hospital. He found a space in the car park, vaulted over the three-foot wooden barrier opposite the accident and emergency department to save himself a three-minute walk, and after hurriedly donning a face mask, sprinted into A&E. There were several dozen people sitting there, just as he had experienced a few days ago. He couldn't see Sam. But further down a corridor he did see Mary, standing just outside a curtained cubicle, talking to a doctor. He rushed up to her, and as she turned to him he saw a large dressing over the left-hand side of her face, which was swollen. She had a black eye and cut face.

'Mary!'

'Craig, I was just about to ring you. Sam's fine, she's been moved to the maternity unit.'

'Thank God,' he said. 'I couldn't get any sense out of the paramedics or cops. Are you okay?'

'Not too bad. Some idiot pulled out in front of us, and in trying to avoid him, I managed to turn the car over. The man driving the other car was worse. He hit a lamppost pretty hard.'

Gillard gave her a hug, and patted her back. 'Mary, you are very good in a crisis.'

A few minutes later, Gillard was sitting by Sam's bed in the maternity unit. She was groaning in pain, but was able to give him a brief smile. She looked untouched by the accident. Both he and Mary were listed as Sam's birthing partners, so he was allowed to stay. He wasn't sure what the rules were but he put his mobile phone on silent mode. The midwife popped her head in to check on Sam's progress, making some checks before announcing that Sam was in labour.

For the next fourteen hours, Gillard watched as his wife struggled to give birth to their child. He held her hand, mopped her brow, made encouraging noises, but most important of all ignored his phone, which continued to buzz quietly in his pocket.

Eventually, when he slipped away to go to the gents, he checked on the many messages that had been left for him. There was one from Alison Rigby, wishing him and Sam the best of luck, and reminding him that she expected him to be back at work in the morning.

Thursday

Grace was born at 5.37 on Thursday morning. A furious little bundle, her face tightly scrunched, she weighed in at a healthy eight and a half pounds. As Craig held his daughter in his arms, she drooled contentedly down the front of his shirt and gripped his little finger. Her tiny fists had extraordinary strength. Gillard knelt by his wife, whose dark damp hair was matted across the forehead. She reached out to the child that she had wanted for so long, through multiple miscarriages. Tears of joy were running down her face, and he felt himself welling up too. There were no tears on Grace's face, but it didn't inhibit her cries. Woozy with lack of sleep, he tried to absorb the bliss of being a new father, to imprint it on his brain, because in less than three hours he had to be back at work. To solve several murders. One life new in the world, others unjustly terminated.

Gillard had hoped to stay with his wife until just before eight. Fat chance. A text from the chief constable arrived just before half past seven, while Grace was tentatively getting her very first food at Sam's breast. The message was characteristically terse: 'New developments. We need you in.' He said heartfelt goodbyes to Sam and her mother, then thanked every nurse or midwife he saw on the way out. A call from DS Singh came just as he was queuing at the pay station. The Sikh gabbled through a carefully rehearsed congratulation, before saying: 'We've got a missing person lead. An Estonian woman named Eva Rebane, aged twenty-six, missing since October, last seen leaving her shared flat in Balham, south London. She had a tattoo of a fox on her shoulder, it's apparently what her name means.'

'Any DNA link?'

'We've sent away to Tallinn for a sample, but the dental records are already on file after the Met tried to match her up to a previous body. This time, they're a match.'

'What about Gary Wray's cleaner? Have you discovered who that is?'

'Rob Townsend is looking at that. Nothing so far from his computer or phone records. The cleaner used by the agency hasn't been there since September last year.'

Gillard thanked him and ended the call. He bought his ticket, and headed to the car. He tried to call to mind the image of his wife and daughter, hugging in bed. But his imagination kept being drawn back to the basement, and the rotting body of a young Estonian woman. Almost certainly killed by Gary Wray. So who really *was* this man? When Wray's body had been found, the picture, based on nothing more than press coverage, had been that of an ambitious entrepreneur, fighting in a tough industry. The taint was already there – like many such types he was accused of being as coercive and controlling in his personal relationships as he was in his commercial ones. Now, the stink of rape and murder had permeated the case. Like Jimmy Savile, the halo of fame had blotted out the shadows.

–

Back in the CID office, and light-headed from lack of sleep, Gillard lurched to the refectory and ordered a large mug of coffee. Word had got around about his fatherhood, and as he absorbed the congratulations from colleagues, his frustration melted away. He berated himself. He was a dad, and needed to treat this as a day of miracles, not mundanity. Sam could so easily have died in the car last night. He showed them his phone, where he had a photograph of Grace in his arms. Finally making his excuses and getting back to his desk, he placed the coffee to one side, intending to catch up with the forensic pathologist's report on the body in the basement. However, sitting on Gillard's desk was a copy of the *Daily Mirror*, with a bold-faced headline.

Basement Body Horror at Wray Home in Guildford

Murdered handbag magnate linked to Nightingale Nightmare rapes

A woman's body found has been found in the basement of a Guildford home owned by murdered De Marr handbag mogul Gary Wray. The remains, naked and wrapped in plastic, were discovered by police on Tuesday in a house in Churchill Terrace, adjoining Nightingale Park. The body is thought to belong to missing Estonian receptionist Eva Rebane, informed sources told the Mirror. Ms Rebane, who a Mirror investigation confirmed once worked as a temp at Wray's business, has been missing since October. Police are remaining tight-lipped on the discovery, but are hopeful that they are close to solving the Nightingale Nightmare, a spate of sexual assaults in the area. The house seems to have been used as a base by the attacker, with several items of clothing belonging to the victims being recovered from an upstairs bedroom.

Wray, killed in a brutal attack in the very same park on Sunday, is the estranged partner of Tia Whitlock, whose High Court attempts to secure a larger share of the De Marr business they founded together failed earlier this month.

A sticky note had been attached to the newspaper, signed by Alison Rigby. It simply said: 'See me.' With a heavy sigh, Gillard rang Rigby secretary's and checked the chief constable was in. Having confirmed that he was expected, he made his way out of CID and into the main Mount

Browne building, reading the full coverage in the newspaper on his way. He was sent straight in, where Rigby was pacing about the room, on the phone to PR chief Christina McCafferty. Seeing Gillard, Rigby clicked her fingers and pointed to a chair by her coffee table. Gillard did what he was told, and sat awaiting his turn. He felt like a lamb, newly arrived at the abattoir.

'…well, you should be on to it, that's what you're paid for, Christina. We should always be one step ahead of the press, not as in this case three steps behind.' She cut the call, and placed the cordless handset onto her desk.

'Craig, who is the mole?'

'I honestly have no idea, ma'am. Everyone was told to keep this confidential.'

'Well, now we're scrambling to catch up, aren't we? I have told you many times that we need to control the narrative of a developing crime story. The red tops do not care for the niceties of evidence. They don't just jump to conclusions, they pole-vault.'

'I agree, ma'am.'

'And they seem to be better detectives than we are, wouldn't you say?'

'Well I'm not sure—'

'How come the *Daily Mirror* found out that Eva Rebane temped as a receptionist at De Marr Couture, and we didn't?'

'They probably have greater resources—'

'Oh I see. So it's *my* fault, is that it, Craig?' She fixed him with the most powerful blue stare of death that he had ever seen. He had to look away. 'I've blown the budget for this case, and all you can do is whine to me that you need more bodies.'

'That's not what I meant, ma'am.' He felt almost woozy with lack of sleep.

'Well, whatever you did mean, it doesn't matter. We now pretty much have to confirm the details of this story. Hopefully we can avoid another press conference, but I'll get Christina to put out a statement by lunchtime'. She picked up her phone, tapped out a number, and dismissed him with a wave of her hand. As he stood up she muted the phone with her hand and said: 'By the way, Craig, congratulations to you and Sam on the birth of your child.'

'Thank you, ma'am.'

He headed out of the building, into CID, and ran into Claire Mulholland. She was clearly delighted to see him. 'Hey, it's the new dad! Congratulations, Craig.' She gave him a big hug.

'Thanks, Claire. It hasn't sunk in yet. Sam was in labour most of the night.'

'You must be absolutely wrecked.'

'I haven't had any sleep,' he replied. 'But apparently Rigby thinks I'm of some use, even in this state.'

'And how is Sam, after the accident? That must have been such a worry.'

'I honestly thought she had died, when I saw the car. But fortunately both she and her mother are fine, bar the odd bruise.'

Claire then asked the obligatory questions about the baby's weight, health and so on, until she said: 'Craig, I'm still trying to tie up some loose ends on the Stapleford case, but if you need me, I'm working out of the small meeting room, where I can get some peace.'

'Okay, that's good,' he said. 'Glad to have you back.'

His phone rang. The forensic pathologist. 'Sorry, Claire, got to get this.' Claire patted him affectionately on the arm, then departed for her meeting room, while Gillard greeted Dr Delahaye.

'Hello Craig. I haven't written my full report yet, but here are my initial findings. The body was in a pretty poor condition, with liquification of much of the viscera. I would estimate she had been dead for at least three or four weeks. Cause of death was not apparent, there being no obvious wounds or major contusions, and no fightback evidence from samples under the fingernails. However, the hyoid bone was broken, which may indicate strangulation. Surprisingly, despite the deterioration in the corpse, it was also possible to observe petechiae in the eyelids, which may back up the hypothesis. Hypostasis, the position of the blood in the body, indicated the victim had been on her side shortly after death. We will be quite limited on what we are able to establish in toxicology, however the one result which I think you will be interested in, is that the internal DNA swab has returned a match with the late Mr Gary Wray.'

'So he raped her?'

'Well, his DNA was certainly found inside her. I don't want to speculate about consent.' The Home Office forensic pathologist was diligent about limiting himself to what the body could tell him, and Gillard admonished himself for making the same mistake a tabloid news journalist might.

–

Christina McCafferty was sitting with Gillard in his office as they pored over a draft press release. There was a real skill in making these as terse as possible while removing ambiguity. The statement simply said that following the recovery of human remains from the basement of a home owned by Mr Gary Wray, forensic examination had concluded that the death was suspicious. Dental records indicated that the body was that of Estonian national Eve Rebane, a former receptionist at De Marr Couture, who went missing in October last year. Following the killing of Mr Wray, police were not looking for anyone else in connection with the crime.

'Yes, that looks good,' Gillard said. 'In a couple of days perhaps we can follow it up with something to the effect that following his death, police are no longer looking for anyone else in connection with the spate of rapes and sexual assaults in Nightingale Park.'

'You've probably seen that the tabloids are already going crazy. Speculating about previous attacks, other cold cases.'

'I've seen some of it,' Gillard said.

'ITV's planning a documentary to air next Wednesday,' she said. 'They asked for my comments.'

'Please tell me it's not Dines?' Gillard asked.

'Afraid so,' she said. Retired Greater Manchester Police DCS Terry Dines was hated by most serving detectives. He'd made a career out of his documentary series *Ten Crucial Police Errors* in which he went from one active case to another second-guessing police decisions.

Gillard groaned. 'I know Dines. He made hundreds of errors in his own career, culminating in losing a vital murder weapon in a gangland case.'

Christina sighed and shook her head. 'So what about the timing of the releases? I mean we could do it all at the same time.'

'I'd rather wait a couple of days until we've spoken to all the victims. There is very little direct forensic evidence, so rather than raising expectations I would certainly like to get a sample of Gary Wray's voice in, perhaps from one of his sales podcasts, so that each of the victims can listen and confirm whether this was the man who assaulted them.'

'That sounds like a good precaution,' Christina said. 'Especially as there's one other matter. The Wray family have announced the funeral for Saturday, now the body's been released.'

'That's the same day as the Stapleford funeral,' Gillard noted.

'So rather than embarrassing the Wray family, and getting an even bigger press deluge, we could wait until early next week.'

Gillard inclined his head. 'I'm not in favour of stage-managing operational matters, but I suppose we could hold off in the interests of tying up all the loose ends.'

They packed up their documents, and Christina prepared to leave. 'You know,' she said, 'I never guessed when we started investigating the killing of Gary Wray that we'd find conclusive evidence of his own crimes before getting much of a clue about his murderer.'

'Maybe one can lead to the other,' Gillard replied. 'It often does.'

—

Gillard drove back into the hospital car park at noon. Technically, he was at lunch, but with a hastily grabbed cereal bar in hand he was intent on seeing Sam and Grace before they left hospital at four. He had managed two quick phone calls during the morning, but there was no substitute for seeing his new daughter. As before, he parked nearest the A&E entrance, and took the shortcut over the fence. Just as he was reaching the line of smokers outside the entrance, he saw a call come up on his mobile from Detective Chief Inspector Mike Welbeck of West Midlands CID. They had been on a training course together in Manchester back in the 1990s, and had hit it off pretty well. Mike had already emailed him a day or so ago, and assuming it was social message, Gillard hadn't yet read it. This time though, he risked answering it.

'Mike, how are you doing?' he asked, as he strode into the building, heading for the maternity wing.

'I'm fine, thanks. I saw the e-fit of the assailant in the Gary Wray case on TV, and realise that we have some CCTV footage of someone who fits the bill.'

'Where? In Birmingham?'

'Yes, Small Heath. A very serious assault on a Mr Prabir Sengupta, a shopkeeper. The man is alive, but in a serious condition.'

'When did it happen?'

'Just after seven on Monday morning.'

Gillard thought about timings. 'Could it really be the same person, Mike? Gary Wray was killed down here in Guildford roughly ten hours earlier. That would be one busy suspect.' He decided to keep to himself that this same perpetrator had been flagged up by DNA evidence in connection with the Ken Stapleford killing in Hove.

'I sent you the CCTV footage. Did you get my email?'

'I'm sorry Mike, I've been snowed under, as you can imagine. I'm just on my way to see my wife in hospital after she gave birth.'

'You couldn't get any leave?'

Gillard laughed. 'I was promised some, but I got hauled back in for the big case.'

'That's cruel.' He laughed. 'Congratulations on being a dad. I don't see much of my kids these days, but at least I had time off for the births.'

Gillard knew that Welbeck was divorced. 'Thanks for the heads-up, Mike. I'll take a look when I get chance.'

'Okay, Craig, it's clearly a long shot, but you'll have to tell me what you think. Honestly, it's like a Bruce Lee film.' Welbeck hung up, leaving Gillard to wonder about the last reference. Bruce Lee? The late martial arts expert.

Making his way rapidly past patients on trolleys, and through crowded corridors, Gillard strode through to the maternity unit, while clicking through his emails to find Welbeck's. The wailing of babies and moans of pain from behind a curtain heralded his arrival as he walked up to Sam's bay. She was sitting up in bed, with Grace in her arms. Gillard gently embraced them both. 'I've forgotten flowers,' he confessed, looking in vain for bunches brought by others.

'You can't bring flowers in here,' Sam said. 'Something to do with bacteria.'

'Ah, yes. Right.' He spent a delightful fifteen minutes with his wife, and then another five with Sam's mother, who had just arrived laden with baby-related purchases.

It was only on his return to the car, after dealing with texts from the chief constable and Vikram Singh, that he turned to the email from DCI Welbeck. The link from the email went to a video in the police file sharing service. It was from a wall-mounted exterior CCTV camera outside a shop in Birmingham. A rotund, middle-aged man in a duffel coat over Punjabi trousers emerged from a car parked at the pavement and began to unlock the roller shutter of a shop. As he bent down, someone in motor-cycle gear and helmet ran into the frame and pressed what looked like a TV remote control into his neck. He jumped like a scalded cat and then collapsed on the pavement. His assailant kicked him, then hauled him to his feet with one hand, kneed him in the groin, head-butted him and punched him for good measure. It was sickening to watch.

Then from the top of the frame, two burly Asian men ran along the pavement to intervene. The assailant turned rapidly and kicked the larger of the two men in the face. The other began to grapple with him, but was effortlessly hurled to the ground in some kind of judo throw. In a blizzard of punches, elbows and kicks that lasted less than ten seconds the two men were left apparently unconscious, while the assailant ran away in the direction he had come. The entire video was less than thirty seconds long.

This needed looking at again, on a larger screen. But some things were obvious. The assailant was in very similar motorcycle gear to the man who had hit Gillard, right down to the same helmet. Not tall, but fast as hell on his feet. Likewise, the sheer economy of the blows meted out seemed to indicate some kind of professionalism. A cage fighter maybe, kickboxer or mixed martial arts expert, something like that. Repelled but fascinated, he watched the video a second time. His own bruised ribs seemed to resonate with the blows.

Was it really possible this was the same person? What enemy could Gary Wray and an Asian shopkeeper in Birmingham have in common? It seemed even less likely than a connection between Stapleford and Wray. It seemed inconceivable that all three could be linked. He called Mike Welbeck on the hands-free as he drove back into Mount Browne.

'I looked at the video, Mike, and have to agree with you. The assailant is identical. I can personally vouch for the speed and power of the guy.'

'So I heard. Based on what I've seen, you're lucky to be alive. He was clearly using some kind of home-made stun gun.'

'That wasn't used on me, but seems to have been used on Wray. It seems incredible, but this must be the same person. I've left a message for Claire Mulholland, the DI in charge of the Ken Stapleford case. We've got some overlap in the MO. All of them showed rapid and effective physical violence, preceded in two of the three cases, by an electrical weapon.'

'But not a police Taser,' Welbeck said.

'Thankfully, that possibility was giving me nightmares. But there are anomalies. In Gary Wray's case, he was stabbed in the eye with what appears to be a sharpened screwdriver. In Ken Stapleford's, it was a knife from the victim's own kitchen. I didn't see any sign of a knife in the CCTV you sent me.'

'No, there wasn't one,' Welbeck said.

'What progress have you made in tracking him down?'

'Almost none. An eyewitness reported seeing the assailant get into a black SUV, but we don't have a registration number or any further sightings. However, I've taken the footage to a number of martial arts and boxing gyms, to see if they recognise the fighting style or the person. There was pretty universal agreement amongst the professionals that this guy is an extremely proficient kickboxer, possibly professional at some stage. The elbows and fist strikes weren't quite so powerful apparently, but still showed speed and agility.'

'But did anyone recognise him?'

'Sadly, no. I got a list of the top fighters in the country, and there's a few hundred. I've got my team cross-checking heights and builds against the CCTV. We reckon the assailant is perhaps five-eight, eleven maybe twelve stone, so in the lighter weight categories.'

Gillard liked this approach. When an inquiry was bogged down, a bit of lateral thinking always helped. The first cross-check he needed to do was with Aaron Randall's Audi. He left a message with Carl Hoskins to see whether the martial arts expert's car had been seen in Birmingham, and indeed whether Randall himself had an alibi for Monday morning.

It wasn't convincing, though. If crime is about motive, means and opportunity, then Randall made sense for the Wray killing, because of his connection to Tia Whitlock. That of course was motive, and his fighting skills were the means. But why on earth would he want to assault a Birmingham shopkeeper? Or Ken Stapleford, for that matter?

–

While he was on the phone to Welbeck, Gillard noticed a call waiting from Claire Mulholland. He said a hurried goodbye to the West Midlands detective, and picked up Claire's line. 'Craig, you wanted to speak to me?'

'Yes. I've only had time to read the summary post-mortem on Stapleford. If you've seen the whole thing, can you tell me whether there was any mention of electrical burns on the body?'

'I don't think so, but let me check.'

'We've now got a strong connection between the cases. That in turn makes it less likely the DNA link is due to contamination. And it could go further than that. There's another case, in Birmingham, seemingly involving the same assailant in motorcycle gear who hit me and killed Gary Wray.'

'Really? A *third* attack! Is that possible?'

'Only just. The man was attacked first thing on Monday morning, so that's less than twelve hours after the Guildford attack. And a home-made stun gun seems to have been used, the kind of thing that might have left the type of burns found on Gary Wray's body.'

'That's incredible. Is there a DNA link from the gloves?'

'Not so far. If Ken Stapleford's DNA has turned up on the face of this third victim too, that would make it an absolute certainty that we are talking about the same assailant. Trouble is, given that the victim is still alive, I don't think there's much chance of lifting any deposited DNA from his face, at least if it wasn't swabbed immediately.'

'I guess paramedics would have been in charge, treating him.'

'Yes. Assuming he was in the same kind of state as Stapleford or Wray, medical staff would have doused his facial injuries with antiseptic, so that's probably goodbye to any DNA trace. I can ask Welbeck, but I don't think there's much hope.'

'Still, Craig, we're definitely getting somewhere.'

'Somewhere, yes, but if any of this stands up, we're talking about a hyperactive spree killer. From Hove at four p.m. on Saturday, to Guildford around nine on Sunday evening, and Birmingham at eight on Monday morning.'

'But what do any of these victims have in common? A retired policeman, a handbag entrepreneur and this guy in Birmingham?'

'I've no idea, but each new incident is extra data, and gives us a much better chance of finding the assailant.'

'In theory, but how?'

'Transport. How did the assailant get to all these places so quickly? It's a long shot, but I've asked Vikram to do an ANPR check. To see if any one vehicle lit up cameras in Hove, Guildford and Small Heath, Birmingham from Saturday morning to Monday lunchtime. Starting with Aaron Randall's silver Audi.'

'That's a brilliant idea.'

'It wouldn't work if the killing had been spaced out over a couple of weeks, because of the huge number of hits it would generate from delivery drivers. But in such a short space of time, we should get a manageable number. If, and that's a big if, the same vehicle was used throughout.'

–

Carl Hoskins was slouched at his desk at Mount Browne, tidying up the loose ends of the Stapleford case for DI Mulholland. He'd just put in the request for a national ANPR check on Randall's car on Monday morning, which he was told would take about an hour. He turned back to Claire's list: he had to double-check all the associates of Tommy Hollis for connections to the Brighton area, and Fir Close in particular. There were dozens of mugshots of this criminal fraternity over the years, not all of whom had been convicted. It was the usual gangland problem of reluctant witnesses. He leaned back in his chair, with his hands cupped behind his head, staring up at the flickering strip lamp. God, he *really* fancied a portion of chips. He had been fighting with the desire all morning, but it was getting the better of him. Since his diabetes diagnosis, and urged on by his daughter, he had embraced a healthier diet. Supermarket fruit salad for lunch was all very well, he particularly enjoyed the pineapple and any strawberries he could find in it. But often it was full of tasteless bits of unripe melon. Today, he'd gobbled most of it down by eleven, and tossed the plastic box containing the remains of the melon and his plastic fork into the bin.

And now the vinegar tang, the salty crispness of hot chips rustling in white papers began to consume him. Still fighting the munchies, he looked at the details of all the vehicles which had been seen or recorded in Fir Close, Hove in the days leading up to the killing. The roofer who had been working at number three, and who had hired the blue Renault van, was called Gerard Daly. That name, common as it was, rang a bell. He looked back at the list of Hollis henchman, and found him. He'd been cleared of conspiracy to murder back in 2013, at the same time that Hollis went down. The address given for the van hire matched, as was expected, the registered address of GGD Roofing Ltd in Brighton. A quick look at Companies House showed that the only director when it was set up in 2009 was Gerard Stanley Daly, which exactly matched the court records. He'd given his occupation at the time of arrest as a scaffolder, which maybe wasn't a world away from roofing. With a growing sense of excitement, Hoskins checked the addresses on record. Daly had been living in Crawley in Sussex at the time of his arrest, and the Companies House records showed a Brighton address. He then looked up the website of the roofing company, but it was a pretty terse affair, littered with spelling mistakes. The only reference to staff was an email address for gez.daley at the website. That could be him.

Going back to the court case, the accusation had been that he was present when a discussion about the killing of a rival had been made. He managed to find an alibi, from an elderly female neighbour, which was enough to sway the jury. Looking at the mugshot, and the CCTV surveillance footage on file, Daly was a stocky individual, who looked quite capable of violence, but he had no known history of it. Had he taken up cage fighting later, perhaps? It seemed unlikely.

The next check was with the Fir Close residents who had employed GGD Roofing. They confirmed a flat roofing renewal job at the back of the house, which had taken two days and coincided with the dashcam records of the van's presence in the close. It was only when Hoskins asked what the job was that the penny dropped. The roofer was replacing worn-out bitumen felt with GRP, glass reinforced polyester.

Immediately after the call, Hoskins googled GRP roofs. It was just as he suspected: they were made of fibreglass and resin. He looked at the evidence bag with the gangster gloves and clapped his hands in glee.

'Claire!' he called. 'I've got something here.'

Chapter Sixteen

Three hours later, Gerard Daly was sitting disconsolately in an interview room at Redhill Police Station. Claire Mulholland and Michelle Tsu stared in at him through the one-way glass from another room, watching him picking at his stained fingers.

'That's fibreglass,' Claire said.

'Caught red-handed then?' Michelle asked.

'Not exactly. He complained when we wouldn't let him clean up first.' Daly had been arrested that afternoon by plainclothes officers of Sussex Police who were waiting for him in a car parked just outside the GGD Roofing yard. He expressed complete bewilderment, but co-operated.

'So what's the plan?' Michelle asked.

'We're assuming that he was doing a reconnaissance for the actual job. The back roof of number three does give some visibility of the front of Ken Stapleford's house.'

'What about the actual killing? The roof job was finished two days before Stapleford was killed.'

'It doesn't rule him out. A different vehicle, maybe, then he went in.'

'There's no DNA, is there?'

'No. There is no match inside Stapleford's house to Gerard Daly. But if Daly was in work overalls, and wearing the type of gloves you probably use when you're working on a roof, all that might shield him,' Claire said.

Michelle looked at her.

'Yes I know, don't tell me. It is still pretty thin. Of course, the officers that made the arrests were cock-a-hoop at the idea that Liam Lewis will now get off.'

'What a surprise.'

'Okay, let's go in.'

Daly looked up as they walked in. 'I don't know what this is all about.'

The two officers prepped the tape, and greeted the duty solicitor, an impatient-looking bespectacled man with something of Captain Mainwaring about him.

'When did you last see or hear from Tommy Hollis?' Claire asked.

Daly sucked his teeth. 'Years ago, before he went inside.'

'Did he ask you to do a job for him? On the quiet?'

He shook his head. 'Like I say, I haven't heard from him and am not expecting to.'

'Do you own a motorcycle or an e-scooter?'

'No.' He looked at his brief, as if the police had taken leave of their senses.

'Where were you last Saturday afternoon?'

'I was watching football with some mates, down at the Welly.'

'The where?'

'Duke of Wellington, Crombie Street, Redhill. I'll be on the CCTV, if you want to check.' He folded his arms, as if there was nothing more to say.

–

Gillard was back at Mount Browne preparing for the three p.m. incident room meeting when DI Welbeck rang him to say that he had spoken to the victim.

'He's been conscious for a few hours, but remains in a bad way, with a fractured eye socket, a broken jaw, and several missing teeth. He seems a tough old bloke, and is likely to make a full recovery.'

'Was he able to tell you anything about the assailant?'

'Not too much. As you recall he was crouching down, unlocking the security shutter for his shop, and describes just feeling this incredible pain. He claims to have heard and seen nothing, and thinks he must have passed out.'

'Does he have any idea why he was attacked?'

'He owes some money to a local family, and has had trouble paying. He assumed it was related to that,' Welbeck said.

'Mike, I think you were right all along. Your case is connected, not only to Wray's killing but to the murder of Ken Stapleford in Hove on the Saturday before.'

'I thought you had charged Liam Lewis with that?'

'Yes, but there is no way Lewis could have committed all three crimes because he was in custody after the first.'

'So how come?'

'Gloves. We think the same pair of gloves was used to assault both victims, because Stapleford's DNA turned up in a swab taken from Gary Wray's face.'

'Do you have the gloves?'

Gillard grimaced. 'Unfortunately no, but it's the only way I can think of that DNA from one victim was transferred to another. We do know Wray's assailant was definitely wearing gloves, as the attacker was in Birmingham, and we have a few microscopic woollen fibres from Stapleford's face.'

'We didn't swab Mr Patel's face and I'm sure it's too late now.'

'I guessed as much, but there might well be other places that DNA was left, perhaps on his clothing.'

'I'm sure we'll still have that,' Welbeck said. 'Leave it with me.'

'Do try the other guys who were attacked. There may be DNA on them from the gloves worn by the attacker.'

'Okay, I'll do that.'

'What's the background of the victim?'

'No criminal record. Married, but separated. A very traditional Muslim of Bangladeshi origin. Seems to have been some disputes within the family, but I can't get anyone to talk about it. However we are concentrating on the debt angle. He owes fifty grand to his cousin, who does have a bit of previous. However the cousin has a cast-iron alibi. Flight and passport record show he was in Dubai.'

'One final thing, Mike. Let's keep these linkages out of the public eye. I haven't even told my chief constable yet.'

'Agreed.' He hung up.

With that uncanny ability she so often displayed, Alison Rigby rang Gillard the moment the call to Welbeck had been cut. 'I'm so glad to find you back in the saddle, Craig,' she said. 'I've just sent some flowers to Sam to give her my congratulations.'

'Thank y—'

'Now I understand we've got a definite forensic linkage between the killings in Hove and Guildford. I had assumed there was contamination by CSI, but when I spoke to DI Mulholland she said independent tests had confirmed the initial finding.'

'That's right, ma'am. And we've got a third possibly linked attack too. An attack on a middle-aged Asian shop-keeper in Birmingham. Fortunately, he's still alive.'

'It sounds impossible.'

'I know, and I don't ask you to believe it until we have stood up the evidence, ma'am. We are not going public with any of this yet.'

'Hmm. So we keep Liam Lewis as prime suspect.'

'At the moment, but the more this inquiry expands, the more potential leads get generated.'

Rigby chuckled. 'I knew I did the right thing calling you in. What's your baby's name again?'

'Grace,' Gillard said.

'Ah yes, well keep up the good work, solve this quickly, and you'll be back to nappy changing duties in no time.' She hung up, leaving Gillard staring at the phone.

Claire Mulholland walked in. 'Craig, I just looked through the full PM report on Stapleford. There actually *was* a description of a burn listed in the PM report. It was probably electrical, of indeterminate age, and on Staple-ford's right hand. I rang Delahaye and he said that he didn't flag it up because the victim was trained as an electrician, and according to the statement, had been undertaking electrical work for neighbours in the weeks leading up to his death. I think he was a bit alarmed to have overlooked something that may turn out to be so significant.'

'Cases turn on tiny scraps of evidence, Claire, we just have to keep our eyes open.'

-

Thursday's late afternoon incident room meeting included Inspector Geoffrey Holt, DI Claire Mulholland, DS

Vikram Singh, DC Liz Tufnell and two of the three detectives who had previously had Covid. On Zoom they had DCI Welbeck in Birmingham.

'All right everybody,' Gillard said, pointing to the photos of Wray, Stapleford and Sengupta stuck on a whiteboard. 'We have three evidential or forensic links between these three crimes. One, it looks from CCTV, and my own visual evidence, to be the same attacker involved in the Wray killing and the assault on the shopkeeper in Birmingham. Second, we have a plausible explanation for the DNA of murder victim Ken Stapleford appearing on the face of Gary Wray. Indeed, we see evidence of the same or similar gloves being used in the attack on Mr Sengupta. Third, we have electrical burns on all three victims, along with some CCTV evidence which shows a home-made stun gun being used on Sengupta.'

'My money's on Aaron Randall,' Liz Tufnell said, turning a biro over and over between her fingers.

'Nah, Liz, not for the Birmingham case,' Carl Hoskins interrupted. 'ANPR showed his car being driven in Liverpool at the same time as that attack.'

'And he's also got an alibi,' Gillard said. 'Rather a good one, unfortunately. He was interviewed by regional TV at his own gym just twenty minutes after our Birmingham shopkeeper was on CCTV being beaten up on Monday.'

Vikram Singh held up his hand. 'Sir, there are some interesting ANPR results on the broader trawl. While there was no single vehicle which triggered cameras in Hove, Guildford and Small Heath, Birmingham over that weekend, we do have a few plates that were captured in Birmingham and in one of the other two.'

'Any of them a dark SUV?' Gillard asked. 'That was the car that the Birmingham assailant was seen to get into.'

'Not exactly. There is a 2014 midnight blue Nissan Qashqai, but that's a crossover rather than an SUV.'

'So where was it?'

'Small Heath on Monday morning, one hit at 07.19 and twice on the B2066 in Hove on Saturday afternoon, 15.36 and 16.27.'

'Definitely not in Guildford?'

'Not at the times we asked for. But I can expand the search criteria, if you want.'

'Who's the owner?'

'A Mr P. K. Umrani of Erdington, in Brum.' Singh looked up. 'This doesn't sound significant to me. He's got every reason to be in Birmingham.'

'Anything else?'

'A white VW van in both Guildford and Small Heath. However the timings are the wrong way round, basically. It was in Small Heath on Saturday afternoon, and Guildford on Monday morning. Are you interested in motorcycles?'

'Try me,' Gillard said. 'The assailant was wearing the gear, after all.'

'A Kawasaki 750 in Hove and Guildford, but the timings are a bit off.'

'Hmm. A powerful bike like that would have turned a lot of heads, but let's chase it down anyway.'

Singh looked down the various records on his phone. 'I don't have anything else. Oh, it seems like Mr Umrani is a bit of a speed merchant. Five speeding tickets in the last week, so he'll be up for disqualification.'

Gillard turned to Welbeck. 'One for you to pick up, Mike?'

'I'll chase it up,' he said.

'Now Carl, what about our fibreglass roofer Gerard Daly?' Gillard asked. 'How are his alibis looking?'

Hoskins looked pained. 'I'm afraid he really was in the Duke of Wellington in Redhill at the time he said. The pub security cameras show him clearly, leaning on the bar, at exactly the time of the Stapleford killing, unfortunately.'

'So that is both of our suspects ruled out,' Gillard sighed. 'Daly and Randall.'

'It looks that way,' Hoskins said.

Gillard sighed. Neither of these two had DNA links to the crime scenes, either. This certainly didn't seem to be getting any easier.

Welbeck raised his hand. 'Just got the results of the DNA tests on Sengupta's clothing, and that of the other two who were assaulted. Two samples match Ken Stapleford.'

'It must be the gloves,' Gillard said. 'There can be no other answer.'

–

Welbeck got back to Gillard quite quickly. 'I've just interviewed Mr Umrani, the owner of the Nissan Qashqai. And it seems he loaned the vehicle a couple of weeks ago to his brother-in-law's sister, who just happens to be the estranged wife of Prabir Sengupta, the man who was beaten up.'

'Aha! That sounds really significant.'

'We've contacted her by phone, and she claimed the car was stolen.'

'When was it reported?'

'That's the trouble, she didn't report it. There's no record of anyone reporting it stolen.'

'This sounds quite fishy, Mike.'

'Yes it does. She claims to be living down in your neck of the woods, in Farnborough. Says she hasn't been to Birmingham for years. Can I ask someone your end to interview her?'

'Yes, of course.'

After he'd taken the detail and ended the call, Gillard looked more closely at the movements of the car. The timings of the ANPR captures worked perfectly for the Hove killing and the attack in Birmingham. He logged on to the system, and brought up everything the DVLA had on this car. The government licensing agency records showed there were five pending speeding tickets, all of them during the period spanning the killings. On Saturday afternoon on the M23, heading north towards the M25 London orbital road, just an hour after Ken Stapleford was killed. Then one on the M6 near Manchester, later that night. Then on Monday morning, one in Small Heath, Birmingham, just after the attack on Prabir Sengupta, then a half-hour later one at roadworks on the M6 heading east for Coventry.

That vehicle had certainly got around.

He needed to flesh this out. He logged into the road safety system and put in a request for a nationwide search for this vehicle on ANPR. He wanted to know every camera it had tripped from the week before to a week after the killings. He also requested the actual photographs. Sometimes from front-facing cameras it was possible to see who was in the car.

It took only fifteen minutes to get the basic data. The Nissan had travelled from the Brighton area on Saturday afternoon, up the M23, M25, M40 and M6 all the way to Glasgow, much of it seemingly at illegal speed. It returned equally rapidly to the M25 in the small hours of Sunday morning, then towards Guildford on the A3. Late on Sunday night, it headed up to Birmingham on the M42, leaving again by late morning, and returning to Guildford. Gillard mapped the vehicle's movements against the timings of the three crimes. Hove, Guildford and Birmingham. The match was perfect. Whoever was in that vehicle absolutely had to be the killer. If they could find the car, they could find the murderer. But where was it now?

Chapter Seventeen

It was gone five when DC Kim Leighton parked the unmarked grey Renault amongst a collection of macho cars outside Lenny's Combat and Martial Arts. The departmental spare, the Renault had dents and scratches, and fitted in reasonably well with the Mitsubishi Warriors, cut down Vauxhall Corsas and aged BMWs with tinted windows outside the gym. It was a 1960s industrial unit set amongst warehouses on the outskirts of Farnborough. She made her way across the car park, pulled open the door and was immediately hit by a waft of male sweat and the echoing shouts and impacts that produce it.

Lenny Vashev himself was identified by a sweatshirt bearing his own name on the back. Not that you'd easily mix him up with anyone else. About six-one, built like the proverbial brick shithouse, and with a bullet head, he was bellowing instructions to two young men sparring in a ring. A man standing next to Lenny nudged him as she approached, and he called a halt to proceedings.

'Ah, you must be detective Kim,' he said, in a slight East European accent. 'Come into my comfy office away from this racket,' he said, gesturing at the dozen or so individuals within sight who were training.

Kim followed him with no high expectations. In the previous day and a half, she had telephoned or visited more than a dozen gyms, martial arts instructors and the

British Martial Arts and Boxing Association. Everyone had been very helpful, but there had been little progress, even when she had attended in person to show the video of the Birmingham attack on her iPad. Like DI Welbeck, almost everyone who saw the video concurred that the assailant was professionally trained, but when asked to hazard a guess as to who this individual was, they were left scratching their heads. It was pointed out to her that 160,000 people in the UK regularly participate in at least one martial art or combat sport.

Lenny offered Kim a coffee from a posh Nespresso system, which she accepted, along with a plain chocolate digestive. 'I had a quick look at the video online,' he said, as the machine hissed and spluttered. 'But if you have a better definition version that would help.'

'We've enhanced it as best we can but it is from CCTV. As I mentioned, this person is reckoned to be about five foot nine, and eleven stone at most.' She showed him her iPad.

Lenny watched the video at full-screen size. 'Whoa, those are good kicks,' he said, as he watched the two bystanders being brought low. 'That's a very good kick-boxing technique. And there is clearly some judo skill. But obviously I can't tell who it is, because of the helmet.'

'How hard is it to fight like that wearing a crash helmet?'

'That is a very interesting question. I've never tried, and I imagine the biggest danger would be limited peripheral vision, and steaming up. It would be hard in a protracted bout, no doubt about it. But against the untrained, even two or three of them, you wouldn't get out of breath.'

'What are your own specialisms?'

'I was Bulgarian special forces. We practised karate, and a little bit of kickboxing. When I first came over here in 2006, my first job was as a nightclub bouncer. I tried a bit of cage fighting, but I couldn't keep my weight down, and I was up against monsters, real killers. I was once offered ten grand to fight a pitbull, but lucky for me I looked up the videos to see what they could do to people. I wasn't going to get my face ripped off like the bloke I saw. No way.'

'So you've no idea who this is?' She played the video again.

'Stop it there,' he said. 'You see, that is a very high kick, the one on the jaw of the biggest bystander. Not many people can kick that high. Not many blokes, anyway.'

'You mean women can kick higher?'

'Oh yeah, it's something to do with the hips. Just like women can do the splits much more easily than men can.'

'So could this be a woman?'

He blew a sigh. 'Well if so, she is built like a man. Shoulder bulk, a stocky upper body, with narrow hips. Even moves like a bloke. Of course, if she'd been taking testosterone, like some of the female weightlifters do, that could fool us. A couple of years of Nebido, the fat begins to shift from hips and thighs to shoulders, and the neck gets thicker too.'

'Do you know any women in Britain who have done this?' Kim asked.

'There's a few out there. Personally, I only met the one. Four years ago, there was a woman who came here, just the once. First time I looked at her, I thought she was half-bloke, half-girl. She'd clearly been weight-training, then stopped. Out of tone, flabby almost. Very shy, wouldn't make eye contact. I thought, no, no, she's not right for this. She said she wanted to do it for her mental health, which I thought, fair enough. It builds self-confidence, self-belief, all that. I thought, a gentle induction here. I do remember it well because she was very self-conscious about her body. Insisted on wearing this shapeless top, as well as full-length jogging bottoms. I thought, she's gonna sweat like crazy. I wondered if she was Muslim, because we have had a couple in the past. Sometimes they are white. But she didn't have her hair covered. And this I do remember, her hair was all spiky, and green.'

'What was her name?'

'I don't recall. But I tell you what I do remember. I went out for a gentle spar with her, like I do with the boxercise ladies. I parry, and they punch. It's normally pretty mild stuff. She was different, she could punch really hard. And from nowhere, she feinted right, I moved forward, then there was this massive Muay Thai high kick from the left. Got me on the side of the head, and I bloody went down, didn't I? Right in front of the whole gym. She'd clearly had a lot of training, but hadn't mentioned any of it.'

'Do you have her details? Address, membership, anything like that?'

'No. We don't collect details of walk-ins, until they have finished their two free sessions. And that was on the first. I left half a dozen messages for her, because I thought she had potential, I could train her. But she never returned my calls. I think she was a bit embarrassed, and never came back again.'

'Can I ask you to come into the station? We need you to do an e-fit.'

–

Gillard was sceptical about Kim Leighton's information. Okay, it was certainly a tenable line of inquiry that the attacks on Gary Wray, Ken Stapleford and Prabir Sengupta were inspired by their treatment of women. But having been on the receiving end of the attacker, he could hardly believe that this actually *was* a woman. He always reckoned he could tell a woman by the way she moved, by proportions, by vocalisations, half a dozen other unconscious assessments. He rang Welbeck to bounce the new theory off him, and he too was dubious. 'When I was in uniform, Birmingham city centre, at chucking out time I've seen quite a few women fight. But from the CCTV footage this appears so clinical, lacking the kind of emotional explosion that normally accompanies female violence,' Welbeck said.

'Yes, I agree, but our informant seems to be telling us that she has some real professionalism. You know something, Mike. We should never underestimate a woman. Let's pursue this with an open mind.'

Thursday evening

Driving into his own street at half eight on a wet evening after a long day, Gillard was as usual running late. Sam's control room work colleagues had dropped in after the end of their shift to see Grace and she had texted him to let him know it had snowballed into a bit of a party. He'd wished they had been able to wait a week or so, but events have their own momentum. The first colleagues had arrived before seven, and some had already left, according to Sam's latest message. She was exhausted, and needed him to help.

Trouble was, there was literally nowhere to park. This was the one disadvantage of the new house in Parkmead

Crescent. It may only have been a few minutes' drive from Mount Browne, but at the time of day that Gillard normally arrived home there were very few places left. Although there were some residents' parking spaces, he hadn't had his paperwork through yet and couldn't use them. The rest of the street was often crammed with the vehicles of those who worked across the other side of the park where the streets were double yellow lined. Unable to find a slot, Gillard parked one street further back, and walked in the drizzle down the road. Trying to unwind and forget about crime for a moment, he popped in his AirPods and texted Sam to let her know he'd be there in a couple of minutes. But some part of his brain must have been still processing in the background because, just a few dozen yards short of his house, he stopped and turned around. The car he had just passed was a Nissan Qashqai. Black or possibly dark blue. Midnight blue? He retraced his steps until he could see the number plate. It was one he knew by heart, having seen it a dozen times on the ANPR and DVLA databases.

This was the same damn vehicle. The one they were looking for.

And someone had left it almost by his house.

He pocketed his AirPods, pulled out his phone and rang the duty DI, John Perry. 'John, you'll never believe this. I found that Nissan Qashqai we've been looking for. It's almost outside my own house. Yes, unbelievable. Talk about hiding in plain sight. Get a CSI team here too, please. I'm hoping the interior will be minging with DNA.' He was about to finish the call, when he said. 'Actually, hold on for a moment. I've changed my mind.' He moved away from the car, towards his own house.

The vehicle could still be in use, perhaps by someone living in this very street. The last thing he needed now was to have blue lights all over the place while CSI went through it. He had everything he needed at home, except a tracker bug. 'On second thoughts, John, can you send me just one plainclothes crime scene investigator in an unmarked vehicle? And I need a magnetic vehicle tracker. Get Vikram to apply for a warrant on this registration number.' He read out the plate. He was told that some-body would be there in twenty minutes. Gillard looked to his own house, where he could see the stained-glass picture window which looked out on to this side. Excel-lent, that could be a lookout post from which anyone approaching the Nissan could be seen. He hurried home, and was just about to put the key in the front door when it opened. Tanya, one of Sam's best friends from the control room, emerged, followed by another woman.

'Ah Craig! Congratulations on the birth of Grace,' Tanya said, pausing to give him a hug. 'She's so beautiful. You must be so happy.'

'I am,' Gillard said. 'Are you leaving?'

'I'm afraid so, straight off shift to get here, and now I have to get home.'

'Ah, could I just borrow you for ten minutes?' he said, moving aside to let the other woman past, as shouted goodbyes were exchanged. 'It's quite an important oper-ational matter,'

'Ooh,' Tanya said, her dark eyes widening, her hands still resting on his shoulders. 'That sounds exciting.' Gillard caught a whiff of alcohol on her breath.

'It's not really, I just need you to stand as lookout,' he said, ushering her back into the house. 'The best place is our picture window halfway up the stairs. There is a car parked along the street, a Nissan Qashqai, and I need you to keep an eye on it for a few minutes until my reinforcements arrive.'

He had no sooner finished, when he heard Sam calling for him, and Tanya responding: 'Sam, I'm going to be a spy for Craig!' *Oh hell, Tanya is actually drunk.*

Sam came out to the hallway, Grace in her arms, followed by Mary and Tom, Sam's parents.

'Oh, Craig I wish you could have got here sooner...' Sam began. She looked wrecked.

He kissed her briefly, and stroked his daughter's fine dark hair. 'I'm not actually finished for the day yet, I'm afraid.'

He watched as Sam's face fell. His own phone was buzzing but he ignored it. 'I'm sorry, Sam, the car we've been looking for is actually almost outside this house.'

'So, you are buying a new car?' Tom asked, jingling the change in his pockets.

'Is this the right place?' Tanya called down. She was sitting on the window seat next to the stained-glass window. 'I can't see through the coloured patterns.'

'No, if you stand on a higher stair you can see through the clear panel above.' She moved and he looked up at her, now balancing precariously on high heels to peer through the top pane.

'Oh yes, I can see now. Which one is it?'

Mary inserted a glass of white wine into Gillard's open hand. 'Here, Craig, it looks like you could do with this.'

'So what kind of car is it that you are in the market for?' Tom asked. Sam's father was a bit of a petrolhead, and always surprised that Gillard's own car was so low-key.

'Are we buying a new car?' Sam asked.

'No. No! Just give me a minute, please.' He realised he was now addressing a small conclave of Sam's friends from work and elsewhere, who had gathered in the hallway, drinks and canapés in hand, to see what was happening. He thanked Mary, handed the glass of wine on to Sam and thundered up the stairs to where Tanya was standing unsteadily looking out. He rested his hands lightly on her hips so that he could stand and look over her shoulder. 'It's that one, the Nissan Qashqai.'

'Righto,' Tanya said. 'I'll let you know if it moves.' She pushed her bum backwards into him. Alarmed, he stepped away and dropped his hands from her hips. 'Spoilsport,' she whispered.

Gillard continued up the stairs, ignoring Sam's calls, and went into his home office. He knew he was going to get it in the neck from Sam for this apparent rudeness, and even more so if she had spotted Tanya pushing her bottom into his groin, but he needed to check that he had a spare forensic kit. As he pulled open drawers, he picked up his phone and returned the missed call from the control room. They confirmed that an unmarked vehicle with one officer was on its way and due to arrive in five minutes. A locksmith had been requested. On his way down, he ran into Sam, talking to Tanya. They were sitting side-by-side, squashed onto the window seat.

'Is it still there?' Gillard asked.

'Ooh, gosh. Let me look.' Tanya stood up, and peered through the glass panel. 'Yes, it's still there.'

'Craig,' Sam said. 'I have to talk to you, especially if we're thinking of getting a new car.' She led him down the stairs and into the kitchen.

'I'm not. Tom just got the wrong end of the stick. Ah, I see the new fridge has arrived.'

'Yes, but they didn't take the old one,' Sam said. 'It's in the back garden now.'

'Is that what you want to talk to me about?'

'No, Craig—'

Mary interrupted. 'The cleaner shifted it, she's marvellous, honestly, but you wouldn't know it—'

'—we lost our buyers.'

'Shit.' Gillard thought about the monstrous bridging loan, and the increasing time it must now span. 'Do we know why?'

'No, the estate agent didn't know. They had seemed so keen.'

'Pound to a penny Trish has got to them,' Gillard said. Would they never be rid of the woman?

Ellie arrived with Grace in her arms. 'Here, does Daddy want to hold her?' she said, passing the baby to Gillard. Ellie and Sam had known each other since college. Gillard cradled his child gently against his chest, which prompted a few *aaahs* amongst the assembled friends. Grace was less impressed, and woke up and began to grizzle.

'She's hungry,' said Mary.

'Join the club,' Gillard muttered, looking at the spread laid out on the kitchen table, of which he hadn't yet had a single bite.

'No, she needs her nappy changed,' Sam said. Gillard, who had shrugged off his raincoat but was still in his work suit, started to lift his daughter back towards Sam.

'Haven't you changed a nappy yet, Craig?' asked Ellie.

'Not when I'm still at work, but I'm happy to get involved afterwards.'

'But you're always at work,' Sam said, then turned to Ellie, and said confidentially: 'It's the perfect get-out clause.'

'So, Craig, have you caught Gary Wray's killer yet?' Ellie continued. She sounded tipsy, too.

'We're getting there,' he said, after swallowing a bite of tuna and mayonnaise canapé that Sam posted into his mouth. 'We're tracking him down gradually.'

'One of Tia's boyfriends, do you think? Or a vigilante?' she asked.

'I'm sure you understand why I can't comment,' he said.

'Frankly, I think he deserved it,' Ellie said to Sam. 'Obviously a complete bastard, the way he treated her.'

Gillard nodded, and swallowed before saying: 'I'm getting the impression that a few people feel that way.'

'Craig!' Tanya shouted. 'There is a man by that car.'

He reversed out of the conversation and thundered up the stairs, manoeuvred carefully around Tanya and peered through the clear panel. 'Ah, I think he's one of ours.' He took out his mobile and rang the number he had been given by the control room. The man he was watching put a phone to his ear.

'DC Gary Collins.'

'Gillard here. I'm watching you from a few doors down. Are you able to get into it?'

'I'm waiting for the locksmith, just a couple of minutes away. But I just fitted the tracker.'

'I would advise you to wait in your vehicle, because I have a feeling that the suspect is somewhere close by and might spot you if you hang around.'

'Okay, will do sir.'

'When the locksmith arrives, I want the quickest possible forensic essentials: dabs from steering wheel, glove compartment and boot hatch, plus DNA tape lifts from headrests. If you can steal the front footwell mats, do so.'

With the car surveillance in safe hands, Gillard felt able to eat, grabbing generous handfuls of crisps, mini pizzas, sausage rolls and pork pie. Everyone wanted to talk to him, but all he wanted to do was to enfold Sam and his daughter in his arms, and then get some sleep. So he went through some mechanical small talk, particularly with Mary, who had plenty of excuses to make about the poor supermarket buffet, given that the fridge had been changed over, and the delivery men were a nightmare, and thank God for getting in someone to help. Gillard assured her that by now he would have eaten roadkill, so long as there was ketchup to go with it. Somehow she seemed offended by this, and turned away. For a bit of peace he let himself out the back door into the garden, where at least the rain had stopped. Feeling that he wasn't alone he turned to his left, and saw the gigantic American-style walk-in fridge that they had wanted to get rid of, almost exactly his height and twice as wide.

His mind was drawn back to their lost house purchasers. Their home in Banstead was worth a lot less than this one, and they really needed to sell it quickly. He didn't want to become an accidental landlord, particularly because Sam would be too tied up with Grace to be able to oversee it. He blew a sigh and stared up into the sky, wondering if the overtime he had done would be enough to cover the interest on the bridging loan.

The buzz of the phone interrupted him. It was DC Collins. 'Sir, just notified the control room that the target vehicle is on the move. I thought you'd like to know.'

'Occupants?'

'One male, carrying a child, and one female. She was driving.'

'Description?'

'We're in the car and it's raining hard now, so we didn't get a good look at them. The male was average height, stocky, wearing a grey hoodie and a woolly hat, carrying a small rucksack. Couldn't see the face because of the child. The female, late thirties maybe, light-coloured hair.'

'Are you following?'

'Yes. We're a couple of cars behind, but the tracker is on my phone, so it's easy-peasy.'

'That's great news. Did you manage to do the DNA lifts?'

'No. The locksmith only arrived a minute before the two suspects, so we didn't get a chance.'

'That's a shame. Still we should be able to get it later. Do keep me in the loop.' He thanked them and hung up. By the time he walked back into the kitchen most of the guests had gone. Sam was talking to Ellie and Mary.

'Hello stranger,' Sam said. 'I didn't know where you were.'

He blew a sigh. 'I'm really sorry this has intruded on our time together. A car we've been searching for to tie together several murders and attacks has just turned up parked on our own damn street. I couldn't ignore it.'

'Well, I think you're doing very well, to be able to juggle work and home,' Mary said.

'If that's juggling I don't recommend a job at the circus,' Sam said. 'These are precious days in your daughter's life, and at this rate you're going to miss them all.'

'Sam, really. What can I do?' He looked at Mary for some support, and she smiled indulgently.

'I'll go and see her now,' he said.

'I wouldn't,' Sam said. 'It's taken me ages to get her to sleep. She'd been crying a lot earlier in the evening.'

His phone buzzed and he looked at it. DC Collins. 'Sorry, I have to get this.' He turned away to answer it. 'Yes, Gary, go ahead.'

'The target vehicle is stationary at the Tesco superstore, Ashenden Road.'

'Can you see it?'

'Yes, but the occupants have already left. We're told that a couple of patrol cars are on their way.'

'What? They'll scare them off! Who called them in?'

'DI Perry. He told us to keep an eye on the car while the uniforms go inside the store.'

'I'm bloody SIO,' Gillard said. 'All right, just make sure that they don't use the blues and twos. I'll be over in ten minutes.' He cut the call. 'Just wait till I get hold of bloody Perry,' Gillard said to no one in particular.

'So you're going out again?' Sam said. Tears sprung up on her face.

'I'm sorry.' He pulled her into an embrace, and she clung to him and began to sob. Over her shoulder he saw Mary mouthing: *hormones*. He hoped so, because the last thing he wanted to do was upset Sam, after everything she'd been through. Not only the protracted birth, but being upside down in a car crash a few hours previously, trying to stay awake for this spontaneous party, and then of course hearing about their house buyer pulling out. And he wasn't here with her to share the burden. However understandable the reasons, he could see why she was upset. Thank God for Mary.

He kissed Sam's neck, and stroked her hair.

His phone buzzed.

Perry.

Gillard gradually released his hold on Sam, took a deep breath and answered the call. Perry began in a rush: 'Craig, look I've heard you're not happy. I'm sorry, I was just trying to be proactive, and knew that you had stuff to do at home, with the baby and everything.'

'Have you got them?' he asked.

'We've got the car; officers are searching it now.'

'But not the occupants.'

'Uniforms are in the store. There's loads of CCTV, so we'll narrow it down pretty quickly. You can't get far with a child in tow.'

'Do you have any idea how many kids go with their parents into a busy Tesco?' Mentally, Gillard was counting to ten. 'John, we could easily have got them getting back into the car if we tried it softly, softly. Remember, this vehicle isn't registered to either of those occupants. It seems to have been passed around a lot of people. The woman who was supposedly lent the vehicle is being interviewed first thing tomorrow, but her description doesn't match those who were last seen in it.'

'Ah, I didn't appreciate that.'

'All right, John. We are where we are. I'm absolutely dead on my feet, and all I can think of is getting some kip, so I formally pass it over to you as duty DI.'

'What time are you in?'

'Seven, I suppose. I'd love a lie-in, but...'

'Have a good night, Craig,' Perry said, and hung up.

Sam was looking at him. 'I'm just going to bed now,' she said, wiping out streaks of tears underneath her eyes. 'Sorry about everything. She waved a hand around the kitchen. I just...'

'We're both knackered, Sam. It's completely natural.'

'Are you coming to bed too?'

'Just one final phone call.'

Sam closed her eyes and nodded, clearly trying to swallow a final disappointment. 'You know, Craig, the one thing that really annoyed me: Tanya said how fanciable you were. She said she really enjoyed being your spy. You know what a flirt she is.'

'She was drunk, Sam. That was obvious.'

'Ah, but that's when the truth comes out.'

He prayed that Tanya hadn't mentioned making a pass at him. There would be no way he would escape blame.

'Sam. Please.' He kissed her on the tip of her nose. She went into the hall and began to climb the stairs. Gillard turned back to his phone. No, screw it. There's always one more phone call. He turned the device off, and went after her up to bed.

Chapter Eighteen

Rainy awoke in the middle of the night after vivid dreams, and momentarily forgot where she was. Then she came to her senses and experienced the mini-grief of realising anew that her ex-husband was dead. She was in the spare bedroom of her sister-in-law, Aileen, in Dundee. She and husband Doug had welcomed her, held her close, and even cried together. Rainy received a sympathetic response to the retelling of the story of her marriage. Aileen, of course, knew Ross' temper of old. She had been on the receiving end of it throughout her teenage years, and had always wondered whether the leopard had ever changed his spots once he became a married man and an NHS consultant.

Of course not.

All three shared meals and a couple of bottles of wine, and yesterday the two women had even indulged in a one-day spa retreat, the kind of luxury Rainy couldn't normally afford. Now, however, she knew that some of Ross' money would be coming her way, so to hell with it. But today, Friday, after three pleasant healing days, she had to go back to face the music. To return to work, to return the many missed calls from colleagues. Above all, she had to face the truth of what she'd done. Once again, her mind went back to how it all started.

She still recalled the distinctive smell as she had made her way down the corridor of the community health building in Reading. The citrus taint of cleaning products mixed with the smell of floor polish. She found the meeting room, and looked through the wire-reinforced glass. There were seven women, a mixture of ethnicities and ages, in conversation and sitting in a circle on plastic chairs. She tapped on the glass and then eased open the door. Everyone looked up. One woman stood and greeted her. 'You must be Rainy,' she said. 'Do come in and join us.' It was Rachel, the woman she had spoken to on the phone. Tall, with tousled blonde hair, and stylish clothing, she was somehow younger and more glamorous than Rainy had visualised her. That in itself made her seem a little intimidating, already several steps above her on the self-worth ladder.

Rainy picked a chair next to a fidgety shaven-headed woman with nose and eyebrow rings, whose forearms were covered with a patchwork of scars, perhaps self-inflicted, including a recent and still-scabbed word, *Hex*. She scratched and picked at the scars constantly. On the other side was a slender octogenarian, wearing a pearl necklace and earrings, who introduced herself as Nina. A large black woman opposite was Anna, then next to her was Loti, a tiny Asian woman with huge brown eyes and dark hair in a ponytail. Assisting Rachel was Scarlett, who ran a women's refuge in Farnborough. She was tall, and had long red hair on one side of her head, the other side green and cut short. Rainy didn't catch the names of the other two, a grey-haired middle-aged woman and a tall teenager with bitten nails.

'You're amongst friends,' Rachel said. 'Don't feel you have to speak; you can, like Hex, simply listen. As I said, you will discover that although your experience is unique, it won't be unknown. It's only by acknowledging your feelings in all their complexity that you can get to the other side.' She turned and gestured to the group. 'Anna here was talking about self-worth. Even though she was the victim of a sustained campaign of public belittlement, derision and control by her husband, she was telling us that she felt she deserved it. Being overweight, feeling unattractive, she felt it was her fault. I think we can all understand that.'

Half an hour later, after listening to more from Anna, Rainy felt able to say her piece. She described her marriage, the happy early years, the deterioration in Ross' behaviour as he became more senior at work, and his huge temper. While she was talking, others were nodding their heads in recognition. She was not alone. Loti, sitting with her legs folded up on the chair, said: 'He sounds just like my husband.'

The session was scheduled to last an hour, but continued for ninety minutes. At the end, Loti produced a plastic box full of samosas, and handed them around. Rachel went to the cafe and came back with a pot of tea on a tray with half a dozen cups. Rainy learned that this communal food sharing was a normal part of the weekly meeting. As they were leaving, Rachel invited them all for a women-only pot-luck party in a week's time at her house in Guildford. 'I know some of you have transport issues, but we have access to the community van, and Scarlett is driving.' The redhead waved a hand and smiled.

Rainy had to change work shifts to go to Rachel's party, but as she sat in the van clutching a bag containing a Tupperware box full of three-bean casserole, the route from her home in Reading to Guildford was achingly familiar. Rachel's home was in a pleasant neighbourhood next to Nightingale Park. As they waited outside the door, the sound of Gloria Gaynor's 'I Will Survive' could be heard inside. The door was opened by a boy of perhaps six years. 'I'm Jack!' he announced.

'I know you are, darling,' Scarlett said, scooping him up in her arms.

'Red and green hair!' Jack exclaimed, fingering her locks as he was carried into the kitchen. The group made their way in, and found there were already thirty women there, and just one man, Will, a stocky, dark-haired individual of about thirty, who was Scarlett's partner. Rainy instantly detected the sweet cloying smell of cannabis, but having not disclosed her occupation, decided to ignore it. After all, she'd smoked dope in her early years as a medical student. She recalled an unforgettable party when three male students had a competition to see who could drink the most of their own urine. That was the night when she woke up on a communally occupied bed next to the man she was destined to marry.

Ross. The man whose behaviour had led her here.

She was introduced to many people at the party, and they freely shared their stories. A young mother whose boyfriend was now in jail, having stamped on her child; two sisters who had run away from their abusive stepfather. Talking to Nina, the older woman she'd sat next to in the first meeting, she was surprised to hear that this woman of cultured tones and refined appearance lived in a women's refuge, afraid for her life. Her moneyed husband, not content with beating her up, had chased her with private detectives and solicitors to cut her divorce settlement if she was seen with another man. Only her continued solitary penury would satisfy him, she said.

Across the room, Rainy saw someone who seemed vaguely familiar. She asked Scarlett who she was, and was told she was Julia, the charity's legal counsel. 'You might have heard of her,' Scarlett said. 'She witnessed the suicide of a gang criminal in a custody suite at Nottingham Crown Court. It was in all the papers. He shot himself with a smuggled weapon.'

Now Rainy realised who she was. Barrister Julia McGann, who Gillard had been convinced was implicated in the murder of her former partner. Nothing ever stuck, however. It was one of the few cases that her boss had never been able to satisfactorily close. The supposed murderer, an abused and vulnerable young woman called Destiny Flynn, had never been found. Gillard had thought she was probably dead.

Julia seemed to have some star quality for some of the women, who crowded around her. Rainy began to feel quite uncomfortable being here with her, having sidestepped a few questions about her occupation by saying that she was a hospital doctor. She made her way to the buffet and filled up her plate, always her reflex when anxious. When she returned to the fray, she got talking to Loti. The story of what he had done to her was horrifying. Failing to conceive her husband a son, she was locked in a garden shed at night, where she would often end up shivering with cold. His extended family all lived in Small Heath, Birmingham, where they ran an Asian food distribution business. She was the outsider, having been brought in from Bangladesh in 1997 to marry him.

'But I refused to be a doormat,' she said. 'I am now cast out from the family, exiled. I came down to live with a cousin in Reading five years ago, and have not been back to Birmingham.'

'Do you have any work?' Rainy asked.

'Yes, fortunately. Pharmacists are in good demand.' She shrugged. 'It's a living, but it's not a life. That man has taken everything away from me, and ostracised me. He told all sorts of lies about me having affairs, none of which was true. Yet he *has* had affairs. And he and his brother boasted of sleeping with white girls, and I mean young girls, passed around.'

'What about your children?'

'My twin daughters, twelve-year-olds when I left, still live with his sister. He has threatened to have them killed if I try to make contact with them again. It was only last year when I was able to see them.' Loti's eyes filled with tears as she told her story. 'And he was furious. He told them he will track me down and set me on fire. He drives a delivery van all over the country. My husband told the children that he has a can of petrol always ready in the van in case he finds me, to save the family honour. Many times, I just can't sleep. I keep thinking I can see his van.'

'This should be investigated by the police,' Rainy said, feeling impotent rage on behalf of the woman.

'The police do nothing,' she said. 'No one has the courage to give evidence. You know, I should have poisoned him, I should have killed him. I had the knowledge, the access to medicines. I just lacked the courage.'

'It's not the answer,' Rainy said.

'Violence should never win.' The voice was Rachel's. Rainy turned to look at her. 'But sometimes in role play getting your own back symbolically is highly cathartic.

226

Are you coming to the refuge fundraiser barbecue next week?'

'Maybe. I'm not sure.'

'It's only a tenner,' Scarlett added, passing by with a tray of food. 'The refuge needs the money. We lost local authority funding last year, so all we get for our tenants is housing benefit, and it's not enough. Some have jobs, but they're usually sporadic and part-time.'

'It's not just about the money,' Rachel said, taking Rainy to one side. 'We all gather round the bonfire, and tell stories. We have a special kind of therapy, that often seems to help. It seems to me, Rainy, that you could do with a little catharsis.'

'All right, count me in.' Rainy handed across a tenner.

'Well done,' Rachel said quietly. 'You know, I know you're shy about it, but it doesn't matter to any of us that you're a police officer, not a doctor.'

'What?'

'Someone recognised you. But any woman can be a victim, Rainy. You don't have to be reticent about your job. You are welcome, and we embrace you. If you prefer, I shan't tell the others.'

'Aye, I would prefer that. I'm already feeling responsible for police failures in all these stories that I can't defend or put right.' She waved her plate to indicate the others.

Rainy looked across the room, and spotted Julia McGann looking at her. The barrister smiled at her and lifted a plastic glass in salute, before turning back to another conversation. Clearly the recognition had been mutual.

She wondered whether she should mention it to Gillard on her next shift. But she never did.

Chapter Nineteen

Friday

Grace woke them at two a.m., then 3.35, then 5.05. Sam attended to her each time. But when she wailed again at 6.30, it was Gillard who finally hauled himself out of bed. As he gently jigged from side to side holding his child, he didn't think it was possible to feel more tired than he had been yesterday. Grace's cries, some of them gentle but others more urgent, were unignorable. At one point he'd considered going to the spare room to get some sleep, but another abandonment of his long-suffering wife seemed unconscionable.

Once she was finally asleep, he rested her gently in Sam's drowsy arms, then took a long, hot shower to wake himself up. He checked his phone as he gulped down some cereal. The latest episode of the search for the occupants of the Nissan Qashqai had the punchline he anticipated. They hadn't been found in Tesco. The search of the superstore's many CCTV feeds had been going on all night, and there were seventy possible suspects who matched the vague description that DC Gary Collins had given of a stocky male in a hooded top, and a light-haired woman in her thirties. They needed better descriptions than that, much better. In the meantime, they had an interview planned with the last person to admit having driven it. The estranged wife of the Birmingham attack victim.

—

Loti Sengupta claimed to have no access to transport, so Gillard had sent a patrol car to Farnborough to bring her in to Guildford Police Station for nine a.m. By the time he and Michelle Tsu got across to the station in Margaret Road from Mount Browne, she was already waiting in an interview room. Looking through the one-way glass from the anteroom, he saw a tiny and rather elegant woman, wearing jeans and a sweatshirt, with her long dark hair in a French twist. Even with her moderately high-heeled leather boots, she couldn't be much over five foot two. This was clearly not the person on the e-scooter. Not a woman of violence. She hardly looked capable of bruising a meringue nest. But she could have been the driver of the Nissan for someone else. Someone who was capable of murder.

Michelle looked through the statement Mrs Sengupta had already given over the phone to Welbeck. 'The alibi is rubbish,' she said. 'Her best mate says she was staying with her all weekend, but there is no independent verification.'

'But she did say she went out shopping on Saturday afternoon and on Monday morning,' Gillard said. 'Maybe we can get the store cameras. Let's go easy on her for now. You take the lead, and be sympathetic. Her story might well give us a motive.'

They went in and introduced themselves. 'Do I need a solicitor?' the woman asked.

'No, but you can have one if you wish,' Gillard said. 'You are being interviewed as a witness.'

She nodded and smiled. She seemed relatively relaxed, which surprised Gillard. In his experience the truly innocent were the most worried by a police interview. The woman seemed cool. When asked, she gave timings for her shopping trips, including visiting Sainsbury's just before six o'clock on Saturday evening. It was clear to Gillard that if she could prove her presence in Farnborough at that time, there was no way she could have been in the Nissan Qashqai, which was already captured on camera on the M40 near Oxford.

'Tell us about your relationship with the victim,' Gillard asked. The answer was as detailed as it was shocking. The opening question brought forth details of her confinement in a locked shed, repeated rape by her husband, and being cut off from the few friends that she had locally. 'He rang Boots, where I was a pharmacist, and told them I had gone back to Bangladesh,' she said. 'That time he locked me in the shed for five days, when I should have been working. He wouldn't let me have a phone, and put a lock on the landline. Eventually I lost the job.'

'And this was all because you couldn't conceive him a child?' Michelle asked.

'We already had two children, daughters. It was because I could not give him a son. Prabir is a very traditional man,' she said with a wry expression. With a little more questioning, she described how she had fled Birmingham with the secret help of a female relative of her husband. 'I was able to rent a room in a house in Farnborough with a friend of hers. I got some part-time work locally as a pharmacist.'

'You must be very angry with your husband,' Michelle said.

'Very hurt, very upset.'

'How did you manage?' Michelle asked.

'I found some helplines, and went to a women's aid group. They were really good.'

'I'm glad that it worked out for you.' Michelle smiled at her sympathetically.

'Were you ever tempted to try to get your own back?' Gillard asked.

'No. I just wanted to forget about him. But I really did want to see my daughters.'

'Have you been back to Birmingham?' he asked.

'No, I was too scared. But I have seen them.' She described how the female relative borrowed her husband's car to bring her daughters down to see her.

'That's the car that was later stolen?' Gillard asked.

'That's right.'

'Yes.'

'When was it stolen?'

'I last saw it just over a week ago.'

'Why did you not report it?'

'Well, at first, I really thought that my cousin, who brought it down, had come to take it back.'

'But Mr Umrani tells us that you didn't contact him or his wife to ask?'

'Well, that car has been around a few members of the extended family, so I wasn't sure. It's quite old, and it's not their only car.'

Seeing how little progress they were making, Gillard returned to the main question. 'Do you have any idea who might have attacked your husband?'

'I knew he was in debt, money borrowed through the community. So I assumed it was related to that.'

'Perhaps you asked someone to beat up your husband?' Michelle said.

She looked shocked at the accusation. 'No. Absolutely not. Of course, there were times when in my head I wanted him dead.'

Gillard's eyes widened.

'It is perfectly natural, is it not, to fantasise about such things?' she asked. 'And yes, at my lowest point, if I'd had the courage, I might have killed him myself. I'm a pharmacist, I know how to source the kind of medicines that would do the job. But I knew I never had that kind of bravery, and I do not believe in violence.'

'That's good to hear,' Gillard said. 'So if we can borrow your mobile phone for half an hour, we might be able to substantiate it.'

'Sorry, how do you mean?' she asked.

'We have a nifty little device called a data kiosk here which can extract texts, emails, photos and phone messages. It could help underscore what you are saying.'

'I see. So you *do* suspect me of somehow organising this attack?'

'It's an obvious line of inquiry, as you have a motive,' Michelle said. 'We'd be stupid not to look at it. Don't take it personally.'

'Don't take it personally! What an extraordinary thing to say,' she said. 'How else am I supposed to take it, when you don't believe me?'

It was a good point.

—

Two hours later at Mount Browne, Gillard was looking at some very crisp CCTV footage forwarded by the research intelligence department. Loti Sengupta's statement said she was with her friend in a Boots store in Farnborough at around nine o'clock on Monday morning. The close-ups in his inbox confirmed that it was definitely her. It was no surprise. He had never believed that this tiny, poised creature would be involved at the business end of a plot to kill her husband, and it now hinged on what could be found from the hundreds of texts and other data recovered from her phone. The readiness with which she surrendered the device made Gillard think they would be disappointed there too.

Gillard asked Research Intelligence Officer Rob Townsend to treat Loti's data as a priority. It took less than an hour for him to email back with a summary of what was on the phone. Gillard skimmed the messages, a series of innocuous-sounding texts and voicemails, with various women in her phone book. These messages, which Rob quoted, certainly did sound like the conversations one might expect within a women's support group, and fully bore out her accounts of the abuse she suffered in her relationship. Rob had also downloaded a few photos of the shed where she said she had been confined by her husband. They showed a tiny hut with a sleeping bag, a bucket, a towel and a bottle of water. Finally there were several messages from someone who was identified in the woman's address list as RM. Rob had put a question mark next to this, but Gillard looked at the number and recognised it. This surely was a number he'd called just a few hours ago.

Rainy Macintosh!

Gillard cross-checked with the records on his own phone. Yes, it *was* her personal mobile phone. Rainy seemed to be a friend or at least an acquaintance of Loti Sengupta. It seemed quite surprising. Then he thought

233

about the death of Rainy's husband. He didn't like the direction this thought was leading.

Rainy would be heading down from Scotland today. He rang her. The phone was off, and he thought about leaving a message. No, it would be better with an element of surprise. He'd try again later.

–

It was pouring when Rainy's taxi arrived at Dundee station, but despite the weather she was in a decent mood. She'd had a better-than-expected stay with Ross' sister Aileen, remaining with her and husband Doug a couple of days longer than planned. After paying the driver, and wriggling out with her umbrella and luggage, Rainy bought herself a couple of heavyweight newspapers, and a single-serving bottle of Prosecco. The ScotRail train, via Edinburgh, was due in ten minutes. With a bit of luck she'd be back in London by late afternoon, and home with Ewan in time to prepare an evening meal. The boy had been staying with the family of a school friend, and had enthused by text to her about the collection of video games he'd been playing.

But of his dead father, not a mention.

Finding her seat, stowing her luggage and settling in for the journey, she now had to get up to speed on events. She'd barely looked at her phone since arriving in Dundee, and stayed clear of the news. But now, well, it was time to catch up on the murder of Gary Wray. She'd already had texts from colleagues saying that Gillard had been attacked in Nightingale Park, and apart from sending him a text wishing him a quick recovery, she hadn't delved into the story. After all she had plenty on her plate, and she'd be back into the fray soon enough. But now she was staggered to read the story in detail, a savage attack on the handbag entrepreneur while he was out jogging. And then a description: police were searching for a someone dressed in motorcycle leathers and helmet, and riding an e-scooter.

She eased off the cork, and after swigging some Prosecco straight from the bottle, flicked through the papers. Plenty of in-depth articles about Gary Wray, and the growing suspicion he had been the Nightingale Park rapist. One of the tabloids speculated that the handbag entrepreneur was perhaps, worse still, a murderer. A body had been found in a house that he owned near the park. The wine ran out long before she finished all the coverage of the story, and she ordered another bottle from the trolley as it passed.

Flicking through, she came across another savage crime, in Birmingham. A man was beaten while opening up his shop on Monday morning. His name was Sengupta. There was something familiar about that name. Reading more closely, the article described an assailant dressed in motorcycle gear.

Just like the attack on Gary Wray.

The attacker had used some kind of home-made Taser.

Just like the attack on Gary Wray.

When they were at the mortuary, McLeod had asked her whether Ross had done recent electrical work at home. 'Is he a bit of a DIY fellow?' he'd asked. She'd almost laughed at the idea. Her ex could barely fix a plug. She'd not given a thought to the implications of the small burn found on his arm and neither it seemed had McLeod.

Concentrating again on the papers, she realised why she recognised the name of the victim. The same surname as her friend Loti from the women's group.

Oh God. Oh my God.

She picked up her phone and left a message for Loti, and then thought about ringing DCI Harry McLeod. Then she thought about the list, and decided not to. The list she had seen six weeks earlier when she'd been to a barbecue at the women's refuge.

Chapter Twenty

Six weeks earlier

The refuge had turned out to be a half-dozen caravans and converted outbuildings behind a run-down farmhouse near Farnborough. There were a dozen women who lived here, some of them with young children. With its small-holding, vegetable patch and goat paddock it felt more like a commune than anything else, but it was homely. Rainy was standing around a bonfire with six other women. Loti was there, and Rachel of course, but everyone else was new to her apart from Scarlett. There was alcohol, a lot of it. Some kind of hot toddy, with more than a nip of whisky in it. Rainy found it very moreish.

Rachel bought out a box full of pieces of coloured card rectangles, each labelled in marker pen with an emotion: guilt, fear, intimidation, self-doubt, anxiety. 'All right, what I'd like you to do is to each gather up two or three of these negative emotions.'

The women laughed as they sorted through. Rainy grabbed a handful. 'Och, I've got three intimidations and a self-doubt here. Has anyone got a spare anxiety?'

Everyone chuckled.

'I'll swap you a fear for one of those intimidations,' said Scarlett. 'My bastard of an ex was very good on the intimidation.'

After a few minutes of laughter and jostling, and some more hot toddy, Rachel encouraged them to move closer round the fire. 'Right, sisters, I want you to hold one unwelcome emotion in your hands. Say after me: "I banish thee, to a place of eternal flame. I have no need of thee. I consign thee to fire, and I am free."'

Hesitantly, they intoned the words. Some of them were slightly giggly, others more solemn.

'...I consign thee to fire, and I am free.'

Rainy watched as each of the women threw a scrap of card into the fire. Rachel, standing nearby, sloshed something from a metal can onto the flames, which roared into the sky. Rainy felt her face burning, her eyebrows beginning to singe. The cards were consumed, curling, turning black, fragments lifted into the sky. Across the other side of the fire, a tall, solidly built woman called Bronwen, hitherto shy and almost monosyllabic when Rainy had spoken with her, raised her arms and punched the air. 'Yes! I am free of you.'

The women worked through their consignment of unwanted feelings, tossing them into the all-consuming fire, waving goodbye to them. For all of its faux witchcraft overtones, Rainy did feel a gathering sense of belonging, a revival of the spirit. Bright faces around the fire, flames reflected in their eyes, a sense of possibility and regrowth. And of course a good slug of drink. Scarlett emerged with another round of toddies, which seemed even fiercer than the last.

'I'm a bit drunk,' confided Loti. 'I'm not used to this.'

'Aye, it's definitely going to be a taxi job for me. I'll have a wee chaser of council juice next or I'll get the bedspins.'

'Council juice?'

'Water, from a tap.'

Loti laughed. 'Well, that's a good one.'

'We've got veggie burgers and falafel inside,' Scarlett announced, indicating one of the outbuildings, which had been turned into a communal kitchen. 'They'll be ready in five minutes.'

'What about the next stage?' Bronwen asked Rachel. 'Can we do that?'

'If everyone is ready for it,' Rachel replied.

'So what is the next stage?' Rainy asked. 'Go roond as a gang and beat the bastards senseless?'

'Ha ha,' shouted Bronwen. 'I'm up for it. I've been going to the gym. They have these boxercise classes where you spar with a trainer.' She mimed a low blow. 'He called me a hellcat!'

Rachel smiled indulgently. 'Well, now we've got rid of the negative emotions, we can go a stage further. To banish from our hearts the source of those damaging feelings. Come inside, and I'll show you.'

Rainy, Loti, Bronwen and a fine-featured woman called Caroline followed Rachel inside one of the caravans. There was a pad of paper on the dining table. 'Each of you must identify the source of your negative…'

'Just write down the bastard's name and address!' Bronwen interrupted. 'Describe him.'

'We've got a little list. They never would be missed,' muttered Caroline to Rainy.

'We've all done it,' said Rainy, recognising the line from Gilbert and Sullivan's *Mikado*, which she'd had to sing at school.

'It all seems a bit, well, vengeful, to me,' Caroline said. 'We women shouldn't become *more* like men, we need to make them *more* like us.'

'Aye, I do agree. But how?'

'Won't work,' Bronwen interrupted. 'Women have had enough! We've got to recognise we're at war, then strike back at them. Incel crazies and misogynistic influencers. We have to steel ourselves for the inevitable fight.' She raised a fist. 'And I'm bloody ready!'

'Sounds like my wee marriage, sure enough,' Rainy muttered. 'Everything but the trenches and machine guns.'

Bronwen was already busy, scribbling down in a spiky hand the name of the man who had made her life a misery, his address, phone number and for good measure, his workplace. Loti followed suit. Rachel copied each across neatly onto a brown paper luggage tag, the kind with a string through the hole. Caroline confessed that she didn't have her ex's current address.

'He took all my money, sold our home, the house I had inherited, and moved abroad while I was on holiday. He even took my cats.'

'Having the address doesn't particularly matter,' Rachel said. 'This is about freeing *you*. Just write his name.'

Rainy poised with her pen over the pad. There were five other names and addresses listed. She knew that Ross had moved recently, to a village outside Glasgow, his home simply having a name, High Bank, and a postcode. It was all stored in her detective brain, as was the slight unease about disclosing it. She scrawled it down, and watched with growing discomfort as Rachel transcribed it to a paper label.

'You're not planning to post this list on social media or anything, are you? As a blacklist?'

'No, don't worry,' Rachel said, with a smile. 'It's confidential.' She tore the sheet with the list off the pad, folded it and put it in her pocket. 'But I keep lists of exes and their addresses in case any of the women we help are attacked. It has happened in the past.'

'That's the job of the police to follow up.'

'Yes, and we know how well that's been done, don't we? Present company excepted, of course.'

The arrival of food interrupted the conversation. Rainy had drunk too much to have the words to challenge this, but it still seemed somehow unnecessary and intrusive. She was surprised to find herself apparently defending Ross' rights, but gradually realised it wasn't him she was defending but the privacy of her own experience. After another round of hot toddies in the kitchen, and some raucous music, they all trooped outside again. This time they each had in their hands labels with the name and address of their former partners, the men who had abused, bullied, repressed and belittled them.

The fire was blazing high now, and was being fed by Hex, the silent woman she'd sat next to at the first meeting. She lugged a stack of four wooden pallets, and dumped them onto the flames before going back for more.

'It works best if you have a lock of hair, or some other object that belonged to them,' Bronwen slurred, clearly drunk. 'That's the way we did it last time.'

Rainy and Caroline exchanged a glance, witnessing Bronwen's transformation from painfully shy to outrageously drunk.

'Nothing wrong with a wee bit of Voodoo, eh?' Rainy muttered to her.

'If only they'd told me, I would have made a clay effigy of Ronald in my sculpture class,' Caroline responded, giggling. 'We could have stuck pins in him!'

'Aye, that would have been a blast.' Rainy realised that for all the nonsensical rituals, it was the community of shared experience that was really warming her. There were people who had lived, suffered, and understood what she had been through. It had the embattled cohesion of an underground church, and she felt enfolded and nurtured by it.

'Make way,' Rachel said. Turning around, Rainy saw Bronwen and Hex carrying an old wooden chair, on which some scarecrow of stuffed male clothing had been tied. Its head was a pair of tights stuffed with paper, and a paper face had been glued on, with angry features in marker pen. It was wearing a football shirt, knotted at the wrists, and trousers which had been tied at the bottom to stop the stuffing falling out.

'Och, a penny for the guy,' said Rainy.

'I've never met any guy worth that much,' Bronwen said, as she let go of the chair and allowed Hex to manoeuvre it towards the fire.

'We're months too late for Bonfire Night anyway,' Caroline said.

'Aye, but I still fancy a baked potato and some bangers.'

'Now it's time to assemble the sources of all your anguish into our little sacrifice,' Rachel said. Bronwen and Caroline tied their inscribed luggage labels to the string waistband of the scarecrow. Rainy followed suit. When they had all finished Hex lifted the chair, strode up to the bonfire, into the heat and smoke, and placed the ensemble carefully into the flames. She retreated gradually, then picked something dark up from the ground.

'Yeah, don't forget that, Hex,' Bronwen said. Hex advanced again towards the flames, which were already beginning to lick around the painted legs of the chair.

The dark object in her hand she balanced on the head of the mannequin, fitting the elastic under its chin.

It was a toy police helmet.

Rainy's stomach turned over, and her disquiet turned to anxiety. This was all going a bit far. The flames had already begun to take hold. The mannequin trembled, then writhed against its bonds as smoke wreathed around it. The nylon tights melted, the helmet sagged, and the angry paper face blackened. As it split a mouth opened, and flames licked out. For just a few horrifying seconds, this homunculus appeared human, arching backwards in agony, a noise like an excruciated shriek emanating from the burning stuffing.

A few of the women cheered as the chair toppled backwards into the all-consuming conflagration, but Rainy could see Caroline and a couple of the others were repelled by the violent symbolism they were invoking. Hex, however was not. She stared into the flames, her expression undecipherable. Then she caught Rainy's glance, and her face hardened, her dark eyes burning bright with something harder and more driven than regret. This was a woman who had already burned every unwanted emotion, but retained a hold on something else, something powerful. She clearly was in a different place, somewhere Rainy never wanted to visit. She turned and scowled at Rainy, mouthing something under her breath, before turning and heading back inside the refuge.

Rachel approached and rested a reassuring arm on Rainy's back. 'We're all worried about Hex. She's a lost soul. Her mother's made multiple attempts at suicide after years of abuse, and has just been sectioned again.'

'She doesn't seem to like the police.' Rainy was thinking about the toy helmet.

'Well, it's understandable. In fact you won't find many here with a good word about the police, given the failure to act,' Rachel said.

Rainy knew the other side of it. She'd been on the training courses, and heard from domestic violence specialists, all of whom were hugely sympathetic to women. Intervening in 'domestics', as they were called, was the most sensitive, difficult and hated of all policing duties. All too often the most diligent of case-building was wasted when the victims were intimidated out of pressing charges, often for understandable reasons. In many cases, the cycle went on and on for years. But it was no use mentioning that here. You couldn't quibble with the agony these women had suffered. She felt horribly impotent, and angry that in all these cases nothing had been done. Was there something she could do about it? Maybe there was. She drained the final dregs of her hooch, and stared into the fire.

That was the moment she had made a fateful decision.

–

After the food, Rainy joined in a conversation in one of the caravans. Loti was recounting to a couple of the refuge residents how she was beaten, and how she still lived in terror of being burned by her husband. Rainy followed Loti when she headed outside, towards the toilet. She watched her disappear and waited until she came out again. She had clearly been crying. 'That was a terrible story, Loti, it broke my heart to hear it,' Rainy slurred, embracing the woman, who seemed tiny and bird-like inside her arms.

'I just need people to believe me. I have lost most of my family.'

'Aye, I believe you. I've got a friend who could find out if your husband has been in the area where you're staying, if it would help you rest easier.'

'Oh yes, that would be wonderful.'

'I'll need his full name and address. Do you recall his van registration number?'

'It's burned into my mind. It's a grey Mercedes Sprinter.' She recounted the number, and Rainy wrote it down, along with the address that Loti was currently staying at. 'Give me a couple of days, and I should be able to tell you.'

'That's very kind. So is your friend in the police?'

'Something like that. Best not ask. This is just between us, okay.'

Loti nodded.

–

Next day, when she was back at work, Rainy waited for a quiet moment when several of her colleagues were on a conference call with the Crown Prosecution Service. She then logged on to the DVLA registration system, and confirmed that Prabir Sengupta was the owner of the van whose number she'd been given. It listed an address in Birmingham. She then switched to the ANPR system. She inputted the van registration, and made a UK-wide trawl of all cameras for the last week. She opted to deploy the data as a map. Sengupta certainly got around. The van had been to London, Tilbury, Cardiff, Manchester, Portsmouth, Leeds, Bradford, Wakefield, Wigan, Carlisle, Folkestone and many points in between. He passed Farnborough a couple of times on the M3, but there were no hits from any cameras inside the town. She could find no criminal record for Prabir Sengupta either.

She filed the enquiries under a bogus case number as a vehicle theft. She knew that there were so many unresolved crimes of this nature that she was unlikely to be caught. It was too small a case for Gillard, which was just as well as he was one officer with such attention to detail that he would find her out. She was really nervous, having never done such a thing before. But she burned with the injustice suffered by Loti, and felt compelled to do something about it.

Present day, Friday

The train was speeding past Doncaster, heading south. She stared out of the window, seeing the unflattering double reflection of her own face as the train clattered under a bridge. Double chin, four-eye glasses and a dismal future. What on earth had she got caught up in? She thought about her son, who she had rung twice a day during her absence. He had largely shrugged off her concerns, wanted to get back to his computer games in whose fantastical depths he seemed to sublimate his loss, his grief and most of his connection to the outside world. He just didn't want to talk. She hesitated to text him, realising that he wouldn't reply. But she needed him. She needed him on her side. He was the man of the family now, yet seemed such a vulnerable boy, and his mind that of a stranger.

She was due back at work on Monday, transferred back to Gillard's investigation. She would have to be strong. But how much of her suspicions should she share with her boss? How much could she let on without illuminating a trail to her own complicity?

She toyed with her phone, her finger hovering over his number. Then she set it aside, and swigged the last of her wine. Finally, she made a decision. There was a nettle to grasp, and it was about time she did it.

She rang Loti again. When she picked up, Rainy said. 'Loti, it's me. I've heard about the attack on your ex.'

'I was shocked,' she said. 'I hated him, but… I wouldn't have wanted… this.'

'I know. Look, I just wanted to offer my support.'

'Oh, thank you. You know, your boss Gillard has just interviewed me about it. I've only just got back.'

'What? Why's he looking at a Birmingham case?'

'I've no idea about that. He and a very nice Chinese-looking detective…'

'That would be Michelle,'

'Yes, they weren't horrible or anything. I suppose it's obvious from their point of view, I was married to him, and he might think I did it.'

'I hope you've got an alibi.'

'I was here, at Bronwen's house. I've not been up to Brum for five years.'

'That's no' a great alibi, to be honest. Still, at least you didn't do it.'

Loti continued to talk about her circumstances, leading Rainy to interrupt: 'Well, I don't know whether you heard, but my ex Ross has been killed.'

'Oh my God,' she said. 'No, I hadn't heard. What happened?'

'He was run over, outside his own home, at midnight. He wasn't dressed for the outdoors at all. It's all totally suspicious.'

'That's terrible.'

Rainy described what she'd discovered, and they talked about it for several minutes. 'Look, Loti. I need you not to mention anything about the information I gave you, about your husband's van. I could get into a lot of trouble, and so could you if it emerges that we've been using police resources to track your ex.'

Loti sighed. 'I didn't say anything. I didn't mention you at all. Anyway, it's not relevant is it, to the fact that he's been attacked?'

'I'm not sure the police would look at it that way. Do you have any suspicions about who did it?'

'Well, he did owe a lot of money to his cousin. But it seems extreme. Look, Rainy. I did tell Rachel how you helped me with the information. That was all right, wasn't it? She's one of us.'

Rainy's stomach turned over. This was not good news. 'Oh no, Loti. I really wish you hadn't.'

'Why?'

'Can't you see what's happening here, Loti? I saw you write your ex's name and address on Rachel's pad, just above where I wrote Ross'. Now, one is dead and the other is fighting for his life.'

'Come on, it's *Rachel*? Really? She wouldn't do anything like that. She is the one always telling us to let go of our negative emotions. You can't really believe…'

'I don't know what I believe, Loti. I really don't.'

The call waiting signal popped up on her phone. Gillard. Her heart skipped a beat.

'Loti, I've got to go. It's my boss.'

As they said goodbye, Rainy closed her eyes and tried to focus. The next few minutes could be the most important of her life.

Chapter Twenty-one

'Hello Rainy, how are you doing?' Gillard asked. 'I'm sorry it's taken me so long to speak to you.'

'Och, that's all right. I got your earlier message anyway, thank you. Besides, you've been a wee bit busy yourself, have you nae? And a new father too.' They talked for a few minutes about Grace, the accident in which Sam and her mother were involved, and the general mayhem at Mount Browne around the Gary Wray case. She began to relax, hoping against hope that this really was no more than a catch-up ahead of her coming back to work on Monday.

'So how is Ewan taking the news?' Gillard asked.

'Not so bad. He's buried his grief, but I'll hopefully manage to get him to open up. I'll have to come back up here for the funeral, as the coroner hasn't finished with Ross.'

'I'd heard it was a hit-and-run,' Gillard said. Rainy knew that she was expected to fill in the gaps.

'It was brutal, and they havenae arrested anybody. But…' This was a slippery slope, and she hesitated to say what she really should be saying: *I think it was murder, and I have a confession to make about my own involvement.* She also knew there was the matter of the electrical burn on Ross' body. All things she should mention. But she couldn't, she really couldn't.

'Do you want me to have a word, Rainy, to make them take it a bit more seriously? I have contacts in Police Scotland.'

'Och, it's rare kind of you, but you don't even have time to see your own newborn daughter.'

Gillard laughed, and then changed the subject.

'Now Rainy, do you know someone called Loti Sengupta?'

An icicle of fear slid down Rainy's back.

'Aye, she's a member of Reading Domestic Violence Support Network. I've been to a few of their meetings.'

'Of course, you have something in common. Is she a friend?'

'Not particularly, but she's been through a lot.'

'When did you last speak?'

'Before I came up north.'

There was a pause before he continued, 'Had you heard about what happened to her ex-husband?'

'I only read the newspapers. So is she a suspect?'

She listened as her boss took a deep breath, clearly deciding how much information to share with her. 'Not at the moment. However, the car which she was using is a vehicle of interest in a number of inquiries.'

Rainy was horrified. Not so much by the potential involvement of Loti in a case, but by Gillard slipping into officialese. 'A vehicle of interest' was police speak used with the press and the public. To use it on her meant one thing. She wasn't a colleague anymore; she was on the other side of the interview desk. A suspect, possibly, certainly no longer trusted. A lonely place. And she knew it would only get worse from here. She had only a few seconds to decide whether to spill everything she knew, or to hold her tongue and hope for the best. In the end she opted to shelve the decision.

'Sir, what are you actually telling me?'

'It's not what I'm telling *you*, Rainy. It's what I think you should be telling *me*.'

She said nothing.

'Rainy, you said you hadn't spoken to Mrs Sengupta since before coming up north. But someone using your phone, the one we are talking on right now, called Loti Sengupta less than ten minutes ago. It's just come up on Rob Townsend's tracing screen.'

Shit! She'd just fallen for the oldest trick in the book.

'Rainy, I need to know why you lied to me.'

'Loti is innocent,' Rainy said. 'But I do suspect that someone used a list of exes which Rachel compiled to start getting some revenge.'

'That's Rachel Meadows, right?' Gillard said. 'We heard that name from Loti.'

'Aye, it's her.'

'Rachel Meadows is a close friend of Julia McGann, as you must know. The woman who I believe was involved in two murders, if not three, but have never been able to prove it.'

'I had been meaning to mention it, sir. In fact Ms McGann turned up at one of the parties. She recognised me, so I was hardly undercover. They knew I was police.'

There was a long, uncomfortable pause. 'Rainy, I have to say I'm really disappointed that you seem to have got mixed up in this, but I'm much more alarmed that you didn't see fit to tip me off that a woman with a criminal connection seems to be so deeply embedded into a women's support group.'

'Och, Rachel is a qualified psychotherapist, she is always the person trying to calm things down.'

'Rainy, four years ago, Rachel Meadows was running a gardening business. We haven't had a chance to investigate her bona fides as yet...'

'Sir, if I had said something to you, then I would just have proved to all these fellow victims that I was police first, and a victim of domestic violence second. I felt their pain, I shared their stories. The police aren't trusted, and with good reason.'

'Someone within that organisation was involved in commissioning, at the very least, the killing of Gary Wray and Ken Stapleford as well as the attack on Prabir Sengupta.'

'And the murder of Ross,' she said. Her voice now thickening with emotion, she said: 'There were electrical burns on his body. It was a deliberate and premeditated killing, and the reason I know it, is because I put his name on the list.'

Chapter Twenty-two

Gillard was there with three uniforms, including a family liaison officer, plus a locksmith, when they knocked on Rachel Meadows' door in Churchill Terrace. There was no reply. That wasn't a surprise. The landline had gone unanswered, and the mobile number Rainy had given them for Rachel was switched off. He was only guessing, but he reckoned that she was the fair-haired woman that had been seen getting into the Nissan yesterday evening, who had somehow vanished within Tesco. At some stage she must have come out to see police swarming around her vehicle, and been spooked. Now she could be anywhere. Unfortunately, Rainy hadn't been able to provide an exact addresses for the bonfire celebration she had described. Vikram was now debriefing her by phone, trying to get as much information about the Reading Domestic Violence Support Network as possible, and the women within. However, it was quite apparent that Rainy's normally precise police brain had been in hibernation during her time at the women's group. She had seemed very hesitant, as if she was being asked to implicate these women who had become her friends. And as for lying to him, why had she done that? A maverick thought had intruded into his brain, that Rainy had somehow been more deeply involved in her ex-husband's death than simply adding his name to a list. He had dismissed the idea, but it kept crawling back.

As he watched the locksmith get out his tools, Gillard thought again about the Nissan. It had travelled to Glasgow at exactly the right time to be involved in the death of Ross Macintosh. Rainy clearly wasn't in it, she was working at Mount Browne and then travelled down to Hove. Meanwhile the vehicle had whizzed up the M6 to Glasgow, collecting a speeding ticket, one of several it had collected over that crucial weekend, in which Ken Stapleford, Gary Wray and Ross Macintosh had been murdered, and Prabir Sengupta left fighting for his life. Could the names of all four men have been on this list that Rainy mentioned? Ross was, and so was Prabir Sengupta. But Rainy hadn't mentioned Tia Whitlock as an attendee, or even part of the group, so how could Gary Wray's name have been on the list? Ken Stapleford was an even bigger mystery. His second wife lived in Warwickshire, and his first was dead. Rainy had not seen his name on the list, or even heard it mentioned in any of their meetings. This idea of a list didn't seem to be a complete explanation of what had happened. And was it Rachel who carried out the killings, or someone else?

The locksmith finished, and the door was opened. Rachel Meadows' home had clearly been left in a hurry. Though the downstairs area was reasonably tidy, all three bedrooms were a mess, with clothing strewn about. Iron-ically it was the one bedroom that clearly belonged to the child, Jack, which seemed to be most orderly, with an extensive array of toys neatly lined up on shelves. The master bedroom and the spare were clearly recently inhabited, and although the beds were made, various personal items remained: a belt, earrings, curling tongs. No toiletries. No phones. Likewise there were no computers, only a printer, modem and chargers at a desk to indicate where a laptop might have sat.

Gillard supervised the uniforms who were lifting fingerprints from mugs and glasses, and hairs from soft furnishings. It would be good to match these up against the samples taken from the Nissan last night. He had already put out an alert for Rachel's own vehicle, a silver Subaru Forester hybrid. There had been no ANPR hit so far. Still, tracking her down shouldn't be too difficult so long as she had her son with her. What he really wanted, and had found no sign of, was a membership list for the Reading Women's Domestic Violence Network. There was a website, with a request for volunteers to start a helpline, which had not been set up. Apart from Rachel, no one was named on the site. There were plentiful accounts of domestic violence, but these were flagged in advance as having pseudonyms. All he had at the moment were the names given to him by Rainy and Loti Sengupta.

–

An hour later, back at Mount Browne, Gillard was listening to his voicemail, a process which to save time he often did while simultaneously reading his emails. As usual, most of them were routine internal messages. Then he came to one with just a few seconds of silence, then a strange almost unearthly sound, like a protracted gasp, before it terminated. He looked at the caller ID number.

Sam's mobile!

He returned the call, but the line was busy. What was it he had heard? It sounded like a gasp. Another incoming call flashed up, from Sam's phone. He tapped on it, and heard her voice.

'Sam, are you okay?'

She laughed. 'I'm sorry about that. I was trying to get Grace to leave a message for you, but she blew you a raspberry instead, then managed to touch my phone and cut the call.'

'You almost gave me a heart attack! I thought someone was strangling you.'

She laughed again. 'No, I'm fine. Things are a bit chaotic.' She turned away for a moment, and spoke to someone else. 'No, honestly it's fine. You can find a spare duvet in the under-bed storage. You can sort yourself out...'

'Sorry Sam.' Claire Mulholland was signalling to him from across the office. 'I've got an incident room meeting in one minute, so I'll have to go.'

'Just a quick update, Mum and Dad are going back to Keswick this afternoon.'

'Yes, I remember you telling me.'

'Helen is filling in.'

'Helen?'

'The cleaner.'

'Oh, yes. Right. She'll be—'

'I've got to go.'

'Oh, and we have new buyers! The estate agent just rang.'

'Fantastic news. Now, I've really got to go. Bye for now, Sam.'

'I love y—'

Craig had killed the call, but regretted truncating that last, most important utterance. Even as he was standing up and pulling his documents together, he texted her quickly.

The moment he hit send, he was aware of an animated Vikram Singh, phone in hand, calling across to Michelle Tsu.

'We've found her,' Singh said. 'Rachel Meadows, in Farnborough.'

It was an hour later when Gillard sat down opposite Rachel Meadows in the rape suite at Farnborough Police Station. Her six-year-old, Jack, was next door, playing with Lego and being supervised by a family liaison officer. His voice could occasionally be heard. Mother and child had been found at the women's refuge, and although a couple of the women there had initially refused to let police in, Rachel herself had voluntarily walked out with her son in her arms.

'So am I under arrest?' she asked.

'No, but we certainly have some questions we'd like to ask you.' Gillard took in the woman's confident demeanour, her blonde, professionally cut hair, her poise. She was wearing a white blouse which showed off her figure, and tight-fitting jeans. He knew immediately that she was not his attacker, nor the one seen on CCTV in Birmingham. Her height was about right, but she was too slim and too, well, obviously female.

'So, Ms Meadows, I'd like to start with the Nissan Qashqai which you have been using. How did you come to have this vehicle?'

'All the same, I'd like to wait until I have a solicitor with me,' she said.

257

'If you like. I'll arrange for a duty—'

'That's okay, I've already rung my own.'

There was a knock on the door, and the desk sergeant's head appeared. 'The interviewee's brief is here,' he said.

Then in walked Julia McGann.

'How are you, Craig?' she asked. Soberly dressed in charcoal grey trouser suit and patent leather shoes, she had with her a hefty-looking solicitor's briefcase.

'I'm fine, thank you.' In truth, he'd been a lot better before she showed her face. 'I didn't think barristers could take this kind of work,' he said, inclining his head towards Rachel.

'I'm no longer practising at the bar. I've joined a specialist law firm.' Her large blue grey eyes scrutinised him from below her dark bob. He'd almost forgotten how attractive she was. She pressed a business card onto the table in front of him. The name of the firm meant nothing to him, but underneath it was the slogan. *By women, for women*. 'We're making quite a name for ourselves.'

'It doesn't surprise me at all.'

Julia took out a voice recorder and placed it on the table.

'All right, if that's how you want it,' Gillard said. 'I'll move us to a formal interview room, set up for recording, and I will have a colleague with me.'

Fifteen minutes later, they were in a much gloomier basement room. Gillard had with him DC Kim Leighton, who had been present when they found Rachel in Farnborough.

'Ms Meadows, can you account for your movements last weekend?'

She folded her arms. 'What time last weekend?'

'Between four p.m. and midnight on Saturday, at nine p.m. on Sunday and at eight a.m. on Monday,' DC Leighton said, reading from papers in front of her.

'Well, on Saturday afternoon Jack and I were at the refuge in Farnborough.'

'That is the women's refuge at Fordbridge Road, where you were discovered today?' Gillard asked.

'Discovered?' interjected Julia. 'My client wasn't hiding, detective chief inspector, she came voluntarily. She was unaware that she was being looked for.'

'I doubt that very much,' Gillard said. 'Numerous messages were left on her phone today, and emails were sent to the website that she runs.'

'Nevertheless, she is not at your beck and call,' Julia continued.

Gillard glared at her, before turning his gaze to Rachel. 'Would anyone there vouch for your presence?'

Rachel smiled. 'Yes.' Yes, of course they would, Gillard thought. No surprises there.

'I take it you are aware of the series of murders and assaults that took place over that weekend?' he asked.

'Well, not a series as such. I heard about the Gary Wray killing, certainly. In fact one of your officers came to visit me to check the back gate from my house on to the park. I was certainly alarmed about it, especially after all those rapes. Which the police seemed not to be interested in clearing up.'

Gillard decided to change tack. 'I'd like to ask you about a Nissan Qashqai.' He read out the registration number. 'This vehicle was owned by a relative of Loti Sengupta, one of your psychotherapy clients, and a regular attendee of your women's group in Reading.'

'What about it?'

'Have you ever driven or been a passenger in this vehicle?'

'Yes, a couple of times.'

Gillard was disappointed at her brazenness. It had the advantage for her that she could explain the presence of DNA in the vehicle which matched that from her home.

'Did you use it at all over the weekend in question?'

'No. I believe Loti mentioned that it had been stolen before that weekend.'

'It has never been reported stolen.'

She shrugged. 'That's not my problem. I'm not the keeper of the car.'

Gillard ground his teeth. Julia McGann may well have been coaching Rachel. He wasn't making any progress. Still, he had some ammunition in his back pocket.

'So just to be clear, any journeys you did take in this vehicle were before the weekend in question?'

'Yes.'

Gillard took out his iPad, and tapped on a video. 'This is footage from a CCTV camera just inside the entrance to the Tesco Extra at Ashenden Road.' He showed the video to her. 'Is this not you?'

Rachel blinked, and glanced at Julia. The image was sharp. It was clearly Rachel, pushing a trolley. If she denied it, they would have her bang to rights because a transaction was made on her credit card just a few minutes later at this very same store.

'Yes, that is me.'

'Can I ask how you got there?'

'I got a lift with a friend.'

'Is this your friend?' He pointed to the stocky figure in the grey hoodie who walked in the shop just after her.

'No. I don't know who that is.'

'Ms Meadows, you travelled with this person in the Nissan Qashqai. You were both seen by police officers taking the vehicle from a spot in Parkmead Crescent. You drove.'

'That is completely untrue,' she said, turning to Julia, who then intervened.

'If you have any evidence of this, detective chief inspector, you had better show it.'

Gillard knew that the surveillance officer's account would not stand up in court. He hadn't been sure who the people were, and didn't even see them leave the car in the Tesco car park. The car had been left some distance from the entrance to the store, and there was no CCTV giving coverage of the parking spot.

'We have footage from within the store showing you and the man in the hoodie walking around together.'

'We got talking in the car park. I don't know him.' She smiled at Gillard.

'I'm not sure where all this is leading,' Julia said. 'What exactly are you accusing my client of having done?'

'We are investigating four very serious crimes, linked with this vehicle. Three murders, potentially, plus one very serious assault. Furthermore, the names of two of the victims were on a list which you, Rachel, compiled during a bonfire party at the women's refuge a number of weeks earlier.'

Rachel rolled her eyes. 'The list was simply a psychological device to allow damaged women to let go of their emotions. It has nothing to do with any actual crime.'

'Don't you think it's a coincidence, Ms Meadows, that they were all attacked in the same weekend?'

'No. I abhor violence, in all its forms. I spend too much of my life dealing with the after-effects of male violence to have any interest whatsoever in something like this.'

'But wouldn't a little revenge be tempting?' Kim Leighton asked. 'A chance to right a wrong?'

'Perhaps you should ask your own Detective Sergeant Rainy Macintosh,' Rachel said. 'She's clearly the source of your information. But I don't think you can rely upon it.'

'Really? Of the women in the group you run, at least two had their former partners attacked on the same weekend—'

'—when I was with friends at the refuge in Farnborough,' she said, smugly.

'No you weren't.' Gillard leaned forward and said, 'Rachel Meadows, I'm arresting you in connection with the murder of Gary Wray and others. You are not obliged to say anything. But it may harm your defence if you do not mention when questioned something which you later rely on in court. Anything you do say may be given in evidence.' He was surprised at the satisfaction it gave him to be able to say this to her. And especially in front of Julia McGann, Rachel's close friend and conspirator.

Maybe he would finally be able to nail them both. He watched as the custody sergeant arrived and escorted her from the interview room. A few minutes later, while he was talking to the desk sergeant, he heard Jack crying inconsolably, as he was taken in the arms of a police family liaison officer towards a woman from the local authority, who was waiting in reception. An innocent casualty in the hunt for justice.

–

It was noon before the incident room meeting could take place. The full team was there: DI Claire Mulholland, DS Vikram Singh, DI John Perry, DCs Michelle Tsu, Kim Leighton, Liz Tufnell, Rob Townsend and Carl Hoskins. DI Welbeck was on Zoom. Rainy Macintosh was expected to arrive at five, but now had to be excluded from active operations. Claire was to break the news to her.

'All right everybody,' Gillard said. 'The news blackout remains in operation. The chief constable has made it clear to me that until we tie these crimes firmly together, we say nothing about the links. Is that understood?'

There was a general murmur of agreement. 'Michelle, what's the latest on forensics. Do we have anything from the Nissan?'

'Yes, lots. There are DNA matches from Loti Sengupta, Rachel Meadows, and fourteen other traces which are not on the system. Fingerprints, likewise, from the two women and numerous others. Interestingly, one set of DNA matches traces found at Gary Wray's property in Churchill Terrace.'

'From the basement there?' Gillard asked.

'No. From the rear bedroom, and various surfaces in and around the kitchen.'

'Good. I wanted you to throw every test you can at those samples. Let's see if we can determine the sex, age and familial linkage.'

'I anticipated that,' Michelle said. 'The tests will take a couple of days to be completed.'

'No link to any of our male suspects?'

'From the car, no. Aaron Randall, Gerard Daly and Jürgen Kempf seem to be in the clear forensically.'

'Well, Kempf traces were found in Gary Wray's flat, yes?'

'Yes, but he had been a tenant there. He hasn't turned up in any of our other crime scenes.'

'Right, John, have we got to the bottom of the fiasco at Tesco?'

DI Perry raised his hand, and asked for the lights to be dimmed. 'Yes.' He used his laptop to project footage of CCTV onto a screen. 'This image, which you will have seen before, is Rachel Meadows entering the store with her son Jack in the trolley chair. If we wait a few seconds,' he said, clicking to a new image, 'we see the person in the grey hoodie, who has a hand basket.'

'So they split up?' Gillard asked.

'Not initially.' He showed a new image, of the two adults in conversation. 'You can see a bit of the face here.'

'Is that a man or a woman in the hoodie?' Hoskins asked. 'Got small hands for a bloke.'

Perry smiled. 'Then look at this sequence, near the checkout. I'll put it on video.' They watched as Jack, once again in the arms of the hoodie wearer, points out of the main windows, where the flash of blue lights could be seen intruding into the store. Hoodie put the child down, and retreated into the aisle behind. Perry switched to a different camera, in one of the aisles where clothing was sold. Hoodie shrugged off the rucksack, opened it and crouched down. The hoodie was unzipped, and a woollen hat underneath removed.

'It's a bloody woman,' Hoskins said. She had a shaven head, a thick neck, but the facial features were unmistakably female. The woman switched jackets, stowing the hoodie in the rucksack, and then pulled out a dark short-haired wig, which she put on.

'Is this our killer?' Michelle asked.

'Maybe,' Gillard said. They watched the video, which ended with the woman using a self-service till, then leaving.

'What time does Rainy get in?' Singh asked. 'She would know.'

'About five, she reckoned,' Michelle said.

'She would know if it's someone from the women's group,' Gillard said. 'But we mustn't assume that.' He'd seen the face before, but where? It certainly wasn't somebody he knew well, but he never forgot a face, even if he only glimpsed it for a moment.

'Hang on a minute,' Gillard said. 'John, can you zoom in on her, not her face but lower?'

'Certainly.' As he zoomed in, the picture became less sharp, but not yet blurry or pixelated.

'I want to know what's in her shopping basket.'

'Why?' asked Hoskins, laughing.

'Because, Carl, I can see she is using self-service till number twelve. If I get a couple of items from her basket, and cross-reference to the time of the transaction, we should be able to work out the name on the card that paid for it.'

'That's brilliant,' breathed Claire. 'Really brilliant.'

'I can see Marmite,' Hoskins said. 'It's a very distinctive jar.'

'Right, that should be enough. Carl, would you get on to Tesco? Get them to cross-reference, if they can, from the time, the till and that item.'

'Righto, sir.'

'Kim, when is our martial arts instructor coming in?' Gillard asked.

'Ah, he came into Margaret Road station this morning. He didn't manage much of an impression for the artist, I'm afraid.'

'Never mind. Send him a copy of this video. Oh, and remember you have to pixelate out everyone but our suspect.'

'Data protection, right?'

'Absolutely. Team, I really think we're getting somewhere.' He looked at his watch. 'I have to go now, Vikram is in charge, you can call me on the hands-free.'

'Can we interrogate Rachel Meadows again?' DC Leighton asked.

'Yes. But treat her nicely. Make sure she's fed. Her brief has a grudge against me, and we don't want to give her any fresh ammunition.'

Gillard's afternoon would be taken up with a trip down to Hove, long promised to Claire Mulholland, firstly to pay respects to Ken Stapleford at his funeral, but secondly to review exactly how the killer could have approached and escaped unnoticed from the retired policeman's home.

Chapter Twenty-three

Ken Stapleford's funeral was packed with police. Gillard counted three dozen officers from Surrey that he recognised, and probably another dozen he guessed were police but didn't know. Alison Rigby wasn't there, perhaps a political judgement based on what was beginning to emerge about Stapleford's past behaviour. He wasn't after all killed while on duty. The dead officer, however, was given the full treatment, with his formal cap on top of his coffin. For all the pomp, Gillard saw no members of Stapleford's family, bar Colin, the brother who lived in Weston-super-Mare. Claire told him she had been hoping that his second wife or perhaps the daughter from the first marriage would attend. In fact it was an almost entirely male affair. The only women seemed to be a few partners of male colleagues.

The eulogy was given by Colin, laden with references to Ken's love of Brighton and Hove Albion, his camaraderie, and his own sporting achievements. Once the formal proceedings were over, Gillard and Claire declined the invitation to come along to the buffet. There was work still to be done. Forty minutes later, they arrived at Fir Close in Hove. Gillard took in the shape of the close, as Claire Mulholland described the locations of the various relevant neighbours and the doorbell camera.

'I really don't see how it's possible to get up the street without being seen,' Gillard said, as he drove slowly around the close.

'That's exactly what I thought,' she said. 'I've been tearing my hair out trying to work out how anyone else but Liam Lewis could have been involved.'

He parked on Stapleford's driveway. 'I take it you've not released the crime scene?' he asked, spotting the police padlock still in place on the front door, and the tattered blue-and-white crime tape.

'No. The coroner was prepared to delay the handover to the family, given that I told him I still had unspecified investigations to make.'

Gillard nodded. That was a wise move. Coroners were often under pressure to release crime scenes back to the family as soon as possible, given that relatives often had nowhere else to live. But once a crime scene was returned it was often almost impossible to recover any further forensic evidence, and any that was found was much more open to challenge in court.

They both dressed up in Tyvek suits, booties and gloves, and Claire took out a key, unlocked the padlock and eased open the door.

The extent of bloodstains in the hallway was still quite shocking. They made their way around one room after another, with Gillard looking at photographs on his iPad while Claire described exactly how the attack appeared to have taken place. They spent half an hour within the house and Gillard could find no obvious hole in the way that she had undertaken the investigation. Finally, they investigated the garden. Claire led him down to the fence, drawing his attention to the bank of brambles beyond and the steep descent to the railway line.

'I really can't see how anyone could get over here,' she said.

Gillard nodded, then turned back to the house. 'However, if they did, they could probably approach undetected unless someone was in the kitchen. And as we know they were both watching TV.' He turned back to the fence and leaned over as far as he could. 'Have you taken a trip by train, behind here?'

'No. I couldn't see the point.'

Gillard pulled the location up on Google Maps. 'Let's take a quick trip on the next service from Hove to Portslade, and see what we can see from the track.' He took a spare pair of blue nylon gloves, and stuck them on the ends of a couple of briars. 'Hopefully we can see these when we go past, so we know which is the relevant garden.'

—

It was half an hour later when the two detectives boarded a train heading west. They had their faces glued to the window on the south side, looking out for the blue gloves. They took many photographs but didn't see anything out of the ordinary, until the gloves were spotted. There was indeed a huge bank of brambles, but just to the right of it, near a signal gantry, was a rusting ladder recessed into the vertical wall behind a couple of electrical junction boxes.

'That's a possibility,' Gillard said. They only had a few seconds to look before the train passed by, but transferring photos to the iPad they were able to quickly look in greater detail.

'You'd have to know in advance, wouldn't you?' Claire asked.

'Well, if the killer was a regular traveller on this route, he might well have noticed the ladder. The services are only once every thirty minutes. I would have thought it possible to get on the embankment from the bridge just here, fifty yards away.' He pointed at the iPad.

Half an hour later they were standing on the parapet of a road bridge which crossed the railway embankment close to the back of Stapleford's home. Though it wasn't possible to see the recessed ladder from there, it was apparent the old and rusty railings here had long been broken, and there was a discernible pathway through the nettles and brambles leading down to the railway line.

'This looks to me a real possibility,' Gillard said.

'I just hadn't considered that access was possible at all,' Claire said.

'It smacks to me of something else, too. Real local knowledge. This is the kind of trespass that would be known to local schoolkids, but very hard for a stranger to research.'

'So what's the next step?' she asked.

'Ring up British Transport Police and get access to the track. They'll probably have to close a section of one of the lines between Portslade and Hove.'

Two hours later Gillard and Mulholland were standing on the cinder track underneath the embankment wall, accompanied by three officials from Network Rail and an inspector from British Transport Police, each of them wearing hard hats and clad head to foot in hi-vis. As Gillard predicted, a short section of the line had been closed off and trains were diverted to share the opposite track. They were led to the junction boxes and the recessed access ladder, and from this angle it was clear that an intruder could climb to within three feet of the bottom of Ken Stapleford's rear fence.

'Have you had many recorded intrusions on the section of line?' Gillard asked the inspector.

'Passengers have reported seeing kids trespassing. It was on our to-do list. But you know how long that list is.'

'I can imagine,' Gillard replied.

The two detectives scrutinised the bottom of the ladder, looking for snagged material. Gillard began to climb, and when he got to the fourth rung looked down. Something shiny was lodged behind one of the junction boxes, and impossible to reach. It was a carving knife, the blade a good eight inches long, of the kind found in any kitchen. He described what he was seeing to Claire.

'Is that significant?' she asked.

'I'm convinced it is.' Gillard's phone rang. He glanced down and saw it was Sam. 'Hello Sam, what's up?'

Claire looked at him as he listened. 'Sam, can I call you back? I'm in the middle of something. Ten minutes, okay.' He hung up. 'Some domestic crisis,' he said by way of explanation to Claire.

'This is definitely significant. In fact I'm beginning to see what happened.'

'I'm not,' Mulholland replied.

'You told me you were baffled by the fact that in what otherwise seemed to have been a carefully planned attack the murderer helped himself to a knife from Ken Stapleford's kitchen, as if they had forgotten to bring a weapon. However, it all makes sense if the assailant had lost the original knife while attempting to climb this ladder over the brambles into the garden.'

'Ah. I see.'

'It actually supports the thesis that the attacker came in this way.' He turned to address the inspector. 'Are you able to retrieve that knife for me? We need to do some forensic tests on it.'

The inspector leaned forward and peered around the junction box. 'I imagine we'd have to remove the housing on the cabinet, but yes, it could be done.'

'Gloves and evidence bag, you know the drill,' Gillard said. 'I'll get CSI to call you.'

He turned to Claire. 'Given that we didn't find anything inside the house, I would be sceptical that we will get any traces.'

'I agree.' She looked around, but couldn't see any possibility of this particular place being overlooked by security cameras. He checked his watch. 'This has been useful, but I think we should be getting back.'

–

It was ten to five. Gillard and Claire were heading along A281, the shortcut from Horsham to Guildford, which avoided having to go on the M25 on a busy Friday afternoon. He'd been making extensive use of the hands-free, getting Vikram checking on the evidence file and watching out for any new forensic results. One exciting new development had occurred. One ANPR camera on the southbound M6 in Staffordshire on Sunday morning had not only caught the Nissan Qashqai, but with the morning light at precisely the right angle it was clear that the woman driving had a reasonable resemblance to Rachel Meadows. There was a passenger, not so clearly illuminated, in the front seat. None of the other cameras had produced anything quite as clear.

'This is good,' Gillard said. 'We are gradually closing down on her.'

'She is very slippery, Craig,' Claire said. 'We have to be careful.'

He recalled that he had agreed to ring Sam back more than half an hour ago, but hadn't yet done so. Just as he was about to request the robot to ring her, a call came in. DC Michelle Tsu. He answered it.

'Go ahead, Michelle.'

'I've been looking into Rachel Meadows' background. The psychotherapy qualification is genuine, from the Open University in 2019. She's not part of any practice that I can see. As you correctly recalled, she did run a gardening company, but it closed during lockdown. Her son is home-schooled. She has no convictions. We've got oversight on her bank accounts, and there is nothing out of the ordinary.'

'I want to know the location of any card purchases.'

'I've looked. There wasn't a single one over the weekend of the murders.'

'So we've got nothing on her at all, except that image capture of her in the car.'

'No.'

'How thoroughly did you go over her home?'

'We were just looking for computer, phone, the usual stuff. We haven't found any of it. When she was arrested, she didn't have a phone on her,' she said.

'Right, that's an obvious line of inquiry. No doubt someone at the refuge has it. I'd really rather avoid having to search that place – it would be very bad PR in the current climate having a bunch of constabulary uniforms barging into a place where women are supposed to be safe from all forms of violence.'

'That's a very good point, sir.'

'Look, Rainy will have the number of Rachel's phone and it should be on Loti Sengupta's phone too. Get Rob Townsend to track down and contact the service provider, and download everything we can. If we can get an email address, so much the better.'

'I'm on to it, sir.'

Gillard cut the call, having been notified of Sam waiting on the line. He took the call and before he could say anything she blurted out: 'Craig, where are you?'

'Ten minutes from home. What's the matter?'

'It's the cleaner. She's—'

He rolled his eyes. 'I thought she was good—'

'Craig, she's locked herself in the bathroom, and she's threatened to kill herself.'

He could indeed hear bellowing in the background.

'What's her full name?'

'Helen Smith.'

'Can you give me an address? Then maybe somebody she knows can talk her out of it.'

'I've only got the agency address, in Farnborough. Besides, she got evicted from her flat yesterday. I was planning to let her stay this weekend, until she got herself sorted out.'

'Are you there alone?'

'Just me and Grace. I'm talking to her, but—'

'Has she got anything in there with her?'

'There are scissors, all sorts of tablets I suppose. I'm not sure.'

'Did you ring the agency?'

'Yes, but there's no reply. It closes at four on a Friday.'

'Did you have any idea she was like this?'

'Well, I knew she has had mental health trouble. The agency specialises in helping vulnerable—'

There was a bang and a scream. 'She's coming out. Oh God, Craig—'

The phone went dead.

'What is it?' Claire asked, alarmed.

He felt his blood drain from his face. 'I think we've found our attacker, Claire. Hiding in plain sight, in my own damn home.'

'With Sam and the baby!'

'Yes, with Sam and Grace.'

Gillard hit the blue lights and sirens as they raced into Guildford's Friday night traffic. While he concentrated on the high-speed drive, racing down the middle of the road between lines of stationary cars, Claire rang the ambulance service, directing it to his home address. Once she had finished the call, she asked him: 'Did you know about this cleaner?'

'No,' he said, getting the hands-free to ring Sam. Engaged. 'I haven't had a moment since Grace was born, I didn't think I'd ever seen her. But now I realise I have, leaving my house when I arrived yesterday, while I was talking to Tanya. It's the same woman who we saw on the Tesco CCTV, with a wig.'

'Sam is very resourceful,' Claire said, biting her lip. It sounded more like hope than confidence.

'Her parents had been with her until this afternoon. They'll be driving back to Keswick by now.' Gillard turned off the sirens and lights as he entered his own street. He would have blocked the street if necessary, but as if by magic, a parking space was available right in front of his own house. The lights were on, upstairs and downstairs as he and Claire raced out of the vehicle towards his front door.

He had his keys in hand, but before he could insert them in the lock, he saw something that turned his spine to ice. There was a bloody handprint on the glass, and a scarlet runnel beneath.

His precious wife and newborn daughter were in there. *Oh Sam!*

Chapter Twenty-four

The day before

Helen was leaning over Grace in her crib. 'Isn't she lovely? Can I hold her?' she asked Sam.

'Yes, of course.' As the cleaner picked up the baby, her sleeve slid up and Sam got a good look at the scars on her forearms. She had already spotted on the right arm the word 'Hex' picked out in nine straight slashes, but on this arm there was a more recent series of cuts, scabbed over and seemingly random. But as the woman held Grace, she could suddenly read them as three letters: A, G and E. Before the 'A' was a blizzard of little cuts, partially obscured by the charm bracelet that Helen was wearing. Turning to gaze at Sam, the cleaner saw what she was looking at, and pulled down her sleeve.

'It looks like you're still going through difficult times' Sam said.

Helen nodded, and stroked the back of Grace's head gently. 'I used to get my moods and that. Because of my dad and what he did to Mum and me, but I'm much better now. Generally.' She smiled tentatively, as if trying to convince herself as much of Sam. 'It's never affected my work, Mrs Gillard, honestly.' She continued to jig the baby gently.

'It's fine, Helen, really it is.' Sam rested her hand gently on Helen's wrist. She flinched.

'What is it you were writing?'

She looked straight into Sam's eyes. 'Rage. I was angry.'

Later on Thursday morning

'Is your husband all right to you?' Helen asked, as she was polishing the big mirror Sam had hung halfway along the hallway. 'I never see him.'

'Yes. He's not here as much as I would like. Still, I suppose I should have known that when I married him.'

'What does he do?' she asked.

Sam normally didn't tell people about Craig's work, but if she was to stay, Helen would soon know. Once all the boxes were opened and the official pictures were on the wall upstairs, it would be obvious. 'He's a detective with Surrey Police.'

Helen appeared to freeze, her arm in mid-sweep. Then she polished away more rapidly, with even more vigour, her jaw set. 'My dad was a policeman too.' She seemed to wipe even harder, making the mirror rattle against the wall. 'He's dead now. Gone. But not up here.' She tapped the side of her head, and turned to look at Sam. She had the emptiest eyes that Sam had ever seen. Dark voids. 'I can still hear Mum pleading with him, on her knees. When I was a kid,' she said, squirting a little polish on the scalloped edge of the mirror. 'In my head I could hear this whining and pleading, as I was falling asleep and as I was waking up. Voices, terrible voices. They never left me alone.'

'Oh Helen, I'm so sorry.'

She shrugged. 'It's life, ain't it. Mental health, domestic issues. The shit that life throws at us.' She managed a brittle smile, then walked out into the kitchen.

Sam looked at this mannish, powerful woman, broad muscular shoulders and narrow hips. Only her hands were feminine, and the set of her mouth. Right from the first moment she'd arrived, shy and almost monosyllabic, Sam had felt pity for her. She had also speculated about whether she was transitioning, or had been. Her short dark bob looked a bit like a wig. Too glossy, with no graduation at the nape of the neck. Mary, more practically, noticed failings in the cleaning schedule. The unemptied bins, cobwebs missed, the breaking of one of the plastic clips on Sam's new and expensive cordless Dyson. Sam wasn't blind to this. From the very moment Helen began, it was peculiar to see a scouring pad wielded on the skirting boards, rubbing away as if her life depended on it, while the washbasins were ignored. Sam had gently pointed out the priorities, and Helen quickly conformed. She certainly wasn't stupid, and seemed to have a real fear of losing the job. A woman called Scarlett from the agency had rung up on the second day to ask how Helen was getting on. Sam had no intention of mentioning the failings. Although today there was one issue that perturbed her.

Helen kept going into their bedroom to look at the baby.

Sam had heard her over the baby monitor. She cooed and aahed at Grace, and on several occasions it sounded like she picked her up. It gave Sam a sense of impending maternal panic, which she had trouble fighting down. It was something of the same feeling she got when Trish's peculiar teddy bear for the child had arrived. Mary had been all for having a quiet word with Helen, but Sam was reluctant. After all, Helen was probably desperate for a child of her own. She was young enough, early thirties, but… Sam had tried to park all the prejudicial assumptions about this strange young woman's chance of finding a partner, but they lurked in the back of her head all the same, curdling in with the pity.

Thursday afternoon

It was the fridge that changed Mary's view. The delivery van arrived at ten o'clock and disgorged a loud mansplainer with a pencil over his ear, and a young skinny assistant whose eyes wandered, unsubtly, over Sam's full post-natal figure. She kept out of the way, as did Helen, while Mary directed the two, wheeling in the new slimline model on a sack truck. When Mary asked them to take away the old one, pencil-ear tutted and laughed. 'No, no, love. We can't carry that monster except on a proper trolley. You didn't tell us it was one of those big American ones. They need special techniques. Health and safety.'

Mary gave as good as she got, and the men beat a retreat, saying that a special pickup could be made, for extra cost. Or perhaps the local authority would oblige. Sam and Helen returned to the kitchen where the old fridge sat as immoveable as an Easter Island statue in the middle of the floor.

'What are we going to do now?' Mary asked. 'You've got some guests tonight, haven't you?'

'Yes. Colleagues impatient to see Grace. They'll be here at seven.'

'We could open the double doors into the garden and get it out there,' Helen said. 'It's wide enough.'

'We'll never shift it,' Sam said. 'It doesn't even have any wheels.'

'I agree,' Mary said, folding her arms. 'I told you we should have used John Lewis, but no, you wanted to save forty pounds.'

Sam bit her lip, and went upstairs to avoid reigniting the argument. Ten minutes later, she heard some noise below and Mary's exclamation of delight. 'You have to come and look at this,' she called up. By the time she got down, the fridge was gone. Mary pointed out into the garden where Helen was just finishing positioning the thing.

'That's incredible, how did you two do that?' Sam said.

'Me? She did it pretty much on her own,' Mary said.

Helen came in, closed the double doors, and dusted off her hands. 'That was a pretty good workout.'

'Well, I felt out of breath just watching,' Mary said.

'I tried out powerlifting, a few years ago,' Helen said.

'Powerlifting?' Sam asked, incredulously.

'Yeah. My therapist recommended I go to a gym, to build my self-confidence and, actually, I found it addictive. Because I was unexpectedly strong, my trainer recommended me for competitions. So at his suggestion I stupidly started to take supplements, which turned out basically to be testosterone. After a year of that my hairline started receding, like a man, and my voice dropped. I was furious. I had a relapse for about six months in which I hated myself and gave myself a new name: Hex.' She lifted her sleeve briefly. 'After I got out from being sectioned, and after Mum's second suicide attempt, I went back to the gym. No drugs this time, no weights. Just kickboxing. Turned out I was good at that, too.' She tapped the side of her head. 'Focused my pain into a laser beam of aggression, that's what my trainer said.' She turned away and picked up a duster. 'I'll do the tops of the doors now.'

Sam glanced at Mary, whose eyes were as wide as her own. Who was this extraordinary woman?

Friday afternoon

Sam stood outside the bedroom door, and called through. 'Helen, I've got a cup of tea for you here,' she said, setting the mug down. There was no reply. Puzzled, she headed downstairs.

'Is she still asleep?' Mary asked 'It's three o'clock in the afternoon, for goodness' sake.'

'What can I do?' Sam said, lowering her voice to a whisper. Helen had arrived at nine o'clock that morning, even though she wasn't due next until Monday. She was carrying a rucksack and a wheeled suitcase. She had been in tears, saying the landlord had kicked her out. Sam had offered her the spare room for the day, and moved all the baby's things into Craig's office.

'Can't she go somewhere else?' Mary asked. 'She must have friends, surely.'

'Not locally, and she's got no money. The landlord kept her deposit.'

'Maybe Craig can do something about that.'

Sam gave a sardonic smile, and rabbit-eared her fingers. 'It would be a "civil matter".'

Mary shook her head. 'She is supposed to be helping you out, not the other way round. You're not supposed to be vacuuming, and we've got to go in an hour.'

'She's a good cleaner, Mum.'

'Well, a bit too thorough, I'd say. I don't know what she used on the shower floor, but it's got a funny green stain.

And that knife block I bought you both last Christmas, I can only imagine she used Domestos on it, because all the varnish has come off, and instead of teak it's more like the colour of bone.'

'Mum, I tackled her about that. She used to be a hospital cleaner, that's why everything gets scrubbed to within an inch of its life.'

'That's as may be,' Mary said, looking at her watch. 'So are you sure you are going to be all right on your own?'

'I'll be fine, Mum, honestly. You've been so kind, but you can't stay forever, I understand that. Craig will be home in two hours, he has promised me faithfully.'

'Yes, well, we'll see about that won't we,' Mary said briskly. She reached for her coat and said, 'I don't trust her.' She flicked her eyes upstairs. 'You need someone properly reliable.'

'Mum. She was abused by her father. She witnessed decades of domestic abuse at home, it's only a couple of weeks since her mother committed suicide. And she is so good with Grace, she absolutely adores her.'

'Well, it's a tragic tale,' Mary said dismissively. 'But you've got a new baby. You've got to decide whether she is here to do the cleaning or to receive therapy.' She shrugged on her coat. 'Anyway, I've got to go. Tom's getting itchy feet.'

'Okay, Mum. Safe trip.' The moment her mother had left, Sam rang Craig's work mobile. Busy. She left a message asking for a return call. Something inside felt wrong. Really wrong.

Friday, 4.50 p.m.

Sam was in the kitchen when she heard the bedroom door open, footsteps, then the slamming of the bathroom door.

That was enough to wake Grace up in the main bedroom, who began to cry in stereo, the sound both direct and through the baby monitor. Sam made her way upstairs, but could hear a much deeper howling and sobbing from the bathroom. Desperate, bereft adult tears. The sort when someone you love dies unexpectedly.

'Are you all right, Helen?' Sam asked, through the door. She was determined not to confront her with her suspicions. Surely it would be best just to keep her calm.

No reply.

'Helen, talk to me.'

There was no reply, but the unmistakable sound of a bathroom cabinet being rifled.

'Helen, what are you doing in there?'

'Don't you have any proper razor blades? The kind that cut wrists.'

'Let's talk about this, don't do anything silly.'

There was a crash and a bang. 'It's time I finished this. Long past time.'

'Please, Helen, I can get you some help.'

'Bit late for that.'

'Have you swallowed anything?' Sam said.

'Nothing of yours, don't worry.'

'What have you taken?'

'You really want to know? Half a bottle of vodka, amphetamines, my old powerlifting tabs.'

'But why, Helen?'

'Because I need the rage. I need the rage to end it, don't you see?' There was a bang, as if she had punched the wall. Sam kept redialling Craig, who had been constantly engaged, but felt now she should probably call the paramedics instead. First, she checked in on Grace, who was grizzling again. She bundled her up, and took her downstairs and into the lounge. Part of her was sure that Helen wouldn't hurt her or the child, but her maternal misgivings could not be quieted. She lay the child down amongst some cushions on the settee, before returning to the bathroom door, still locked, where now there was silence. She had her phone in hand but was going to give negotiation one last try before calling 999.

'Open the door, Helen, let me in.'

No reply.

'I'm going to call for an ambulance, if you don't let me in.'

'Yeah, well get the cops while you're at it. I'm sure they want their share of the action. And there's been plenty of that, believe me.'

'Helen, please.'

Sam stepped away and redialled Gillard. He finally picked up. 'Craig, where are you?'

'Ten minutes from home. What's the matter?'

'It's the cleaner. She's—'

'I thought she was good—'

'Craig, she's locked herself in the bathroom, and she's threatened to kill herself.'

For the next half minute, while she talked to Craig, she had her eye on the bathroom door.

'Did you have any idea she was like this?' he asked, finally.

'Well, I knew she has had mental health trouble. The agency specialises in helping vulnerable—'

There was a bang, and the sound of shattering glass. The door was unlocked, and flung open. Helen stood there, wearing a loose T-shirt and shorts, her face puffy, eyes bloodshot. Without the wig, her sparse spiky hair made her look masculine, the cords on her neck tense.

Behind her, the mirror-fronted cabinet was shattered. In her hand, above her own head, Helen had a wickedly sharp sliver of the mirror, like a dagger. Blood was already running down her arm, dripping from her elbow.

'She's coming out. Oh God, Craig—'

As Helen moved forward, Sam screamed and dropped the phone, which tumbled down the stairs.

'You want to see me do this, yeah?' Helen asked.

'No, I don't! I want you to stop,' Sam said, retreating down the stairs. 'Stop.'

'I can't.' Helen reached down, pressed the point of the shard just above her left knee, the muscled flesh puckering, then released on penetration. Bright blood welled up. Growling in pain, she then drew the sharp point from just above her knee up along her own muscled thigh. Streams of red spilled down.

Sam screamed, thundered down the stairs, fled to the lounge and scooped up Grace into her arms. She could hear the creak of the stairs as Helen descended slowly.

'I'm not going to hurt you, Sam, or your baby,' Helen called out. 'I only kill men, the very worst men.'

It sounded like she was standing by the front door. 'But I do want you to understand how I have suffered from men. Men in the police. Men like your husband.'

'No! Craig is a good man.'

'He's a cop, Sam. It's the armed wing of the patriarchy, Rachel explained it. Two types of man are attracted to be in the police: the man of violence, and the authoritarian personality. Which one is your husband?'

Sam looked at the phone, whose screen was now cracked, and dark. There were only two ways out of the house. The front door, which meant getting past Helen, or the rear doors into the garden. Helen had locked it after she'd moved the fridge yesterday, but where on earth was the key? Even if she got into the garden, there was no way out. Sam looked around and spotted the landline handset, which Craig had disconnected a few days before. Could she just plug it back in? She didn't know if she had time.

Helen called out to Sam. 'Last Saturday afternoon I murdered my own father. Stabbed him to death. I can tell you, it gave me more pleasure, more release, than any sex I've ever had.'

Sam trembled, hugging Grace to her, and stood in the doorway between kitchen and lounge. They were ten yards apart, watching each other. She didn't know what to do, except to play for time, until Craig arrived. 'But why, Helen?'

'A lifetime of reasons. It started when I was five. It was my first trip to the swimming pool, but I still remember the look in his eyes when he claimed to be drying me there. He asked, "Does that feel nice?" Bastard raped me when I was eight. He was off work, supposedly sick, and waited until my mother went out shopping. He gave me my teddy to hug because he said it might hurt. It did, and it made me cry. It always made me cry, even when it eventually stopped hurting. I knew it was wrong. I thought it was my punishment for something, I kept asking: "Daddy, why are you hurting me?" For years I wanted to please him, thinking if only I did the right thing then it would all be better.'

Sam looked away as Helen drew the shard down her inner arm.

'Ah, shit, that really hurts,' she gasped. 'By sixteen, I'd been through everything. I took drugs, I sought out oblivion, made a good friend of the shadows. I had casual sex with anyone, male or female. But I kept waking up and then I wanted to be dead. At twenty-three I thought, if I can't be a woman, maybe I should be a man. After all, if you can't beat them join them, right? I went for a couple of NHS sessions about gender reassignment, but didn't have the patience. That's when I started at the gym, first time.'

Helen began to sob, and wiped her face with a bloody arm. Sam could no longer distinguish what were tears and what were runnels of blood.

'He used to beat Mum, usually late at night. I would hear her pleading. In my head, I still hear her, begging, weeping. Each time, there was a shout from him, a blow, then a silence, then her tears. She told me years later that he rarely hit her where it would show. He had these gangster gloves, with hard knuckles, seized from a drug dealer's torture chamber. He would punch her with them, but always low down, where the bruises were hidden by clothing. Guess what? I found them gloves last Saturday, when I was hiding in that upstairs room at his house. And I gave the bastard a good going over with 'em.'

'Was there no way to make it up, to put your feelings to him?' Sam asked.

'I've been to his house before, a year previously. It had been my last attempt to try to salvage some kind of relationship with him. Waste of time. As I left, I promised myself that if Mum died, I would come back and kill him the next day. I looked around. I was already planning it, and I reckoned I'd found a way to get in unseen.' She halted. 'Shit, they're here.'

Sam heard the creak of Helen running upstairs, then the front door opened, and her husband called her name. She shuddered with relief and shouted out to him. 'Craig, thank God.'

Chapter Twenty-five

Gillard stood in the doorway. He could see no one. 'Sam, are you okay?'

'I'm here by the lounge, with Grace. Helen's upstairs, and has self-harmed with fragments of the bathroom mirror. Be careful!'

He looked up the stairs, and saw the blood spattered on the new oatmeal carpet, the gory handprint on the banister. There were no stains along the hallway towards the kitchen. Behind him the front door opened again, and Claire arrived by his side. 'Paramedics should be here in two minutes,' she whispered. 'Two patrol cars are with them, a firearms unit is seven minutes away.'

'Go to Sam, she's in the lounge,' Gillard hissed, pointing to the kitchen. 'Make sure there's a back exit available. There are double doors, and a key somewhere. I don't know what we're facing up here,' he said, beginning to climb the stairs.

Claire rested a hand on his arm. 'Craig, no! You should wait here until reinforcements arrive.' She lowered her voice. 'You know how dangerous this woman is.'

'She is a victim as well as an assailant, and has an important story to tell. I can't risk her bleeding to death.' He continued to ascend, the treads creaking beneath his feet. 'Helen,' he called out. 'I'm Sam's husband. Help is on its way. You need to staunch those wounds.'

There was no reply.

He reached the halfway point, the small landing by the picture window, where the stairs turned left and headed to the first floor. He continued upward until he could see the landing. The carpet sparkled with fragments from the mirror, and was spattered with blood. The bathroom door was open, the spare bedroom door closed, with bloody handprints on it.

Behind it, he could hear sobbing.

'Helen, let me in.'

There was no reply, so he gently turned the handle, and eased it open. The woman he saw standing there in front of the bed had criss-crossed her entire body with fresh cuts, across her legs, arms and abdomen. Her clothing was drenched in blood, her T-shirt and shorts ripped. He wanted to assess whether she had given herself a deep stab wound, one that would be immediately life-threatening, but his eye was immediately drawn to the mirror shard, held in her left hand, next to her own head.

'I'll do it, I promise,' she warned him.

He didn't doubt it. She had started to, after all. But he wondered whether he could disarm her without provoking a fatal wound to either of them.

'Take a deep breath, Helen. Together we can make this better, but you have got to help me.'

'No, I'll wait until they arrive with the guns. Going out in a blaze of male violence, that would be appropriate right? A Hollywood death for a crazy bitch.'

'You're not mad, Helen. You need help.' He prepared himself, sizing up whether he could seize her left wrist before she used the shard on herself. The scimitar-shaped fragment offered an unnatural grip, sharp edges undoubtedly hurting her hand, the blood clearly in evidence. He moved forward gradually, trying to reach her left wrist and intending to push her onto the bed two feet behind her. A soft landing, where she couldn't kick or punch, that's what he wanted to engineer. She slowly pivoted the dagger away from him, drawing him closer, like a balletic scene. Only then did he spot what she had concealed, low, in her right hand. The device he'd seen in the Birmingham CCTV.

While he hesitated over whether to go for her dagger arm or the stun gun, she struck instantly, ducking and pivoting her weight, exploding into action. Her right arm connected with his hip.

That searing instant blasted him: a blue arc, the smell of burning, and enveloping it all a pain so intense that he thought he was being fried alive. He heard a high-pitched scream of agony he later realised was his own. He was thrown against the door frame by some unstoppable force, and while trying to stabilise himself, felt a powerful knee to his groin. It felt like his balls were rattling around inside his skull, like some agonising pinball game. As he stumbled backwards, feeling sick, he realised he was no match for this woman. If she wanted him dead, it would happen.

He was aware of Sam's screams in the background and Claire Mulholland climbing the stairs. His right hand was now on the door frame, his left trying to grab at the home-made Taser. He got hold of Helen's right wrist, slippery with blood, but she kicked his supporting leg away. Falling, he lost his grip altogether, and tumbled backwards down the stairs, hitting Claire on her way up. She crashed right down and banged her head on the newel post at the bottom. Gillard landed on his back on the mezzanine landing, and before he'd risen to his knees, Helen was on him. She pushed the stun gun into the side of his head, and again the world seemed to explode. He came to with his head halfway out of the picture window into the street, the back of his neck resting on sharp fragments of glass. Helen was kneeling on the lower half of his body, that same shard of mirror next to his throat.

'Helen, no! Leave him, alone, I beg you! Please!' Sam shrieked from the bottom of the stairs.

Gillard could see in his peripheral vision that Sam had edged up a stair, and Claire was there too, on her knees.

'Stay down there both of you, or honest to God I will slit his throat!' Helen warned.

'Stay back, Sam,' he rasped. 'We can talk this out.'

'She killed her father,' Sam shouted.

'You're Stapleford's daughter, from his first marriage, aren't you?' he said.

'More's the pity. I promised myself I'd kill him, if Mum died. I'd been planning it.'

Gillard needed to play for time. 'You came in from the railway line, didn't you?'

'Very good. Yeah. It was funny, because the last time I went to see him, a month after he moved in, he showed me. It was his escape plan, if any of the criminals he'd ever put away came for him. It was over the back, and down onto the railway line. There was a hidden ladder.'

'How did you get the timing right, though. To kill him during half-time?'

She emitted a short bitter laugh. 'Even when I was a kid, he always left the back door unlocked during the day. I guessed he still would, and planned to come in when he'd be watching a match. The hard part was working out which one. Not a home game, or an easy-to-get-to away fixture. Anyway, I eased open the door, and could hear him in the lounge laughing and joking. My mistake was to assume he'd be alone. They had the TV sound right up, so it was easy for me to sneak up the stairs and hide. But I didn't know what I was going to do. Then, as luck would have it, the other bloke left at half-time. I came down, grabbed a knife from the kitchen because I'd dropped my own. I was even able to walk right up behind him. He called out: "Hey, Liam, take a look at this replay". That's what he said as he turned, and saw me. You should have seen his face! I zapped him on the hand. He went down and I just went mental with the knife. I was out of there in one minute, over the brambles down the ladder, along the railway line to the bridge where Rachel was waiting in the car.'

'She gave you a lift?' Gillard said.

'Yeah. A lift and the list. I was on a high with the rage, seventh heaven, amazing. Then she said, "There are others, you know." She showed me the names and addresses. "Each of them is like your father", she said. "There will be no better catharsis. You'd be doing a favour for the women who aren't as strong as you, who can't do what you can do. You will aid all womankind." We went up all the way to Glasgow, in the end, for that surgeon, and did that horrible guy in Birmingham on the Monday morning. The one who imprisoned his wife. I wish we'd killed him.'

'What about Gary Wray?'

'Ah, now that was just luck. On the way up to Glasgow, we were talking about him, about what a pig he was, getting away with everything just because he was famous. We got back to Guildford, and I was just buzzing with energy. Two down. So Rachel said, "Why don't you go into the park, see if you can catch the rapist?" She lent me her electric scooter. I just prowled around for half an hour, waiting by those bushes where the rapist always struck. Then I saw this jogger. He looked at me in my motorcycle gear, and initially I imagined he thought that I was the rapist. But I recognised him from the TV. What a piece of luck! When he came round for the second lap, I got him. Easy.' She laughed. 'That's the thing about killing, you know? Once you start, it gets moreish. I was just buzzing, because I'd thrown off a lifetime of repression. I'd taken my own existence, and shaped it myself. It was exactly what Rachel said would happen.'

'She led you astray, Helen. It was a wrong turning.'

'Ha! Typical cop, always blame a woman. Short skirt, yeah, she's asking for it. Friendly on Facebook, yeah, well that's consent isn't it? Had a drink, well it's disgusting and a come-on. Never mind that the men are always drunk. Well, they have needs, don't they? Even my own mum said it.'

She growled, and gripped the blade harder, blood from her hand dripping onto Gillard's face a few inches below hers. 'This is what *you* make me do. It's men, always men,' she said, forcing Gillard's neck harder against the broken glass. He could feel the burn of the cuts, the welling blood.

'There's a war coming,' she growled. 'When women fight back. Has to be. Rachel predicted it, is preparing for it. She's got a plan. Against the patriarchy, the Incel nutcases, the abusive cops, the rigged court system. Power in our own hands. That's the answer. It's Armageddon.'

He struggled to find a way to get his arms free. One was pinioned underneath her knee, and the other was hanging out of the window, surrounded by sharp glass. And he could feel the deadly points of the stun gun, in his side, a hair trigger from agony.

'Now, now,' she said, chiding him and holding the blade closer still to his throat. 'Lie still.'

'You have lots of mitigation, Helen, it doesn't have to end in disaster,' he said. With his head half out of the broken window, Gillard heard the arrival of the ambulances and police vehicles, sirens going. The crackle of radios, urgent shouts, and the slamming of metallic doors. It should have given him hope, but instead he felt a premonition of disaster. The boys in blue would goad her to do something terrible.

She laughed, a bitter little chuckle. 'Three cheers for the bloody cavalry, eh? Come to take down another nut job. I'm damaged goods, see? Not right up there.' She twisted the point of the shard in her temple, until a teardrop of blood popped to the surface, and started trickling down the side of her head.

He could hear but couldn't see the arrival of officers at the foot of the stairs.

'Armed police!' they yelled.

'Back off, filth, or I slit his fucking throat! I am not joking!' she bellowed back, lowering herself so that she was almost moulded into his side, away from them, the sharp edge resting painfully against his extended throat.

'I never understood it, that my daddy could be a policeman,' she whispered into his ear. 'Someone there to catch bad people. And do this to me. So I thought I must be bad. That's how a child thinks.'

She ignored the continuing calls from downstairs for her to release her captor. 'Funny that it's all a fuss if a woman hurts a man, isn't it? Not the other way round. I mean, when we were living at Mount Browne, in a police house, Mum rang 999, and asked for the police. They sent the man from next door, one of my dad's best mates.

No arrest, just a chat and a laugh. I hoped it would be better after that, but nothing happened. See? Nothing ever happens when it's a man.'

'That's just not true,' Gillard said. He could feel the pulse in his neck against the blade.

'I never understood it until Rachel explained to me. Coppers *are* the problem. The police attract men who like power over others, men who don't like women, men who retreat from equality into the old world. Men of violence. After Sarah Everard, she told me in our sessions that it would never change. When women are angry, well, it's the time of the month, isn't it? Or, she's just an old bag. An ugly bitch. A miserable slag, a tart. Rachel was really good at explaining. She told me that words like this, men use as a protective barrier against women. Men put us into boxes of inferiority, to hide our individuality, label us, because then it's easier to hurt us. Me, they'd think I was a fat, ugly lesbian, right?'

'Not all men are like that,' Gillard croaked.

'Maybe, but they cover up for the others, don't they? Just a bit of banter, is what they say. You know, my dad worked with Kincaid, didn't he? On the girl F case. He boasted that he buried the case. The poor girl who committed suicide. My mum told me all about it. But I'm girl F too. And there's a hundred girls for every letter of the bloody alphabet, all ignored, all abused, all crying out for help.'

Gillard heard the sound of an automatic weapon being cocked. Heckler & Koch, standard for police firearms units, quite distinctive. They were right outside, presumably aiming for what they could see of her head through the broken window.

'Don't shoot!' Gillard yelled.

'Helen Smith,' someone shouted from outside through a loud hailer. 'There are armed police all around. Release your captive, and let's bring this to a peaceful end.'

She lifted her head and yelled out of the window. 'Go to hell!'

'Keep your head down,' Gillard warned her. 'They might just shoot.' He was aware of the military momentum of sieges, the hair-trigger mistakes, the screw-ups that were all too common.

'Why do you care?' She gave him a strange quizzical look, but shrank down back to her previous position, almost entwined around him like a lover, her lips close to his ear. He had one arm free now, but the blade above his throat dominated his attention, and the twin prongs of the Taser resting in the small of his back.

'Back to my story. By fourteen, I was old enough to understand, but what was I going to do about it? I started on myself. I slashed my wrists. That was only the first time. I realised that I could punish myself with self-inflicted pain, because that's all a woman can do. A woman can only hurt herself, because men are stronger. They put me in care a few times, but Mum needed me. She attempted suicide twice.'

There was a negotiator downstairs now, a woman. Smart move, Gillard thought, but he knew he had to pay attention to his captor, in whose unstable hands his life hung.

'Hex, it's me, Scarlett,' she called up. 'What on earth are you doing? This can all come to a peaceful end.'

'Judas! You joined in against me with the police.'

'No, we've got to talk this out,' Scarlett said. 'We are against violence, remember? That's what brought us all together at the refuge, and the women's group. You can't win by choosing male tactics. You're hurting women by doing this. Don't you see?'

'Scarlett, I've *already* won. Three dead abusers, three bastards who can never again hurt a woman. That's better than your load of leaflets, website pages, coffee mornings and funding drives, all that shit which is just us women preaching to each other while the men carry on!' She turned back to Gillard. 'Right, I've said my piece now. The bastards can have me.' She released her hold on his neck, and let him pull his head back in through the open window. She allowed him to clamber to his knees, but still held the Taser, its prongs sharp in his side, as he stood up, her human shield.

'Let go of the hostage. Now!' someone yelled, a male voice, drowning out Scarlett's softer tones. Gillard could now see down to the foot of the stairs, the two marksmen, four other officers, and at the open door the woman with hair both red and green. Claire Mulholland, and Gabby Underwood. And Sam, tears streaming down her face.

They're going to shoot. He suddenly knew it.

No!

The bangs were deafening.

Chapter Twenty-six

Five minutes earlier

Once the police had swarmed in at the base of the stairs, Sam was hustled away to her own kitchen by Family Liaison Officer Gabby Underwood. Sam held Grace tight in her arms, the baby crying gently as if somehow she knew that something momentous was happening. Sam was chewing her lip, never having imagined her own precious husband held hostage within her own home, the one place they should all be safe. Once the armed officers had arrived, two at the base of the stairs and three more outside, her heart sank. They could all hear Helen's voice, telling her story, mainly to Craig but audible beyond.

Eventually she persuaded Gabby to let her approach, to try to negotiate. But the police had already found someone else. Scarlett from the refuge. She said the right things, the voice of reasonableness, of calm and compromise. And when Helen began to rise to her feet, bringing Craig with her, she thought: it's all going to be over.

Then, the shouts from outside.

And then the shooting. Five deafening shots. Mayhem, screams, panic.

Her husband falling, to his knees, two bright red flowers blossoming in his abdomen. Helen dropping too. Blood everywhere.

'No, Craig!' she screamed, and then fainted.

–

Chief Constable Alison Rigby drew the meeting to order. Around the main boardroom table at Mount Browne was the silver commander in charge of the siege, the head of the firearms unit, and at her side, the head of the Independent Office for Police Conduct for Surrey. She stared at each of them in turn, her eyes a relentless blue.

'Gentlemen, this has been the most monumental screw-up I have ever come across. Right from the start it was badly organised. Little attempt was made to get civilians to safety. As a result of which Gillard's wife witnessed the shooting of her own husband, in her own home.' She addressed the head of the firearms unit directly and the man quailed. 'A bullet from one of your officers penetrated beyond the staircase and missed a week-old child by all of four inches.'

'To be fair, ma'am, we arrived to find a chaotic situation. We had assumed that the blood was mostly Gillard's, not that of his assailant, so we thought—'

'Negotiations were still continuing, that much was obvious,' Rigby said. 'Who gave the order to shoot?'

The silver commander and the head of the firearms unit looked at each other. Two thickset men, wondering how to shift the blame. 'I think we gave the men permission to fire when they had a clear line of sight,' the head of the firearms unit replied.

'You *think*? These decisions are supposed to be crystal clear. I have lost the best detective I ever employed because you failed in your job.'

'He's not dead, ma'am.'

'Perhaps not, but he'll never work again. A bullet in the spine, a punctured lung. He may never walk again. There are huge lessons to be learned here.'

–

Detective Inspector Claire Mulholland and DC Michelle Tsu were interviewing Rachel Meadows at Margaret Road Police Station in Guildford. This was the third time in two days, and once again Julia McGann was present as her solicitor.

'So, Ms Meadows you admit that you picked up Helen Smith from Hove after she had killed her father?' Claire asked.

'No, that's not what I said. What I said was I gave her a lift. I had no idea what she'd been doing. I just knew that she was distressed. And yes, she did talk about an argument with her father.'

'What about the blood?' Michelle asked. 'She must have been covered in blood.'

'I really didn't notice any,' Rachel said. 'She was wearing dark motorcycle leathers, so I suppose it didn't show.'

Michelle rolled her eyes in disbelief.

Claire said: 'DNA samples and blood matching that of Ken Stapleford were recovered from the Nissan Qashqai that you admit you were driving. And that's after it had been shampooed, scrubbed, and disinfected by you. There must've been a heck of a lot before.'

'As I say, that car had been driven by a lot of people before I got it.'

'I think my client has been very clear on this point,' interjected Julia McGann. 'She has repeatedly denied being involved. There is no crime in giving a friend a lift. She was also a psychotherapy client.'

'So why did you give her a lift up to Glasgow that Saturday evening?'

'I didn't. She drove herself while I stayed at home with my son.'

'What about this?' Michelle said passing across a photograph. 'It's an enlargement of an image taken by a speed camera in Staffordshire early on Sunday morning, which clearly shows there are two people in the vehicle which was returning from Glasgow.'

Rachel only glanced at the photo, before sliding it back. 'You can't tell who these people are.'

Claire held it up. 'While the passenger is obscured by shadow, there is enough light to see the driver is light-haired, like you, wearing a green sweater that matches one we found at your house—'

'Oh please,' Julia interjected. 'Millions of people have similar items in their wardrobe.'

'—and there is a distinctive bracelet, on your right wrist, on the steering wheel, which exactly matches one we found in your home.'

'You can't even see it!' Julia said.

Michelle smiled. 'Here is the enhanced close-up.' The bracelet with two distinctive gold stars was clearly caught in the early-morning sunlight. There was also a ring with a stone on the middle finger. 'You're wearing the exact same ring, right now. On the same finger.'

Rachel covered the ring with the other hand.

'Too late now,' Michelle said, wagging a finger.

'For the tape, the interviewee covered up the ring,' Claire said.

'You'll never get a conviction on that,' Julia said, folding her arms.

Claire smiled at her, and turned off the tape. 'You really don't do professional distancing, do you?'

'I'm her friend as well as her legal representative. You don't have to tell me how to do my job.'

Claire restarted the tape and turned her attention back to Rachel. 'Right, so if you say you didn't go to Glasgow on the Saturday night, where were you?'

'I was with Scarlett and some of the others at the refuge.' Rachel looked smug. 'They'd already given statements to that effect.'

'Actually, two of them have changed their minds,' Claire said.

'Who?'

'We will disclose that in due course.' She held up an envelope. 'These are new witness statements taken since the shooting. I think that rather opened the eyes of some of your former clients. At least they can tell the difference between right and wrong.'

Rachel extruded a sarcastic smile. 'You got nothing on me, absolutely nothing.'

'Really?' said Michelle. 'Well, I have news for you. Your friend Hex, Helen Smith, as of this morning, is now out of danger.'

Rachel looked shocked and said nothing. Julia nudged her subtly in the ribs, so she said: 'Thank God! Oh, I'm so relieved. I was really worried,' Rachel managed, putting a hand over her mouth. But to Claire's eye she looked annoyed about the woman's unexpected survival.

'Yes, she's even tougher than you thought,' said Michelle. 'Five bullets, and it looks like she's going to live.'

'Police bullets, fired as she was surrendering her hostage,' Julia reminded them. 'Another heavy-handed operation.'

'That's an inquiry for another day,' Claire said. 'But I was able to get fifteen minutes at her bedside this morning. She had some interesting things to say.'

'Like what?' Rachel said, with her arms folded.

'She said it was you that drove the car that ran over and killed Ross Macintosh.'

'I don't even know who you're talking about.'

'He's on the list,' Claire reminded her.

'What list is that?'

'The list that you handed to Helen Smith, on the Saturday afternoon when you picked her up in Hove. The list that she said you encouraged her to use to rid the world of male abusers.'

'Do you have this list?' Julia McGann asked. 'Can we be sure it ever even existed?'

'Unfortunately, we have been unable to recover any phones or computers belonging to Ms Meadows. But we have witness evidence from those who saw the list, and knew it existed,' Claire said. 'The vulnerable women, who you exploited in order to justify the killing spree that you wanted to arrange. They've seen through you, Rachel. The spell is broken.'

Claire had to give it to her. At a point like this, many suspects, even hardened male ones, would show some emotion. Worry, upset, even rage. Not Rachel Meadows. Utterly impassive, cool and detached, still with that hint of tousled glamour.

Michelle lifted a battered metal biscuit tin from the floor, and placed it on the table.

'Do you recognise this box?' she asked Rachel.

'No.'

'That's strange, because it was recovered from your office at the Reading Women's Domestic Violence Network.' She lifted off the lid, and revealed a dozen devices similar to the home-made stun gun that had been used by Helen Smith. 'Do you recognise these?'

'No,' she said.

'Your DNA is all over them. One of four boxes full of these dangerous weapons, more than fifty in total. We have reason to believe you made these illegal devices following instruction from a YouTube video. The specifications conform exactly.'

'No.'

'What were you planning to do with them?' Claire asked.

'No comment.'

'Are you planning a women's army? To fight male aggression? To right the wrongs of society?'

'That is simply conjecture,' Julia said. 'My client doesn't have to answer that.'

'All right,' Claire said. 'Let's get back to direct evidence. Ms Smith told me that on the same day she murdered her father, you and she drove to High Bank, Alderley Lane, Kirkintilloch, an address to which Mr Macintosh had recently moved. Ms Smith put on her wig, walked up to the door and rang the bell—'

Julia interrupted. 'Perhaps you could explain exactly how my client was able to find out where this man lives, if as you say he had only recently moved there?'

Claire knew exactly what the brief was angling at. That Rainy Macintosh had added her ex-husband's name and address to the fateful list. 'We are still investigating that,' she replied.

Rachel and Julia exchanged knowing glances.

Claire looked down at the statement in front of her. 'After ringing the bell, Ms Smith waited for the victim to come to the door, whereupon she explained that there had been an accident on the lane outside. Being a doctor, the victim walked down the drive followed by Ms Smith. Upon coming to the road, in front of the vehicle in which you were still in the driving seat, Mr Macintosh asked who was hurt. Ms Smith then said, and I quote: "You are, you abusive bastard." She then pressed into his back a home-made electric shock device. He collapsed and while he remained stunned you then drove slowly and deliberately over his body.' She looked up and stared at Rachel.

'What a pack of lies,' she said.

'Is it not also true, Ms Meadows, that you went to a 24/7 tyre-fitting place in Staffordshire, and paid cash to have all of the tyres changed on the Nissan on the following morning?'

'Let's see the evidence, detective inspector,' Julia said. 'Without it, this is simply a hopeless attempt by a troubled and imaginative young woman to shift the blame for crimes she has committed. However much we may sympathise with her awful straits as an abused youngster, we have to see this statement for what it is: desperation.'

Claire turned over the page on the statement. 'Ms Smith has, as you know, confessed to the killing of Gary Wray in Nightingale Park, Guildford. She said that you provided the electric scooter, and gave her a place to stay.'

'Well, I don't deny she stayed with me. She also stayed at Gary Wray's house after his death. She'd been a cleaner there for some of his tenants. She was frightened to return to her flat after what she said was her argument with her father, fearing that he might come after her.'

'He was dead!' Michelle exclaimed. 'Pinned to his settee with his own carving knife.'

'Look,' Rachel replied calmly. 'We all know that now, but I just trusted her at the time.'

'Was she staying with you on the night before she was shot?' Claire asked.

'Yes, but that morning I advised her to leave, because of all the police activity locally.'

'You did that simply to protect yourself, didn't you?' Michelle asked.

'No.'

'Did you know she was going to go to Mrs Gillard's home?'

'No. I wasn't aware that she was cleaning for them. Scarlett handled all the agency work. Obviously, had I known I would have suggested anywhere but there!'

'She was by all accounts upset, when she arrived. She said she'd been kicked out.'

'That's not how I would describe it.'

'All right,' said Claire, looking down at her notes. 'Let's go back to the weekend of the killings. She said that you persuaded her to come with you to Birmingham, on the Monday morning.'

'That's not true. I just let her use the car.'

'So you were at home on Monday?'

Rachel thought for a moment. 'Not all day, but yes.'

'With your son, Jack.'

'Yes.'

'That's very interesting, Rachel, because Helen Smith told us that Jack was in the car with you two for the attack in Birmingham, and afterwards all three of you went up to see your aunt, at her farm near Bakewell.'

At this, both Rachel and Julia blanched.

'We've traced and talked to your aunt, just half an hour ago,' Claire said. 'And she confirmed that she babysat Jack for two hours while you drove up onto the moors.'

'This is utter nonsense,' Rachel said, weakly. Claire thought she hadn't even convinced herself.

'And this is where it gets really interesting, for you both,' Michelle said, leaning forward on her elbows, and pointing her pen at Rachel and then at Julia.

Claire continued: 'Helen Smith told us that you had yourself claimed to have killed an abusive man, two years earlier, and were eager to show her how it didn't have to weigh on your mind for the rest of your life. You drove her up onto the moors to show her the disused mine shaft down which you tossed his body.'

'That is ridiculous.' Rachel turned to Julia, but the solicitor was staring forlornly at the table.

'Derbyshire Constabulary has opened an inquiry into the matter, at our request,' Claire said. 'But I don't think we will find the body of a man, will we Rachel? The body we will find will be that of the missing eighteen-year-old girl, Destiny Flynn.'

Chapter Twenty-seven

The intensive care unit bustled with medical professionals as Sam, with Grace in her arms, followed the doctor to see her husband. She was being allowed five minutes only, as he was shortly to be prepared for a second operation to remove a bullet. When she saw Craig, grey and shrunken in the bed, she hardly recognised him. Wired up to machines, heavily sedated, he didn't even seem to be aware of her arrival. She had been told that his heart had stopped twice, the second time while in theatre, but he had fought back. One bullet had passed through his left hand, into the left side of his chest and through his lung before hitting a vertebra, and then passing out of him and into Helen Smith. The second bullet, fired from outside the house, had passed through his shoulder before hitting Helen in the jaw. Three other bullets hit her but not him.

After calling his name a couple of times, quietly, Sam sat gently on the bed next to him and held his hand. She squeezed his fingers and got a response from him, his fingers tightening slightly. There was a fluttering of his eyelashes too.

'Craig, I thought you were going to die. I couldn't believe what happened. There was such confusion. But I saw enough to see that you were trying to save your captor's life. For all that she had done, you were aware that she was not evil, just very damaged. Manipulated perhaps, by others. I love you for that, even though I'm angry with you too.' She wiped tears from her eyes. 'For putting yourself in danger by going up the stairs to her when you didn't have to, by working so bloody hard that I couldn't even reach you early enough to warn you.' She stroked the baby's head. 'The doctors tell me that your spinal cord is damaged, which means you might not be able to walk again. I shall try to be brave, for you, and for Grace. I can't imagine what the future holds for us, but there is one very important thing to make us look on the bright side.' She kissed Grace on the side of her head, and the sleeping child stretched and gurgled as Sam laid her down on her father's chest. 'Give Daddy a kiss, Grace,' Sam said, tears streaming down her face. 'Hold him close, because he risked his life to make us safe. And with enough of our love, he will get better.' She paused to still her sobs, and then kissed him on the cheek. 'Craig, I love you. We will get through this.'

Chapter Twenty-eight

A month later

An unseasonal dusting of March snow covered the Derby-shire Moors, as crime scene chief Harry Abbott watched his investigators. They worked hard in the biting easterly wind, their Tyvek suits billowing, to access an ancient lead mineshaft. Getting exactly the right location had been difficult, even with the help of testimony from Helen Smith, who remained in hospital. The weeks had passed until the discovery of a vital clue: a single size three girl's training shoe, close to the entrance of one shaft. Sodden, discoloured, and with its lining beginning to dissolve, the trainer still had information to offer. The laces were done up. The chances were that this shoe was lost while the body was being moved.

It was a further two hours before the next break-through. Abbot had persuaded a skinny police recruit, just nineteen, but an experienced potholer, to be lowered down the awkwardly aligned and narrow shaft. It was fifteen degrees from vertical for the first twenty feet, and then doubled back on itself. Light could not penetrate to the bottom which was reckoned to be sixty feet below the surface.

As the lad was lowered down, Abbott looked up. Two police vans and a grey people carrier were approaching on the narrow track from Bakewell.

'Looks like he's here,' Abbott said to his deputy.

The vehicles arrived and a bunch of well-known senior Derbyshire officers emerged. Two unknown female plain-clothes officers, well wrapped up in coats, emerged from the people carrier and went to the rear door, which had a ramp. After a minute or two they extracted and pushed round a wheelchair, with considerable difficulty, over the rough hummocky grass to within ten yards of the shaft. In the wheelchair sat a rugged-looking man in his fifties, just wearing a suit despite the cold.

'Hello Harry, I'm DCI Gillard,' he said. 'Have you found anything?'

They showed him the shoe, now in a clear plastic evidence bag.

'The size looks about right,' he said, then gazed across the moors to the soft snowy horizon. 'But even if yields a DNA sample, we need more.'

Just then, a shout came from down the shaft, and Abbott went over to the edge to hear what was being said. He listened with mounting excitement and hurriedly made his way back over to Gillard. 'Human remains, sir. Probably female, and a matching training shoe on the other foot.'

'I want to see the shaft,' Gillard said, and turned to one of the female detectives with him, who'd introduced herself as Michelle Tsu. She passed him a pair of crutches, and the other detective, DI Claire Mulholland, helped him to his feet. Gillard was clearly in a lot of pain, and each faltering step showed in the set of his jaw. Laboriously, he made his way over the snowy tussocks, and was helped down into the depression from which the shaft ran.

'What are the chances of DNA surviving down there?' he asked.

'It's quite acidic soil,' Abbott replied. 'But there's bound to be some part of her that is not deteriorated too much. And then we still have the teeth.'

'If it's who I think it is, there are no dental records. We tried that route already. But we do have a DNA elimination sample.'

'Do you have any suspects in mind?' Abbott asked.

Gillard looked across at him, and gave a shrewd smile. 'Oh yes. One is already on police bail, but I'm itching to arrest the other. Julia McGann. The moment we get a DNA confirmation just let me know.'

He turned and beckoned Michelle and Claire to help him make his laborious way back to the wheelchair. As they began to manhandle the chair towards the van, Abbott called out to him: 'I'll send Surrey Police a copy of anything that we find, sir.'

Gillard leaned, as best he could and looked over the back of the wheelchair. 'I'll be back,' he said. 'I'm not going anywhere.'

Epilogue

Rachel Meadows never admitted her guilt, but was sentenced to thirty-five years for the murder by ligature strangulation of Destiny Flynn, and of conspiracy to murder three men. When her computer was eventually found, hidden in an outbuilding at the women's refuge in Farnborough, there were plans for the creation of a nationwide female vigilante force, armed with stun guns to mete out justice to suspected abusers. She had written a long manifesto, ready to encourage female recruits from all over the country, starting with universities and colleges. She also had a slogan: *If the police won't act, we will.*

Julia McGann confessed to her part in the plot, and admitted that it was she who killed gangster Terence Bonner two years earlier with a smuggled gun. She was sentenced to twenty-five years. Helen Smith's plea of diminished responsibility was accepted by the court in the killing of her own father Ken Stapleton. However, she was convicted of murder, attempted murder and conspiracy to murder in the cases of Gary Wray, Ross Macintosh and Prabir Sengupta. She will serve her sentence of life imprisonment in a women's secure psychiatric hospital.

Rainy Macintosh was reprimanded for her role in obstructing the investigation, and was taken off front-line duties. But her abuse of police resources to help Loti Sengupta was never discovered. Craig Gillard remains on sick leave, and is undertaking intense physiotherapy to regain the use of his legs. The Independent Office for Police Conduct has launched an investigation into the botched firearms operation. In the meantime, Claire Mulholland has been promoted to DCI, pending news on Gillard's recovery.

And that went better than anyone expected. Gillard took on his physiotherapy with determination and good humour. He was warned it would be tough, but put in long hours on the exercises along with some in-patient time at the spinal injury unit, which included an operation to repair a damaged vertebra. Determined not to lose the use of his legs, he amazed doctors with the speed of his improvement. He was told that running ever again was out of the question, and cycling doubtful. Swimming, though, was definitely going to be part of his regime.

Chief Constable Alison Rigby only waited two weeks before sending Gillard some cold cases to review. 'A brain that good cannot be allowed to go to waste,' she told him. He and Sam spend much more time together than at any time in their marriage, and are both delighting in their daughter. Grace loves nothing more than to sit cradled in her father's lap while he re-examines Surrey's unsolved crimes on his computer. As Sam has wondered: 'Maybe she'll grow up to be a detective herself, one day?'

An Excerpt from The Two Deaths of Ruth Lyle

The first instalment of the upcoming series, The Talantire Thrillers by Nick Louth

Chapter One

Saturday, seven p.m. Good, bang on time. The suspect's car, a dark BMW estate, slid into the car park of the Royal Oak. The rendezvous chosen carefully. Halfway to Dartmoor, she wouldn't be recognised. Detective Inspector Jan Talantire watched from her own darkened vehicle, in the shadow of the pub's gable. Ignition off, no lights. She was just thirty yards away, but able to scribble down the registration number in her pad. Six years old, one rear brake light not working. The BMW came to rest in the position she had expected, opposite the lounge, nose towards the pub so the driver could see in. The suspect was silhouetted in the glare of the pub window, broad-shouldered, hair short at the sides, shaped above, and a neat beard. Her electronic intel looked correct, so far. She waited as he emerged from the car. Tall, tight trousers that gripped at thigh and calf, some kind of formal jacket. He made his way around to the rear of the vehicle, opened the tailgate. Bent over whatever was inside, both hands busy.

Interesting.

The suspect closed the tailgate then made his way, empty handed, into the pub, wiped his feet carefully, and could soon be seen through the front window. He took a seat within view of his vehicle. Clearly wary, no drink as yet. A bit nervy, perhaps. Good, he appeared to think the stakes were high. So did she. Things had gone on long enough. She had just ten minutes to wait, her decision. A policy. She risked the interior light, which she was pretty sure could not be seen from inside the pub. Took a final glance in the mirror at her disguise. Long indulgently dangly earrings, chestnut hair, high-lighted just yesterday, full bodied, down at her shoulders, the work ponytail banished. Eye make-up, fairly extensive eyeshadow, eyeliner underneath to emphasise her big blue eyes. And lipstick; not the full crimson, but a softer shade, which she reapplied quickly. A small handbag, containing both work and personal phones. She took a quick glance at each, then switched them off. It was something she rarely did. But this time it was essential not to be disturbed.

She smoothed down her trouser suit, checked her lap for crumbs from the cereal bar she had gulped down as a precaution against a rushed exit. Slid down the sleeves of her white blouse, and added a bracelet. Nothing flashy, but smart. She pulled off her flat work shoes, and slid on the royal blue high heels she had kept in the passenger footwell. That would add a couple of inches to her height, making her five-ten. She saw the suspect check his watch. Two minutes to go. Okay, time to make her move. She slid out of the door, into the March chill, walked gingerly around the puddles and made her way to the pub entrance.

The warmth of the place slid over her, as she turned to the table. She was within five yards before he looked up. A cautious smile.

'Hi, you must be Jan,' he said, standing up and offering his hand. Nice smile, great teeth. His profile said over six feet, but he was barely taller than she was. Maybe five-ten at most. A lie, but maybe a forgivable one. As long as he hadn't lied about his age. That looked spot on.

'Glad to meet you, Adam. I'm sorry I'm a bit late.' It was deliberate, a calibrated time to build expectations.

'I hadn't noticed.' *Liar. But a nice liar.* 'Glass of wine?' he asked, getting ready to head to the bar. *Imposing expectations, not so good.*

'They have a nice plum porter at the moment, so I'll go for a half of that.' Her first challenge. He hid his surprise well. She sat and glanced down at the menu, but with a sidelong glance checked him out as he headed to the bar. Yes, the trousers were tight, but at least properly belted. Firm bum. Clearly fit. Some kind of stain near the vent of his jacket. *Come on, turn it off, you're not at work now.* But still she saw him looking back at her reflection in the bar mirror. Good sign.

Back with the drinks he sat down, looked through the menu and asked: 'Did you say you were a vegetarian?'

She laughed. 'No, no, not at all. You must be mixing me up with someone else.' *Come on Jan, be fair. He's probably got a few dates on the go.*

'Sorry,' he laughed, and flexed his eyebrows in acknowledgement. That attractive smile again. She found herself grinning back at him. *Steady on, Jan. This is date one, five minutes in.*

'Try the pan fried pork chop with garlic mash,' she said. 'Very good.'

'Garlic?' he asked, leaving the rest unspoken. Flirtatious. *No, I wouldn't kiss you tonight if you were glazed with honey.*

'Or there is the home-made pasta vongole. If you like seafood.'

'I love seafood,' he said.

The conversation flowed. Until the inevitable question.

'So Jan, your profile said you worked with social services?'

Here we go. 'That's basically right.'

'So with adults or kids?'

'A bit of both really. Of course I spend my day like most of us do behind the computer terminal bashing away on a keyboard. A bit boring, really.' This was a line she had polished with all the previous dates. She wasn't going to tell him what she really did. Kiss of death on the first date, surely.

'Yeah, tell me about it,' he said. 'I'm a technical editor. For consumer electronics. So what about this kid that disappeared? Is that one of your responsibilities?' he asked.

Eek, that's a bit near the knuckle. 'I'm hoping that case doesn't fall to me.'

Alice Watkins, aged seven, had disappeared a day and half ago. Playing in the garden of her home one minute. Gone the next. It had made the papers already, but was at this stage still primarily a uniform job. Door-to-door, trawling the stream at the bottom of the garden. Appeals for witnesses. But the anxiety had spread through the entire Barnstaple office, amongst not only all the officers, but the receptionists right through to the man who fixed the photocopier.

'I suppose she's dead,' Adam said, as he called the waitress over.

'Let's hope not.' She changed the subject, and asked him about his work. He was a technical editor. 'I used to be based at home but it was driving me mad, so I rented a shared office. I found it was important to be able to relax when I was at home, knowing I wasn't at work. Different headspaces, know what I mean?' That smile again.

They talked about music, and found Latin jazz in common. He was impressed to hear that she ran, and even more impressed by the distances. 'I'm a member of Black Bull Harriers,' she said.

'I used to run a bit, and go to the gym. Bit more of a fair-weather exerciser, I suppose.'

They ordered and the food came quickly; she didn't even notice what she was eating.

'So tell me about your day, Jan,' he asked. This was good, and a nice change. She had suffered at the hands of conversational broadcasters, who didn't listen but simply waited for the next opportunity to talk. There was Brian, who had droned on and on about investment and pension strategies, and Aaron, who had stared almost without interruption at her breasts while describing his software sales business. And it wasn't as if the topography beneath her peach-coloured jumper was particularly mountainous. Still, like Everest, they were simply there. Presumably to be conquered. Not something Aaron would ever get the chance to do.

'Managed to get out of the office a bit today,' she said. 'Can't tell you about the case, you know, data protection.' *Saw an old man dead, sitting on the toilet with his trousers round his ankles. What a stench.*

He smiled and nodded. 'I was correcting the English instructions for a tumble dryer which had originally been written in Chinese. It's bread and butter for now but it's difficult to see this kind of work lasting once artificial intelligence gets going. I'll be out of a job.'

Jan went to the toilet. She felt his eyes on her as she walked away from him. Once she was inside she switched on her work phone, an act of habit. Three text messages and a voicemail from DC Stephen Dowling, who was on duty covering Barnstaple and Ilfracombe tonight. Dowling was just twenty-two, a probationer, and had been on one of her situational judgement training courses. She had given him a helping hand over the first few months, but this was now getting a bit out of hand. She was on a date, for heaven's sake. With a sigh she checked the message. 'Sorry to bother you when you're off duty, ma'am, but I'd appreciate a bit of help. I got two uniforms here and a dead body.'

She rang him. 'Ma'am, thanks for calling back.' His voice was high pitched, squeaky almost, as he gabbled away. 'We've got a big crime scene here in Ilfracombe, and I mean massive. I'm a bit out of my depth. DI Lockhart is the duty DI but he's stuck out in Snozzle and told me to get on with it.'

St Austell, locally known as Snozzle, was down into Cornwall, two hours' drive from Ilfracombe.

'What's happened?'

'We've got an elderly lady. She's been stabbed, blood everywhere.'

She looked into the bathroom mirror, seeing tiny creases in her brow. The arrival of work mode. In the harsh light of the bathroom her eyeshadow made her looked like a panda, and at this rate just as likely to get a mate.

'Okay, don't touch anything—'

'And, sorry ma'am, I've been sick.'

'Please tell me, not on the crime scene.'

'I got out as far as the hall. It's down me jacket though.'

Fantastic. Amateur night. 'Let me speak to the senior uniform.'

'There's only me and PC Moody at the moment.'

Christ, it gets worse. Philip Moody was even more junior than Dowling, and dim with it. Talantire stared into the washbasin, seeing her date going down the plughole.

'What about CSI?' she asked.

'They can't get here until morning. The main crew is in Exeter, because there's been a hit-and-run with two injuries, and the second crew's in Penzance.' Another Saturday night escapade. *Why don't we have enough officers?*

'All right, Stephen. I'll be there in half an hour.'

'Thank you so much, ma'am, it means a lot to me.'

'I'm not doing it to help you, Stephen, I'm doing it because it needs doing right, and if we get it done right now that saves an awful lot of fuss tomorrow. Is the crime scene secure?'

'Yes. It's taped off. We called a locksmith to get a padlock, he'll be along directly.'

'Good. Have you rung the duty forensic pathologist?'

'Yes. I'm waiting for confirmation whether he can come.'

'Have you taken some photos?'

'Yeah, but we've got no evidence markers.'

'But I take it you do have booties and gloves?'

'Gloves, yeah, but I got puke on the first pair and I spose that's got my DNA, and we didn't know we needed booties when we first went in, so there's footprints and that.'

Jan could only imagine what mess the crime scene might be in. Thank God she had only drunk half of her beer. She didn't like anyone smelling alcohol on her breath. She splashed water on her face, and then with rapid and practised movements used some cream and make-up removal pads to tone down the slap. She looked at the lipstick marks left on the tissues and wondered if she would ever see Adam again. She hoped so.

Heading back into the restaurant she saw him playing with his phone. He looked up and smiled, then did a double-take to see her emerging workaday face.

'I'm really sorry, Adam. Something's come up at work. I have to go.'

'Really?' He clearly didn't believe her and looked a little downcast. 'Is it the little girl?' he asked, staring at his hands. It was almost as if he wanted it to be the case, something definitely serious enough to justify abandoning the date. Anything as long as it wasn't about him.

'Look. I like you, and I think we should meet again. But I have some secrets I can't share with you right now.' She pulled out a twenty and a ten, which she guessed would cover what they'd eaten so far.

'No, it's fine. I'll get it,' he said.

'No, you won't. I insist. I'll message you later in the week.' As she left, she felt his eyes on her. Not assessing her figure this time, but assessing whether she had told him the truth. That it clearly mattered to him was a good sign. Maybe not all was lost.

Chapter Two

It was a half-hour drive to Ilfracombe, and she was in her own car. At least she didn't have to put up with the annoying ticking from the unmarked Ford she had been allocated. Once the heater started up, it sounded like a bomb waiting to go off. The grease monkeys hadn't been able to replicate the noise when they drove it, and hadn't found a cause. She used the hands-free phone to ring into the control room in Exeter, to find out the state of play. The male call handler summarised what they knew so far: 'Female, mid-sixties, founded stabbed in a rental property in Mercer Lane, in the town centre. The alarm was raised by a neighbour who had heard a violent argument two days ago—'

'Two *days* ago!'

'Yes. And hadn't seen the lady emerge from the house. He knocked on the door this morning, and again this afternoon, and finally rang us on the non-emergency number shortly after five. Our first officer, PC Moody, arrived at 8.15 p.m. and shortly after effected an entry.'

'And the rest, as they say, is histrionics.'

Jan thanked him, rang off and checked the time. The initial call was nearly four hours ago. Not an outrageously slow response for a non-emergency call. In some parts of the country they were not answered at all. Fortunately she always kept a go-bag of forensic coveralls, booties and gloves in her own car as well as in her official unmarked vehicle. Next to it in the boot was a holdall containing wellies, torch, DNA swabbing kit, yellow plastic evidence markers and fingerprint lift gel strips.

She arrived at the address. Mercer Lane was about three streets back from the harbour, a narrow and twisting lane, jumbled with terraced Victorian cottages, the odd lock-up garage, but hardly any on-street parking. Two squad cars were now there, blocking the road, and there were five uniformed officers visible, along with a sizeable crowd of rubberneckers. Beyond them she recognised the looming presence of Inspector T. P. Carnegie, and heaved a sigh of relief. Known universally as Wigwam because of his initials, Carnegie was six foot two, mid-fifties and bespectacled, with thinning hair. He was operationally a safe pair of hands, if only he would keep them to himself in the office. Never turn your back on Wigwam was one of the first pieces of advice she was offered when she started at Barnstaple five years ago. To be fair, Wigwam was much better behaved these days after Maddy had 'had words' with him a year ago, but a reputation like that once earned wasn't easily lost.

Carnegie was talking to Dowling and Moody, gathered around the entrance to a stone-built house. Bluebird Cottage, according to the glazed tile sign outside. The wooden door was slightly ajar and light from inside filtered out into the street.

'Very kind of you to turn up, Jan,' Carnegie said.

'That's all right, I wasn't doing anything much.'

'We're a bit stretched here.'

'Retched, I heard.'

Carnegie rolled his eyes in agreement. The smell of vomit by the doorway was overpowering. She glanced at

Dowling, who looked decidedly sheepish, in a damp zip-up fleece jacket that he had clearly made some attempt to clean up.

'Who's been inside?' she asked him.

'Just us two,' Dowling said.

'Show me your holiday snaps, then.'

'It's pretty ghastly,' Dowling said, passing across his phone. She swiped through half a dozen images. A blood-drenched woman was lying spreadeagled but fully dressed on a kitchen table, with eighteen inches of a wooden crucifix protruding from her chest. The Christ figure in silver rested with his feet on her blood-soaked blouse.

She blinked away her shock. 'Right. I'll go and suit up.'

'I'll sign you in, then ma'am,' said PC Moody, shrugging a clipboard.

Five minutes later, now wearing her Tyvek coveralls, gloves and booties, and armed with gel lifts and swabs, Jan made her way back through the growing crowd, past the uniformed officers and up the step. She eased the door open. It was an unusual cottage, that was for sure. A short hallway, with a kitchen off left, but her eye was drawn to the long lounge with a high vaulted ceiling, and tall narrow windows at the far end. To the right, a spiral staircase in metal led up to a gallery bedroom. The flagstoned floor was marked with bloody footprints, from what might well be constabulary boots, as well as the spattered remains of Dowling's lunch. Before moving in, she took a gel lift from the light switch by the door, and followed it with a DNA swab. She didn't have any stepping plates, but carefully placed her feet around the right-hand edge of the hallway. There were two women's coats on the coat rack, and she took fibre lifts from the collars. She moved forward methodically, taking samples as she went, finishing with the round brass handle of the kitchen door from which the bloody footprints originated.

Only then did she allow herself to ease open the door and take in the full horror of the crime scene. The poor woman had been gagged with a pair of tights, and from the smell had clearly lost control of her bowels in her final moments of life. Jan set down plastic evidence markers then concentrated on taking pictures, more than a hundred images for this room alone. She crouched for low angles, and stood on tiptoe for top-down perspectives. Under the table she spotted a handbag and retrieved it, putting it into a plastic evidence bag. *If CSI can't get here until tomorrow, what other evidence can I secure that may be lost by then?* There was one crucial element.

Time of death.

The longer the delay, the harder it can be to establish exactly when the victim has died. Though there are standard countdown calculators of time against body temperature, these can be thrown by environmental factors. If the ambient temperature changes, because for example the central heating comes on, a body may retain heat for longer. She looked around the kitchen. A rather swish newly installed set of cupboards, worktops and drawers. Hardwood. A well-equipped rental, with lots of money spent. Loads of pans hanging from ceiling hooks, Brabantia utensils on a wall rack. Knives, lots of 'em. This wasn't just domestic envy, it gave her an idea. She did fingerprint lifts of the two principal drawers before sliding them open. Bingo! She was right.

A meat thermometer. This was a brand-new digital device with a steel probe the size of a darning needle. She turned it on, then noted the room temperature, 16°C. Carefully she approached the body, hoping that she wasn't going to get into trouble with the forensic pathologist for making a fresh hole in the victim. With her gloved hand, she lifted a section of unbloodied blouse, exposing the woman's waist. She rested a thumb against the pale skin. Cool, but not cold. Flexible, so presumably beyond rigor mortis. She took a photograph of the unblemished skin, before pressing in the long probe to its full depth. She waited while the digital readout temperature climbed. Then when it had stabilised, she photographed the display. It showed 19.2°C, about half a living body temperature. She'd have to look it up precisely, but it didn't seem out of kilter with the reported witness statement, hearing the noise of an argument two days ago. That could well be when she died.

She was just wondering what else she could do when the phone rang. Detective Superintendent Michael Wells, her boss.

'Hello Jan, thank you for giving up your Saturday night to help us out here.'

'I'd like not to make a habit of it,' she said, looking at the impaled body in front of her. 'I'd rather be sitting at home watching *Strictly*.'

'Well, as you are aware we are having a resourcing crisis.'

'That's been true for as long as I've been in the police service, sir. With all due respect I think it's high time that the police and crime commissioner managed to get us some more resources. Half the time we've got one overnight duty DI covering the entire region. It's not enough.'

'I hear what you're saying. Jan. Now, about this body. I was getting garbled reports about a crucifix of all things.'

'Well whatever else was garbled, it wasn't that. Sir, this is the clearest case of murder I've ever seen. We need CSI here as soon as you can possibly get them, along with the duty forensic pathologist.'

'Well, we've got a couple of crime scene investigators on their way now. I understand Dr Piers Holcomb will be there by eight a.m. It sounds like we need to keep the body in situ until he is there. And Jan, I'd like you to be SIO. Carnegie and the uniforms will hold the fort overnight but I'd like you to be in charge by the time Dr Holcomb arrives.'

'All right, sir.' She had been due the whole weekend off, but had already accepted from the first moment she started removing her make-up in the Royal Oak that she was going to be hard at work until her scheduled duties resumed on Monday.

Jan looked around to ensure she hadn't brought anything into the crime scene apart from the evidence markers. She then carefully retraced her steps. Emerging outside into the narrow street, she was blinded by the flashguns of the press. Though kept back a good twenty yards by the crime tape, they were using their long-lens cameras to good effect. What they really needed was a good crime-scene tent, so they could work around the cottage entrance unobserved. As things stood, residents were staring out of upstairs windows opposite, and could see exactly who came and went. There were a dozen uniformed constables present now along with Inspector Carnegie.

She called him over. 'We're going to need to have the houses opposite cleared. We can't have all these people gawking down at us. And seeing how cramped the street is, we won't be able to get the mobile incident room down here.'

'I've already made arrangements for tomorrow,' he said, pointing down a narrow alleyway. 'We're taking over the Stag and Hounds in Exeter Row. I've notified the pub company.'

Jan remembered a good night in the Stag, well over a decade ago when she and fellow trainee Caroline had gone, off duty, to see some heavy metal band and got very drunk with some locals. They only narrowly escaped being arrested when the police arrived after a window got broken outside.

'That should be perfect. Refreshment on tap,' she said.

'Sorry to disappoint, it's closed for refurbishment, but they haven't yet started on it. There's no booze on the premises.'

'Spoilsports,' she said.

'It'll be ready first thing, and it's only fifty yards from the scene.'

'Great. I'm heading off home now for a bit of shut-eye.'

'Thanks for coming in, Jan. Much appreciated.' He pointed to a bin bag by the side of a patrol car. 'Stick your overalls in there.'

She passed him the evidence bag containing the handbag. 'I hope there is some ID in there. We need to find out who she is.'

'The landlord's emailing me the rental contract. Tenant wasn't a local, apparently. Been here seven or eight months.' He shrugged the bag. 'I've appointed one of the PCSOs as evidence officer until tomorrow. He only did the course last week.'

As Jan walked away towards the car she reflected how few experienced officers there were around. Everyone seemed to be straight off a training course. That's all very well getting to use the latest gizmos, but there is no substitute for experience.

When she was inside the vehicle she checked her personal phone for messages on the dating app. Nothing from Adam. Oh well, probably the end of that. They hadn't even swapped surnames, so at least her cover was intact. She drove home, and got in about a quarter to eleven. She was just cleaning her teeth when her phone buzzed. A message through the dating app from Adam.

'Hi. Hope work wasn't too onerous. Meet up again next week?'

She grinned into the mirror, a little beard of white foam dripping from her chin.

Chapter Three

Mercer Lane was still taped off with two officers in attend-
ance when Jan arrived shortly before eight on Sunday
morning. As she got out of the car she met Detective
Sergeant Maddy Wells and DC Dave Nuttall, both from
the Barnstaple team, along with a new officer, wearing a
trouser suit and a fawn hijab.

'Jan, this is Primrose Chen, she's the new digital evidence officer,' Maddy said. 'Joining us from the Met, no
less.'

'Welcome, Primrose. You've caught us on a very busy
day, so you'll be straight into the action.'

'That's perfectly fine,' she said, with a slight American
accent. 'I like to be busy.'

'Then you'll love CID,' said Nuttall, his trademark
leather jacket unzipped to reveal a denim shirt that
matched his ripped jeans. He was as usual chewing gum.
He was late forties, thick-framed glasses, dyed dark hair
slicked back, like a superannuated teddy boy.

'Where's Wigwam?' Jan asked Maddy.

'He's going to join us later on.' Seeing the puzzled
expression on Primrose's face Maddy explained how the
uniformed inspector had gained his nickname. 'What
you'll find, Primrose, is that it's best not to use nicknames
to people's faces.'

'Especially if your nickname is wanker,' Nuttall interjected.

Maddy and Jan shared a glance. Primrose's face had
coloured slightly, as she glanced towards Nuttall.

'Don't worry, he's just trying to be funny,' Jan said.

'Of course, we'd never use that as a nickname, Primrose,' Maddy whispered, leaning towards her. 'The reason
being that there are no end of wankers in Devon and
Cornwall Police, and we wouldn't know who you were
talking about.'

'Right, let's get this show on the road,' Jan said. Nuttall
had the keys and let them into the pub through the side
door, and it all came flooding back to her: the smell of stale
beer, the sticky carpet with its paisley pattern designed to
hide the stains. The hand pumps and the taps, this week's
guest ale or cider sensation. Above them a low nicotine-
stained ceiling with its exposed mock beams. The round
tables with curlicue cast-iron legs, perfect for smashing
your shins on and far too heavy to throw. The jukebox
was gone, replaced by a quiz machine. There was no sign
of the pool table either.

Maddy went to the windows and drew the curtains,
while Nuttall and Primrose brought in whiteboards,
magnets, paper and marker pens from the unmarked van
outside. Jan set up a laptop and projector screen, and in
ten minutes they were ready to run.

'Right, I can confirm that Dr Holcomb is there now,'
Jan said. She opened an envelope and pulled out a sheaf of
photo enlargements, fixing them to the whiteboard with
magnets. Right at the centre she put a shocking image
of the poor woman impaled by the crucifix, gagged and
drenched in blood.

'It's like something from a horror film,' Nuttall said. 'I wonder if her head spun round.'

Jan stared him down. 'A bit of respect, Dave, if you don't mind.'

From an envelope she pulled out half a dozen clear plastic evidence bags. 'Mobile phone, purse with bank cards, passport. All the usual stuff, but no driving licence. She is Mrs Ruth Lyle, aged sixty-nine, a widow, formerly of 106, Alexandra Terrace, Exeter. According to the landlady she'd been living here since June last year.'

'I'll do a financial check,' Maddy said, 'and follow up all the ID information.'

'Good. Primrose, I need to get inside that phone and find out who had been messaging her, any images or videos and of course the movements of that phone in the last fourteen days.'

'Okay,' Primrose said. 'I'm told that you now have a data kiosk in Barnstaple. Otherwise I'll have to send it to Exeter.'

'Yes, we got a spanking new Aceso Dual, although hardly anybody knows how to use it yet.'

'Wow, that's a cool device. It can be used in the field as well as a desktop. I'm quite familiar with it.'

'Dave, I want you to liaise with the uniforms, your immediate task is finding next of kin. I also want you to find out everything you can about the building: who had access, where the keys were kept, and run a criminal background check on the landlord. And you will need to get a DNA sample from him.'

'Right, boss, I'm on it,' he said.

'Finally, we need to find any CCTV in the area. The assailant could only have come from two directions, and there must be some coverage. I'll be asking Inspector Carnegie to co-ordinate that... ah, speak of the devil.'

Carnegie arrived in his usual baggy suit, with a colourful tie – balloons and bottles of champagne – so badly knotted so it didn't lie flat on his shirt. 'I'm sorry I'm late, Jan. It's taken a while to persuade the neighbours opposite the crime scene to vacate their house.' He glanced at the whiteboard, the photographs and the name of the victim now written up in marker pen.

'Ruth Lyle? That's a bit of a coincidence.'

'Why?'

'It's the same name as a young girl who was murdered in the town half a century ago.'

Nuttall snorted with derision, and began to chuckle.

Carnegie fixed him with a stare. 'Have you not heard of the famous case, Nuttall? I would have thought a sharp sleuth like you would be aware of some of the criminal history of this county.'

Nuttall shrugged and continued chewing. 'Well, it's hardly the same person, is it?'

'Obviously not. But I was brought up here in Ilfracombe and my father was the coroner at that time, and I can tell you that the crucifix murder was a pretty big deal in 1973.'

'Did you say crucifix?' Jan asked. She removed one of the enlargements on the whiteboard, and handed it to the inspector. 'Our victim was impaled with this, which to me looks like a crucifix.'

'Good Lord,' Carnegie said, and grabbed a seat back to steady himself. 'Good God.' He went pale.

'Hold on a second,' said Maddy Wells, typing at her laptop. 'Yes, there it is. In the *Devon Argus* newspaper database. Headlined "The Devon Vampire Murder", it says Ruth Lyle was sixteen when she was found dead on April Fool's Day 1973 with a crucifix in her heart—'

'Hang on, that's exactly fifty years last Thursday,' Jan said.

'—The crime was unsolved for six years until a youth by the name of Gawain Entwistle confessed to the killing. Entwistle, a neighbour of the victim, was considered retarded—'

Nuttall sucked his teeth. 'Ooh, you can't say that nowadays.'

'—and was sentenced to life imprisonment,' Maddy continued.

They were all staring at Wigwam, who looked like he was in shock. 'Are you all right?' Jan asked.

'I just cannot believe this,' he muttered. 'That case devastated Ilfracombe, the entire community was in shock. And now, fifty years later…' He stared back at the whiteboard, his eyes glazed.

'It's a very long time for a copycat killer to wait,' Nuttall said.

'True,' Jan said. Nuttall might be annoying, but there was nothing wrong with his detective antenna.

Carnegie was holding the photograph and his hands were shaking. 'I just can't believe this. I was only six when it happened, but my mother told me that this case almost destroyed their marriage.'

'Listen to this,' Maddy said. 'The original killing took place in the Dimpsey Chapel. Where is that?' She turned to Carnegie.

'I've heard of it, but I don't think it exists now,' Wigwam said. 'Probably demolished after the killing.'

Primrose was busy at her laptop. 'I've found a record online from the Ilfracombe Civic Society. The Dimpsy

Chapel was originally known as St James without West-gate.' She looked up. 'Such crazy names in this country.'

'Dimpsy means shaded or dusky,' Jan said. 'Westgate still exists and was presumably part of the old mediaeval wall. So if without means outside, it's pretty close by.'

Maddy was busy on her laptop as they were talking. 'St James without Westgate is on a map from the local antiquarians. I just found it.' She squinted at the screen. 'You can't zoom in much, but it's actually on Mercer Lane, so it must be very close to Bluebird Cottage, which is number eight.'

'I found some press pictures from the time,' Nuttall said, pointing to his laptop screen. 'Two or three of the buildings in the lane have been demolished, but this is the same wrought iron lamp sticking out of the wall.'

Jan looked over his shoulder. The picture showed a press of helmeted police around an arched doorway into a narrow stone wall. There was a number by the door, and by zooming in Nuttall identified it as a four. 'Okay, so it was number four Mercer Lane. It doesn't look like a historic church. All right, there is one easy way to sort this out.' She grabbed her coat, which had been lying on the bar behind the whiteboard. 'Come on everyone. School trip.'

One minute later the assembled detectives made their way out of the incident room into Exeter Row, carefully locking it behind them. They made their way up the pedestrianised shopping street, past Boots and Claire's Accessories, and turned left into Mercer Lane. A female PC guarded the lane, closed off by an arc of blue crime tape. Ten yards beyond it was a CSI van, behind which a white tent was connected to the front of the cottage. A few passers-by were taking selfies.

'Has Dr Holcomb been?' Jan asked the PC.

'The forensic pathologist? Yes, he just left a few minutes ago. The body has been removed, but there are two CSI staff still inside.'

Someone called from the tape barrier, a good-looking young man in a bomber jacket and jeans. 'Hi, detective? I'm James Harvey, *North Devon News*. Can you tell me what happened here?'

'No comment,' Nuttall shouted back.

'Is it true there's been a murder?'

The detectives ignored him and ducked under the tape, then made their way along the lane until they were opposite Bluebird Cottage. The historic Victorian-style lamp protruded from the wall high up to the left of the door. Nuttall, who now had the 1973 photograph on his phone, held it up to show Jan.

'Looks like the same place,' he said.

Jan almost felt faint at the revelation.

'This just cannot be true. A girl called Ruth Lyle was killed here in 1973, and then fifty years later almost to the day, a woman of the same name is killed with an identical murder weapon at the same location.'

To be continued…

CANELOCRIME

Do you love crime fiction and are always on the lookout for brilliant authors?

Canelo Crime is home to some of the most exciting novels around. Thousands of readers are already enjoying our compulsive stories. Are you ready to find your new favourite writer?

Find out more and sign up to our newsletter at canelocrime.com